After the Ruin

HARRIET GOODCHILD

HADLEY
RILLE
BOOKS

AFTER THE RUIN

Cover art © Yana Naumova
Cover design © Heather McDougal
Map of Ohmorah, the Later Lands and Lyikené © Douglas Reed
Typeset in GFS Didot

ISBN 978-0-9892631-5-3

Published simultaneously in the United Kingdom and the United States of America by:

Hadley Rille Books
Eric T. Reynolds, Publisher
PO Box 25466
Overland Park, KS 66225 USA

Edited by Terri-Lynne DeFino

www.hrbpress.com

For Louisa & Jane, best of friends,
and for Douglas, best of all.

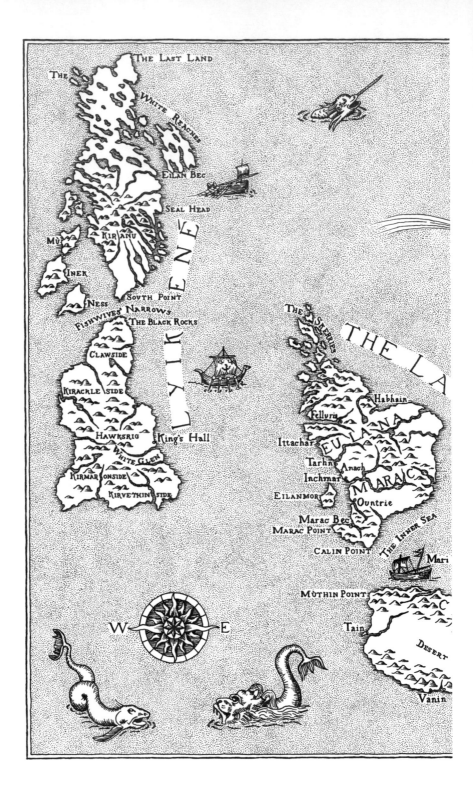

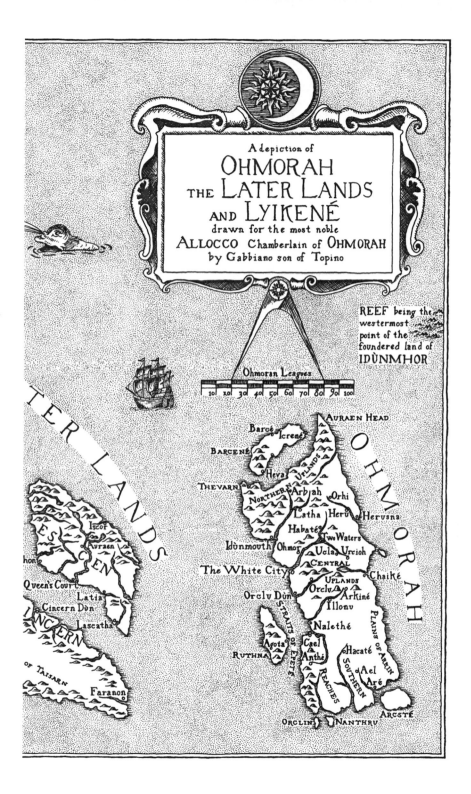

A depiction of
OHMORAH
THE LATER LANDS
AND LYIKENÉ
drawn for the most noble
ALLOCCO Chamberlain of OHMORAH
by Gabbiano son of Topino

REEF being the
westermost
point of the
foundered land of
IDÙNMHOR

Ohmoran Leagues

10 | 20 | 30 | 40 | 50 | 60 | 70 | 80 | 90 | 100

TER LANDS

OHMORAH

AURAEN HEAD

Barcé
Icrené
BARCENÉ
Heva
NORTHERN UPLANDS
THEVARN
Arbiah
Orhi
Latha
Herù
Herusna
Habaté
Idùnmouth
Ohmor
Two Waters
Uclas
Urcioh
CENTRAL
The White City
UPLANDS
Chaiké
Orclu Dùn
Orclu
Arkiné
Illonu
PLAINS OF ARRIN
Nalethé
STRAITS OF EPETE
Agota
Cael
Anthé
Hacaté
RUTHNA
SOUTHERN
Ael
REACHES
Aré
ORCLINJ
NANTHRU
ARCSTÉ

ESCEN

Iscot
Auraen
hon
Queen's Court
Latia
Cincern Dùn
Lascatha
INCERN
OF TAISARN
Faranon

Who's who in *After the Ruin*

In Felluria

MARWY NINEK, the Tion; ageless, beautiful and broken.

YATTA TALA, a weaver of cloth and a judge of men.

  BAESINA YATTA, her daughter; a spinner of threads.

  ISSA BAESINA, her granddaughter; a sempstress.

ASSIOLO, an outlandish musician in search of better days.

† *METIUS ESTUI, king of Eulana.*

  † *KETALA IITHA, wife to Metius Estui.*

In Lyikené

TE-MERIKU, the king; a red-haired bastard.

KISTORU, a hill lord; foster-father to Te-Meriku.

  ALA, his wife.

    † *IMACAH, their son.*

† *HADÙHAI, the old king; a man farsighted in his age.*

THODÙHAH, helmsman to the king.

  MARIS, wife to Thodùhah, daughter to Hadùhai.

    LIÙTHÁNWY, their daughter; grey-eyed and desolate.

    ITHÁNU, husband to Liùthánwy; a whaleman from the north.

ARDÙVAI, the nightwatch; a black-eyed rogue.

  ALMECU, his brother.

RENÙKU, a fatherless boy; ward of the king.

KALANU, a shoreman of the king's company.

† *IMACAH MOR TAMARHAK, a hero of old tales.*

In Faranon

AVERLA, fire made flesh, a golden witch.

  THORN, TWIG and LEAF, her minions.

  GRU, her manservant.

  CASARCA, her maidservant.

In Ohmorah

ALLODOLA, lady of the White City; a woman of the First People for whom a hundred years are as but one.

† *ALLOCCO, her chamberlain; a man of the First People who, long ago, stopped the sun and brought the world near to its ruin.*

  † *ALCEDO, his son; a white-haired boy drowned in the flood.*

Here, there or anywhere

KENU VANITHU, a dwarfish piper who longtimes has set the world a-dancing to his tunes.

EDO INCITHU, a fat mercatman of Cincern Dùn.

SILUS DANATU, his nephew.

TORÙKOTU, a man of blood who sets no curb upon his will.

THE KING OF THE BORDERLANDS, a quiet king with a borrowed face, clad in rags and starlight.

THE LIÙTHION, the kindred of the borderlands; spirits of wind and starlight, no weight upon the world.

THE LIÙTHION, one of that kindred clad in flesh, who sent a wave to quench Allocco's fire.

† *Dead and gone into the dark, living only in memory and thought.*

List of Chapters

This is what happened

Well, he's taken her by the lily white hand
And by the grass green sleeve
And he has laid her down at the foot of an oak
And he has never once asked her leave, my boys,
He has never once asked her leave.
            Tam Lin, Traditional

I have said before: stories link together, like beads upon a chain, like dancers joining hands to form the figures of the dance. Did I say this before? Because there are so many stories, it is easy to forget there are as many tales that never can be told. These are as many as the lives not lived, as many as the roads not taken, as many as all the things that might have been. I can tell only of words that were spoken, or of deeds that were done: of might have been, I cannot tell.

But might have been is the ghost that haunts us; might have been is the dream that fades fast in the morning; might have been is the star seen sidelong from the corner of our eyes. So it is that might have been slips between the edges of my tale. It cannot be otherwise. There cannot be a tale of might have been.

This tale begins, like many another before it, with a man and a woman. It begins in Felluria, a long time ago. Since that time much has changed but Cal Mora still stands between the sky and the sea.

Above the shore, there stood a tower and, in that tower, there was a room. The room had a door and that door was locked. There was a hearth within the room and, in that hearth, there was a fire and, in that fire, the key to the door burned red as any flame. Against the wall, there was a bed and, on the bed, there was a sheet and, on the sheet, there lay a flower and every petal of that flower was red.

Beside the bed, there was a table and on that table was a knife. Above the knife, there was a beam and, from that beam, a noose was hanging. Beneath the noose, there was a chair and, in that chair, a man was sitting. His hand had locked the door. His hand had put the key into the fire. His hand had placed the knife upon the table. His hand had tied the noose. His hand had laid the flower upon the bed. He looked at all the things that he had done, and smiled.

Before the door, there stood a woman. She beat her hands upon the door but the door was locked and she could not open it. She crossed the room and knelt before the hearth. She reached out her hands to the key but the fire burned and she could not take it.

On the table stood a jug and, in the jug, the wine was red as blood. The man stood up from his chair and poured wine into a cup. *In the morning*, he said, *the fire will be dead and the hearth will be cold and the door will be opened.*

The woman looked at the knife lying upon the table, at the noose hanging from the beam, at the man drinking his wine. She saw the knife was sharp, and the knot was firm, and that the man was smiling.

Only your strength and your will stand between us tonight. Do you have the strength, he asked, *to drive home the knife? The will to kick away the chair?*

The woman picked up the knife and tried the edge against her palm. Five drops of blood fell onto the floor. She put the knife against her breast but her hands shook and she laid the knife again upon the table, and still the man was smiling.

The woman stood upon the chair. She put the noose about her neck and kicked the chair away.

The man watched her dance upon the empty air. He had tied the noose and he knew the strength of it. He had whetted the knife and he knew the edge to it. He counted out a hundred heartbeats and took the knife in one hand and the rope in the other. With the knife he cut the rope and with his hand he loosened the noose.

The man laid the knife upon the table and the noose upon the fire. He laid the woman down upon the bed. The blood was red upon her hand and the mark was red around her neck and her eyes were black with fear and pain and hatred.

Strength and will are not enough tonight, he said. He lay down upon the bed beside the woman, and smiled. *All of Felluria is mine and I will take it.*

Above the shore there was a tower. In that tower there was a door. Behind that door there was a room. In that room there was a fire, a flower, a jug of wine, five drops of blood upon the floor and the blood and the wine and the flower and the fire were red. In that room there was a man and there was a woman and the night was black around them.

In the morning, when the fire was cold, and the flower was dead, and the wine was drunk, and the blood was brown, the man took the key out of the hearth. He unlocked the door and, when the door was open, the woman walked out of that room and the man laughed as she passed him.

That is what happened in Felluria, a long time ago. Much has changed since that time, the tower has fallen and the man is gone, but still Cal Mora stands between the sea and sky.

1: Once there were roses here

First he played the notes o noy, *Scowan erla grae*
Then he played the notes o joy, *Far yorten han grun orla*
An then he played the guid glabber reel, *Scowan erla grae*
That would mak a sick hert heal, *Far yorten han grun orla*.

King Orfeo, Traditional

It was the equinox and spring just beginning to creep across Cal Mora's flanks when Assiolo first came into Felluria. The wind blew cold from the mountain and he pulled his hat more firmly down upon his head and drew on gloves of kidskin, pausing a while upon the road to look towards the grey stone walls waiting at its end. Down by the water's edge, oystercatchers followed the retreating tide and he turned to watch one bird fly fast across the shingle calling to its mate.

At noontime he rapped hard upon the wicket gate in the great door, doffing his hat when the porter's face showed at the window.

"May I come in?" In this place, his accent was as outlandish as his garb and the door remained shut fast against him.

"What's your name?" the porter asked, mindful of his charge.

"Assiolo." Both courtesy and commonsense demanded more but he gave his name and kept his silence.

The porter tried again. "Where're you from?"

"The east."

The porter scratched his head, thinking a moment, then named the furthest east he knew. "From Escen?"

Assiolo smiled. "East of Escen," he answered, "but it was one from Escen first told me of Felluria."

"Who might that be, then?"

"A piper, in seeming a beggar and a dwarf, in truth like none other in the world. You call him Kenu Vanithu in these Later Lands. He told me once a wandering musician could find a welcome here, and so I took up my lute and came to see if he spoke true." He turned a little, to show the porter the lute case slung across his back.

The porter snorted, his face somewhere between a sneer and a laugh. "That rogue? He's not been by in all the years I've kept this door. And you from the east?" Assiolo nodded, and the porter's sneer was plain. "Next time you tell a lie, make it a better one: There've been no ships from the east these last five months. Edo Incithu, he's always the first of the mercatkind to these parts and it'll be a month before we begin to look for him."

Assiolo shrugged. "No ships? Well, man, this is your place and I must bow before your knowledge of it but, ships or no, I am here. I have given you my name and surety of that name so either let me in or fetch one of your betters who might see what you do not and at the least grant a stranger a night's rest before casting him again upon the road."

The porter hummed and thought and sucked his teeth a while but opened in the end the inset door to let Assiolo step across the threshold into Felluria. But no further, for there he made him wait before the second gate until the steward had come from the great hall to judge what best to do with him, and clear it was the porter hoped only that he should send him on his way. But – alas – the steward nodded at his naming of Kenu Vanithu and led him off across the courtyard and up a stair and down a corridor to a room where there was a bed, and an oaken kist with a jug and ewer, and a window looking across towards the hall.

"This room is kept against the piper's coming," he said, "but he's not been by since I was in my cradle. Yet since you know him, you may have it now."

"And the terms? I've silver enough, or ivory." Assiolo was looking at the door. It had no lock to it, neither a latch on the inside to keep the world at bay, nor bolt without to make a prisoner.

"In the piper's name you asked, and Marwy Ninek will offer you what he is given. On those same terms."

"Oh, I can sing for my supper," Assiolo answered after a moment's thought, a bitter smile upon his lips that never touched his eyes. "Whatever I was, I am no more. In these lands I too must be a beggar."

The steward paused, his hand upon the door. "There is water in the well and peat to make a fire in the store beside the kitchen. Follow your nose, and you will find the privy. If you come to the hall, you will be fed. The rest is none of my concern."

Assiolo held up his hand to stay him. "One question: Did Marwy Ninek make the piper welcome?"

"Once, it is said. But that was long ago, when she was very young. He has returned betimes, so I've been told. Each time she gave him food and shelter, she listened to his songs and stories, and, when he came to take his leave, she said no word to keep him."

Alone in the piper's unlocked room, Assiolo took off his coat and opened his bag. There was little there, a razor with an ivory hilt, a couple of changes of clean clothes, a map within its case and a book, a little thing clad in bright silk embroidered over with flowers. He put the linen and the map away in the kist and set the lute down on its lid. The day was cold, the air was chill so he went out to bring back a basket of peat and set a fire within his hearth. As it smoked slowly into life, he leant upon the windowsill turning the pages of the book a while and, though he did not weep, his eyes were very bright. But in the end he shook his head to clear it, laid the book aside and sat upon the bed-end, leaning forward to the fire to warm the stiffness from his fingers. Then he took up the lute to tune it, and after played a while and so the afternoon slipped slowly away.

The shadow of the hall had filled the courtyard when there was a tap upon his door. Opening it, Assiolo saw an old woman on the threshold, scowling up at him. "I'd heard this room was full again with a beggar musician and came to see for myself. You're better favoured, lad, than that rogue but are you better omened?"

"Mistress, I cannot say, the future being a book no man can read."

"How'd you get in? The gate was locked against strangers."

"There are many ways," he said, holding his voice level, though a smile lurked at the corners of his eyes, "to open a locked door but the one I favour is first to knock and then ask entry."

She scowled, and ducked around him into his room. He shrugged at her discourtesy and closed the door behind her. The draught was making the fire smoke. "Why'd you come here?" she demanded. "East of Escen's a long, long way."

Assiolo turned himself slowly around, a hint of laughter twitching his lip, showing her the walls, the bed, the fire. "Anywhere's good for a beggar, so they say, but I'd say here's better than most for a man who wishes to sleep warm and dry."

The old woman pursed her lips whilst she considered him. "Whatever you are, you're not a beggar, no matter what tale you told before the gate." She picked up the book and opened it, thumbing through the pages curious as a child. "What's this?"

Assiolo sighed, seeing himself a fool for leaving it in plain sight. "Old tales of love and longing."

Though it was clear a book was to her an unfamiliar thing, she took care and gave him no excuse to take it from her. She turned the painted pages and he waited for her question. "Here's a pretty thing," she said at last, pointing to a picture. She held the book towards him. "I never got the knack of letters: read me your riddle."

Assiolo took the book and glanced at where she pointed. No fool, this woman, she knew well what it showed. How could she not? This was Felluria. The naked body of the king hung from the apple tree, the woman below the tree stretched up her hands in agony towards him. Of all the tales between its covers this was the one he favoured least, having known cruelty enough firsthand not to want to read of

it and yet, when his mother lay dying and he sat close by, to read
and to distract her, she had not let him leave it out. *Read it*, she had
bid him. *The world is as it is. It changes nothing if you close your eyes.*
So he had read and, when the tale was ended, looked up to see the
piper listening at the door, his hands full of white roses.

The old woman's voice jerked him back into the moment. "Read
it, lad."

"It says," Assiolo read aloud, closing his mind against the memory,
making the words as any other on a page. In a moment, seeing her
face blank, he paused to find the words to turn one language to
another and make a new beginning. "In your speech it says, *At the
back of the west wind, in Lyikené, there was once a man. His hair was
red, his arm was strong, no man could stand in fight against him, but he
was not —*"

She cried out, "Enough!" Holding up her hand, fingers crooked
in the sign to avert misfortune. He obeyed, and shut up the book.
"Some tales are better left untold in any tongue," she said. "I'm Yatta
Tala, a weaver to my trade. Who are you, lad?"

"Assiolo."

"And the rest?" When he did not answer, she stepped towards
him and clasped a bony hand about his arm, pinching hard, speaking
harsh. "There must be more to you than that. That tale you started
ended here," she told him, "but that book's from as far away as you
are."

He looked down into her face and gently peeled her fingers from
his wrist. "I left it all behind, mistress, in my own country. Here, I
am only Assiolo."

"Yet you brought that story with you. Tell me, Assiolo son of
nobody, is that likely to be chance?"

He did not answer for there was no need. She had known from
the moment she saw the king hanging from the tree it was not
chance had brought him here. Instead, he answered the question he
had already turned aside with a jest. "I had a mind to make a new
beginning. And if things go awry, then it's no great matter: I have
nothing left to lose."

The old weaver fingered his coat cast carelessly upon the bed,
considering the weight and quality of its black wool and silk satin
lining, turned her eyes to the red silk of his shirt and the finespun of
his britches, the needlework where the neck of his linen shift showed
beneath his collar, and laughed. "A better kind of nothing, lad, than
you'll find here." Turning the pages of the book, she stabbed her
finger at another picture: a man following a twisted dwarf through
the trees of the wild wood. "Tell me true: is that piper at the back of
this?"

That was a question he did not care to answer, but his silence told its own story. Her laughter stopped and her face was sharp and wary. "Aye well, you're not the first to listen to his stories. Scratch the surface of any tale and you'll see that face staring back at you."

"When I was a child, I loved him," Assiolo answered, mildly.

"There's many of us that could say the same, lad. Even I was young once. Even Marwy Ninek. But we're no longer children and love is not enough, not in Felluria leastways."

"Neither am I a child. You asked, mistress. I did but answer to your will."

She sniffed, turning from him to the lute. "That's a pretty toy. Can you play it?" He nodded, a smile again creasing the edges of his eyes. "Well, give me a tune, lad, and show your substance."

He thought a moment, deciding what might suit the time and the place and the thought, and played, giving her first a jig and then a reel and laughed aloud to see her foot beat out the time for all she held her face impassive.

"Well," she said, when he was done, "that set is of this country. How'd you come by it, Assiolo?"

Laughing still, he answered, "Why from that piper, of course. He knows most the tunes of most the world."

"So it's his tunes you'd have us dance to here in Felluria."

He shrugged. "In truth, I'd given it but little thought. They're pleasant melodies enough in any country and no great thing to turn them from the pipe." She frowned, and he said lightly, "Aye, I've thought myself a rebec might be better suited to their style but my fingers have more skill upon the lute. I've other songs that are all my own if you don't care for his."

He played again, a music made on a summer's evening in his mother's garden, woven through with the blackbird's whistle and the wind in the apple trees, with her shy, sweet smile that had drawn him from his father's shadow out into the sunlight.

"That's pretty, lad," she said when the last lorn notes had faded to silence. "Who was she?"

His grief was yet too raw to speak aloud and, besides, his mother deserved better than to be spoken of to a stranger. He answered, shortly, "A woman I loved in my own country, too little and too late."

She laughed again, the hard, harsh laugh of a woman who has lived a long time and seen much that is wrong with the world and all the creatures in it. "That tells me more than all the rest together. You're but a man as other men, Assiolo, for all your outlandish manners. No doubt you'll set us all a pretty dance until we trip and break our hearts against you."

Assiolo came down to the great hall to find his dinner and to give a song in return, knowing that most of what he played would fall fresh on western ears, years old as it may be in his homeland. The food at the common table was plain but plentiful, broth with barleycorn and turnip, sausage of pigsblood and oatmeal, salt cod and black bread and strong brown ale. He ate what he needed to turn aside his hunger, casting now and then a glance towards the high table where there was chicken stewed with saffron, and red wine to drink with it. And whilst he ate, he listened to the talk around him.

It had been a long, hard winter and wild things had grown hungry. Some said it was a dog-wolf that had learnt to raid the sheepfolds, others swore it had been a bear. There were graves beyond the gate, scraped out in midwinter, for two shepherds who could have said for certain, had they lived long enough to tell their tale. Marwy Ninek had paid the death-fee without question or stinting. She always did, they told him with approval. Assiolo kept his ears open when they spoke of her, but learnt only that she was an easy mistress and a quiet one, taking her due and nothing more.

After the food, when the tables were cleared and more jugs of ale set down upon them, the steward nodded to him and he took the musician's place by the fireside. Mindful of his company, he played dance tunes, easy on the ear, undemanding on the mind so as not to distract men from their talk or their womenfolk. With half an eye, he watched the company mill around the hall, a sea of strangers' faces, burly, bearded westerners shaped to the land and the sea. A woman whispered to her companions and a set formed for dancing. Assiolo gave them the tunes he had played for Yatta Tala, and each time through quickened the rhythm until their faces flushed with laughter as they kept time with clapping hands and thudding feet. And at its end, he let them sink exhausted on the benches and changed pace and mood into a song:

> "The white flower is open, the hawk's on the wing,
>   The sun is a-rising, it is time to begin.
>   The sun is a-rising, the east is a-flame,
>   The hawk in the sunlight cries out your name.
>
> "The hawk in the sunlight slips out of sight,
>   The shadows are falling and fading the light.
>   The shadows are falling down gentle and deep,
>   The sun is a-setting, time now to sleep."

When his song was done and the last grace notes had slipped away into the evening, Assiolo stood, lute in hand, and bowed to the company to let another take his place and he a cup of ale. A woman's voice asked, "Who is this lutist?" and he saw a pathway clear before him to the high table, and felt hands at his back pressing him forwards.

He had read his father's books and listened to the piper's stories. He knew who Marwy Ninek was, and what she was; he knew she had been born a king's daughter and yet was no more a woman than the piper was a man, but he had not seen her face before, though she had sat the evening through in the centre seat, the old weaver Yatta Tala at her side. He stepped forward, bowing low, kneeling before Marwy Ninek with all the grace and courtesy he could summon, as if he had still been a lord of the White City, and heard her speak, soft with an accent he had not heard before, even this evening in Felluria, speaking this tongue as it had been spoken long, long ago before the stone walls around them had been built, asking, "What is your name?"

"Assiolo."

He looked up, their eyes met and in that meeting his world was changed forever. He had read of such things in old tales but never before believed them true. Yet there she was, so close he need only put out his hand to caress her cheek, so close one step was all he needed to clasp her to his breast, and hold her tight, and never, never let her go. For a moment, looking into the depths of her eyes, he was certain she had known him as truly as he knew her for, in that moment of first sight, she had stretched out her hands a little way towards him, caught in her breath in a soft gasp, a whisper, "Assiolo," but then her face closed, became again a lovely mask of blankness.

"You have a fine touch on the strings," she told him. Her voice was calm and gracious, as if he were only another wanderer upon the road, who gives a tune, a song, an evening's pleasure and is gone on the morrow, forgotten by noontime. *And that*, he thought, *is all I am to her*. But he had seen her hands reach out; he had heard her whisper, *Assiolo!*

Words rose to his mouth before he had the time to check them. "I desire only to please you."

Marwy Ninek stared at him, as a woman might when a man's familiarity displeased her. And yet he would not look away, having spoken only the truth and being not one whit ashamed of it, and in the end it was she who turned down her eyes. "Play again," she bade him, sitting back in her chair whilst Yatta Tala set out the pieces for a game of fox and geese.

"What would you have me play?"

"An it please you," she answered, and did not look at him. Above her head stretched the banner of Felluria, black as her hair with a

five-petalled flower broidered upon it, a bright bold pattern of orange
and crimson. And now, as he looked towards her and beyond her,
he saw the same flower carved upon each boss of the roof above his
head, lithia the firestar that grows on barren stone and is the first of
all its kind to seed itself upon scorched ground.

Assiolo thought a moment, thrumming at the lute to steady
himself and still his breathing. "*Banish misfortune,*" he said, though
no one heard him. "Let the tune be the charm." But all the time he
played he felt the shame of it, that the tales of the ruin Torùkotu
had brought her were all true and not all the tunes in all the world
were enough to give her peace. The world was as it was and, if he
loved her, he could not close his eyes to it.

In the weeks that followed, spring spread itself in green across the
moorlands and the mountain until only Cal Mora's peak stood hard
and grey above the stone walls. In those weeks Assiolo began to
know Felluria, and to be known there. Yatta Tala in her sly, dry way
saw to that. She was a master-weaver and, often in the afternoons,
he would find his way to her workshop where she threw her shuttles
back and forth and watch the patterns form across her loom. There
were other women there: Baesina Yatta, her daughter, at the spinning
wheel; Issa Baesina, her granddaughter, at her embroidery, her bright
hair plaited through with coloured ribbons, red and green and gold.
They made him welcome, after a fashion, setting him tasks of wool
to card and silk to wind, teaching him songs out of Eulana.

Of Marwy Ninek in that first month he saw as much and as little
as any in that place. A strange life, he knew, she had in her: never
to sicken, never to grow old, never to quicken, never to wither or to
fade. There were others like her in the Later Lands but where he did
not know: the piper had not told. Watching sidelong in the evening,
picking up the threads of conversations, he learned she could talk to
fishermen of mackerel, and to shepherds of sheep; she could spin
a thread fine and strong as cobweb; could tell a tale and mend a
quarrel; that she spoke to old women of the past and of the future
to the young; later, when the sea lanes opened and the mercatmen
came, first from Cincern Dùn and Tarhn, later from Marihon and
Escen, he watched her sit down with them to drive a hard bargain
for their wine and silks and spices but, always, there was a space
around her that no man could cross, be he fisherman or mercatman
or beggar-musician from beyond the eastern sea. She was the Tion
of Felluria: she had lived a long time and to each generation she was
the same.

And yet, Assiolo thought, watching in the evenings with a lover's
eye, *that is not all she is.* Each night, lying in his narrow bed, he

would read, by candlelight, the tale of Torùkotu and Ketala Iitha, though he had it by heart, and wish again it were not true.

One evening, perhaps a month after he came there, Marwy Ninek sent for him. It had been a warm day for such a time of year and warmth lingered still in the stone walls of Felluria. A green tracery of lithia patterned the stone but the flowers had not yet opened. They walked together in the court beyond her hall and, on a stone bench beside the door, sat Yatta Tala, an old woman enjoying the evening sunshine. He bent his head in courtesy as they passed her by.

Marwy Ninek pulled a strand from the wall, twisting the stem through her fingers as they walked. "Why did you come here, Assiolo?" she asked, though she did not look at him. She looked only at the lithia, at its green leaves, at the stains its dark juice left on her skin. "Surely not to sing to strangers in return for a bed and pickings from the common table?"

Though she would not look at him, Assiolo looked nowhere save at her. "If you did not give me that bed, I must sleep on bare ground beyond the wall. If you did not feed me, I must in the end go hungry. I have my lute and my voice and little else besides."

She cast the broken stem aside and raised her eyes towards him. There was no sign of her age written on her face, no thread of silver woven in the tight braid pinned fast behind her head; she looked a woman young and lovely, only her eyes were no woman's eyes. They looked out wary on the world, filled with a depth of loneliness that was very hard to look upon. But he had marked, these weeks he had dwelled within her walls, that no man of Felluria would look her in the face.

"I am not a fool, Assiolo; do not take me for one." Marwy Ninek spoke a little louder than before, and Yatta Tala turned her head towards them. "I have seen many men in my time: some were kings and some were beggars and you are like to none of them. What is your purpose in Felluria?"

"I thought, after my mother died, 'twas time to make a new beginning. And so I changed one future for another and came to take my chances in the west."

One step would be enough to catch her up into his arms, to stroke her hair and kiss her face and promise her his love and care and kindness forever and for always. He had loved her in a moment and, surely, it had been the same for her. She had reached out; she had gasped his name in that moment of first seeing. No sign of that now in her eyes that looked at him so cautious and so fearful. And yet, Assiolo thought, she had asked for him to come to her; and yet, he thought, seeing the flush upon her cheek, she was still there. That was not a little thing. Perhaps it was a beginning.

Assiolo took three paces back and said, quietly, "When I walk beyond the walls, I see the blackthorn is in flower and green leaves on the elder; there is celandine scattered on the grass and violets in the ditches; there are briars by the roadside, sweet enough at midsummer for all their thorns. But, inside these walls, there is lithia and there is nothing else."

Marwy Ninek said, so soft he could scarce hear her, "Once there were roses here. The wind blew from the sea and killed them." She laid her hand against the wall, spreading her fingers across the grey stone and the green leaves. As if she drew strength out of the stone, she raised her head and told him, clear and cold, "Lithia grows where other flowers cannot."

Memory swooped 'cross time and place into a summer's night time in his mother's garden. Her roses shone white in the moonlight, perfect in every way but that they had no scent. She had loved them for his father's sake, and he had grown to love them for hers. Reaching out, he had pulled the finest from the tree and stared a while before crushing it between his hands. A limping step behind him, a stunted, twisted figure with a face out of a nightmare, a voice out of a dream. *She's gone, lad. What you could, you did.*

Broken petals spilled from his fingers as tears spilled down his face. *Not enough.*

Love never is, the piper said. *But it's no little thing for all that.*

"There were roses in my father's garden," Assiolo told her, "though that too was near the sea. He built a wall to keep the wind at bay."

"But that was in an eastern land. Here, when the wind blows from the west, no stone walls are enough to check its path."

His heart ached as he looked at her. In seeming she was like a woman, and one full young and slender, with small, high breasts and a waist to snap between his fingers. Such a little time since he had first seen her, and already her face haunted his dreams. But in his dreams she smiled at him, sweet as a briar rose at midsummer. It was a grief to him he had not seen her smile, that here and now she was so lovely and so fearful. Her fear was a greater barrier than ever a locked door or a stone wall could be.

Assiolo said, marking in his memory the curve of her cheek, the dark arch of her brow, "Kenu Vanithu told me once he had a mind to see again roses growing beside the sea."

"And you did not think to ask him why?"

On that lovely, bitter evening in his mother's garden, the piper had plucked a rose from another tree and breathed in its drowsy perfume. In the sunlight it had been red but all colours were quenched to black beneath the moon. *I once saw roses such as these*, he had said, *wine-red and scented sweet as summertime, growing upon stone walls beside a western sea. Before the ruin, lad. Since then, nothing but a memory, a thought of might have been.*

"When I asked," he said, thinking still of the story in his mother's book, "he did not answer."

"No," she said, her face bleak as midwinter, "there never is an answer. Yet you left your life behind for sake of an old tale: there are no roses here. I think it is you who is the fool, Assiolo."

"I left behind the man I was, his father's son. Here, he is of no matter and I can be the man I want to be."

"Did you hate him so much, your father?"

"He did great ill," said Assiolo, "to the world and to me. While he lived, I feared him; now he is dead, I cannot forget the things he taught me. When I was a boy, I loved Kenu Vanithu far better than my father; when he took ship into the west, I begged him, *Let me come with you!* But he left me behind." He could not keep his voice quite steady as he told her, "Oftentimes, I think of what might have been, had he done otherwise."

"When I was very young," she said, softly, "I also begged him, *Let me come with you.* Like you, I was left behind. Like you, I think of might have been."

Their eyes met. Marwy Ninek did not move towards him, she did not move away but in that moment the space between them grew a little less. Yet still he could not reach out across that space to draw her closer to his heart. Might have been would never be. He had been shaped by his father's vengeance, she by Torùkotu's rage and the past hung heavy on them both.

"Will you walk with me upon Cal Mora's braes," he asked after a moment, "and show to me your country?"

She shook her head. "You are a stranger here. Yatta Tala, perhaps, if you ask her, or else Baesina Yatta. Not I. Since these stone walls were raised, I have not passed the gate."

Assiolo looked up at the stone walls above him: one hundred feet high they stood, and ten feet thick with a tower at each corner and another above the gate. This was not his place but he must shape himself to fit it, because it was hers.

He longed to offer comfort but it was a gift she would not take. Not yet. He said, quietly so the old woman would not hear, "I know what it is to meet a will stronger than my own. Do not think I'll ask for more than you can give." He bowed his head in courtesy and stepped back, that she might pass him by to seek the shelter of stone walls.

"Well, lad," Yatta Tala caught at his sleeve to make him sit down beside her, "that looked to me like a wooing. So you've a mind for roses, like many a lover afore you."

Assiolo laughed, hard in his throat. "How bold it is you think me!"

"I've said before, you are a man as other men. I'm as like to be surprised to see a wasp seek honey: she has a lovely face, and much else besides. Did you think yourself the first to ask her?"

"No harm in asking."

"That depends, both on the question and the manner of the asking." Again her dry laughter, as at a jest he could not see. "Oh, it's not you I spoke of, Assiolo, though you're braw and bonny. I'd have thought a goose as like to seek a fox."

He met her gaze a long, long time, and when she spoke again it was of another matter. "You need other clothes, lad. That finery is well enough but plain suits everyday. I had sons once – they left enough behind them. It'll do for you."

"Why?"

Her laugh was dry as the rustle of firestar leaves upon the wall. "Charity, lad. Why else? Good for my reputation to ludge a beggar." She looked up and her eyes were hard and bright as chips of glass. "You've a fine touch on that toy of yours, and a fine voice to match it, but you'll need more than that if you're set on staying. What will you do when we've heard all your songs thrice over? Turn juggler or fire-eater? What trade were you brought up to, Assiolo son of nobody?"

Caught by surprise, Assiolo stared at such a question. Trade? He had been reared a lord of the White City, to rule in the lady's name and his father's shadow. He knew its histories, its laws and languages, the manner of address for each degree, the dances of the lady's court, the cost of everything and the price of nothing.

The weaver pressed her case. "Do you know aught of fishing? Of sheep and goats? Of butchery or tanning? How to sow a field or reap a harvest?" At each he shook his head. "Come, lad, what are you, thirty summers? You must have learnt something in that time, even in that eastern land of yours."

Many things, of course, and he had left them all behind with his books and silks and servants. Once his father had stopped the sun at noontime: better to starve naked by the roadside than be a man such as his father. The weaver's eyes stared into him, asking her question. In his homeland, no one would have dared speak in such a way, knowing what he was. But here he was, after all, a beggar and so, in the end, he answered, "I know something of leechcraft."

"Well, there's a thing. Can you set a bone and stay a flux and bring a fever down?"

"All of that."

"And the winter sickness?"

He shrugged. The question was a trick. "As much as any other," he said. "Speak the charms and burn the herbs and keep him waking long as can be. No leech can stand against the winter sickness, once sense is lost. In truth, I have not seen it much – it is a trouble in the west?"

"Forty years ago, it fell heavy on Lyikené." Yatta Tala spat into the dust to avert the ill fortune of the name. "Not heavily enough."

Forty years ago, he thought, he had not been born and Hadùhai had been the king in Lyikené. Hadùhai had lived past the winter sickness; his son had died, and his son's son in his cradle; years later, when his time came, he had given his sword to Te-Meriku the sea eagle. In Ohmorah, the lady Allodola had sworn fealty to him, as to Hadùhai and every king before him. *Abasing herself before a boy of scarce eighteen,* his father to him scornful said, *a red-haired whelp out of the sheepfold.* Allocco too had spat into the fire to avert misfortune. *Who his father was no man can say. I think Hadùhai grew foolish in his age to give the mastery to such a man.*

It was neither the time nor place to speak of such memories. "What should I do?" Assiolo asked.

"Make yourself known to the kitchens, lad. They'll give you run of the gardens for such herbs and simples as you might need. And then go find the butcher's wife if you know a cure for colic." She sniffed and scowled lest he should think she had weakened into kindness. "Another fine boy she had but her rooms are close by mine and old bones need their sleep."

—+— —+—

The buds were swelling on the tree and the spring moon, the first after the equinox, had waxed to its fullness. A new year in Lyikené; a time of beginnings. To his displeasure, Te-Meriku found he had to dance at Liùthánwy's wedding. How could he not? A wedding in his hall, the bride the last king's grandchild. Women's feet beat out the rhythm against the pipe and drum. He had to watch her spin laughing down the line of men who played at catching her, listen to the silver bells like apples ringing in her hair.

"Are you happy?" he asked her, when it was his turn to swing her round. "Is this what you want?"

There was no time for her to answer. The pattern of the dance pulled her away from him and into a place where he could not follow, for all he was the king.

Thodùhah the helmsman stood at one end of the hall, his duty done, his daughter gone. The bridegroom waited at the other, ivory on his arms, amber at his neck, his hair twisted with gold silk into the clansman's knot. A whaleman from the north, with red hair several shades darker than his own; he had come a-courting with ivory and tales of a sun that never set. Thodùhah, liking neither him nor the clan he came from, had asked a high price for his daughter, and the northman agreed to it, easily, lightly, as if they spoke of little things that did not matter.

"Smiling!" Thodùhah had said to him, smashing his cup down on the table. The red wine spilled across it in a pattern neither man could read. "Smiling, as if she were a hawk to come to his hand or a hound to follow at his heel. I asked her *why him* – of all the men in all Lyikené? She said she would take what was offered, since she could not have what she wanted. When her mother asked the same, she said she'd a mind to dance on ice beneath the northern lights."

For a while, they drank in silence, as they had done often of an evening in the years since the old king died. At last Thodùhah spoke again, pouring another draught for both of them. "You are the king," he said. "You could end this nonsense in a heartbeat."

"What should I do to end it?" He stared at the surface of his wine and thought of water running through his fingers, soaking away into the sand, and drank to drive such thoughts away.

"Kiss her," said Thodùhah, deep into his cups. "You've kissed every other woman in this place, and half the men besides. Kiss her, or kiss him – either will serve to drive him from her."

He laughed, and choked on his wine. When he could breathe again, he said, "When I asked, she said me *No*. Would you have me take her unwilling?"

"I'd not have him take her at all! The dead are dead, Te-Meriku, she'd be willing enough if you'd but remember it. I'm her father, man – I've seen the way she looks at you."

His wrath rose up against his helmsman like stormwinds from the sea. There were memories he would not share, words he would not speak, even with Thodùhah. "How many rods of bronze is he giving you? How many horns of ivory? Count them and be thankful." He tossed back the last of the wine and stood up from his chair, turning at the door to fling his anger at the man. "You'd have had nothing from me – even if I wanted her. Why pay for one when I can have all?"

A sennight since, he had looked around his hall and seen her standing quietly whilst two men balanced out her fate between them with seven clanlords standing by as witness. Her grey eyes, clear as running water, met his for a moment but showed nothing of her thoughts. He turned from her towards the count, so much of bronze, so much of ivory.

Outside the hall, the rain was falling down. The hills were hidden behind the mist, the past was gone, the future might never come.

The sea and the sky were grey, and that was all. He looked up and saw her, still looking at him. The factor brought the tally-sticks to show to him; then, at his nod, broke each across his knee, giving half to Thodùhah and the other to the northman. The price was paid, the thing was done. And, all the time, she watched him, seeing all, saying nothing. He thought again of water slipping through his fingers, slow rain falling upon a silent sea.

The music played, the women stamped, the men cheered and whistled as Liùthánwy span the last few places down the hall. The whaleman held out his hands to catch her, swinging her up into his arms, carrying her away into another life. She shook her head in answer to his whispered question and all the silver bells rang out in a lovely, empty ripple across the music and the noise. Two men swung the doors wide open as the northman reached them. "A kiss, a kiss!" the cry went up and he paused a moment on the threshold to press his mouth hard down onto hers.

Beyond the doors the moon cast down its cold light, white and sharp as ice across his court. Te-Meriku called for wine as the bridegroom stepped into the night and drained the cup to silence the ringing of those bells.

I, Lyikené: Two halves of one whole

I've got no tax to pay and I heed no master's bell
Who would be a king when a beggar does so well?
And a-begging I will go, and a-begging I will go.

A-Begging I Will Go, *Traditional*

"Apples," says Imacah, "such an incredible fierce desire to eat apples."

"There are apples a-plenty in your father's store."

"Those are not the ones I hunger for. The apple I would eat does not grow on any of my father's trees."

What can he do but laugh, to hear such daring? "You would not!"

"I would if you were with me!"

"Am I not always with you?"

"You and I," says Imacah, "two halves of one whole."

He leans into Imacah's embrace; a pledge, a promise, a boyish trick to steal an apple from another man's tree. Such a little thing, an apple, so small a weight upon the world.

What is the price set on a man's life? An apple? A sword? A kingdom? Standing alone beneath the tree, he wonders, as he has wondered many times over many years, if it were he broke faith with Imacah or Imacah with him?

"I envy you, Te-Meriku."

He turns to Imacah and grins, letting his disbelief write itself across his face.

"No, truly." Imacah sweeps his hand across the air, a gesture that contains the hillside and the hall. "You are free from all of this. All your deeds are your own. No one says of you it is because of your father."

To drive this mood away, he answers, "That, oh most noble Imacah mor Kistoru, son of a thousand years of clanlords, is because my father was a filthy beggarman."

He sees Imacah's eyes dance with sudden laughter and feels himself relax.

"Nay, a thief," Imacah counters, "stealing the bread from the mouths of honest men!" Though he is watching for the blow, he is laughing so much he almost fails to block it. "A whoreson rogue who got you on his mother!"

Imacah's left is faster than his right. He doubles up, reeling with laughter. Just out of reach, Imacah chants triumphant, mimicking the factor's high tone, *"A cheating, lying, drunken scoundrel, fit only to be whipped along the wayside!"*

He recovers his breath, feints and knocks Imacah down into the heather, holds his arm against his throat. "Say that again!"

Imacah twists, pulling his legs from under him, rolling clear and to his feet.

They scuffle across the hillside, half in play and half in earnest, striving each to outdo the other. They are matched pretty even but, this time, 'tis Imacah has the best of it, back-heeling him as he shifts his balance, closing for a throw. The world spins round and around, a tumble of green and gold, no sound but the drumbeat of his blood. Dazed by the fall, dazzled by the light, he lands clean upon a bed of springy heather and Imacah kneels astride him, pinning his arms above his head. No sight but Imacah's face against the light, dark eyes laughing into his. He cannot move, he cannot speak, he can scarce even breathe. A moment's pause and then his breath comes quick and ragged as Imacah lets go his wrists and unfastens the buckle of his belt, grinning all the while to have the mastery.

Later, later, sated, satisfied, they lie on their backs, side by side, looking up into the sky. "There!" Imacah points. "Perhaps it seeks its brother."

The great bird drifts across the emptiness of blue. Its burnished wings outspan a man, its yellow eyes outstare the sun, ever and ever it strikes from the high sunlight, a deadly, necessary thing with no purpose but the one. He screams to it, shouting the name they share, and hears it mew in answer.

"What is it like?" Imacah asks. "To be the sea eagle?"

He does not answer. He follows the eagle with his eyes and mind, riding the currents of the air as in a dream of flight. Three eagles are the symbol of Lyikené; three feathers from an eagle's wing his only birthright. Sometimes, when he is alone upon the hillside, he hears the rush of wind through the feathers of its wings as it stoops to its desire. Once he killed a hare for it and lay an afternoon in the heather watching whilst it gorged. Before it ate, it looked at him, sidelong, from one yellow eye and then the other. He could not read the meaning in its look nor tell if there were thoughts behind those eyes.

Watching now, he sees the eagle has no weight at all upon the world. It does what it must, soaring free of the past and of the future, beyond the purposes and meanings men make for themselves. At last its wide circles lift it out of sight and he remembers he is only a man.

He says to Imacah, "The king has sent for me."

Imacah rolls over, propping himself on his elbow. "Aye well, you'll never go unnoticed—not till you learn to keep that hair covered. There's none other like it in these hills. It flared up brighter than the torches on the streambank."

As he knows not his father, he may not bind his hair as Imacah does into the clansman's knot. Instead he lets it tumble down around his shoulders, turning what should be a badge of shame into a flag of triumph. He shakes his head, laughing the world to scorn. The breeze catches up his hair and, for a moment, he sees Imacah as through a flicker of flame. The day he became a man, Imacah got up from his place among the watching clansmen to stand with him and untie his own hair, grinning all the while to see his father's rage.

Perhaps remembering, Imacah twists a strand, bright and light as a fire's red heart, about his fingers, says, "But for those torches we'd have had those apples."

He pulls free and draws the knife from his belt, a handspan of hammered bronze, the bone hilt chased about with gold. It is the finest thing he owns, made by the king's own swordsmith; its pair hangs at Imacah's side. The two together cost Kistoru dear, and dearer still the cost to a hill lord's pride to see his son value his gift so lightly.

"I would the moon were dark tonight," he says, trying the edge against his finger, "so I could set myself a second time against the king's men and this time have the mastery."

"So too would I!"

They clasp hands on it and the thread of blood on his hand smears onto Imacah's to seal the pact. The shadows lengthen across the afternoon and Imacah's mood falls back upon him, the eager light dies from his face. "But tonight I must sit at supper to hear my father tell again of the days when he was young. A wonder and a scandal he is not himself the king if half his tales are true."

He has forgot the king in thoughts of his revenge. Since he must answer to him within a sennight, he asks, "What is he like, the king?"

"An old man," says Imacah, screwing up his eyes against the light. "Not like my father. You can see in his eyes he thinks but not what he is thinking." He opens his mouth as if to speak, closes it again, but in a little time says it anyway. "If the fine is more than you can pay, smile and say nothing. Then come to me."

"Nay, I'll put a patch over my eye and sit me down by the wayside to beg for it! A fine sight I'll be, don't you think, on the road to your father's hall? He's called me a beggar often and often—let him see the truth of it!" Stretching out his hands, he whines, "Spare a bit for the poor beggarman that lost his eye a-fighting for the king!"

In his patched-up cloak and cast-off clothes he hits his mark too well. Imacah winces and his hand moves in the pattern to avert misfortune as he mutters, "A pox on the king, and on my father! I grow sick of hearing I am one thing, you another. Let's away, both of us. Forget this place. It never was your home and I wish it were not mine."

"Go where?"

"*Somewhere,*" *Imacah says,* "*anywhere.*"

"*Anywhere's a good place for beggars, so I've heard tell,*" *he answers,* "*somewhere's better still, and nowhere's best of all. But since I came from nowhere I'm not minded to return.*"

"*I did not mean it as a jest!*" *Imacah crouches down in front of him, puts his hands upon his shoulders and shakes the laughter from him.* "*Into the north! Let's you and I go join the whalemen. In a season we could have ivory enough to get a ship.*"

"*And set her face towards a star and sail into a dream?*"

There are ships in the far distance, their sails all the colours of the sea and sky, but none of them is like the ship they have built for themselves a hundred times on afternoons like this. Behind closed eyes he sees her, the grey gull's head and the long sweep of her black folded wings, swift and low upon the water, bearing them into another life.

"*Think on it, two handspan for every man aboard and double for the man who sights her,*" *says Imacah.* "*We'll never have enough elsewise, not if the moon were dark a month of nights. Only when my father...*" *His voice tails away to silence and in a moment he mutters,* "*and then it is too late.*"

Weighing Imacah's words against the king's summons, he wonders if the eagle will return; decides what it will mean if it does. When he stares up into the sky it is empty but for the scudding clouds. Waiting, wishing, he counts out a hundred heartbeats, then fifty more for luck. It does not come and so he shakes his head. "*Too late already, this year.*"

"*I thought you'd come with me.*"

He smiles, holding Imacah's hand between his own. "*I'll follow you to the edge of the world in a sackcloth but now's not the time to prove it. Nay, listen,*" *he says, not letting him pull away,* "*think on it a moment: it's a twomonth's journey to the north country and 'twill be the equinox in but a sennight. An we go now, we find the boats drawn up, the ice four fathoms deep and the whalemen hunkered down for the winter. No work and no welcome for strangers with bellies to fill. A long winter's night and nothing to do but wait until the sun remembers to rise.*"

"*There's always something to do on a winter's night.*"

He snorts with laughter. "*Aye, well, so you've shown me, but I'll want a warm bed up in the north. See sense and wait awhile—it'll all still be there in the springtime.*"

"*We should not wait.*" *Imacah's lip twists with the petulance of the boy he is no more, suddenly his father's son.* "*We should seize our freedom! Be what we desire and not what they*"—*he gestures to the hall*—"*would have us. Here we're caught in a pattern not of our making.*"

He spreads wide his hands. "*We are what we've always been, a clansman and a bastard. Look me in the eye and tell me it matters.*"

"*You know it does not!*"

"*So why haste away now?*" he asks. "*It cannot be because they caught us 'cross the water. Or because of your father's thricetold tales. Nor even what the king would say to me.*"

A son is the father's and so Imacah is always called Kistoru's son. In truth he is far more like his mother, being dark of eye and hair. He has the same trick she does of pulling at his ear when he is uneasy. He does it now. "*You had a girl, that time my father called the clansmen out to his hunting.*"

"*And so I did—what's that to do with anything?*"

"*What was it like?*"

"*If you do not know, I cannot tell.*" He grins, watching the thoughts run across Imacah's face. "*Try it for yourself.*"

Imacah scowls. With his thumbnail, he rubs the bells from a sprig of heather and scatters them into the wind. He does not look up but mutters between his teeth, "*My mother starts to talk of marriage.*"

He laughs, hard and harsh, at the thought of it. "*Then she's a fool. Surely Ala knows she's as like to pick apples from an orange tree as see your wedding day. She's eyes in her head and knows well how to use them.*"

"*She hopes that she sees wrongly. That it is a little thing that does not matter. That if you were not here, I would see reason. All these three things together.*" Imacah tosses the bare twig aside and starts to strip another. "*Always she rattles on at me, weighing up one woman against another till I wish them all sunk in the sea and she beneath the lot of them!*"

"*You're not a maid who might be forced.*" He shrugs, settling himself back into the heather. "*When she asks you, tell her, No!*"

"*Then she weeps and wails and tells me she is lonely. She wants a daughter since her own is dead.*"

To that there is no answer. Imacah rants on a while, then glances sidelong at him. "*Tell me true, what was it like?*"

This time he answers without jesting. "*Neither the simple thing I'd thought it, nor the mystery you'd have it. She was amused to find how little I knew, and made sure I knew much more before the morning.*" He glances at the shadows falling across the hill, the woodsmoke rising from Kistoru's hall. "*You'll be late for your father's stories.*"

Ignoring this, Imacah says, "*I know all I need.*"

He knows Imacah's face better than his own but, when he looks up and meets his eyes, the hairs rise on his neck. In unthinking answer he reaches out and their fingers knot together. This is what matters. This is all that matters. He leans across and kisses him, and all else is forgotten. There is neither past nor future but only he and Imacah, together in this moment, forever and for always.

That moment passes into another, and another. In the time after the sunset, Imacah draws breath at last and whispers, "In the north, the whales will care nothing for either of our fathers. Let's away and find our freedom."

"In springtime," he promises, "in the springtime. I've a mind to meet the king, and a score to settle with his company. Let's make sure the clans remember us, when we are gone."

As they walk down the hillside, Imacah's arm about his shoulder, he takes up the story of their future. "The next year we'll go a-raiding into the Later Lands like heroes from the piper's tales, like Torùkotu himself, you and I against the world. A hundred fights we'll start, each on a different shore, and then a hundred more, and by the time we're through Imacah will no longer mean Tamarhak's son. No one left alive will say your deeds came of your father!" Above the hills the stars are pricking into light. He points westwards to Liùthai the seastar, ever the first to shine out of the sunset. "And when we've tired of the Later Lands, we'll set our ship towards that star and sail into the west, further than any king has dared to go, and live forever and a day beyond the sunset."

Imacah's laugh rings out into the halflight. "I wish it could be now."

"Soon," he answers, "soon."

2: The king across the water

"Oh where hae ye been, my long, long love,
  These seven long years and more?"
"Oh I'm come to seek my former vows
  That ye promised me before."

The Daemon Lover, Traditional

The long day of midsummer, and again the piper must step empty-hearted through the sunlight. All around him, music played as in every year since women danced with men beneath the flowering trees. But this was not his time, this was not his place: today his song was silenced and he could make no music on his wooden pipe.

Another song sounded in the sunlight, a tongue of fire and sunlight flickering around the trees. Around and around him were many songs, and many voices singing them, but this called to him as those did not. In all the years of his life only one had sung this song, and she was long years gone.

He walked out of the meadows towards this song, he walked beyond the orchards to the places where apple trees gave way to birch and ash and rowan and, as he walked, the day grew brighter and the song sweeter yet, calling him out of his long past.

When he found his ear had not deceived him, when at last he saw her, his heart was filled with fear, but her song was not yet ended and in such singing he could take only joy. She sat in sunlight, a golden witch in the golden wood, combing out her golden hair. Slowly, slowly, she turned her head that he might see her beauty bright as the sunrise, might watch the sweep of the comb through her long hair, might know her song was sung for him alone. And the web she wove of song and light and golden hair caught him and held him fast.

At last she stilled the slow motion of her comb, at last her song fell silent. She held him a long time in that silence and, when she put down her comb and stretched out her empty hands towards him, when he could move again, he gasped for air as if he had been drowning.

"It is as you see – I am here. As in the long ago," she said, beautiful and terrible as the sun at noontime, "I ask, and here you are to answer, my piper."

"I had not thought to hear you sing again, Averla," he said, his heart beating out a new rhythm, "or see the sweep of your yellow hair."

"Oh my little piper, is it my song you fear to hear, or the echo in your own heart? A fine dance you have led since we were last together, limping before with all the great ones following after."

"Not you, Averla!"

"Never I! Allodola you tamed to piety, the Liùthion has grown safe and heavy in the flesh you clothed him in and Allocco is dead. And here I sit, and I am neither tame nor safe nor dead! And there you stand – that thought you knew all things – suddenly to know not all the world dances to your tunes."

He cried out, "What do you want?"

She began to braid up her hair, the twists ripe and heavy as summer wheat between her fingers. "I want what I have always wanted. But what is it that you want?" She fastened her braids about her head and drew up her hood to cover the corngold of her hair. She smiled to see his face. "I know you, better than any other in this world. I know that you are lonely. I know you are afraid. You should have taken what I offered." Her voice dropped to a whisper, caressing the words as she spoke them. "Do you lie awake at night, my dear, and think of all the things that might have been?"

"Enough, Averla, please enough!" he cried out, and, though he could not weep, his eyes were very bright. "If I cannot have the whole, I will take nothing."

"Even of me?"

"Even of you. I never wanted a night spent in your arms, tangled in your yellow hair. I want what you will never give."

"And so you went your way, your endless way along the road, and tried to drive me from your mind. I think you did in Escen – I never thought till then you were as much a fool as any man, seeing only a pretty face and not the thought that lies behind it. You were never such a fool with me!"

"With you I had no hope, Averla. It is not much to say in your favour, that you were never kind."

"Did you want my kindness, monster? You flung hers in her face and left her. Little fool! Perhaps you spoke too soon and frightened her; perhaps she would have loved you if you had given her more time. Now she is dust these many years, and might have been will never be. But that other one still lives, that first you charmed and then left lonely. Another took your leavings. And now Allocco's son turns his face to a new future. And so do I." She laid her hand upon his arm and drew him down beside her. "Tell me, my dear, if a man should chance to kill a king, what does that make him?"

The wood was full of sun and birdsong and the movement of the wind in the trees. He did not see the sunlight, he did not hear the birdsong. He saw only Averla, he heard only her laughter. "Poor monster, poor musician, to live so long and know so little! You closed the gate, you trapped me in this shell of flesh and now the world is a crooked place for all you try to make its ways run straight."

—┼— —┼—

Marwy Ninek woke upon midsummer's morning, as she had woken on so many other mornings, to an echo of a man's laughter.

The fire is not yet burned out, the night is not yet ended, and I am not yet satisfied.

Closing her mind against the memory, she got up from her bed, washed and dressed and went out to face the day. Later, she looked around at the men of Felluria. Torùkotu was long years gone but here were the living he had left behind. Behind her eyes, she saw him, standing beside the open door, laughing across the years. She opened her eyes and saw him still, here and there across her hall. His red hair grew on the blacksmith's head, the fisherman beside the fire wore his smile and a young shepherd held a crook with his long hands. All of him was here; he had never left Felluria, though with all her strength and all her will she had brought darkness down upon him. He had scattered himself across the land and, like the seeds of lithia, taken root in the stony ground. She looked at the women in her hall, at the shepherd's lass handfast with her man and shivered at the sight, wondering how she could bear to have him touch her.

Her gaze fell on another man, the outlander Assiolo. He sat in the window with his hat in his hand, looking out beyond the sunlight into a distance only he could see, a sprig of firestar in the lacings of his shirt. He wore the clothes now of Felluria but still looked like a stranger, pale-faced, clean-shaven, his brown hair cropped to his chin. All around him flowed the hubbub of the morning: games of draughts or fox and geese between ships' captains, mercatmen doing business amidst their tally-sticks and counting beads, children riding hobby-horses between the tables, but he sat surrounded by a little space that none would cross. She had seen in these last months many men turn their eyes away from him, and jests at his smooth cheeks fall away in face of his mild stare. He was a young man, this outlandish stranger, but he had seen more of the world than many old men in Felluria.

She crossed her hall towards him and, as she passed through the noise and the bustle, men drew back from her path, turning their eyes away. Assiolo rose up as she came close, bending his head in greeting, and she sat down in his place. Casting about for something to break the silence, she said, "You have a name now for music. Even Yatta Tala says she has not heard your like before."

"Not to my face. To my face, she says that fools and children like

new toys awhile and cast them aside when another comes their way."
He spread out his hands, smiling ruefully, and almost she smiled
with him. "And to that I have no answer, since it is the truth. Is
there aught you wanted of me?"

"Nay, only to hope you will play this evening."

"Alas, I must crave your pardon. I have no songs to fit the day. It
is midsummer," Assiolo said, "the world is full of light and out of
balance." She trembled, and steadied herself against the stone wall.
"I will find Yatta Tala," he said, "or else her daughter. You are not
well."

"Yatta Tala will be at her loom, and younger women making
ready for midsummer. I am quite well. Except..."

"Except?" he asked, very gently.

"I have the headache; last night I had bad dreams." She had
not thought to say such a thing. A dream was of no matter in the
sunlight; a dream had no hands to hold her, no flesh to thrust at her.
She stood up from her seat, and he stood back to give her room.

"The wind can blow your dreams away, if you will let it," he said.
"Beyond stone walls, where the wind blows free, you will find green
grass beneath your feet and blue sky above you."

"I shall walk in the court. The sky is as blue there as beyond the
walls, and the grass as green. And the wind blows."

Marwy Ninek bowed her head and waited for him to leave her.
Instead Assiolo turned his brown eyes towards her and she thought
again how unlike he was to the men of Felluria, this quiet stranger;
he would look her in the eye, unafraid, unashamed.

"May I walk with you?"

She started at the question, and all else was drowned out by the
thunder of her heart. No man of Felluria would have dared ask such
a thing. In Felluria, men answered if she spoke to them, or else kept
silent in her presence. She leant against the wall, seeking strength in
the touch of cold stone. Assiolo must have seen, but she saw not one
whit of discomposure in his face.

"It's a fine, fair day," he said, "and I would store up sunlight
against the weeks of rain that are sure to follow it."

The stone was firm beneath her touch, grounding her; in her
hall, the men and women of Felluria passed together through the
morning, laughing and talking, planning the hours ahead, bright and
unafraid.

"If you would rather walk alone," he told her, "you have only to
say. I'll not press you if I am unwelcome."

His eyes were mild; his face was still; he waited for her answer.
Marwy Ninek swallowed once, she swallowed twice, and told him,
"I'll walk with you within the court."

"I am glad," he said, and, though she did not look at him, she could hear in his voice that he was smiling.

Beyond the walls, Cal Mora rose up, its flanks patched with bracken and with ling; beyond the walls, the wind was blowing through birken trees and pine; beyond the walls, seabirds called across on the shore; beyond the walls, the briars were a tumble and a tangle, the sweetest roses with the sharpest thorns. All these she had seen, many times across many years, and she had turned her back on all of them for sake of her stone walls.

The gate was open; the road beyond the gate was dusty with noontime and summer, stretching up onto the moorland, stretching out towards the shore. Assiolo paused a little time, looking up towards the mountain. She stood beside him. "A fair place, in the summertime," she told him, "drear and dreadful when the rain beats down in winter and there is no shelter."

He glanced at her, but if he had a question he did not ask it. "And tonight the fairest night of all, I've heard, for those with a mind to keep it on the hillside."

"No doubt tonight, if you've a mind for it, you'll find a bonny lass to tumble with you in the heather."

"I never kept midsummer but once," he said. There was a look on his face she had not seen before, a bitter smile as at some black memory. "Let lovers play at love and others bide quiet within stone walls."

Marwy Ninek turned from the gate to the garden behind the hall. Assiolo followed. Children were playing there, some noisy game with bat and ball. She settled herself on the soft grass in a patch of sun beneath the wall and in a moment he too sat down, close by enough to talk easily, too far to touch. Between them grew a patch of harebells, nodding and trembling in the breeze. He leant his back against the stone, a young man in the sunlight, watching the children's ball bounce across the grass and the clouds pass across the sky. The grass beside the wall was scattered with tormentil and daisies and, like a child, she picked the flowers, threading them into a chain of silver and gold to wear about her wrist. And somewhere, far, far in the back of her mind, she was glad he did not mean to keep midsummer upon Cal Mora's braes.

"You said you have bad dreams," Assiolo said. "Tell me your dreaming. Perhaps two can bear what one cannot."

"They are dreams, dreams only," she answered shortly. "They have no weight in the waking world."

The children ran and chased each other across the grass; the swifts screamed of summer in the high air; the swallows swooped to their nests beneath the eaves. The shadows lengthened across the afternoon as the midsummer sun slowly sailed towards the west. Marwy Ninek sat beneath her wall, making her chains of flowers. Assiolo sat close by but, as she worked, she looked only at the flowers twisting around her fingers.

"Sometimes," he told her after a long time of silence, "it can ease a mind to tell a dreaming."

"Sometimes," she answered, "there are stories which should not be told."

She looked at the shadow of her hall, at the swallows' nests beneath the eaves; the day was bright, the sun was warm, the night was far away.

Assiolo picked a harebell, a little thing, fragile and delicate beside the daisies and the tormentil, and held it out before her. "It bends when the wind blows but the wind cannot break it. It takes a living hand to do that, and the mind behind that hand."

The wind blew across the wall and she shivered, pulling her coat around her. Assiolo spoke across her thoughts, "There are men within the world will crush a flower beneath their feet and think nothing of it." She fixed her eyes on the chain of flowers about her wrist, on the harebells in the green sward, forcing herself to stillness. "My father was such a man," he said, "I think Torùkotu was another."

The children's voices could have been calling from another world. Assiolo sat very still and straight against the stone; he did not move towards her, he did not move away. When the constriction on her heart had lifted, when she could breathe again, she let her words fall into the space between them, "Long ago, I drove him into the dark."

"But his deeds still hang heavy across your mind and memory. I have eyes, and I can use them."

"His will was stronger than mine."

Assiolo made no move, he said no word. His eyes were following the flight of swifts, the wide sweeps of scimitar wings 'cross the azure sky. She forced herself to speak though her words hung heavy on her lips. "That night was his revenge – he did not even want me for myself: the one he wanted slipped through his fingers at the last. Ketala Iitha cheated him with death – I was all that was left of her, the only part he had not taken." She saw Assiolo holding the harebell in his hand, tracing stem and calyx with one finger, very gently so that he did not crush it. "It was a long time ago, and always it could be yesterday. Torùkotu taught me fear that night, he taught me hatred. He taught me that sometimes all I can do is not enough to keep me safe. Now I am but a broken thing."

Threading the harebell into his shirt, Assiolo said softly, "I do not think you are broken. I think, when you were very young, a man made you look upon all the evil in the world and, since then, you have been long years alone and long years afraid. But look around, here are stone walls to turn aside the wind, here are the people of Felluria, who love you."

"All this is nothing," she answered, and cast aside her flowers. "There were stone walls long ago, and people then who loved me. The walls fell, the people died and I was left alone to live on after the ruin.

"When I was young, the piper told me stories, he sang me songs among the roses to drive away my loneliness. At summer's end the roses died. He took the name I gave him, he gave me lithia and left me. Firestar flourishes when all else dies, as fair upon the ruins as on a king's hall." She pulled a sprig of firestar from the wall and wound it around her wrist, its flowers like sparks, its dark juice staining her skin. "It is a long time since I was young, Assiolo," she said, making her voice hard as the stone walls about her hall, cold as the wind that blew down the braes of Cal Mora. "What was done cannot be undone."

"That is true," he said, "but because the past was terrible does not mean the future must be. Perhaps the worst days are gone and better ones remain. The future is not yet written, even in Felluria."

She looked up into his face, into his brown eyes, and, almost, she believed it could be so.

—+— —+—

Three windows to the king's chamber, one looked east and one looked west and the third towards the south, and all were open to midsummer's night. Beside the bedplace, the king's sword rested, waiting for the morning and his hand, and, in the bed, the king slept, lapped in fur, cushioned on feather, his hair tumbled around him, its fire quenched to blackness and shadow. There came a laughing murmur through his dreams, a teasing caress light as a whisper of silk against his sleeping skin, the scent of elderflower and honeysuckle drifting out of the night, and the king sighed and shivered into waking. Eager, ready, he reached out, to pull her close and take what he was offered.

She was not there that should be. His grasping hands met only the yielding softness of sealskin; he was alone, no body in the bed beside him. Fully awake now, puzzled, he looked around and saw the long-haired star beyond the window, low in the eastern sky, sickly and yellow in the time before the morning, casting its beam onto the bed. Desire fled away into the night, leaving cold fear behind it. No living man had seen this star but, like every king before him, he knew its name, he knew its meaning and closed his eyes against its light. No man could look into that light and not be blinded.

"Do you know me?" asked the light.

"I know you," he answered. Behind closed eyes he saw her lying next to him, smiling eyes blue as the sky at noontime at midsummer, clad in the golden mantle of her hair. "What do you want of me, Averla?"

"What I have always wanted. But that is not why I am here. I am here for you, Te-Meriku. Twice now the piper has turned your fate from one future to another. Let me do likewise. You need not die an you serve me."

She leant forward into her kiss and her hair spilled over and around him, rippling in honey-heavy waves across his breast. Her strength was greater than his for all her skin was soft and white; he could not turn away and, from behind his closed eyes, she looked down at him, smiling. A moment's pause, and then he felt her hands a-roving, teasing, caressing, moving down, down, down, across his naked skin, her lips following, an edge of pain behind the pleasure. He was tangled in her hair, struggling against strands like seaweed, the long sea grass that ripples in the current, that knots and twists around a man and drags him to his death. He writhed and twisted to reach the great sword so close beside the bed, straining until his fingertips of his right hand could all but touch the carved ivory of its hilt. Averla caught his wrist and pressed him back onto the furs, such strength in her white fingers; though with his mind he saw a woman, his eyes were blinded by the light. With sure touch and certain knowledge, she asked and he felt his treacherous body answer, then, laughing, she straddled him. He groaned and shuddered as, between one heartbeat and the next, all self and sense and understanding were consumed by light and fire.

Averla stroked his face, gently brushing back his hair as if indeed she loved him. "You need not die, my dear, no more than this little death, an you yield to me," she told him, as he lay beneath her, soaked in sweat and shame.

"Is that what you whispered to Allocco? When, by your art and his, the world came close to ruin?"

She sat back smiling. "So says the piper. You were not there, you cannot know. But now you are here and I am here, so answer me, Te-Meriku: will you take what I offer? I give fair payment for your kingdom. I'll swear it is enough for any man, even for you."

He pulled himself free, hoping he hurt her, crying out, "Other men, Averla, not me. I am the king, and I will keep my own."

"And so you say me *No!*"

He closed his hand on the bronze sword and pricked its point against her throat, backing from her, as from a venomous thing that could corrupt by touching. "And so I say you *No!*"

"You think, because you are the king, no man can kill you? You think, because my brother wears your face a while, that you have weight upon the world?" Averla's voice was cool and steady, she did not move, she did not flinch, though the bright bronze pressed at the blue pulse beneath her chin. A long moment was counted out, a hundred heartbeats and then a hundred more, and the king's hand trembled. He could strike with all his might and not one golden hair be severed. Averla took the sword from him, easily as he might part a child from its toy, and laid it 'cross her bare knee. The crack of breaking bronze filled his ears, sharp as a branch snapping in the frost. She took his right hand, turning it palm upwards to read the map of his life.

"Poor fool. You have lost much, Te-Meriku, and you must lose more, an you say me *No*. When I am done, you will have nothing, not even your life: another shall come to take the kingship from you, to stand upon the further bank and close the gates of evening, sealing the tree beneath the other sky. Then there will be not day nor night but world without end, forever and for always."

He had been years the king and knew well how to judge truth in a man's words, or a woman's. But though Averla wore a woman's flesh she had never been a woman: maybe she spoke truth, maybe she lied, maybe his future was writ in stone, maybe in running water. Such things he could not know: the future was a book no man could read. But one thing he did know: true and certain was his kingship, a rock to cling to whilst all hopes were wrecked around him.

"You cannot reach the tree," he said, "you cannot cross the water. That marks the boundary and the limit. Even for you, Averla, there are things that cannot be."

"And so you think you have the mastery? You? A western barbarian without even a name to call his own."

The king reached for the pieces of the broken sword; closing his hands upon the hilt of ivory and gold, he opened his eyes though the light dazzled him. It was the hardest thing he had ever done. He had been wrong to think a heart could not break twice; he had not thought he could know such pain and live. The sea eagle has eyes that can outstare the sun but he was only a man and the light blinded him.

"I am the king in the west," he said. "I guard the tree beneath this sky, as have all the kings since Imacah mor Tamarhak: while I live you will not have your own again."

"If you set yourself against me, Te-Meriku, you will die." Averla's voice was the thunder after the lightning, her face the sun at noontime and her breath the desert wind that withers all flesh to dust. She waved her hand towards the eastern window, where the balestar hung and spread its yellow light across the land and sea. "You see that star now with your mind's eye. Soon, soon, even in the reckoning of men, it will rise as herald of my right and my victory. For all his vows of love and all his tears of loss, Allocco did not live lonely in his exile. He left a son behind him, a son with all his strength and will and knowledge. He is already in a place where your kin made a devastation. And I shall make him mine, my tool, my creature. It will be very easy for him to come to hate you. He will snuff out your life easy as a candleflame and walk where I cannot, the king across the water."

She kissed him three times, on his brow, on his cheek, on his mouth; her lips burned him, his tears hissed into steam and he knew himself a man alone in a sea of fire and pain. Then Averla kissed his eyes and he screamed out in terror, seeing clearly the future he had made for himself. There could be no escape, though he keep all his oaths and promises.

A hand shook his shoulder, a voice called in his ear, "Te-Meriku, *Te-Meriku*." The king opened his eyes to grey light and fading shadows, looked up into a sleepy face exasperated to be disturbed at such an hour. "You left me little time enough for sleeping," she told him, "I'd think you'd let me have it."

He stared to see the woman in the bed beside him, round and sweet and rosy, in every point unlike Averla. "I dreamed."

"All men dream. Others do it quietly."

Dazed and stupefied by dreaming, uncertain whether this was trick or seeming, Te-Meriku reached out to touch her breast and fumbled for her name, finding it after a moment's thought. "Hadùwy."

She slapped his hand gently away, laughing a little. "Not now. In the morning, if only you will let me sleep."

Sitting up, he looked around his chamber, seeing the sword in its right place at the bedside, his clothes and hers tumbled carelessly across the floor. All was as it should be, no stars beyond the window, only the grey light seeping across an overcast sky, the patter-pat of raindrops on the roof. "Sleep then," he said, "but, in the morning, I'll hold you to that promise."

Her laughter was a charm against ill-fortune. Night terrors fled away into the dawning and he relaxed, himself again.

"How strange," she murmured, turning her back and settling down again into the sealskin, "to be the king and have bad dreams."

II, Felluria: The first days of the fall

She sits alone within stone walls when, unexpected, the dwarfish piper comes to her. Without the walls, the briars grow, a tangle and a tumble, poor flowers with just a touch of sweetness but strength enough in root and stem to stand against the salt wind and the storm. The walls make a little space of shelter from the wind and within the walls are other roses, red as blood, white as snow, drooping their heavy heads against the summer's warmth, scented sweet as summertime.

"I am glad to find you, Thelis Ketala," he says. "There is something I must give you."

She shakes her head. "You call me by a name that is no longer mine."

"Forgive me," he says. "I knew the one who was Marwy Ninek before you. You are nothing like to her."

He drops a ring onto her palm. A man stands forever on the surface of the stone, his empty hands outstretched beneath the bare tree. She stares awhile before she asks, "Why give the king's ring to me? You should take it back to Metius Estui."

"Metius Estui pulled it from his finger when the wind blew from the west. He bade me tell you to keep safe within the stone walls of Felluria."

"I will keep it safe and give it back when he returns."

He sets his hand upon her shoulder. "The king is dead," he says, "the king will not return. There's another in his place in Eulana, lass, a man of bronze and blood."

She does not move, she does not look at him. She hears her own blood beating in her ears, louder than any drum.

Beyond the garden, women's voices rise in a lamentation. "Metius Estui called the young men to his company, a sixmonth since," she says, hearing the names within their cries. "I think they too will not return."

The ring is hard and heavy in her hand, its red stone dull as old blood. A chip is missing from one corner, a blemish that was not there before.

"No, lass, no," he answers, softly, sadly. "A childish folly, to think to turn back the tide with a wall of sand."

Behind her and above her, grey stone is laced across with the clinging tendrils and leaves of firestar. The evening light, golden as honey, spreads itself across the garden. Faces pass behind her eyes, taking flesh only in her mind. She bites her lip, thinking of the blacksmith's second son. All men must die, but this is the first time death has swooped so close across her life, brushing her cheek with its black feathers. She draws a deep breath and pulls her coat tight against the wind, bends her head into her hands. In her heart is a pain she has not known before.

The piper asks, as if he read the thought unspoken, "Was there one amongst them you think on more than the rest?"

Her answer is no more than a breath carried away upon the breeze. "The end has come before the beginning."

The piper turns away, to sit cross-legged beneath the wall and put his wooden pipe to his mouth. He blows, his fingers dance and music fills the garden, spills out into the evening. All other noises fade away, even the harsh cries of women fall back to nothing in face of this jarring, jangling melody. There is nothing its maker has left to learn of suffering, of pain and loss and disappointment, of hope trampled down into despair. He plays, and sorrow swells her heart to bursting until, when she can bear no more and presses her hands across her ears, opens her mouth to beg for silence, the tune becomes a little thing, a sweet tumble of notes rippling across her troubled mind like a stream across Cal Mora. It swells and grows and all the rest is washed away. The past is gone, the future is changed but, here and now, is music.

At last his fingers are still and he sets the pipe down on the grass beside him. Within stone walls women still weep but the first raw shock has tempered into aching misery.

She asks, "What is your name?"

"I have no name; I lost it long ago, along with all the rest. Kenu, they call me, the monster."

"Not I. I will not call you monster."

The piper holds out his hand. "Not you? It is of no matter. A word, no more than that."

She turns the ring upon her finger, studying the device upon the stone. She has known it her whole life long but never yet paused to parse its meaning. The firstborn tree she knows full well. It grows by day beneath one sky, by night beneath another and two kings guard it. One offers death, the other oblivion, but this king's hands hold neither sword nor apple.

"Which king is this?" she asks. "Who stands beneath the bone-bare tree and offers nothing?"

"Nothing, lass, and everything."

She looks up, puzzled by his riddle. He smiles and says, " 'Three kings beneath the tree are seen, of day and night and might have been.' "

Lines out of a childish game. She played it herself ten years ago, casting her stones, singing and skipping from square to square. He reaches out to touch the ring. "There's hope here, lass, and longing, all you could wish for, all that might come to pass if the world is as it should be."

The laments of women rise above the garden. She shivers, remembering how the verse ends. "'There is no time for might have been.'"

He shrugs. "I've said before, lass, I'll say again: dreams and tales are not a life."

In a little while, as twilight folds itself around them, she whispers, "What of my mo—" She pauses on the word, puts another in its place, "Ketala Iitha?"

The piper thinks a little time before a short, sharp answer. "She lives."

"Will she come to me?"

"I have no firmer grasp upon the future than any man," he says, "but, for my part, I think it better she does not."

She looks into his face and does not understand.

"There are choices turn one future to another. So will it be for you, I think, should she come here," says the piper. "There's a red king in Eulana, lass. Salt in the meadows and blood in the trees."

She traces a finger across the carved stone of the ring. The broken edge is sharp; this is a recent hurt. A flash of memory: a woman weeping beneath an apple tree, the petals falling down like flakes of snow. "If she asks," she whispers, "what can I do but answer?"

His eyes are not the eyes of a man. They have looked on many things no man will see. "Choice comes," he says, steady and unblinking, "and oftentimes we call it necessity to ease the weight upon our hearts."

"Even you?" she asks, thinking of the stories she has heard, the tales she has been told.

"Oh, I above all others," he answers, a note of mocking laughter in his voice. "Who am I to judge necessity? I chose, and know the penalty of choice. No hand but mine has shaped my future." He takes back his hand and bows his head. "I have told the tale I came to tell, and now I must away."

"Stay yet awhile," she says. "It grows lonely in Felluria."

"The world is very big," says the piper, "and cares not that we are in it. Many times, in many places, I have seen such things to make me wish to lie down and sleep, nevermore to waken. But the world is fair as well as foul." He reaches out to touch the red rose tucked into her hair. "I've lived a long time, lass, and there are few things sweet as roses on a summer's evening."

There is a note in his voice she has not heard before. She remembers the blacksmith's boy, his face flushed red as any rose, twisting his hat between his hands. "The roses are lovely but yet the women weep."

His answer is very soft and very sad. "Love is all we have to set against the dark; the pity is 'tis not enough."

The ring is heavy on her hand, his news heavy on her heart, the laments of women heavy with the weight of might have been. Were she a woman she could weep and lose herself in an ecstasy of grief. She cannot weep. Instead she tells him, "Your music says all words are not enough to say."

The piper's smile twists his face into a grimace. "You do me too much credit, lass. I'm but a poor beggar, wandering my days across the world because I have no home to call my own."

"I know what you are," she says, "you are my kind if not my kin." She takes the rose from her hair and holds it out to him, the crimson petals quenched to black in the twilight. "See, I'll give you payment for your play."

He takes the rose. "And tomorrow, if I will not stay?"

"I will scatter the roses on the ground and trample them."

"Nay, lass." He laughs, suddenly merry, and even in the midst of grief her heart catches a spark of laughter from his golden eyes. "They are too lovely and too delicate for such a fate. I'll make a bargain with you. Whilst there are roses in this garden, I'll sing to you each twilight."

For a month and a day, the roses bloom. Each evening, as the sky grows bright, she waits beneath the tower with a rose in her black hair; each evening, as swifts give way to bats upon the summer twilight, the piper comes to her.

She sits quiet those summer evenings, sometimes conjuring the blacksmith's boy to mind. The piper is little, he is twisted, hideous in the slanting evening light, as unlike the blacksmith's boy as midnight is from noontime. He is many things but he has never been a man: he will not follow a king's call to glory and destruction. And, all across those summer evenings, something is ending, something else beginning but so gently, so quietly, she does not notice either the end or the beginning.

Meeting her by chance upon the uplands, the piper shows her the marks pressed by hares in the heather and a lark's nest on Cal Mora-side; in the evenings, he teaches her the many names of stars and the many words for rain. "You are so young," he tells her, smiling at her joy, "I've lived a long time; I forget what it is to be so very young and see the world for the first time."

Beyond the garden, the west wind blows saltspray to blight the briars; beyond the garden, women weep and grief makes stone of old men's faces; beyond the garden, stormclouds gather and thunder echoes across Cal Mora-side. But, within the garden, stone walls turn aside the wind and make a space of shelter from the storm. Falling asleep, alone in her narrow bed, she whispers, over and again, "Bela, Belata, Morigu, Te-Ata, Yatta, Issa, Tascu, Ku," seeing in her mind's eye the eight stars of the hawk rising above the black bulk of Cal Mora.

"I have a gift for you," she says, one evening as she sits with him, watching a great moth drifting in the dusk above the roses. "Perhaps it will make good what was lost."

"Ah, lass," he says, "you've given already more than a beggar dares to dream of."

"I'll ludge many a beggar for your sake," she answers, "but this gift is for you and none other. It's a new name I give you: Vanithu, the musician."

His face is hideous in the halflight. He does not smile, he cannot weep. He rises, clumsy, to his feet and kisses her once upon the brow. "Hope is the hardest thing there is to bear, love is not enough, but yet we love and hope and dream of a future better than the past."

"Even you?

The moment stretches out between them; a step not made, a word not spoken. An owl beyond the walls calls out, "Who will? Will you?" His fingers brush softly 'gainst her cheek as he takes the red rose from her hair. He tucks it in the pocket of his coat and limps away into the dark.

Later, later, after the ruin, she looks back and sees clearly. All that was hidden is now plain, like flotsam washed up to the tideline.

After that night comes a day of storm when rain beats down upon Felluria and the wind from Cal Mora whips up the roses and tosses broken flowers upon the grass. By the evening the rain has passed, and the wind, but she can find no rose that has stayed whole.

The low sun slants from beneath heavy clouds. It falls upon Felluria and the firestar sparking red upon the walls. It lights the piper, who sits cross-legged against the wall in his coat of ragged blue. "There will be no music tonight," he says very gently, "you cannot pay the piper."

"The roses were payment for your play. All the rest was freely given, by you as by me. I have eyes," she says, "and I can see."

She does not know why he says nothing. She does not know why he turns from her. She sits and watches as he pulls lithia from the walls and twists the stems into a crown. In the western light the flowers burn between his hands like a circle of fire. "You gave me roses," he says, placing it on her head, "I give you lithia. Roses are sweet upon a summer's evening but the wind blows and they are scattered. Firestar clings hard to the stone and the wind cannot break it."

She holds out her hands to him but he steps backwards out of reach.

"I came to say farewell," he says, suddenly harsh, suddenly hard. "Summer is over, the roses have fallen and the wind blows me away."

"Will you come back?"

Long and steady he looks at her from strange golden eyes. "There are few to whom I give that promise. There are many ways across the world and I seldom walk them twice."

All around her on the grass are sticks and twigs and the bruised heads of roses, a ruined garden in the first days of the fall. "Stay with me," she whispers.

He shakes his head. A little gesture, curt and quick, as he might use to flick away a fly. "I've stayed too long already. I knew 'twas folly but the roses were so very sweet. A pleasant time enough, a dream amid the roses, but I must wake and go my way. Some things end, lass, before they begin: best this is one of them."

"The men died," she says, "but you are not a man."

"Nor am I fit for loving. All that I ever had in me to offer up as love for love blew away on the wind before ever I reached Felluria. You are very kind," he says, slowly, deliberately, "and very lovely, but music and dreams are not a life. Think what I am, think what I did. You saw more clearly before you heard my songs and stories."

"Oh, I have eyes," she says, "and I can see. It was for you as for me, this month among the roses." The blacksmith's boy had flushed red as any rose. They are nowise alike, the piper and the blacksmith's boy, but for a touch of roughness to their voices, eyes that look this way and that, anywhere, everywhere, save upon her face. "You are afraid," she says, and he does not gainsay her.

She stands and stares down at him for a long, long moment. He bows, cold, full courteous, then pulls his hat down on his head and turns away.

"Wait!" she cries out as he puts his hand to the gate. "You must not go." She pushes herself before the gate to bar his way. "Stay," she begs him, "stay. Next year there will be roses."

"I cannot stay. This is not my place."

"Then I'll come with you."

"And forsake Felluria to pad the road with me? Nay, lass, you don't know what you ask."

"You must stay, or else must take me."

He shakes her hand from his arm, his voice is harsh as she has not heard it in a month of music, hard as stone grinding against stone. "Not Imacah mor Tamarhak in all his pride dared say must to me!"

"He was a man! I am a Tion, as are you."

"A Tion!" He laughs. She flushes. "Listen, lass: 'tis not yet eighteen years since the Tion died and you were born. You have her place, her name, her life: never to sicken, never to grow old. For a long, long time, if the world is as it should be, you will be Marwy Ninek, the Tion in Felluria. But now—now you are a child, soon you will be a woman and know a woman's hopes and fears." She cannot move, she cannot speak, she can scarce even breathe. "In a long, long time, when all you know has

changed, when all you love has passed from the world, when the tales of your youth are no more told, when even your name is forgotten, come to me, Thelis Ketala, and I will call you Tion."

This month of summer evenings, she has listened to his music and his stories; she has seen only his golden eyes and known only his sorrow and his kindness. These are a part of him, but it is not the whole, perhaps not even the greater part. There is a fire burns at his heart that scorches all he touches.

She bows her head, unable to meet his eyes. Perhaps he reads her thoughts upon her face for he says, dry as the wind through summer grasses, "I see you begin to understand. Tamarhak's son named me fairly when he called me monster. What I am, I am, and so I cannot stay."

She stares and stares and does not answer. All she has known before this night could be bounded in her heart and yet still leave it empty.

"One thing else," he says, touching his finger to the ring, tracing the branching pattern of the tree, "if Ketala Iitha comes to Felluria, if love fails and hope falls short and the future is more than you can bear, an apple plucked beneath the other sky will bring an end to sense and self and memory."

He nods once in farewell and limps away into the dark, a hideous, twisted, stunted creature.

3: A double-edged blade

Mony a one for him maks mane,
But nane sall ken whar he is gane:
O'er his white banes, when they are bare,
The wind sall blaw forever mair.

The Twa Corbies, Traditional

Assiolo was tumbled out of sleep by the knocking at his door. Alert, uncertain, he lay in the dark, waiting to see what followed it.

"Assiolo." A woman's voice. "Are you there, lad? 'Tis I, Yatta Tala."

"A moment." He fumbled for his shirt and britches and, half dressed, opened the door to see the weaver with a lantern.

"Have you a strong stomach?"

He remembered a night in his own city, the reek of spilled blood, its stickiness upon his hands and swallowed hard upon the memory. "Strong enough. What's amiss?"

"A thing to show you, not to tell. Put on your shoes and follow me."

Yatta Tala led him across the court, up a staircase, down a corridor and towards an open door. Three shepherds were there, and a fourth upon the bed with bloody bindings round his arm and chest and face. The three men looked to Yatta Tala, their question written on each face.

"You've seen Assiolo afore now," she told them. "He's other callings beside music."

"You'll vouch for him?"

She nodded and pushed him forward to the bed. "If you're a leech, now's the time to show your craft."

The men drew back a little, to let him look at their companion. "Does she know?" one asked her.

"I doubt she knows her own name, tonight," the old woman answered. "I'll look to her in the morning; it's that lad there matters now."

Assiolo asked, "What happened here?"

"On the mountain," said the oldest man. He faltered into silence and looked from one of his companions to the other. They nodded for him to go on. "A wolf."

"Got into the sheepfold," another told him. "Fool here tried to drive it off."

"Should have made a light," the first man said, stepping back.

Assiolo turned the clouts away from the boy's face to see what lay beneath. Yatta Tala held the lantern close and steady, looking where the men would not. A sight to turn the stomach to be certain: half the flesh hanging from the bone, his right eye missing. The beast had worried, too, at his arm; there were bite marks there and scores from claws tearing deep into the flesh. Blood welled beneath his fingers, slowly, certainly. The boy's flesh was pale; he had lost too much blood already.

The weaver spoke beside him. "That's what you must face, lad. Can you do it?"

He took a breath and let it out slowly to steady himself. "What I can, I'll do." Her hand gripped his a moment, a touch of comfort he had not looked for. He met her eyes and nodded. "We need more light and warm water. Clean cloths. And make a fire, the boy's half frozen with his fear." As he gathered his thoughts, he heard her say, "One of you, go wake my daughter. Then his mother."

He had thought him in a swoon and been glad of it but the lad stirred beneath his hands. Lips moved but no words came forth from his ruined face, only a moaning whimper and soon he began to thresh upon the bed.

As a man passed him, Assiolo caught at his sleeve to hold him back a moment. "Go to my room. In the box beneath the bed there's tincture of poppy. Bring it, and the willowbark beside it." The man stared, baffled, and Assiolo sighed. "Bring the box. I'll find what's needful."

The others stood close by the window, rubbing bloody hands against their sides. "Where is that water?" Assiolo asked the weaver. "I'll need spirit too to wash these wounds, and needle and sinew to close them." He glanced from one man to the other. "If he's a sweetheart, tell her she'd best brace herself. Whatever I do this night, he's left his looks upon the mountain."

"He's sweet on the blacksmith's girl," one offered, "though she'd not look..." His words trailed away. "He should have made a light."

At his side, his companion put his head into his hands and muttered, "Upon the hill, upon the equinox, and did not think to take a light."

"It was a wolf?" Assiolo asked, looking closely at the wounds on the boy's shoulders.

"Aye, man, a wolf."

Assiolo looked from man to man, and kept his silence.

At last the water came, and light enough to work by. Spirit was found for him, and a needle. Sinew there was none fine enough, so silk was brought instead at Yatta Tala's order. The boy's right arm had been so mauled and torn there was no hope to save it. He had to use a butcher's cleaver for that, there being nothing better suited to the task. At the thud and crunch, one man hastened out, his hands pressed hard across his mouth. Yatta Tala snorted, "Five brats he's sired and found excuse to stay away each birthing."

Strange to laugh at such a time, but laugh he did. "Some can look and not be sick; others never get the knack of it."

There were others in the room now, quiet women with strained faces. Assiolo saw, from the corner of his eye, Baesina Yatta building the fire and offering clean rags each time he cast a bloody clout aside. Yatta Tala never moved from her place beside him, shining the light where it was needed. A brown-haired woman, her coat over her nightgown, her hair still in its rags, took one look over his shoulder and sank sobbing to the floor. Baesina Yatta slipped an arm around her, cradling her head against her shoulder, murmuring soft words that had no meaning to them. *Too old to be his sweetheart*, Assiolo thought, *his mother, likely.* If her son had once resembled her he had no way to tell. He worked on, and all the while the boy's blood welled up in slow gouts beneath his fingers.

In the time after the morning, he set down his needle and his salves and washed his bloody hands. The boy lay stiff and still, wrapped in clean linen, in the unnatural sleep of poppy. His pulse was weak but steady, counting out his life from one moment to the next.

Suddenly, all his own strength was gone. Assiolo sank down shivering upon the floor in the dull grey light, pressing his face into his hands to drive back the sights he had seen that night. For a few moments, the only sounds were the quiet sobbing of the boy's mother and the patter-pat of rain against the window.

"Assiolo." Baesina Yatta was shaking his shoulder, gently. "Assiolo, drink this."

He took the cup and drank. Something sweet and hot, with the fiery kick of barleyspirit behind the sweetness. Nothing in the world had ever been so good. Never in his life had he ever been so tired.

The old weaver raised her own cup to him. "Good work, lad."

He pushed himself onto his feet. "I'm away to find my bed. When he wakes, make him drink honey water. Nothing stronger. I'll come back in the evening to see how he does."

Yatta Tala opened the door and, as he passed her, he said, very softly so that the weeping woman would not hear, "Praise me in three days, if he is yet living."

He slept the whole light through, and all the day he had bad dreams. He beat his fists upon a wooden door but the door was locked and all his strength was not enough to open it. He walked beneath bare trees, the hunter and the hunted in the wild wood. His mouth filled with saltwater as the sea rose up around him and clinging arms kept him from his heart's desire.

Assiolo woke after the sunset. His clothes were lying where he had cast them down but there was a tray upon the table that had not been there before and steam was rising from the jug beside the ewer. Stupid with dreaming, he wondered how this could be until he remembered: there was no lock upon the door. He washed and shaved and dressed, found appetite to eat a little, though oatcakes and pickled herring were not much to his taste, and went out to see how the shepherd did.

Baesina Yatta was keeping a watch at his bedside. "His mother has other bairns. I thought it better she filled her day with them."

He did not like what he saw. The young shepherd's face was flushed with fever and he tossed restlessly upon his bed. The stump of his arm was clean enough and, by some miracle, his face, but the flesh of his neck and shoulder was ugly and red, swelling around the wounds. Looking at it, Assiolo swore beneath his breath in his own tongue that he had not the skill or luck to make a better job of it.

He set poultices a-heating to draw out the corruption and spread a salve of woundwort and cobweb across the angry flesh, muttering a charm against ill-fortune as he did so. He could not feel it catch, and wondered if its words had value in a place where none but he knew their meaning. Turning the words to the speech of the Later Lands, he heard in them all the sense and none of the meaning.

The lad reached out with his left hand to catch his wrist and pull him close. He tried to speak but his tongue would not form the words in his ruined mouth; all that came forth had no more meaning than a child's babble.

"Hush now," Assiolo said, "no need to fret. Your mother'll come shortly. Until then, I'll look after you."

Evening passed into night time. The poultices gave but little ease, more soothing to the boy the touch of Assiolo's hand upon his arm and the sound of his voice. Because he did not know him, he could think of little to say but sang longtimes in his own tongue, the old songs of ships and kings and rowan trees his nurse had sung him in his childhood. When he offered water, the boy drank thirstily. His touch was warmer now, heated by the fire burning in his flesh. What sense there had been in his eye was fading fast; it darted here and there, flinching from the light, seeking out the shadows.

"Is there ice in this place?" Assiolo asked Baesina Yatta. "If not, bring well water, cold as you can get it. And find another to watch those bairns. His mother's place is here, I think."

He had not pitied him before. Last night he had been but a mess of mangled skin and bone to be reshaped as best he could. Now, holding the boy's hand, he laid his left hand lightly across half his face to hide the ruin and caught a glimpse of what he had been and what he might have been. Tears welled up in his own eyes, at the horror and the waste.

Baesina Yatta returned, and Yatta Tala with her. Somewhat to Assiolo's surprise, there was ice, cut in the winter from the lochan in the corrie beneath Cal Mora's peak, stored in sand and sawdust in an icehouse beneath the north wall. A while later, the butcher came with it, his arms filled with a dripping bundle of sackcloth. Assiolo packed it round the boy, thinking to match one element against another.

Time passed, spreading itself as a shadow across the floor, counting itself out in the boy's rasping breaths. What he knew of leechcraft he had used; what he knew had not been enough. The boy's mother came in and he gave up his place to her. Last night she had wept but now she was done with weeping; love, beautiful and desolate, shone from her face as she looked down at her son.

The night crept by, slowly, slowly. The boy moaned and fretted, though none could take his meaning. Each time the candle burned an inch, he gave him poppy; each time the ice melted, Assiolo helped the women change his dripping sheets; between these times, the mother sat at the bedhead, holding her son's hand, stroking his brow and crooning lullabies, as if he were again a babe in arms and not a great lad past seventeen.

Beyond the walls, across the shore, the tide was turning to the ebb. Beyond the walls, across the shore, a curlew called out of the dark. Assiolo's thoughts were an undertow of memory, dragging him down into the past. Himself, alone within his father's house, an afternoon like many others in those years before he found his way into the space of peace his mother granted. He looked from the lad to the woman. The love in her face was greater even than her fear; feeling his eyes upon her, she turned and her smile pierced him like a shard of glass.

Broken glass reflecting a splinter of memory. Fallen petals in his mother's garden. The piper, speaking across the months between that evening and this. *She's gone, lad, what you could you did.*

His own voice crying out in an agony of truth, *Not all!*

Assiolo bent his head, remembering his mother's smile. She was dead and cold and in her grave, and death the end of all things. Upon the bed, the shepherd moaned, struggling against pain and bad dreams. He was not dead, not yet. And, whilst breath remained, there were ways to remake the bonds of life to flesh nor was it too late to use them.

He had found the book after his father died, taken it unknowing from the shelf to read upon a summer's day. And all the time he read, sitting in his father's place, his father's red wine to his hand, the sunlight did not move and the wind did not blow and all around was silence. When he had done, he shut up the book with trembling hands, knowing himself forever altered. For knowledge gained cannot be forgotten until the mind that holds it is broken or the flesh that carries it is dead. In the deathchamber in Felluria, Assiolo closed his eyes and those words wrote themselves across the page in his father's hand, shaped themselves in his mouth in his father's voice. He was his father's son: he had the strength, he had the knowledge, all he needed was the will.

All the time there was shrank down into a moment, his to do with as he willed. The boy fell still. The song fell silent. All the light that was in the room gathered itself around him, waiting for him to speak and change one future to another.

His mother smiling from her bed. Her kiss, her whisper, *It changes nothing to deny the truth.*

Assiolo swallowed once, he swallowed twice, and kept his silence.

The light faded. The moment passed. Upon the bed, the boy moaned and tossed against his mother's lullabies. Assiolo sighed and opened his eyes. He was not his father, only his father's son and, though he knew the ways, he would not use them. He beckoned Baesina Yatta close and told her softly, "The boy is dying. Let his mother have the last of him."

"A wolf," Assiolo heard one man say to another as they dug in the stony ground beyond the wall, "'tis time to go a-hunting."

'Twas true, no doubt, that there were wolves upon the mountain. 'Twas as true, no doubt, that there were bears and boars beyond the mountain in the wild woods of Eulana. All these would maul a man, if he were foolish enough to put himself in the way of tooth and claw and tusk. But he had seen the shepherd's face and the rents upon his neck and he knew, beyond all doubt, no wolf or bear or boar had torn his flesh.

Assiolo bent his back to his work and did not speak of it, for what was plain to him was plain to others also.

The boy was laid, clay-cold in his cold grave, whilst the wind from the mountain made the torches shiver and flicker in the twilight. Dry-eyed, his mother watched as the bitter earth was piled atop him; blank-faced, his mother stood whilst his fellows spoke for him, and, when all was done, she set down her lantern upon the grave, to burn and burn and keep him company until the morning, and then she turned away. Assiolo stood an arrow's flight distant, in the shadow beneath the walls, thinking of the words he had not spoken, the deed he had not done, and wished, watching, listening, seeing her grief, he could regret them.

He had no stomach for his meat that night and shook his head when any asked him for a song. He supped his ale and stared into the dark inside him, and all the while his father's bright gaze stared back, dazzling as all the things that might have been. Late in the evening, Yatta Tala told him, in her dry, sly way that, as was the custom when any died afore his time, the steward had, at Marwy Ninek's behest, offered the death-fee to his mother: six ewes with their lambs, three measures of barleycorn and an iron knife with a handle of ivory out of the northern sea.

It was not forbidden, in Felluria, for any man to seek out the Tion in her rooms behind the hall. What need to forbid a thing that was unthinkable? But, because it was not forbidden, Assiolo went that night in search of her and tapped upon the door.

"Marwy Ninek, Marwy Ninek, let me come in."

There was no answer. He had not expected one.

Her door was oak, studded with iron. No locked door could keep him out, if he desired to open it, but an unlocked door was another thing entirely.

He said, softly as if the door were not there, "It is I, Assiolo." No answer; behind the wood, only silence. "I came to tell you of my father."

The quiet dark swallowed his words. Perhaps she listened there, perhaps not. He could not know unless the door was opened, and that he would not do. If she was there, if she opened it, then he had a hope of saving her.

He said to the door, "My father was a great man in his time, a noble lord of high degree, most wise, most learned. He lost what most he loved. He did not forgive, he did not forget and, in the end, he had his vengeance, though it cost him his life."

A little sound behind the oak, a rattle and a rustle. So she was there, listening. "I do not think you another like my father, caring for nothing but his own hatred. Please," Assiolo said, "will you let me in? I gave you a promise and I shall keep it. There is no need to fear me – I wish only to speak with you."

He stepped back. Slowly, slowly, the door swung open. Marwy Ninek stood on the threshold, her black hair bound tight around her head, a dark red shawl over her grey gown.

"What do you know of vengeance?" Her tone was dull with exhaustion or with misery.

"Oh, I know. Better than any man alive, I know. I've told you of my father but never yet his name. He was Allocco, lord of Idùnmhor, chamberlain of Ohmorah, who stopped the sun and broke the world. He died, a dozen years ago, but he is a heavy weight upon my heart forever."

He heard her gasp, saw her eyes widen. Then her face hardened against him. "Do not play me for a fool, Assiolo. Time out of mind ago, the piper closed the gates against Allocco's fire. Those tales were old when I was a child."

"If you've heard those tales, you'll have heard too my father came of the First People, for whom a hundred years are as but one. I, being born in Ohmorah, have not his life, but 'tis true: I am Allocco's son."

"And if it's true – what's that to me? Dead, you say – dead men have no weight upon the world."

Assiolo spread out his hands towards her, the great scar plain on his left hand, if she had eyes to see it. "He fed his grief and had his vengeance. And it was the innocent who suffered, the blameless and the weak."

He saw her flinch, he heard her gasp. "Did you come here to judge me?"

Assiolo shook his head. "I have not that right. No man in the world may rightly judge you. But still the shepherd boy is dead, as dreadful a death as I have ever seen."

"Tascu Kai," she said, so quietly he could scarce hear. "His name was Tascu Kai. I held him in my arms when he was a month old."

"I did not know him but it is a grief to me I had not skill enough to save him. Tomorrow," he told her, "or the next day, or the next, for his sake, men are going hunting. Maybe they will find wolves, maybe they will kill them."

She stared and stared, and gave no answer.

"It is of no matter," Assiolo said shortly, " 'twas no wolf torn his throat, no more than 'twas a wolf taught you fear. So I shall say what no man here will say: the boy was not the first to die, because Torùkotu crossed the sea but, I promise you, he'll be the last." Against her gasp, he told her, "I am no man of Felluria and I too am going hunting. I will make an ending."

Fearful, trembling, she stared at him, eyes wide with shock. Almost he could hear the thunder of her heart. "You know what happened, after the ruin? You know what I did?"

"So I do – the piper told me when I was a boy. An apple picked beneath the other sky will make an end to self and sense and memory. There, such an apple brings an everlasting dream of borderlands, a dance upon the wind. This side the water their gift becomes a curse."

She drew back, closing the door against him. Assiolo put out his hand to stay her. "Please," he said, "let me come in. We must talk, you and I, before I go away."

At last Marwy Ninek nodded, so Assiolo stepped past her into her outer chamber. She lit a taper at the fire and set one lamp a-burning on the mantelshelf, another on a dresser, and curled herself on the woollen rug before the hearth, hugging her shawl around her thin shoulders. The room was cold and rain spotting in through the window at his back. He tried to close it and could not; a tendril of lithia had crept in and clung to the stone beside him. He pulled at it until the tough stem snapped. The bitter sap left a dark stain on his scarred palm but he could close the window against the rain and fasten the shutters against the dark. Outside the window, outside the walls, an owl called across the night, *Who will?*

"In the east," he said, winding the strand of firestar about his hand before slipping it into his pocket, "my father twisted the world to reshape it in his image. Here all tales begin or end with Torùkotu." She did not look at him. "He set his mark to shape the pattern of these lands: a red king in Eulana, salt in the meadows and blood in the trees."

She bent her head down to her knees, pulling her shawl tighter. "The king died, and the king will not return."

"The king Metius Estui died," Assiolo answered softly, and watched her shiver for all she sat so very close to the fire. "So yestreen did the boy. But there is a red king still in Eulana. I have not heard that he is dead."

She scrambled to her feet to pace the room, counting out her steps from wall to wall.

"I know what you did," he said, and, though he had not raised his voice, he saw her shudder. "I know why you did it but, though I've heard many tales in my time, I've never heard one that told the death of Torùkotu."

Marwy Ninek answered fierce and quick, her hands on the dark stone of her walls, "I stole an apple from the tree and then came back to face him. This time, it was midwinter, when the dark turns against the light; I hated him and he did not think enough of me to remember broken things are dangerous." For a moment, he saw her hatred rise and set her face ablaze; then its light died and left behind desolation. "If ever there is a time for vengeance," she said, "it is midwinter, when the world is dark and out of balance. But all my strength and all my hatred were not enough."

"I know." He did not say, *Midwinter's night is very long, much darkness, little light.* He did not say, *It is fear gave him the mastery.* He did not even say, *The only end is death.* What need to say such things, when she knew them all already?

"Metius Estui is long years dead," Assiolo said. "So is Ketala Iitha. They went into the dark a long time ago and all that suffered then

have followed – save one. The dead have no need for pity; they have
no need for vengeance. They died, they blow as dust on the wind,
now only you are left to live and to remember. All things must end,
all men must die."

"I had not strength enough to kill him. A hundred men within his
hall had not strength enough." She met his eyes and asked, "What
is it to you? Let him run mad until the world's ending – it will not
be long enough!"

"The boy died!" He flung the words at her, cutting through the
silence like a knifeblade. He met her eyes and for that moment the
mauled shepherd stood between them, an image born of memory
and lamplight. "Aye, think on that! What was Torùkotu to him? A
senseless, useless death before his time."

Marwy Ninek flinched and sank upon the floor, pressing her face
into her hands.

He had gone too far. The weight of all the things that might have
been, had Torùkotu not come into Felluria, pressed down upon her,
crushing her as a flower beneath a man's heel. Assiolo looked, he
saw and let his anger die away into the dark, leaving only sadness
behind. Quietly, as he would speak to a frightened child, he said, "It
is a double-edged blade, revenge. It destroyed my father: I'll not let
it take you too." Very softly he said, very gently, "Torùkotu is but a
man."

"A man no longer."

"I know. Those apples lose their virtue 'neath this sky." He sat
himself down an arm's length from her, his back against the wall.
The shadows waned and waxed around them as the draughts seeped
through the shutters and under the door. "Tell me of Torùkotu."

"Those tales you know as well as any in the Later Lands," she
answered, looking straight ahead so he could not see her face, her
voice empty as a broken heart. "What need for me to tell them?"

"Because you are here and I am here," he said. "Because the boy
is dead. Because what Torùkotu did has great weight still, upon the
world and on your heart."

Marwy Ninek looked into the glowing ashes of the fire, into a
great distance beyond the fire into the past, and Assiolo knew she
looked towards a man only she could see. With her eyes fixed on
the firelight, she told him, "He followed his star, he sailed out of the
west and made himself king in Eulana."

"That is the truth, but not the whole truth. Tell me of Torùkotu."

"He tumbled the towers of Felluria into dust and left a ruin
behind him."

"That too is truth, but not the whole. It was not for Felluria you
sought out the tree beneath the other sky."

Turning at last towards him, she asked, "What would you have me tell you?"

"Everything."

She cried out, "Must I?"

Assiolo saw the panic rising in her eyes, every nerve and muscle tensed against him like a wild bird on the verge of flight, because he was a man, because he was the stronger and too close. He said, offering his hand, "My promise holds. I desire only to stand as your friend and drive back the dark around you. But I need your trust."

With a little sigh, she took his hand. Her fingers were cold as the grey stones all around them and he chafed them between his own to warm them. "He is not here. Only I am here." Quietly, he asked her, gently, "Do you trust me?"

Her whisper was a thread drawing them together. "I trust you, Assiolo."

"See, beginnings are not so very hard." He put his arm around her, settling her into the hollow of his shoulder, comfort for the comfortless. "Tell me now the whole. Two can bear what one cannot."

So she told him. Told him of a child's first angry cry, of men lying in their blood among the broken walls, of firestar petals floating on a dark drink, of a woman's body burning on a pyre, of a man's rage because he could never know his heart's desire. She paused then, to press her trembling hands against her face. Assiolo whispered, "Tell me the rest."

She clasped her hands tight in her lap, weaving her fingers together to steady them, and told him of climbing a stair to darkness, of a locked door, of a fire and a knife and a noose, of a man's smile that curved his face into a grin and never touched his eyes. Assiolo could feel her every shiver, the flutter of her heart measuring out these moments.

Her whisper died away into the dark. Above his head the wind rattled the shutter, far louder than his murmur, "Tell me the rest."

She took a breath and told him. Told him of all the ways a man can use a woman if he cares not how he hurts her, if all that is left to him is his anger and his grief, if he thinks only of himself. And then there was nothing left to tell, and she bent her face into her hands and sobbed aloud for all that had been done that night, for all that had been lost, for all that would never be. She could not weep but she could mourn, great dry gasping sobs of pain and rage and misery and all the time Assiolo held her lightly, loosely, his hand gently stroking her hair and love and pity aching in his heart. He said no word to comfort, for what use were words at such a time? Beyond the window, night passed by and darkness faded into a sour, grey morning and, all the while, the autumn rain fell down like tears upon the stone walls of Felluria.

—┼— —┼—

Beyond the hall the wind blew, whipping out of the west into a gale, but inside the hall all was warmth and firelight. There were bowls of apples on the king's table, little yellow apples, round and ripe and ready, and any that would eat of them could do so. There were apples too carved into the roof beams and rowan branches bound above each window and the door, green leaves and blood-red berries.

After a five days' absence from the hall, Maris nar Ardùwy sat again in her place amongst the women, setting small stitches in the collar of a tiny smock. The king paused by her chair to greet her as was her due.

Another woman would have risen to make courtesy. Maris did no more than bow her head, stately as any queen. She had been mistress of the women's side, a king's daughter with a hundred generations of clansmen to her back, when he was a wild lad with neither name nor future roaming Kistoru's hills. Marking the nature of her work, he asked, "How does your daughter?"

"She has a fine girl-child, Te-Meriku, lusty and like to live."

A beat of time before he answered, "That news I had of Thodùhah three days ago. I asked of Liùthánwy."

Maris's grey eyes met his, steady and unsmiling. "All goes well with her. Ithánu has her in good care."

His mind slipped back to a winter's morning; awaking to the stifled sound of a woman's bitter tears. A little thing, slight and brown. Blood on her thighs and his. Surprised, concerned, to see such misery after the pleasures of the night, he had asked, *Did I hurt you, Liùthánwy? I had no thought to.*

With a sob, she had flung her arms around him, pressing her face into his shoulder. He had felt, rather than heard, her whisper. *No.*

He had stroked her hair, a clumsy comfort for distress he did not understand. *Then why are you weeping?*

If you do not know, I cannot tell.

Maris looked like her daughter might in thirty years. Because of that he said, speaking urgent, speaking low that others might not hear, "If she had asked, I would have answered."

Her lips tightened slightly as she shook the creases from her work. For a moment, the silence between them rang with all the words he had not spoken. She set aside her sewing, saying, "When she was a child she trotted at your heels. Once she became a woman, I doubt you gave her a second thought before she said you no. She touched your pride but not your heart."

All this was true and yet it was not all the truth. But what there was between a man and a woman was not to be spoken of before another, even if that other be the woman's mother.

Looking down into Maris's closed face, he wondered how much she knew, how much she had guessed. In answer to the thought unspoken, she placed her hand upon his arm and told him, not unkindly, "In the springtime, when she's strong again, she'll away into the north to Ithánu's hall, and the babe with her, and that's an end of it."

She had kissed the hollow of his neck and looked up at him, smiling through her tears, rain-grey eyes shining like light on the water. He had drawn his finger across the curve of a tender breast and felt her sigh and shiver at his touch. A moment's pause, then she rolled onto her back and pulled him down to kiss her, shaping herself to his desire, warm and willing as any he had lain with.

Maris met his eyes, steady, level, Hadùhai's daughter. He had been twenty years the king but in this matter 'twas she who had the mastery. In a moment, she took up her sewing. He bowed his head and turned away, crossing his hall to his own carved seat, summoning Edo Incithu, the fat mercatman of Cincern Dùn, with a curt nod. But, looking around his hall at the men and women of the Sea People, he thought again, as so many times over a score of years and longer, there was one not there that should be. He called for wine and drained the cup. The dead were dead and had no weight upon the world.

The dead were dead and he must look to the living. He drank his wine, red wine of Escen, the fire in its heart kindled by a fiercer sun than shone ever on Lyikené, and, unrequited, memory flooded him. He was as like to turn its course as the spring tide rising 'cross the shore. Not the soft flesh of women nor the firm flesh of men could slake that longing; no other face could take the place of that one nor yet the passing years ease the weight of loss upon his heart. The scent of apples sickened him. Any might eat that wished to but never him. He had lost his taste for apples long ago.

The mercatman took the seat beside the king's, in face and figure as unlike him as any man could be, an outlandish sight in the king's hall in Lyikené. To the delight of children, he had pockets full of sugarplums; to the disdain of men, he grew his beard and cropped his hair; to the envy of women, he clad his fat figure in a gown of wool soft and warm as could be wished for, woven, he said, when any asked, from the underfleece of the hillsheep on Cal Mora.

The king drowned his ill-temper in his second cup and asked, "Have you seen aught of the piper this last year?"

The mercatman shook his head. "Years since our paths crossed," he answered, "must be a dozen, more likely a score. He was down

near Marac Bec five years past, so I've heard tell, and rumour says
he went eastwards after."

"Eastward?" asked the king. "To Escen?"

"East of Escen. But east of Escen I don't go, nor any of my
kind. We fear you and your bronze sword, Te-Meriku, and keep the
covenant and our lives."

The king laughed lightly, appreciating the boldness of the lie.
"And glad I am to hear it. 'Twould grieve me sore to kill you after
the wine you've carried 'cross the sea this year. There's mercatmen
enough but none other can match my taste so neatly. Well now, Edo
Incithu, since the wind blows and you must bide here a few days
longer, tell me tales out of the Later Lands."

"What's to tell?" The mercatman spread wide his hands and
smiled. His business done, his profit made, nothing now for him to
do but wait for the wind to drop. A pleasant way to pass the time,
drinking by the fireside telling travellers' tales, even if his drinking
partner was feared all across the Later Lands. "In Escen, the queen
has a new favourite, the master of her horse; the lord of Marihon died
in a cherry orchard and his widow found comfort in a twomonth
with his brother, much to her son's misliking; I did not touch in
Ountrie this year, having burnt my fingers last, and the old prince of
my homeland has a son."

The king whistled through his teeth. "Rhenniu Vorr was old in
the days when Hadùhai was king."

"Five wives he's had afore this lady, and never a whelp between
them." The mercatman looked sidelong over his winecup. "Well, a
young husband may get a child but an old one surely will. Let's see
if he can give the boy years enough to hold the place when he is
dead."

"I think death itself's forgotten him," grinned the king. "As for
the boy, we do things better in Lyikené. Is any man his father come
again?" The mercatman smiled behind his beard, knowing this king's
beginning. He ran on a little while, telling tales heard in the golden
hall of Tarhn or a port town on Eilanmor or the three harbours of
Marac Bec. Perhaps not all his tales were true but all were worth the
telling. All the while, the king laughed and listened, delighted as any
boy to hear of places he would never go and people he would never
see. But at last, when the stream of story ran dry and the mercatman
began to make his graceful pleas of weariness, the king filled up his
cup and asked, "And in Felluria?"

The mercatman looked up sharply, hearing the change in his
voice. "No news at all, Te-Meriku, unless you'd hear me tell of the
weight of fleeces and the strength of barleyspirit."

"The best part of the kingship is that I may wear the wool and drink the spirit and leave all thought of weights and strength to others. Edo Incithu, the tale I'm looking for is not one you've told and so I'll ask you plain."

"Ask, Te-Meriku, and I'll answer if I can."

"I had heard tell that a man born in the east, a man little like to other men, a warlock, had come into the Later Lands, likely to Felluria. Is such a rumour true?"

"A warlock!" The mercatman's face creased into a laugh. "No, and no two-headed cats neither, nor yet a three-tailed pig. What tales you barbarians tell before your fires!" The king caught up his laugh, spreading his hands wide to own himself the fool. "There was, 'tis true, a stranger in Felluria," the man went on, "I never heard him speak of his homeland, nor yet raise the dead or make fire burn in his bare hands," the king snorted his laughter into his wine, "but an old woman there had an eye for him, and she's as good a judge of men as any in the world. I even saw Marwy Ninek look to see if he were there of an evening, and that's a thing unheard of in Felluria."

"A man to charm old women, then. What was he like, this stranger?"

"Like enough to other men. Quieter than many, a musician. I did not mark him much – he neither brought nor bought." The mercatman's round face furrowed. He said, hesitantly, doubtful of his reckoning, "Now I think on it a little, he had the look of one who'd known the piper. You know the look, Te-Meriku."

Something about the eyes, a look of loss and longing. "I know the look." The king's voice was low and dangerous. About the hall, other men fell silent, hearing his tone if not his words. Thodùhah looked up from a game of fox and geese and, catching the king's eye, came to stand beside his chair.

"A stranger, a musician," said the king, slowly, "and one like to have known the piper. Hardly no news at all. What was his name?"

"That I can tell you. Outlandish as it was, it stuck in my mind: Assiolo."

The king let out a long, low breath. "Now there's a name to conjure with."

The mercatman looked from king to helmsman and back again. In Lyikené an honest man scorned to hide his face behind a beard and kept it bare that anyone might read it. He read what was written on those faces and felt his entrails turn to water, seeing two smooth-cheeked barbarians who would kill a man as soon as look at him. He asked, uncertain of the ground on which he stood, "Te-Meriku, what is this man to you?"

"His father's son: Assiolo mor Allocco."

At Allocco's name all fell to silence 'cross the hall. The lord of Idùnmhor had stood in light and fire beside Averla and stopped the sun at noontime to make a day stretch out forever. He would not die, and so the rowan at the gates of morning died in his stead and all the fire beyond the gates spilled out into the waking world. And after, after, when the Liùthion's flood had quenched that fire, when Averla had slipped away into the light, when the piper had closed those gates, when the sun had set and Idùnmhor had sunk beneath the waves, Allocco came out of the east to Ohmorah, and with him those men and women of the First People who had lived beyond the long day's ending. The mercatman drew in his breath, knowing those tales as well as any in Lyikené, his fat face grey and moist with fear. He fumbled for his seat and gave no answer.

The helmsman spat into the fire, making the sign to avert misfortune for good measure. "'Tis but a day since the equinox," he said, "and this gale'll blow itself out by noontime. Not too late for sailing, Te-Meriku, if you've a mind to take him."

The king laughed, harsh and hard in his throat. "Years since, Thodùhah, I had a mind to follow my star into the east, taking Torùkotu as my pattern. Think you the time has come when I too should sack Felluria?"

"For one man, and a stranger?" The old man sucked his teeth, considering the question. "What need for a sack?" he said at last. "Marwy Ninek'll give him up soon as you ask it. She knows, none better, how it will end if she sets herself against you. Bid her open the gate while he is sleeping."

The king picked an apple from the bowl and tossed it from hand to hand. Old tales ran through his mind of glory and destruction. What was the price of a man's life? An apple? A sword? A kingdom?

"His father's son," said Thodùhah, "a heavy weight upon the world. Best strike and be done with it."

"I saw him, once, when I was new made king and sailed east of east to take fealty of Allodola," the king remarked. "So too did you, Thodùhah. A brown-eyed boy of eight or nine, standing in his father's shadow."

The helmsman spat again into the fire. "Aye, well, children grow."

Is any man his father come again?

Te-Meriku stared into the fire, remembering bad dreams, balancing a stranger's fate against his own. The flames burned bright and dazzled him, a white light flickered at the back of his mind, a whisper, a promise. No doubt was but the draught creeping from the shuttered windows made him shiver. *How does it feel*, Imacah asked out of the shadows at his back, *to know the time a man must die?*

The future was not yet written. He could not know the words to turn it to one of his own choosing, only those fitted to his mouth. The king looked up and tossed the apple to his helmsman, grinning. "He's broke no oath nor taken arms against me. I never yet killed a man for his father's deeds. An I did that, there'd be none but bastards left living in Lyikené."

"That pride'll be the death of you, Te-Meriku," the old man chided. "Well, what's to be done, if not that?"

"Little enough that can be. There's one here can do it." The king turned to the mercatman. "Next year, Edo Incithu, and each year after," he said, "you come here as you have done and you tell me news of Assiolo."

The mercatman shrugged, thankful it was no more. "Easy enough."

"There's one else to think of," said the helmsman. "Not likely to be chance he's fetched up in Felluria. Scratch the surface of any tale and you'll find one face looking back at you."

"That's true enough," answered the king. He filled his cup and drank it off. "Well, man," he said to the mercatman, "should your path cross the piper's, you might mention I have questions I'd like answered."

"I'm as like to find a pearl in an acre of shingle."

"Even so," Thodùhah said, reaching out his hand towards the wine. Perhaps it was no more than chance that his sleeve fell back to show clear the little knife bound to his forearm. "I'd count it a great pity to have to ask you exactly how he travelled east of Escen. I'd rather ask the price of martenskin to wrap my pretty grandchild in."

The mercatman had gone to his bed and Thodùhah back to his wife. The king sat late and long in the shadows of his hall, watching the fire die and drinking up his wine. Shadows in the hall, and the weeping, wuthering wind casting hard rain against the shutters; shadows in the hall, and the lamps burning low as, by ones and twos and threes, the dregs of the evening drained away, sliding and slipping into the dark. Two clansmen, a hill lord's sons new down from the mountains, drunk beyond all reason, caroused and clattered their way into the night and the door banged hard behind them. Twenty years ago and longer, in another hall, in another life, he had been another such, staggering and slurring, weaving his way towards his bed, Imacah's arm around his neck. Had they known that they were happy those evenings in Kistoru's hall, thinking no more of the future than the past?

He turned his mind from thoughts of Imacah. The dead were dead and it changed nothing to think on them.

"Waking still, Te-Meriku?" The nightwatch padded from the dark across the hall to take his place beside the door, black-haired Ardùvai, son of a thousand years of clanlords, wearing his new office lightly. "Why keep a dog and bark yourself?"

The king stretched, kicking the fire into life. "This wind has made me restless, and news from across the sea. Will you give me a game afore I seek my bed? I'll wager you a five of ivory, my fox against your geese."

Ardùvai laughed. "Did you not know – my geese had Thodùhah's fox pinned tonight. I'll take your five and triple it that I can rout you fox and geese." He laid a tally-stick upon the table in answer to the king's raised brow. "The substance to back my bragging."

"High stakes!"

"Why play for less?" Ardùvai found a cup and filled it, sitting down across the table as the king set out the pieces.

"I can give you twenty years, man."

"Aye, you can, but you've been distracted by the kingship those twenty years while I had nothing better to do than beat my brother across the board." His roguish smile danced in his dark eyes as he moved the first goose. "I'll warrant I can take you, Te-Meriku, both ways."

The king grinned at his impudence and brought the fox into play. They were not six moves into the first game of the pair when a scream pierced the night, high and thin as a rabbit 'twixt a fox's jaws. It ended suddenly as it had begun. Both men started round, their game forgotten, hands reaching for their knives.

A second scream, closer and shorter than the first. "With me, Ardùvai," said the king softly, moving towards the door.

The night beyond the door was full of rain, driving almost flat against their backs. They rounded the corner into the lee of the hall where light spilled from kitchen windows, pooling in puddles on the stone.

The clansmen had found a woman. The younger held her arms above her head, his hand clamped across her mouth. In the rain his eyes were all a-glitter, watching his brother thrust and strain.

The nightwatch stared to see such a thing within the king's own boundaries. The king himself made no such pause. In some times, in some places, it was counted a shame to kill an unarmed man. Not here. Not now. He seized him by the clansman's knot and jerked him backwards from his pleasure, at the same moment sweeping his knife across his throat. Blood spurted and bubbled; the deed done, he cast the thing that had been a man aside and knelt beside the woman. She flinched from him, another man, bloody and too close, and tried to pull her torn gown across her breasts. He murmured something, too quiet for other ears to hear, and covered her with his cloak.

The other had started up, leaping beyond a knifeblade's reach to set his back against the wall. Now, his own knife glinting in the lamplight and the rain, he stepped forward with all the arrogance of seventeen, half cut still, a hill lord's son that had been taught to know no man his master. "My brother's blood," he said, slurring only a very little. "I'll have your own in payment."

"Is it possible," the king asked, soft and dangerous, "you do not know who she is?"

"A slut from out the kitchens."

"A woman of the Sea People who dwells within my hall."

"Your hall?"

In answer, the king rose up and stepped into a pool of lamplight, his hands bloody, his red hair slicked to his head, his face harsh and unsmiling. The clansman's knife clattered to the stone. "Te-Meriku!" he gasped, shrinking against the wall, his bladder bursting with his terror. His mouth moved as if he would speak, but he swallowed down his words. At such a time, in such a place, there was nothing he could say. His eyes flicked, once, twice and again, between his brother and the king.

Tossing his knife from hand to hand, the nightwatch laughed to see such pride pricked, a hollow, mocking laugh that had no kindness to it. "Shall I kill him, Te-Meriku?"

A long, long time of silence as the king looked the clansman up and down, seeing his youth and fright, his hands outstretched in supplication; a second, longer still, as his eyes turned to the woman huddled in the heavy folds of his cloak. "Did he take you?" he asked.

She shook her head. The king turned back, considering the man again. In the halflight and the rain, not even the nightwatch could read the thoughts behind his face, hard and still as a figure of stone. "His father has no other son," he said at last. "I'm minded to let him live."

The young man mumbled something. It might have been his thanks, a gabbled oath, a babbled promise. Whatever it was, it was of no matter to any other there. "He can live a long time," the king said to Ardùvai, "in his father's hills. But no place else. Hold him."

The nightwatch forced the man to his knees, pinning his arms behind his back. The king stepped close, his bloody knife in his right hand, and cupped his chin in his left, tilting it up to stare hard into his eyes. Nothing in those eyes now but fear. Not even shame.

"No fire," said the king, and scored the right side of his face from eye to chin. The clansman screamed and struggled but hard hands held him fast. The woman leaned forwards to watch, a little smile curling the corners of her mouth. "No water," the king said, slashing open his left cheek. "Go back to your hills, boy. See if your clan will give you a place. There's none for you elsewhere until the seas run dry, until apples grow on an orange tree, until your cheeks are clear again. An I, or any other, see these marks outside those hills you're a dead man surely as your brother."

Ardùvai let him go and he slumped forward, his cheeks shiny with rain and blood. The king turned away, scooping the woman into his arms to carry her into the hall.

"If you are wise," the nightwatch whispered, handing the man back his knife, "you'll go tonight. No word. No thought. Just go. They'll be hunting you come sunrise."

III, Lyikené: A man amongst many

But when he came the king before
He was clad all in the red silk
His hair was like the strands of gold
His skin was as white as the milk.

Willy o'Winsbury, *Traditional*

Sunlight falls into the king's hall, onto the king's red and the king's bronze, onto the king's white hair, onto his face the colour of old ivory. The helmsman asks, "Who is it stands before the king?"

He answers, "I am Te-Meriku."

After that answer, there is a space of silence in the hall, bright and sharp as the blade of a bronze sword, his to fill with the names of men. There are men here could fill it with a hundred generations, could name their father's fathers until the time of Imacah mor Tamarhak himself. Other men, not him. He has no name to offer but his own.

The king himself asks, "No more than that?"

"What more can any offer you? Is any man his father come again?"

A second silence full of staring eyes and quick gasps of breath around the hall, here and there a mutter:

"In the shieling, with the lambs—"

"Kistoru?"

"No! Some beggar's whelp."

The king looks up, and, for a long, long moment, their eyes meet. It is like looking into a flame, into the heart of a fire. He cannot look away and there is no shadow where he can hide. All that he is, and was, and will be, is laid bare by that fierce, bright gaze. The hall is full of men but all the rest are of no matter: they are alone within this moment, he and the king.

The king's laughter rolls out around the hall, and the moment is broken. "Is any man indeed? Come, Te-Meriku, sit down beside me and we will talk together by and by."

And so he does, and so they do, but Hadùhai the king has no thought to chide a bastard whelp caught 'cross the boundary. He speaks instead of himself, near fifty years ago, a young clansman sitting down beside the king in this same hall. He speaks of the tree across the water, the firstborn tree that grows at the gates of evening and is his to guard beneath this sky. He speaks of his bronze sword that, with his will, keeps the balance the piper made so long ago. "The king knows the king," Hadùhai says, last and late. "No man is born a king in Lyikené. Instead the king asks and a man answers."

All the time the king speaks, he listens, his eyes fixed on the flames, watching the patterns shift and change across the evening.

Hadùhai asks his question, offering the sword.

Hands shaking, heart a-thunder, he takes the sword and gives his answer. And, with a word, the world is changed forever.

"I am still myself!"

"You are the king."

"I am not king."

"You will be. And what am I, when you are king?"

He reaches out. "You are Imacah."

Imacah does not move towards him, he does not move away, but the distance between them is wider than any sea. "A man amongst many in the king's hall."

"You and I," he says, and hears his own voice pleading, "two halves of one whole. What is there has changed between us?"

"You went out wearing my sword at your belt, you came back with the king's." Imacah's eyes are fixed upon the sword, its hilt of ivory and gold, its sheath of fine red leather. He reaches out but does not, quite, touch it. He asks, "Do you even know what you must do with it?"

"I know." Of course he knows. He is, after all, a man of Lyikené. This sword is his beginning and his end.

"How does it feel," asks Imacah out of the shadows, "to know the time a man must die?"

He does not answer. There can be no answer and that Imacah can ask the question marks out the space between them. Instead he says, "I love you." He lays down the king's sword, sets his hand on Imacah's shoulder, and says again, "I love you." Never before has he had need to speak these words aloud but the world has changed, and Imacah, and love no longer is enough.

Imacah twists laughing from his curving fingers towards the winejar. "A toast," he cries to any who will hear him. "Let's drink tonight to Te-Meriku the king!"

A roar goes up into Kistoru's hall. He is surrounded, raised up onto men's shoulders; even Kistoru is close by in the throng, shouting out the chorus, "Te-Meriku the king!"

The roar is too loud and deafens him; the wine is too strong and sickens him; men's grasping hands are dragging him down into darkness deep enough to drown in. He looks around in search of Imacah but, when their eyes meet, he sees only another man, one of many in Kistoru's hall, raising his winecup. "Te-Meriku the king!"

He wants to scream, "I am not the king!" but there is a stop upon his tongue. He cannot scream, he cannot speak, and so he drinks and laughs, as Imacah beside him drinks and laughs, his arm across his shoulders, and no one else can see the space between them.

4: In the likeness of a man

It was mirk, mirk night, there was nae starlight,
They waded through red blude to the knee
For a' the blude that's shed on the earth
Rins through the springs o' that countrie.

Thomas the Rhymer, Traditional

"Now, here's a thing," said Yatta Tala to Assiolo, after she had rapped at his door and not waited for an answer, "I had Marwy Ninek come by this morning, wanting broadcloth enough to make a coat. *Will it be proof against the rain?* she asked me, *Will it keep out the weather?*"

He gave no answer, seeing she wanted none. She eased herself down upon the chair by the fireside, and went on. "And here's another, it's not just a coat she's wanting. Boots, the cobbler told me, stout enough to walk knee deep in snow and keep feet dry and warm." She paused, looking sidelong to his face. "Well, lad?"

Assiolo looked up from the tuning of his lute. "I'd ask no less of coat and boots than that they keep me dry and warm. Are opinions so contrary in the west that this is a great matter?"

She laughed, slyly, drily. "I did hear one thing else, and I'll let you tell me if it be a great or little thing: three nights ago a man knocked upon a door that'd been a long time shut. It being opened, he went in and did not come out until the morning."

His fingers grew suddenly clumsy and overtightened the string. It snapped, whipping itself against his thumb.

"Nice work, lad," said Yatta Tala, grinning. "A fine thing to come here a beggar in the springtime and by leaf fall to have tupped the Tion herself. They'll be making songs about you soon."

He flushed. "What there is between a man and a woman is best kept between themselves."

"Nay, no need to stand on your pride. It's all one to me whose bed you sleep in, so long as she be willing."

Mindful of the strings, Assiolo laid the lute aside before he answered. "That you made me welcome, mistress, I thank you; that you ludged me, I am in your debt; that you are my elder, I honour you. But I'll not talk to you of things that are no concern of yours."

"So she's not let you yet." The old woman cackled at his pride. "She will, never doubt it; I've seen the way she looks at you. But, lad, what did you do to make her think of coats and boots that's wanted none of them in all my years and longer?"

"Told her I'd been overlong within stone walls and had a mind to pad the road again." He smiled at the surprise upon her face and said, "You're not the only one to look kindly on a beggarman."

Whatever answer she had looked for, it had not been this. Tightlipped, disapproving, she muttered, "So you're away?"

Assiolo nodded. "Soon as I have coat and boots to wear. The wind blows cold down Cal Mora."

Yatta Tala looked hard at him, pursing her lips as she tried to get his measure. "A strange time to choose, just as the days are growing shorter and the nights colder and she looking at you so longing. Most men give first thought to their own comfort, and beggars and rogues no less than others. Where's it you're headed, if not her bed?"

"Somewhere's good for beggars; anywhere's better still, so I've heard."

She sniffed and pushed herself to her feet. "Well, if you've no mind to answer, Assiolo son of nobody, I'll say no more than fare ye well upon the way."

"Mistress!" Assiolo called her back just as she reached the door. "Forgive me," he said, more gently, "I had no mind to discourtesy. It is only, I cannot stay here now. The boy is dead and his death's heavy on my hands."

"Because you could not save him?" He bowed his head. "That's foolishness, lad. I watched you that night. I saw your strength, I saw your skill. Rest easy, if it troubles you; all you could, you did."

"Not all." Two short, sharp words and yet so hard to say sweat broke out upon his brow. Those words lingered long between them, and all the while the old woman looked him up and down. He said, slowly, with difficulty, "There are some things it is not good to speak of, in sunlight or in darkness. There are words have power beyond their meaning."

"There was a moment, when the boy lay dying. I saw —"

He looked up and met her eyes; she shook her head as, beneath his gaze, the memory slipped from her mind, like water through her fingers. "Something," she muttered, "a trick of the light. And she let you in..." Yatta Tala looked clear at him, asked him very sharply, "Are you sure you did no more than ask her?"

Assiolo nodded, not daring to speak. He had said too much already. He forced himself to look no more towards her, held himself as still as he was able, breathing slowly in and out to mark the moments.

"I've lived a long time," she said at last, "and known men enough to judge them. But you, lad, you I cannot read."

"I made a choice before he died," Assiolo said, slowly, heavily, staring at his hands, "and then a promise after. I made a promise once I did not keep – I'll not make another. I cannot stay."

"But you'll come back? You've a place here."

"Look for me in springtime," he told her, taking up his lute again to mend it, "and have an eye to her when the cold wind blows."

Yatta Tala paused, her hand upon the door, as if waiting for him to speak again. But he had said all he chose to and kept his mind upon the lute, taking out the snapped string to put a sound one in its place, finding the tuning to make it sing sweet and true beneath his fingers. So in a while she went away, closing the door behind her.

When he was done the day was gone and yet Assiolo did not light the lamp but instead let his room fill with the soft shadows of an autumn evening. He sat on the windowseat, watching the bats flickering beyond the window from their roost in the attic above the hall. He was not old, not even in the reckoning of men, but the years were gone forever when he could hear a bat's shrill in the halflight.

There came a quiet rap-rapping at his door. He kept his place, knowing Yatta Tala would push it open whether he answered or not, yet the door stayed shut and in a moment he heard another soft scratch and a whisper, "Assiolo?"

"I am here," he said, his heart a-thunder.

The door opened. Marwy Ninek stood just beyond the threshold, the folds of her red shawl huddled close around her. He could not move, he could not speak, he could scarce even breathe.

"Yatta Tala told me you were away tomorrow." He nodded. She swallowed once, she swallowed twice, her eyes fixed on his face, as if she were learning it by heart, and said, "I have a gift for you, an you will take it."

Assiolo stood to meet her as she took three paces into his room and dropped something small and heavy onto his outstretched hand. From its shape he felt it was a ring. He closed his hand upon it, knowing this was a gift not lightly offered, not lightly to be taken.

"Once it was worn by Metius Estui," she told him, "he had it from his father before him, and he from his. He put it away the night he saw square sails beneath the long-haired star. Few things are left from those days, before the ruin."

Few things indeed, he thought, as he looked down into her face, *and you the sweetest of them all, and the most delicate.* "The king died," he answered, very gently, "and the king will not return."

"It is a ring, no more than that." She reached out and taking his right hand, slipped the ring onto his finger. "It is only a ring," she said, and he heard in her voice that she loved him, "but no other will wear it if you will not."

It fitted if it had been made for him; quickly, it warmed against his skin and, quickly, he grew accustomed to the weight. "I will wear it my whole life long because you give it," he answered, his heart twisting with pain at the thought that he must leave her. He turned his hand, weaving his fingers into hers, hardly able to believe that she was here, so close beside him he could smell the scents of thyme and lavender mingled in her hair.

"Assiolo," she whispered, "this is not your place; you need not do this thing."

"It is my place now," he answered, holding her cold hands in his warm ones. "I gave you a promise and will keep it, and see, I have the coat you sent to keep me warm upon the road."

After she had gone, Assiolo looked more closely at the ring, lighting the lamp to see by. Silver, set with a square cut stone: it could only be a seal ring. The stone was dull and red, one corner chipped, the device on it a man beneath a bare branched tree. As he turned it in his hand, he saw the stone had been carved by an artist skilled as any in his city but the ring itself was no better than any village smith could make. In his homeland he had had far finer rings but its meaning was its value, not its substance. Keeping that thought in mind, he pinched out the lamp and, in the darkness after the light, looked out to see the eight stars of the hawk hanging above Cal Mora's peak.

Assiolo paused at the top of the brae to look down towards Felluria. Slowly, slowly, he had climbed up through the bracken and the heather until he reached the rocks beneath the shoulder of Cal Mora. It had been no little thing to walk beyond the gate beneath the emptiness of sky, no simple thing to stand upon the shore where there was no shelter from the wind, no easy thing to clamber up Cal Mora's side amidst the heather. Now he had found her, he did not want to let her go; now he had passed the door, he did not want to close the gate behind him. As he walked out that autumn morning, an iron knife at his belt, the strand of firestar wrapped in a scrap of cloth in his pocket, he had passed three great grey wolfskins pegged out to cure in the late sunshine.

Up here he could see great distance. Beneath him the little waves of Loch Mora danced in the sunlight, above him was clear air and emptiness until the sky dropped down to meet the mountains. All this was hers, the mountains and the moorlands, and a high price she had paid for it.

He rested, cushioned in the heather, and looked down the brae. The sky above and the sea below were blue and there were fishing boats out in the sound beyond the loch mouth. Her hall stood peaceful in its place between the mountain and the sea, wrapped safe within its walls. Yet, up here, he could see what could not be seen closer: a pattern of light and shadow traced upon the land, the scars where other walls once stood. He shivered at the sight despite the sunlight.

Above him, in the empty air, an eagle swept across the land and sea, circling slowly, seeing all. It marked the fish swimming in the water and the hare crouching in the heather, the children playing on the foreshore and the sheep grazing on the high pasture. Yet nothing that it saw was of concern to it and soon it slipped away on the wind into the sunlit distance of the west. When it was gone out of sight, Assiolo turned his back upon Felluria to walk down the path into Eulana.

Longtimes Assiolo walked, sleeping each night in a different bed or in none at all, in barns and sheds and bothies, wrapped in his blankets beneath the autumn stars. For a while, his way was easy; a wandering musician might find a living on the road, if he kept a courteous tongue in his head and did not outstay his welcome. That he had no mind to, anywhere along the way; he had left his heart behind him within stone walls and gave no thought to either company or loneliness. For a while – then rain gave way to snow, moorland and meadow to the wild woods of Eulana, autumn to winter, and he still walked the roads alone, stained and ragged, dejected as any other beggar.

I am going hunting, he had told her, *I'll not turn back until I have pulled down my quarry.* Fine words from any man, braver still from one who knew no more of hunting than to send an arrow to the kill after other men had set the nets and flushed the quarry, and stood close at hand with spears and knives to step in between their lord and danger. Often and often, when the rain poured down to soak him or the wind blew cold around him, when wastrels mocked his music and scolds drove him from their doors, Assiolo wished he had left those words unspoken, for day by day his resolution slipped away. Only in the evenings, turning her ring upon his finger, remembering her eyes as she gave it to him, did he whisper into the dark, *I gave a promise, and will keep it. Tomorrow*, he told himself at such times, *I'll say the words to draw it* out. *Tomorrow, I shall make an ending.*

Yet ever in the morning, in the cold daylight, he could not summon the strength he needed, finding he loved his life too well to run the risk of losing it.

Day on day, the light grew less, darkness rising in Eulana as the year withered and died. Winter deepened. Ice crept. Snow fell. Assiolo shivered on his way. The cold in Ohmorah had never bit hard and cruel as this. Still, he had not the will to make an ending, though all around winter lay heavy on the land, snow on the meadows, frost on the trees and springtime but a hope and a memory buried deep in the cold ground. Instead, at the wild wood's edge, he lingered a sennight in Habhain town to thaw his bones, paying good silver for bed and board and fire, and, at its end, went away with cap and gloves of martenskin, better proof than broadcloth against the frost.

All through the light, he walked alone beneath bare trees and though sometimes he saw the snow stained red always he could see the marks of wolf or lynx or bear. Those hunters had eyes and ears to find their prey, and tooth and claw to bring it down. He had eyes but could not see the thing he sought; he had ears but heard nothing in the silence of snow. A small voice at the back of his mind whispered it were better so: one thing to speak boldly within the stone walls of Felluria, quite another to walk boldly through the wild wood. He was a fool, that voice whispered, and this the price of folly. When he had been a boy, he had not strength enough to stand against his father: now he was a man, he had not strength enough to set himself against a monster.

At dusk Assiolo had not yet found shelter. Wandering those woods, he knew himself indeed a fool to come so far from the haunts of men. Nor could he rest beneath the trees, so bleak and bare and lovely in the frost, but must stumble on, knee-deep in snow and clear, bright cold that burned fierce as fire through boots and coat and gloves. He had passed all hope of comfort, all hope of rest, when he saw a light beyond the trees, a little light burning steady in the dark, a hope when hope was lost. Banging his hands against his chest to warm them, he fixed his eyes upon the light and went on. No sound but the crunch of his footsteps in the snow. Sharp and sudden in the night, an owl cried out, *Who will?*

Assiolo started round, flooded with fear, then laughed aloud, shaking his head against the owl's question.

In the forest was a clearing and in that clearing grew a briar, bare as any thorn. Behind that briar, there was a house and, in that house, there was a door. Above that door, there was a lantern and, in that lantern, was a candle and the candle burned and burned and drove away the dark.

The windows of the house were shuttered tight, not a chink of light showed through. At Assiolo's back, the night fell down, blackness without stars. Only the light shone, clear and steady, a candleflame against the dark. Assiolo stepped out of the wood into the clearing and thumped with his gloved hands upon the door.

No answer. Assiolo tried again, calling through the lock. Still nothing. He stood back, looking around, considering his choices. There was nowhere else that he could go. The door was locked but the lock had not been made could keep him out if he wished to be within and, on such a night as this, there was nothing he wished more than to be warm and dry with stone walls standing between him and the dark. He drew the glove from his left hand and laid his fingers 'gainst the frosty oak but, from courtesy, before he said the words he knocked a third time with his bare hand.

A rattle and a scratching from within and the door opened. Light spilled onto the snow, warm as a welcome. A serving man stood on the threshold, a spare, grey man, who bowed his head and stepped aside to let him pass. Assiolo stepped from the dark into the light and with a soft click the door shut behind him.

"Thank you," he said, as the man took the lutecase from his back and helped him off with gloves and hat and coat, kneeling at his feet to pull off his sodden boots and offer houseshoes in their place and a woollen robe to wear against the chill. The room the grey man led him to was bright and soft with candlelight, a fire burned in the grate, fragrant with pinecones, and, though it was near-midwinter, on the mantelshelf above it was set a bowl filled with white roses. A lovely place at any time and loveliest of all when outside was drear cold and wilderness.

"My mistress is not here," the man said, "but, my lord, when you came into this country, she bid me make you welcome, give you food and shelter an you needed it." His voice was quiet and colourless, a grey voice fleshless as the man himself.

"Who is your mistress?"

"If you do not know, I cannot tell."

"But she cannot be of this country. It is most strange," Assiolo said, looking all around, "to find a house like this in such a place."

For this house was little like the dwellings of the Later Lands, cottages of lathe and daub and thatch or else great halls of stone where a lord kept all his company. This place was most like a house of his own country, fine stone and painted plaster, dressed wood and marble stairs. "Do you keep this house alone?"

"There are others here, my lord. They will come when they are needed. We are always ready, root and stalk and leaf, twig and stem and thorn. We serve."

"How long has your mistress kept this house?"

"Since the king died, my lord."

"Yet I heard no word of it in Habhain, nor elsewhere in Eulana."

"It is not everyone has the eyes to see, my lord. Another man might pass close by and never see the light."

Assiolo nodded, lulled by warmth and softness. He turned his ring upon his finger, trying to call her face to mind. Felluria was long ago and far away, his promise as words spoken in a dream that could not bind on waking. It was comforting, after so long amidst the other and the strange, to walk upon a silken carpet and sink into

a soft chair before the fire, to be himself again with no need to please
or flatter.

"Rest now, my lord," the grey man said. "There is wine to your
hand. I will bring food by and by."

The food he brought was rare and delicate: golden soup sprinkled
with the seeds of pomegranates, truffled quail stuffed with its own
eggs and fish baked in fromenty, sweetmeats of marchpane shaped
in the likenesses of fruit. The wine was hot and sweet and spiced,
redolent with citrus and with cinnamon. Assiolo ate and drank, then
drowsed beside the fire, drifting gently between sleep and waking.
Music rippled through his dreams, a song of light and fire. A step
behind him, a rustle of silk beside him. She leaned over him in a
sweep of golden hair, and, soft as rose petals, red lips brushed his,
offering a teasing taste of honey. Laughing, he reached out to pull
her down beside him but she slipped twisting through his curving
fingers. "Assiolo," she whispered over her white shoulder, "Assiolo."
She went ahead, a flicker and a flutter, plain in the shadows, hidden
by the light, and he followed after, tracing out the patterns of the
dance beneath the flowering trees. Yet though he yearned and ached
and longed for her, always he was just too slow to catch her, pulled
down by the weight of his right hand.

The snap of resin in the fire woke him. Aching and stiff with cold,
he looked around, confused. Bare rafters above him, brown bracken
beneath him, a grey morning glimpsed through the open door.

Assiolo shook his head against the sight and the light fell back
into its proper place. The fire burned warm, the room was bright
with lamplight. Properly awake now, he stood to walk around the
room, to run his finger across the snowy petal of a rose and cast
his eye across the patterns of the carpet. On the further wall was a
curtain of grass-green velvet broidered over with white roses. A bell
chimed softly in the distance and he counted the time aloud: the
eighth hour of the first; he had slept longer than he had thought.
Beyond the shuttered window it must be morning, even in this north
country.

The door opened silently and the grey man stepped in, bearing
a tray. "Forgive me, my lord. You slept so sound I could not show
you to your bedchamber."

"It is of no matter."

When he had eaten, the man led him to a dressing room where
cans of hot water were set ready and silken robes warming before the
fire. This window too was shuttered tight. He did not seek to open it.
What need to look without when all within was so pleasing and so
perfect? Assiolo washed and dressed, taking pleasure in the supple
fall of silk against his skin. In the glass he saw again the lord of the

White City, his father's son before whom men bowed low in duty and in fear. Only his ring was out of place, a crude thing, and heavy; he stared and stared and wondered why he wore it. Remembering, he smiled and brought it to his lips. She was so sweet and foolish, putting such faith in a trinket.

He opened a door and found a bedchamber. On the table by the bed there was a book, tales of the long past. He took it up to read of the piper and of Imacah mor Tamarhak, the first king in Lyikené to balance the world along a blade of bronze. He read, and remembered much that had slipped his mind since he had left his home behind him. The morning passed quietly by, each hour marked by the bell. At noontime, cramped by reading, Assiolo put down the book. From the corner of his eye, he glimpsed his reflection in the mirror, dirty and unshaven, a beggarman clad in a stained coat of broadcloth. Startled, he wheeled around to face himself and saw his proper shape looking haughtily back, a man of high degree in crimson and in black.

Laughing at his folly, Assiolo walked back along the lamplit halls, past rooms fine as any in his father's house, to the first chamber with the roses and the curtain. As he had hoped, he found wine waiting by the fireside, the table covered over with white linen and a spread of food to tempt his appetite: a soup of mint and peas, a duck with the fat crisp on its breast, new bread with a crumb white as snow, a plate piled high with strawberries and yellow cream to eat with them. If he did not care for red wine, there was white, fragrant with elderflowers and sweet as a summer's evening.

He ate until he was sated and looked about to find a pastime for the afternoon. His lute was waiting in a corner but, when he took it up to play, his hands were stiff and stupid, as with cold. He flexed his fingers in the warmth rising from the fire but each time he plucked the lutestrings the notes were slurred and ugly, a jangle of discord in that lovely place. Assiolo closed his eyes. In the silence, in the dark, he shivered as cold bit deep into his bones. He could scarce feel the frets beneath his fingers.

"My lord?"

He opened his eyes to the grey man standing before him. "Where am I?"

"You are here, my lord."

"And so I am. But all is not as it should be. Here sometimes is elsewhere. The fire is hot," Assiolo said, "the house filled with light and yet I am so cold. Read me this riddle."

"The answer, my lord, is to your hand."

Assiolo laughed aloud that it should be so simple. He drew the ring from his finger and cast it aside onto the table, a little thing

of no value, binding him to the hard cold of another place and
another life, to a foolish promise given without thought. The warmth
and light soaked softly through his flesh as he sank into the chair
beside the fire, a glass of white wine from the south country close
by his hand. The serving man moved quietly around the room,
clearing broken meats away, stoking the blaze, lighting the candles in
the chamberstick upon the table. Assiolo played his lute, each note
chiming soft and sweet and true; cheered to have his own again, he
sang,

> "There are three things I fain would see,
> A rose, a king, an apple tree,
> Then all that might have been could be.
> But might have been is never seen
> Though snow falls white and leaves grow green."

He paused, breaking the tune between one phrase and the next. The
words he sang were true, he knew, but he could not quite remember
why. It was a verse learned so long ago he had forgotten when, so
far away he could not remember where. He rubbed his hand across
his face, trying to call the memory to mind. The serving man refilled
his glass and, as he set the decanter down beside the candelabrum,
Assiolo noticed, from the corner of his eye, what he had not before
and stared hard at him.

"My lord?"

Assiolo cast his eyes round and around the room: the fire, the
chairs and tables, the bowl of roses, the grey man waiting patiently
to serve his will. All was as it should be – it had been no more than a
trick of the light. The thought slipped from his mind; Assiolo shook
his head, strumming the lute, "It is nothing."

The afternoon passed by. He had books to feed his mind, pictures
to feast his eye, music to delight his ears. The fire was hot, the roses
without a thorn, the man quiet and attentive, trimming the candles
that he had clear light to see by. At length, as Assiolo reached out
for his wine, his left hand passed before the lamp and his shadow
followed it, twisting itself across the wall. He looked once, he looked
twice: all was as plain as the hand before his face. Holding that
thought tightly in the forefront of his mind, he said softly to the grey
man, "You have no shadow."

"I have no need of one, my lord."

The serving man reached out to pick the ring from the table and,
quicker than thought, Assiolo snatched it up before the grey hand
could touch it. Cold shivered through him and he caught in his
breath with shock, his heart beating fast and loud as any drum.

"What are you?" he asked. "Friend or foe?"

"Neither, my lord. My mistress set me in this place to serve and so I do."

"What am I to your mistress?"

"Your father's son."

The grey man drew back the grass-green curtain and stepped aside so Assiolo might see clearly. A double portrait hung there, a young man and a white-haired boy. The boy's face he knew well, having seen its likeness every day in his father's study. The man's picture could have been his own, but for the eyes. His father's eyes had ever been blue as the midsummer sky. Assiolo stared and stared, seeing him so young and merry, laughter lighting his face, a white rose held in his right hand, his left set on his son's shoulder. His father's very self but not the man he knew. The man of this portrait had been lost long ago, burned by the fire, tumbled in the flood; the one that lived on, after this boy's death, had shared his face and nothing more.

"My mistress's paramour," said the grey man softly, "and her son."

Assiolo held out his hand but did not quite touch his brother's painted cheek. Slowly, deliberately, he forced himself to calmness and said, "It was not chance brought me here."

"No more than 'twas chance brought you from your homeland to Felluria. No more than 'tis chance Te-Meriku is king in Lyikené. The piper sets his pieces on the board, so does my mistress. He made the king in the west, my mistress shall break him. She has no mind to die beneath this sky, she who was light and fire everlasting the other side of the sunrise."

Assiolo shook his head, feeling the weight of the ring heavy in his hand. "Such things are no concern of mine. I am not your mistress's plaything, nor yet the piper's."

"My lord, you asked for shelter and I answered. An you stay, all this shall be yours, forever and for always. All desire satisfied, all needs met. Such a little thing my mistress wishes in return, no more than that you turn aside and finish what your father started."

A rustle and a whisper, a shimmer and a shiver, light flickering to form. A dream glimpsed in a golden wood, soft round breasts, and sweet red lips, and a fall of golden hair.

Assiolo closed his eyes against the light and his hand upon the ring; standing in the darkness and the cold, he summoned another sight to mind: Marwy Ninek upon the threshold, her hand outstretched, the scents of lavender and thyme rising from the softness of her hair.

A moment measured out in a hundred heartbeats, and then another hundred more, and he had fixed her image firm enough not to lose it with his eyes open. "You will tell your mistress this," he said, "although I am my father's son, I have no quarrel with the king; although I have my father's art, I will not use it against him; although I am free from the oath my father swore, I do not seek to be more than other men."

"My lord, you are your father's son. All that was his, is yours. What he left undone, you must complete. It is for you to give my mistress back her own."

"I left it all behind," Assiolo said, pulling the curtain back into its place. "I lived half my life in my father's shadow – better to freeze in the wild wood than be a man like him. I shall go my own way and make my own choices."

"There are few men, my lord, within the world can do such things. You are no longer one of them. You have eaten the food I set before you; you have drunk from the cup I offered you. In the end, my lord, she will be your mistress, as she is mine, and you will serve, as I do."

"You are not a man. It is not for you to say what can and cannot bind me," Assiolo said, slipping his ring back into its place. He stood up and took three steps across the room towards the fire. Lifting the bowl of roses from the mantelshelf he cast it down upon the floor. It smashed and shards of glass – of ice, said his mind – scattered across the floor in a flurry of petals. He stooped and held a glittering splinter up before the grey man's face, then drove it hard into the ball of his right thumb and shook the red drops into the fire. "I have eyes," he said, "and I will see. Let the world be as it is."

His blood sizzled and hissed amidst the embers and the light swirled and tumbled around him, flickering and twisting the sight of his eyes from one seeming to another. His skin burned and burned but whether 'twas from ice or fire he could not know. He closed his eyes, setting his will against this place, making his mind into a knife to cut its bonds upon his senses.

"Let the world be as it is," Assiolo cried aloud and, opening his eyes, at last saw clearly. He stood alone within a charcoal burners' hut, half of stone, half of timber, with a pinefire burning in the hearth and a bedplace piled with dry bracken. The petals of white roses were nothing more than snowflakes drifted across the floor. A briar grew by the open door, a dry branch tap-tapping on the wood. He reached out his left hand to touch a grey thorn. "Let the world be as it is," he muttered, feeling the cold bond of the ring upon his finger.

The light was steady and there was nothing more. This place was as real as the red blood running from his thumb. "I've grown careless among the single-sighted," he told himself, "to be taken in by such a trick as that."

This place was real, all else but a trick and a seeming, of no more moment than a dream, yet on his lips was still the taste of honeyed wine and strawberries. Assiolo dropped to his knees outside the door, scooping up snow to cleanse his mouth. He sat back on his heels, shivering, turning his ring about and about his finger, flinching from the thought of might have been. The ring was a tie of his own choosing; 'twas his own promise bound him to his love. And yet, and yet, he bent his face into his hands, they had been so nearly severed. He had feared, and his fear near cost Marwy Ninek her future. His breath came fast in anger and in shame; he closed his eyes and she was the only sight behind them, reaching out to him from the folds of her red shawl, a touch, a whisper, "Assiolo." She was his love, forever and for always, and he would keep his promise, live and die a man like other men, not like his father's son.

That night, midwinter's eve, before he slept, Assiolo made a patterning of dry sticks and dry flowers in the earth before the fire and set the ring down in the middle. He pricked his finger with his knife and let three drops of blood fall down upon the strand of lithia. "I will meet you on the morrow," he said, "and we shall see who has the mastery."

Assiolo was woken from sleeping by the white owl's call, *Who will?* Lying in the dark, he heard the owl call again and stepped from his bed into the cold. He stood at the door and saw ghostly wings sweep across the darkness, freezing the night time with its question: *Will you?*

The night was lovely, dark and deep, the longest night that would break into the shortest day, the dark eye of the year. He looked from the door in the time before the dawning. Any man of Eulana would close the door, any man of Eulana would lie down upon his bed and pull the blankets above his ears and leave the grey dawn and the wild wood to the owl. But he was not a man of Eulana. Turning the ring upon his finger, he remembered all the tales he had been told, of dead kings and broken walls, of hatred and of vengeance. A third time, the owl called out: it asked, and he would answer. Today he would keep his promises.

He pulled on his coat, his boots and gloves, he pulled his hat down over his ears and stepped out into the halflight, his knife in his left hand. The snow was thick upon the ground, the hoar frost glittered on the branches, the moon a sliver of silver above the bone-bare trees.

He walked an hour within the wood, and then another after it. He walked beneath the white trunks of birch and the grey branches of rowan. Aspen rattled empty boughs above his head and pinetrees were heavy shadows in the dull light before the dawn. Then the world was filled with ice and fire as the sun rose in its glory, its long, low beams slanting sideways through the trees.

Death came at him out of the sunlight through the naked trees. Once, it had been a man; it was a man no longer. Its hair and beard hung in a rusty pelt around its shoulders. It had no name or memory under the morning sun. Those had been stolen long ago: all that was left was its strength and its purpose. It hunted the day in the wild wood, a nightmare crossed into the waking world, and all wild creatures hid themselves away. In the moment of stillness before he could no longer think, Assiolo knew all the tales he had heard were true.

He had a knife and it had none but no knife was enough to give him the mastery. It knew neither fear nor pain, had no thought of past or future. It came at him and he fell beneath its strength. He twisted beneath it, rolling in the snow. Its feet were bare and trampled him; its teeth were sharp and worried him; its nails were claws and tore his flesh. He slashed upwards but its pelt turned aside the blade, then teeth closed in his arm. He ripped himself from its jaws, dropping the knife, screaming out his pain to the morning. There was no answer: in such a place, at such a time, there could never be an answer. He had not known how greatly he feared death until death came out of the sunlight and rent his flesh, spilling his red blood upon the snow.

It had no words and nor did he. Whatever he had been, he was no more; neither past nor future left to him, only the horror of the moment. Assiolo tore himself from death's embrace and fled between the trees. It followed, its stinking breath rasping in the cold air. It was a dreadful race and one he could not win. He could not outrun it; he could not hide from it: what it saw it hunted, what it hunted it caught, what it caught it killed. He ran from it, in and out of trees whose branches whipped at him, through thickets whose briars tore at him and almost over the bank where the frozen river blocked his way. Then there was nowhere else for him to run. He closed his eyes and stood alone in the cold and dark, conjuring her face to mind. It was her past pursued him; if he failed now, she could never find her freedom. He summoned all his strength and will, opened his eyes and turned to face the thing that hunted him, the monster shaped of her rage and pain and terror. It had the likeness of a man but it was not a man; it was not even a beast. It was a wild thing out of the wild wood with biting jaws, with tearing claws, with yellow eyes that stared and stared and did not see.

It lunged at him and he stepped back, slipping and sliding across the ice. It came after him and the river groaned beneath its greater weight. Assiolo slithered to the bank and found a stone. The wild thing turned after him, its breath foul and panting in his face. He smashed the stone into its face and red blood sprayed over him. It staggered at the blow and fell upon the river and the ice broke under it with a crack like the world's ending. Then Assiolo closed with it, flinging himself upon its shoulders, forcing its head beneath the water with all his strength and all his will until the stream washed its life away and all was silent again beneath the empty sky.

Long after it was dead, Assiolo pulled it from the water. It lay upon the riverbank and all the horror of its life was gone. Dead, it rested at his feet, empty as any other corpse when the man within has slipped away into the dark. He sat, shaking, through the short afternoon, staring at his hands that killed it whilst the blood ran red out of his arm to stain the spotless snow.

The sun set beneath the world and midwinter's night fell down upon the wild wood. By one and two, by threes and multitudes, stars flickered into brightness above the ghostly trees. Then Assiolo saw the stranger in a ragged cloak standing in the starlight on the further bank.

"Will you help me?" he called out. "He cannot lie here to feed the ravens and the wolves."

The stranger crossed the water, stepping lightly across the broken ice. He came to his side and knelt there, saying, "You are hurt." He put his hands on Assiolo's arm and bent his head to breathe on it. His touch was gentle as the falling snow, his breath cold as the north wind and, when he took his hands away, Assiolo saw his arm was whole again.

"Here's a sight," the stranger said, "the king of Eulana lying at the streamside. All the rest she took from him when she drove him from his hall but that she could not take."

The ground was frozen hard as iron but together in the starlight they brought stones from the bank to pile above the corpse that it might lie quiet and safe.

"I had not known that I could kill," Assiolo said, as he set the last stones in their places.

The stranger sat back on his heels to look at him. His face was pale, his hair was black, his eyes were dark as a night without stars. "And are you not a man, as other men?"

"Where there is necessity, there is no choice."

The stranger smiled. "There are many choices on this side of the water. Nay," he shook his head to still Assiolo's protest, "it is not my part to judge you. All the tales you've heard are true."

Assiolo thought for a while, and asked, "Then what am I?"

The stranger laughed, a ripple of starlight across the frozen stream. "Surely you know that? But, if you do not, the answer is to your hand." The stranger took his hand to turn the ring and trace his finger 'cross the carving on the stone. "Here and now, you are the king beneath the bare tree."

"A strange, poor king in a tattered coat. They will not crown me on the morrow and the king's hall lies ruined beyond the forest."

"It is neither the crown nor the hall makes a man into a king. He who kills the king is the king. In Eulana, as in the west."

Long moments passed, a beating out of time in slow heartbeats between the starlight and the snow, and then the stranger asked, "Do you know what you have done?"

"What I came here to do," answered Assiolo. "Turned a monster into a memory, and set my love free to walk safely beyond stone walls."

"She made a man into a monster."

"He was ever that. All I've done today, I'd do again tomorrow." He remembered the ragged shoulder of the shepherd boy; saw again Marwy Ninek crouching in her fear beneath stone walls. "No, more than that – I would gladly lie myself beneath that stone so long as he lay clay cold beside me. I love my life, but not so much I could not bear to lose it in such a cause."

"Fine words, from any man, and finer still from a king," said the stranger. "The future is not yet written; you do not know what you can lose and yet live, or what you may have to bear before your death. Come with me now and you will never know." He held out his hands and smiled. "Come, cross the water and dance with me, free of the past and the future. In my country, there is music such as you have never heard; there, you may slip sideways into a dream and all the sorrows of the waking world will never come to pass."

Assiolo did not take his hand. Instead he asked, "Who are you?"

The stranger stretched out his arms to the night, to the silence beneath the trees and the stars above. "Before the first tree grew, this was my kingdom; when the last tree is dead, it will be again my kingdom. On midwinter's night, when all lands are borderlands, I walk awhile this side the water. Only on midwinter's night can there be two kings beneath one sky." He smiled and asked, "Surely you know me as well as I know you, Assiolo, Allocco's son of Ohmorah?"

Assiolo looked once and saw the stranger had left no mark upon the snow; he looked twice, and saw his feet were bare; he looked three times and saw the stars tangled in his hair. Then at last he remembered all the tales he had been told and knew who stood at his side in the frost and darkness of midwinter's night.

"Yes," he said, "yes, I know you."

"I came not for the dead but for the living. Come with me, Assiolo, come with me 'cross the water, and dance in starlight on the empty land, forever and for always." The king of the borderlands held out his hands, offering an apple; very gently, he asked, "Is this fruit not what you wished for, those years alone within your father's house?"

"Those years," Assiolo answered, "not now. I left my father's house and found a new land, and a new love to keep me in this land."

"As you wish," the king bowed his head, "I do not take the unwilling. But he lies dead beneath the stones, and you have kept your promise. Beneath this sky you have made an ending. But after any ending, there is always a beginning."

"Aye, so there is, waiting for me within stone walls. She's waited a long time and she'll wait forever if I follow you. I will have my life and my love, and roses in the summertime. Neither roses nor love bloom in the borderlands."

"Nor do men grow old and die beneath my sky. It is not so in the waking world. There, all men must die. And, when you lie dying, she must bear your death. Does she have the strength, Assiolo, does she have the will?"

He was silent. He could not answer for he did not know. He had his father's art, he had his knowledge but not his life. The years would fall on him as on any other man. All he had to set against the past was love.

"You are free as any other man to make your choices, and turn one future to another," said the king. "I asked and you have answered. Tonight, after the ending, we have met on your side of the water; we will meet on mine before the beginning."

The king leant forwards and kissed Assiolo softly on the brow, bidding him farewell. "Go carefully beneath the sun and moon.

It was raining as Assiolo came down the brae towards Felluria. Not heavy rain, light drops of the mist that clung about the mountain. He had not been able to mark the point when he had reached the top of the pass but now as he came down he could smell the sea on the wind blowing into his face. He came out of the mist at last and saw the grey keep on the lochside beneath Cal Mora on a damp spring evening. The windows of the hall shone out with light, welcoming in the dusk. His feet were weary so his pace did not quicken at the sight but his heart was glad, for she was there and with her he could make his happiness.

At last he came from the high ground onto the road beside the loch shore. Down by the water the oystercatchers followed the

retreating tide and he heard one bird fly fast across the shingle calling
to its mate. So long since he'd been here, so many other sights seen,
sounds heard in the months between that time and now, but for a
moment all that time was swallowed up in a pied bird's cry and he
was in his place again.

When he reached the gates they were already closed against the
night. Assiolo rapped with his gloved hand against the wicket gate,
and when no answer came banged again, much harder. At last it
opened a chink, and the porter stared long to be sure that he saw
truly before he held the door wide to let him pass.

He went on across the courtyard to the door on the inner side,
then up the twisting stairs behind the hall. Before the door, Assiolo
paused a little time counting out his heartbeats in the dark. Then he
saw the light from within spilling like hope from the gap beneath
the door and raised his hand to the doorknob.

It was not locked. It was never locked. Assiolo opened the door
and waited at the threshold. In the moment before Marwy Ninek
raised her face and looked at him, he saw everything in the room
and knew that he would always remember this moment, the first
perfect moment of his life. He saw the fire burning in the grate and
the sprig of appleblossom standing in a blue vase on the mantle. She
sat sewing in the windowseat, black-haired and slender, wrapped in
her red shawl. Then she looked up and saw him, and cried out his
name in gladness and in welcome.

Assiolo smiled and stepped into her chamber. Unrolling a canvas
packet on her table he laid out a bundle of thorny sticks each ending
in an earthy boll.

"Roses," he told her, "I found them growing on a river bank near
Habhain."

"There have been no roses in Felluria for a long, long time. They
died along with all the rest, the day the walls tumbled into ruins."

"That tale you told," he answered, thinking she was lovely, wishing
she would smile again as she had smiled in that first moment when
she saw him. She flushed and looked down at the roses. He said,
"The walls of Felluria have been sound and strong these many years
and it is time there were roses blooming here again."

"There was a man," Marwy Ninek began, but her whisper died
away to silence, and she touched the stems gently with one finger.

"That tale you also told," Assiolo said, "and I am here to tell
its ending." He held his voice quiet and steady. "That man is dead;
dead at midwinter and gone into the dark. There is no longer any
need for fear."

A little while they stood together, either side the table. He had
come back to her; now it was her turn to find her way across the

space between them. He smiled and whistled a lovesong as he packed up the roses and left her.

"So you came back, lad," said Yatta Tala, sharp and dry as ever, as he sat down beside her next morning and reached for the jug of ale.

"Aye, mistress, I came back."

"And will you tell me where you've been?" Assiolo shook his head, and in a moment she took up his laughter. "Or what you mean to do?"

"Well," he said, still laughing, "a sixmonth since you heard all my songs thrice over. I've a mind to turn my hand to gardening. I've thought, often and often, these stone walls are high enough to turn aside the wind. Let's see if I'm right."

"One thing to make a garden," she told him, "another one to keep it. I take it, then, this time you're set on staying."

"Forever and for always. If she'll have me."

"Oh, she'll have you, lad," and she looked across to Marwy Ninek in a night-blue kirtle, moving through the hubbub of the morning like a swallow in the sunlight, "she'll have you, never fear it."

And, in the days that followed, Assiolo saw, from the edges of his eyes, that Marwy Ninek was watching from her window as he made a garden within the stone walls of Felluria, planting a rowan tree at one side and an apple at the other, setting the rose trees of Eulana between them. And the leaves grew green, and the buds grew heavy and, as the year turned towards midsummer, the first flowers opened so all could see the roses he had brought were red: red as blood, red as wine, red as the flames at the heart of a fire.

IV, Felluria: Open the gate

Four-and-twenty Hielan' men
Cam' frae the Carron-side
To steal awa' Eppie Moray
For she wadna be a bride, a bride,
She wadna be a bride.

Eppie Moray, *Traditional*

Felluria is full of women; of the men, only the old remain, and boys. The eldest boys were children when she was a child. Sometimes, with the other girls, she had played with them. She did not know then what she was, no more than they did, and the future was of no matter. Only the long days of summer had substance in their minds, playing on the seashore with sticks and stones and seaweed, building castles in the time between the tides. Always the sea rose up and washed them clear away. A childish folly, to think to keep back the tide with a wall of sand.

The blacksmith's boy had brown hair curling to his shoulders, hands strong enough to force his will on iron, gentle enough to cup a wild bird's egg upon his palm. Lying in her narrow bed, she thinks on things that might have been, had she given another answer, had he come home, had the world been other than it is.

Three sennight since, before he limped away, the piper said, "You are a child." But she is no more a child and she will never be a woman and some words must not be spoken. Nor must she ever show, with a word, with a pause, with a passing thought across her face like light across the surface of the sea, that she remembers once she bore another name.

Often, as she climbs the stair, she hears the woman weeping in the night time, a stifled, helpless sobbing, such a little sound set against the clamour at the gates. The first night, she sat beside her and laid an arm, cautiously, around her shoulder. The woman did not move towards her, she did not move away. She sat, still as a figure carved from stone, and all the while the tears ran slowly down her face, heavy as raindrops down the windowpane.

"Promise me," the woman says, "the gate will be locked; promise me, you will not let him in."

"I promise," she answers.

"Swear it," the woman says, shaking her by the shoulders, her eyes burning in her curd-white face, her black hair a tumble and a tangle, "swear it, by land and sea and sky, you will not let him in."

"*I swear it,*" she says, obedient as a child repeating its lesson, moving her hands through the patterns of the oath. "*I swear by land and sea and sky, Ketala Iitha.*"

The words lie hard and heavy on her heart, binding her thought and deed; the word she cannot say forms itself in her mouth, shapes itself upon her lips. She looks into the woman's face, a mirror to her own, and swallows hard. The truth is there but it cannot be spoken and, besides, she did not come here to seek or offer comfort.

The woman keeps to her chamber in the black tower, weeping, weeping because her king is dead. She walks alone within the stone walls of Felluria. The smith says no word against her but she is no longer welcome in the forge. Since the woman came, the dead stand between them with silent tongues and empty eyes. She closes her eyes and sees his son, red-faced and awkward, turning his hat in his hands.

"*When I come back,*" he had asked, flushing at his daring, "*will you walk with me along the lochside, and see the sweetbriar flower so bonny?*"

She had looked up into his face and laughed. "*Perhaps,*" she said, over her shoulder, slipping away across the empty garden, "*perhaps.*" Her footsteps behind her were a pattern pressed in frost, melting to nothing as the sun slanted 'cross the walls.

She can still hear her laughter, still see his cheek flushing red as any rose above his new-grown beard. Easier to think of him than of the piper. The piper came when he was dead, offering music amidst the sweetness of roses. Now the piper pads the road alone and the roses have faded; she presses her face into her hands, wishing the blacksmith's boy were there to hear another answer.

Instead, the red king comes a-calling, standing before the gate with empty hands, and she must stand upon the wall and give him answer. The sunlight catches in his hair and conjures it to flame, a dreadful, lovely sight. She stands on the wall, her promise heavy on her heart, a dead man's face behind her eyes, and says him, "*No!*"

He meets her eyes, then, laughing, turns away. She is very young, she knows little of the world, but she is not fool enough to think he has gone for good.

In the evening, women come to her, young and old, all with grey faces. Their words are hard as their eyes, stony with grief. "*She is one,*" they say, "*and we are many. Our sons died for her king's sake, so too our brothers and our husbands. It is not so much he asks for.*"

She pulls a strand of firestar from the wall and twists it through her fingers. The roses are gone, the music and the dream of summertime. This is all that is left.

"*Open the gate,*" the women say, "*and let him pass. Let him have his own.*"

She cannot meet their eyes. They are older than she is, these women of Felluria; they know more of the world. They have lived, and they have lost, and they have suffered. She tries to speak, "She is my..." Her words trail into silence and she says instead, "I gave my word and I will keep it."

She turns away so she will not see their faces.

Later, later, when she is alone, she presses her hands across her mouth to keep from screaming. She cannot keep faith with all she loves, and so she has to choose.

The woman sits for hours in the seat beneath the window, staring beyond the court, beyond the walls to the little space of sky. She carries food to her and watches while she picks at it, crumbling the bread, leaving the meat untouched. Her face has grown thin, little more than skin stretched across the skull, her flesh wasting away even as her belly swells with the red king's child. The woman never speaks of the child to come and nor can she: her silence binds her tongue fast as any cord. She has seen other women in like state sewing little clothes, hemming sheets small enough to fit a cradle, knitting bonnets and mittens so tiny they seem fit only for a doll. This woman's hands twist themselves to stillness, one clutched tight within the other, and always they are empty. Her child will come into the world undowered. Only one evening, taking away the tray, she sees the little knife she brought to cut her meat is not in its place.

"He killed my king and took me 'neath the tree he hung from," the woman says, in answer to the words unspoken. "Why should I not kill his son?"

She meets her eyes and keeps her silence. It is not for her to judge her, nor to stand between her and her hatred.

Not that day, nor the next day, nor the next, but soon, the red king returns. He brings tree trunks to make a ram to crash against the gate. He makes tunnels in the rock beneath the walls and lights fires to crack the stone. All through the autumn days, lithia burns on the walls of Felluria but, every day and every night, the red king's fires burn brighter than any flower upon the stone.

The woman keeps to her chamber in the tower. It is left to her to walk about Felluria and see fear etched on the faces of her people. The walls are high, the gate is oak, the well is fifty fathoms deep, they have stores to last all winter. None of this is enough and all there know it, certain as they know their own names.

The ram beats against the gate, a drumbeat rhythm counting out the time until the end.

She presses her brow against the smooth cold of the windowpane to ease its ache. "What do you seek?" she asks, knowing the answer in her heart. "Why did you come to me?"

"To make an ending. Where else would I go, when all the rest is lost?"

"There are many ways to make an ending."

"But few gentle as lithia." A cold, soft death, as easy a way into the dark as any could wish for. "The piper gave you lithia. It is a fit flower for a Tion, bright without and dark within."

The Tion died, and she was born: that is the only truth has weight upon the world. "And yet," she thinks, "were I a woman, looking into a mirror in twenty years, this is how I would look, if the world treat me unkindly." The future she will never have is written on this face.

"And when you are dead?" she asks, thinking of the ram against the gate, of the fires beneath the walls, of a man's smile that curves his lips into a grin and never reaches his eyes.

"Walls can be rebuilt," the woman says. "He will not touch you: you are not a woman." She stands straight, bracing herself against the weight of the child. "What is he to you?" she asks. "What is any man to you?"

She thinks of the blacksmith's boy, of roses and of lithia, and does not answer.

"You will live to see many mornings after he is dead," the woman says into her silence, "and always be as you are now. You will not suffer, as I have suffered."

The evening before the equinox, the woman's pains come upon her. At sunset, she leaves her to the midwife's care and pulls lithia from the walls of her hall, sets it a-boiling over her fire. The dark juice stains her fingers; when she returns to the room within the tower, the woman sees the stain and smiles.

The child is born in the time before the morning, just as the gate is breached. The woman stretches exhausted upon her bloody bed, her face hungry for the child. Her voice is no more than a whisper, "Give it to me."

The midwife ties off the cord and cuts it; steps forward to give the child to its mother. It bawls, red-haired, red-faced, its father's son. The woman's eyes are black pits of rage and hatred as she reaches out, the knife in her right hand.

Beyond the window, the rain falls softly down like tears upon the stone and night thins into a grey morning behind Cal Mora. She rests her head against the pane, long enough to see the fires flowering in the ruins, long enough to see the men of Felluria—the old men and the boys—broken amongst the broken stones. She turns, sickened by such sights, and steps between the midwife and the mother, holding out her empty hands. "Give me the child," she says, "I'll do what is necessary."

It quietens as she takes it. Awkward and unaccustomed, she settles it into the crook of her arm. It is heavier than she would have thought, solid and warm, streaked with its mother's blood. The woman offers her the knife but she shakes her head.

"I have lithia ready in my chamber," she says. "There is enough and more than enough for two. Let it go gentle into the dark."

"Very well." The woman nods after a moment's thought. "The means are of no matter, so long as 'tis done and done quickly."

A small mercy, she thinks, as she carries it away through shadows thick with smoke. This is a child begun in fear and rage and hatred; this is a child that should never have been born, blood and death its only birthright; this is a child, naked and nameless in her arms. Its eyes, the clouded blue of birth, stare towards her and beyond her and, all at once, she knows her limits. In her own chamber behind the hall, she wraps it in a scrap of sheepskin and puts it to rest within an oaken kist.

No time to think now of the future. The brew of firestar sits boiling on the fire and the woman has waited long enough. She pours the dark drink into a cup to cool, scattering red petals over it. The child stirs in its nest of sheepskin and she stoops to tuck the edges fast around it to keep it warm since it must bide awhile alone. Its eyes gaze into her own, deeper than the sea, empty and ageless. She cannot read the meaning in its look, nor tell if there are thoughts beyond those eyes.

The stones of the court are slick with blood and rain. She bends her head and keeps to the shadows, looking neither left nor right, but even so she sees such things to haunt her dreams forever. The red king has passed the gate. The walls are tumbled at his feet; he deals out death at every hand, a dreadful sight in red and bronze. A severed head rolls from her hastening foot into a puddle, comes to rest with empty eyes staring into the empty sky. She closes her eyes against the sight and her mind against the knowledge and carries the cup to the woman.

Later, later, she calls the face to mind and knows it as the blacksmith's youngest son. But by that time, the smith himself is dead and his widow has no tears left for any but herself.

The woman drinks with neither word nor pause, her face aflame to meet her end. When the cup is empty she sets it down and lies back against her pillows. For the first time since she came into Felluria, she smiles and, for a moment, she is again as she had been before the red king came from the west, her beauty shining lovely as the moon rising through clouds.

"Thank you," the woman says, holding out her hands, "for all you have done."

"The Tion died, and I was born. That is the truth," she thinks, "but it is not the only truth."

She bends to kiss the woman's cheek; here and now, she dares whisper the word she should not speak. In answer, the woman holds her close and strokes her hair, murmuring the name that is no longer hers.

Beyond the room, walls crash and tumble with a sound like the world ending; beyond the room, fires burn; beyond the room, men die screaming, cut down by the thrust of a bronze spear, by the stroke of a bronze sword; beyond the room, Felluria falls into ruin. But, within the room, there is a moment when all the rest is gone and truth is left behind, lying like flotsam along the tideline.

The moment passes and they draw apart. She waits a little time beside the woman, watching as her eyelids drop, watching as she falls softly into sleep and from sleep into the dark. Only when the woman's quiet breaths cease, and the blue pulse at her throat throbs no more, does she leave her and walk down the stair into a grey morning and a desolation.

5: Honey 'midst the roses

I'll weave my love a garland, it shall be dressed so fine
I'll set it round with roses, with lilies, pinks and thyme
And I'll present it to my love when he comes home from sea
Oh, I love my love and I love my love, because my love loves me.

The Loyal Lover, Traditional

Upon midsummer's morning, Marwy Ninek looked from her window. As on other days, as she had hoped she would today, she saw Assiolo working in his garden where his roses had grown strong in the shelter of stone walls. So had he done on many days since springtime, but today was not quite like other days, even in Felluria. She sat a long time in the windowseat, combing her hair, remembering the past, considering the present, and all the while, as she watched Assiolo go quietly about his work, the patterns of the midsummer light played 'cross the walls where lithia burned red and gold.

At last Marwy Ninek bound up her hair and went out into the garden. There were a few green apples setting on the tree, and brown berries on the rowan. She cupped an apple in her hand and thought of another apple long ago hanging upon another tree. Once, an apple had been only an apple. Nevermore. Memory clung, like lithia upon the wall. Memory twined, like firestar across the stone. She pulled back her hand and shivered in the sunlight.

Assiolo knelt beside his roses, patiently digging out the roots of dandelions and bindweed, untangling the clinging tendrils of firestar. Perhaps he had seen her, perhaps he had not, but when she came close she heard that he was singing.

"Into the wood I chanced to stray
All upon midwinter's day
There stood a stranger in my way
The dark was softly rising.

" 'Oh who are you that I do see?
Who stands beneath the apple tree?
Who holds out its dark fruit to me
All with the starlight shining?'

" 'I am the sky, the stone, the sea
All mortal men bow down to me
From love and death I'll set you free
I am the starlight shining.

" 'Come put your left hand in my right
Come dance with me this winter's night
Forget the sunrise and the light
Know always starlight shining.'

" 'Oh no! This dance is not for me
Mine is the rose upon the tree
And my love yonder waits for me
All in the darkness sleeping.'

" 'If that's your will go on your way
Pick roses on midsummer's day
But roses wither and decay
All into darkness falling.'

" 'I'll take the fate that falls to me
The rose is lovely on the tree
And my love, she's worth more to me
Than all your starlit dancing.' ' "

She asked, shyly, hesitantly, "What is that song?"

"An old tune," Assiolo answered. "I heard it first in Eulana."

"I know the tune," she told him, "and bitter words to fit it. But the song you sing is all your own."

"They were the words that fitted," he said, "the time and the place and the thought."

"What happened in Eulana that you should sing that song?"

He sat back, brushing the earth from his hands. "I met a man within a wood. He took my hand, and looked in it; he offered me a future but, in its place, I chose another I had made."

He smiled at her, and, at that smile, though she had grown accustomed to him in the days since spring time, it was as if he were a man she did not know. Her blood beat within her with a pulse strong as the drumbeat of midsummer and she heard herself cry out because she was afraid, of him, of herself, of the future that opened wide as the blue sky above her. Assiolo must have seen, he must have heard, but nothing showed upon his face.

He was here, and she was here, and it was midsummer, the world all out of balance, a day of light and fire and life calling out to life in the short night. She stood in the garden he had made her, between the rowan and the roses, so close to him he had but to reach out his hand to touch her. She met his eyes and at once turned down her own, knowing he could see the flush upon her cheek. Though she did not want to leave him, she dared not look at him and found herself looking instead upon a red rose on the tree beside them. Not even the roses long ago had been so perfect and so lovely but, as she touched it, she started back with a little cry of pain.

"What is it?"

She showed him: a thorn beneath the flower, a drop of blood upon her finger.

"Alas," said Assiolo, "the sweetest roses have the sharpest thorns." He reached out across the little space between them and took her hand to wipe the blood away. "But for all that, it is still a perfect rose." He picked the rose and snapped the thorn from the stem. "The rose is lovely," Assiolo told her, "so too are you lovely." Gently, gently, he tucked the red rose into her hair. His fingers brushed against her cheek, then he cupped her face with his left hand, just enough to tilt her face a very little towards him. He said softly, "I am going to kiss you, love, one kiss, if you are willing."

Marwy Ninek closed her eyes, bracing herself against the past made present, her heart beating out her fear so loud that surely he could hear it.

"Open your eyes, love, look at me. Am I so terrible?"

Assiolo's hand beneath her chin was yet as gentle, his voice as soft, drawing her back into the sunlight. Never in her life had she known a touch like this, so strong and yet so delicate. She opened her eyes and saw him, brown-haired, brown-eyed, a quiet man who could look on the worst the world could offer and not flinch away, who knew the darkness in men's hearts and yet kept kindness in his own.

"Oh," she breathed, "you are still Assiolo."

"And not become a monster?" She shook her head. "One kiss," he said. He bent his head towards her, his mouth brushing her lips lightly as the flutter of a butterfly's wing, then stepped away, to stretch himself upon the grass near the rowan, a young man in the sunshine taking his ease after a morning's work. He held out his hand. "Come sit beside me, it's a fair, fine morning."

"No more than that?"

"No more than that." He drew her down, settling her in the crook of his shoulder and, after a little while, as she relaxed against him, she felt his hand begin to slowly stroke her hair.

"I did not know..." Her thought trailed away to silence.

"How could you, love," he asked, "knowing only Torùkotu?"

"What do you want of me?"

His smile started in his eyes. "What any wants of his true love. To walk with you and talk with you and lie with you between the sunset and the morning."

She gasped and tensed, trembling like a lute string before it snaps. As if he had not felt it, Assiolo said, "If I can't have you, I'll never take another. You are the beginning and the end of my desire."

She could not move, she could not speak, she could scarce even breathe. Still Assiolo stroked her hair, his hand soft and soothing as his voice. "Hush, love, hush. You asked and I answered but there is no need to fear me. I am in no way like to him."

Her answer was a ragged whisper, so low he had to lean close to hear it. "You are a man."

A little laugh quivered the corners of his mouth. "That I cannot help."

Her heart fluttered like a moth against a windowpane; perhaps he felt it or else heard the sudden quickness of her breathing, for at once he put all jests aside. Sitting straight, he told her, "Though I am a man, I swear to you, by land and sea and sky, there is no need to fear me." As his hands swept through the wide patterns of the oath, they drew a golden thread of sunlight out of the air. The oath complete, Assiolo pulled the thread tight, its brightness fading as he tied it in a knot to bind his heart and mind and will. Settling her back into his shoulder, he took her hands between his own. "Listen, love, I would rather lie every night alone than once with you unwilling; tell me, any time, any place, thus far and no further, and I shall heed you."

She looked down at her fingers knotted into his. "Assiolo, I cannot give you what you want."

"Not now, love, perhaps not for a long, long time," he answered, quite comfortably. "But the day will come, I promise you, when what is now impossible will become so very, very easy, when what is now a great thing becomes a little one. Until that time, it is enough that you are here and I am here and that you trust me."

"Oh, Assiolo." Half a sob, and half a laugh. There was so much she could not say; the world was so much bigger than she had thought. She put her hand up to his cheek and he turned his head to kiss it.

A rustle and a whisper, a shimmer and a shiver, light flickering to form, half-seen from the edges of his eyes. Assiolo started round, looking to the bright sunlight falling down within her walls.

"What is it?"

"I saw, something." He narrowed his eyes against the light, and then turned back to her, shaking his head. "Nothing. A trick of the light."

A breath of wind swirled in the rose trees, stem and leaf and twig and thorn tossing in the breeze. Assiolo shivered, though the day was yet as warm and the sun was yet as bright, and crooked his fingers 'gainst misfortune, making the light fall back into its proper place. Then, all the rest of the morning and for a long time into the afternoon, they sat together, mostly in silence, sometimes talking of little things that did not matter, and all the while she felt his heart beat out its rhythm whilst he slowly stroked her hair.

—+— —+—

Averla dabbled her fingers in the pool and the world reflected in the water splintered into a scintillation of light. "A pretty pattern, is it not? True loves and happy endings. A monster slain, a darkness lifted, a captive heart set free amidst the summer roses." Her smile tore pieces from the piper's soul and left his heart bleeding in his breast. "Often and often, I've heard you tell this tale, or else another like it."

"Many times, Averla, in many places." To a girl, in a garden of red roses. To a boy, in a white city far, far across the sea. "All my tales are true. And this one is no different."

Many times, long ago and far away, she had smiled at him, and he at her. Then they had had the sunlight, and their music, and the rowan tree to shelter them, and no more need to think of what might come than of what had passed already. Sometimes, it seems a moment can last forever.

Her red lips curved into a smile. "This tale is not yet ended."

All things must end, the piper thought. The rowan tree had died. They had been parted by the fire, the wave had torn them asunder and what had been broken never could be mended. Aloud he said, "When your creature asked, Assiolo said him *No!*"

Beneath the birken trees, Averla's eyes were clear and empty as the vault of the summer sky and told him nothing of her thoughts or of the things that she remembered. "Assiolo has eaten at my table and drunk from my cup. I have marked him for my own. He's no more the boy in Ohmorah who loved you better than his father."

"He is only a man, Averla."

Smiling still, she asked, "Only a man, my monster? Are you so sure?"

He could not answer. He could do no more than look at her, dazzled by the light.

"Only a man? Allocco's son! Who walked into the year's dark eye to kill Torùkotu and made himself a king!" She leaned closer and he was lost in her blue eyes. "Say it is not true, my little piper, and I'll say he is only a man."

He could not gainsay her. All of this was true. He closed his eyes, he pressed his hands across his face and cried out to her that she might have mercy, "He has put such things aside."

A ringing peal of mocking laughter. " 'Twas you who left him to his father, knowing full well what Allocco would teach him. I have eyes, my monster, and I can see."

"Let him alone, Averla, let him live out his life in freedom!"

"None of us is free, my piper. You set a limit to our freedom when you closed the gates of morning." Gently, she took his hands and, gently, she pulled them from his face. "I chafe within those limits, monster, within this world of flesh and death you trapped me in. So I will watch Assiolo, and I will wait, my dear; then, at the right time, I will ask."

—+— —+—

The days slipped by. Summer slowly settled into autumn and cast a mantle of golden bracken 'cross Cal Mora's braes. The roses had passed their season, the swallows had fled south. Only lithia burned bright, its turning leaves flickering across the walls in flames of orange and of red. The apples had ripened on Assiolo's tree, round and rosy bursting with sweet juice. This afternoon, he had picked them and sat now in the windowseat, eating an apple and staring out into the halflight and the rain. A poor harvest this year, scarcely enough to fill the bowl beside him. But the tree was strong and growing and next year there would be more.

He heard a gentle scratching at his door, a whisper, "Assiolo?"

"I am here."

Marwy Ninek stepped into his chamber and let the door shut quietly behind her. "You were not at dinner."

He flushed. "I had no thought to slight you. Merely, I had no wish to sit another night turning aside a mercatman's curiosity."

"Edo Incithu seeks no more than tales to tell along the way. There's no harm to him—he comes by every summer. So did his father and his grandsire."

"That's as maybe, love, but I do not care to have my name made free with from here to Cincern Dùn. I've told him, thrice, as much as I've told any man in Felluria. Where I was and what I did last winter are no concern of his."

Assiolo held out his hands and she came to him, sitting down beside him to rest her head against his shoulder. He kissed her hair, her cheek, her mouth, and felt her lips flutter gently against his. "I missed you," she said. "I did not know how much I had grown used to you beside me until you were not there."

He dropped a kiss onto her hair. " 'Twas but an evening, love. Tomorrow he's away on the noontime tide and I'll be in my place again. To play too, if you wish it."

She nodded, curled at his side, soft and sweet and warm beside him. He took an apple, pared and peeled it and gave each second piece to her. At their backs, beyond the pane, the rain fell softly down upon the court and the grey evening shaded slowly into black, pierced here and there by lamplight from unshuttered windows. Sitting in the quiet shadows with her light weight pressed against him, breathing in the faint perfume of rosewater rising from her skin, Assiolo felt again the poignant pleasure of her presence. He could not tell how he had ached for her those long months after midsummer, how over and again desire mounted into need that could find no satisfaction. He could say no word and give no sign, knowing her trust was yet but a fragile thing a thoughtless word or clumsy touch could shatter in an instant. Always he must wait for her to ask, trembling, hesitant, and answer, gently as he could.

When the apple was all eaten, they talked a while of little things: the songs he would sing on the morrow, Yatta Tala's feud with the butcher's wife, the many names of stars and the many words for rain, and all the time they talked he waited for her to call to mind how late it was and leave him.

Yet she made no move, nor did he wish she would. But her voice grew quiet, her answers short. "Come, love," he said at last, "I'll walk with you to your chamber."

Marwy Ninek shook her head and asked, "May I stay with you tonight?"

He could hear nothing above the thunder of his heart. The cords of his throat knotted and his breath came quick and shallow. He did not realise until he felt her struggle how tightly he was holding her.

"I did not mean," she faltered, staring into his face with wide and fearful eyes.

"I know." He forced himself to speak slowly and with calm. "It is enough that you are here. The rest will come in its own time." She did not answer. Like a hare within the heather, she quivered beneath his touch and he cursed himself for a fool. "Sweet, it does not matter. There is no lock upon the door. Let me walk you back and I'll see you in the morning."

"Do you want me to stay?"

He could only answer with the truth, holding her cold hands in his. "Yes, love, I do."

She nodded, and gripped his fingers tight. "Then I will stay."

He had not thought before that moment there was space within his heart to love her more. Now, seeing her courage and her trust, he knew he had been wrong. He raised her fingers to his lips and kissed them. "Thank you," was all he said, but it was enough.

"I love you, Assiolo," she whispered, turning her hand and weaving her fingers into his.

"That I know full well."

Assiolo pulled the pins from her hair and let down the heavy braid so it tumbled past her shoulders nearly to her waist. "The women wore it so in my own country. You cannot know," he said, untwisting the strands one from another, "how often I have wished to see your hair set free."

He turned his eyes away whilst she stripped to her shift and climbed into the bed, pulling the covers tight against her chin. He likewise stripped to shift and breeks but, as he put out his hand to snuff the lamp, she said, "I am afraid of the dark."

"No matter, love," he answered, "there's oil enough to burn 'til morning."

"Are you quite certain?"

"Certain sure, and I can always make a light." Knowing her fear, he told her, "Be easy, sweet. If you wake in the night it will be my body in the bed beside you. A man, but one that loves you."

When he lay down, she did not move towards him, she did not move away, but lay rigid as a figure of wood, staring up into the shadows. "You're cold," he said. "Let me hold you."

"No more than that?"

"No more than that." He moved across the space between them and gathered her into his arms. "See, I am still the same. There is no lock upon the door and there will be no darkness." Assiolo held her close and sang quietly in his own tongue, a little song, a lullaby, to ease her softly into sleep.

A rod of flesh within her mouth, throbbing, thrusting, choking. A moment's gasping respite before hard hands forced her to her knees.

I had your maidenhead an hour ago—let's try another way.

She screamed as he drove into her, a pain greater even than the others he had taught her.

Marwy Ninek pulled herself free of the man's arms to crouch against the wall, a wild thing trapped and cornered, knowing nothing but its fear. Her breath rasped against the cold night air and then a quiet voice spoke, drawing her back out of that dreadful night. "Hush, love, hush. He is not here. Only I am here."

She looked up and saw him, brown-haired in lamplight, his face creased with concern and sleep. He was a loving voice whispering her name, a gentle hand reaching out to brush her cheek, a living promise that the past was dead and gone. She moved back into the shelter of his arms, resting her head upon his breast. Assiolo stroked her hair, crooning little words of love, holding her close and soothing bad dreams away.

His heart beneath her cheek beat out the moments, counting out the time between the past and present, and slowly she relaxed. "No need to fear him," he said, when at last she had stopped shaking, "cold stones lie heavy on his bones. You are alive and he is dead, and that is all that matters."

"I cannot forget."

"I cannot change the past," Assiolo said after a long while, "only give you good memories to set against the bad."

The horror of the night time flickered, dreams and memories knotting together into a choking coil, dragging her back into past darkness. "You want to do what he did."

Calm and quiet, he answered, easy as in his garden in the summertime, "No, sweetheart, never that. I want only to please you. There are many ways a man can please a woman – I think it time that I began to show you."

The door was unlocked, the lamp at the bedside burned and burned and drove away the dark, Assiolo's touch was gentle but still she was afraid, remembering all the ways a man found pleasure in the night time. She closed her eyes and gave no answer.

"Look at me," he said, and so she did, seeing herself reflected in his brown eyes. "You are my dearest love, my present and my future; I will in nowise hurt you or give you cause for grief. So, will you let me make a beginning?"

Love and fear battled in her heart but, looking into his face, into his tender smile, she could not see a monster, only the man who loved her. She laid her hand against his cheek and answered, "Yes."

"I am glad," Assiolo told her, turning his head to kiss her hand. "I promise, love, there will be no pain, no darkness and no fear. You are quite safe with me."

For a while, the gentle movements of his hands seemed no different from any time before but then he began to circle her breasts, fondling them through the linen of her shift. His touch was ever light and delicate but still she gasped, aware of every fingertip against her tightened flesh. The strange sensation stirred and deepened when she felt his lips upon her neck, nuzzling a line of little, licking kisses down to her collar bone, then grew deeper still as his mouth took the place of the fingers caressing her breasts and his left hand went a-roving down, down, down, tracing a pattern across her waist and belly, until it came to rest between her thighs. She caught her breath at the thought of what might come next.

"Enough for tonight," Assiolo said softly, drawing his hand away. "Well, love, does it please you?"

She had spent so long remembering another man's brutality she had no words to answer him. Instead she flung her arms around his neck, holding him close as could-be, crying out his name over and over. He stroked her hair, and kissed her face, and every touch of hands and lips showed her his love and care. "I told you true," he whispered. "Only I am here. All the rest is long ago, forever and for always."

In the dull autumn morning, his body chilled to numbness, Assiolo climbed out onto the rocks at Loch Mora-side and shook saltwater from his hair. Still shivering, he pulled on his shirt and britches and picked his way across the shingle shore, scarce able to feel the stones beneath his bare feet. As he came close to the gate, he saw Yatta Tala pulling tall plants of sticklewort beneath the walls. "You'll do yourself a damage, lad, in that cold water now the leaves have turned."

He had been taught courtesy in boyhood and must stop since she had spoken, though the west wind bit hard through his damp clothes and he had no wish to talk. "My thanks for your advice, mistress, but I know best what I can bear."

She straightened herself and peered at him with hard, sharp eyes. "What's the matter, Assiolo? I've seen you courting slow all summertime, sweet as honey 'midst the roses, but now you've got her where you wanted her it's sea swimming every morning."

"Let me go my way through my days," he muttered through chattering teeth, "and I'll freely leave you to go yours."

She grinned at his discomfort. "Ah, but I sleep easy in my bed at night. Can you say likewise? Or have you a need to cool hot blood?"

"Here and now," Assiolo said, biting back sharper words to baulk her of her sport, "my blood is cold as the rest of me and I'm away to my chamber to find dry clothes and a hot drink. If there's something of import you would say, say it quickly."

He paused, shaking with cold, against her answer. Yatta Tala scowled and twisted another plant from its root. "Here's a useful thing," she said, dropping it into her basket and setting to another, a malicious gleam in her sharp eyes, "that laps your craft with mine. I use it to colour wool, tell me the purposes you'd put it to."

"A wholesome tonic," he said, brushing his hand across the hairy leaves of agrimony, "it purifies the blood and cleanses the water."

"Aye, so it does but old men find it has another virtue." She ran her hand along a golden spike and cackled at his flush. "I'd stick with camomile for that hot drink, Assiolo. Soothing to mind and body."

He gathered the shreds of his dignity about him. "Mistress, when I want advice on herbals I'll ask it. Until such time, I'll leave you to deal with your concerns and keep mine to myself."

She looked him up and down, letting her eyes linger long in an appraising stare, until he wished her sunk in the depths of the sea. "I hope she yields before the wintertime. You might not last 'til spring."

Discourtesy or not, he could take no more. And, with her laughter ringing in his ears, he turned his back on her and walked away towards the gate.

—|— —|—

There was yet a line of bothies across Kistoru's hills, each a windowless room with a roof of turf and timber, a hearth built into one wall and a bedplace into another. The shepherds used them in the summertime when the sheep were on the uplands. Now the flocks had been driven to low pasture and the bothies were all empty. They had no locks upon the door and any might make use of them who chose to.

Te-Meriku crouched beneath a rowan at the burnside to clean and skin a pair of rabbits. He still knew all the trackways in the white glen though it was twenty years and longer since he had last set a snare here. As he worked, the eagle swept across the brow of the hill, mewing on the wind. At such a sight and such a sound, memory stabbed, sharp as the blade of a bronze knife: an afternoon spent on the hillside in the heather and this same bird as witness. He closed his mind against that day, thought only of muscle, flesh and sinew, the careful movements of his knife, the softness of fur, the stickiness of blood. When he was done, he wrapped the guts in the skins, still with their heads attached, and flung the bloody bundle hard and far into the heather. A wingbeat and a rush of air as the great bird stooped to its desire, beating the crows away to claim an easy meal. Before it ate, it turned sidelong to look at him from one yellow eye. *What is it like, to be the sea eagle?* He met its eye without an answer. He did not know, he could not tell: beyond these hills, he was the king; within them, only a man without even a name to call his own.

He wiped his knife upon the turf and washed his hands clean in running water. Using the store of wood stacked ready by the door, he built a fire within the hearth and set his dinner roasting, flavoured with a handful of thyme from the hillside. Then he leaned his back against the wall and sat looking out over his own country as the last light set the bracken blazing near as fierce as the fires of sunset burning in the west. A fair, fine evening to sit and do nothing but watch the shadows creep across the hill and smell woodsmoke in the twilight, listening to the senseless murmur of the burn and the mindless whisper of the wind in the rowan trees. A pleasant thing to be alone, and watch the stars slowly prick into life and the hills become black shapes against the dusk. He sat in silence as all about him evening thickened into a night made only deeper by firelight spilling out from the open door.

A step beyond the dark, a shadow swelling and clotting into a man glimpsed sidelong from the edges of his eyes. His heart beat hard and fast as memory shaped itself a moment into flesh, pale-faced and slender, black hair bound up in the clansman's knot. Te-Meriku's mouth opened, a name long years unspoken hanging on his lips, but then the man stepped out of the dark and memory showed itself no more than a trick played by light and shadow.

"What are you doing here?" the king asked roughly. "I said no word to bid you follow."

A little light laugh in the darkness. "And am I not your night-watch? I guard the door while you are sleeping."

No hint of laughter in the king's answer. "Insult to injury, Ardùvai. As well say you think me a weakling or a fool that cannot guard my life myself." A knifeblade glinted in the firelight falling from the bothy door.

"I think as little as I can, Te-Meriku." Ardùvai grinned as he walked towards the firelight. "What I am, I am, and what I am, you made me. But if there's any of that coney left I'll eat it up and gladly. I've been following my nose since the light was lost. A finer scent than roses on a summer's evening."

"Insolent pup," growled the king but all the same his face twitched into a smile. He slid his knife back into its sheath and gestured to Ardùvai to sit. "Eat your fill."

Ardùvai tore a leg from a rabbit and started to eat. Te-Meriku leant back against the bothy wall in silence, staring into the gathering night. In a little time the nightwatch pulled a flask from his pocket and offered it. "This'll drive away your mood and ease your sleep."

"And give me a sore head in the morning?"

"The morning's no concern of mine; I'm but the nightwatch. Come daylight, my duty's done and I'll leave you snoring with an easy conscience."

"I had no thought to sleep tonight but I'll drink with you full willing." Te-Meriku sniffed the flask, then drank and tasted woodsmoke and peat, seasalt and heather honey. He nodded his thanks and drank again. Ardùvai laughed. "Red wine of Escen's well enough but that's the soul of our own country."

"So too it is, and this the very heart's blood." He cast a sidelong glance towards his nightwatch. "The man that makes it guards it closer than his wife's good name. How'd you come by it?"

"Ah, leave a man his secrets." Ardùvai's voice was full of mischief. "I'll let you have a firkin if ever you take me fox and geese."

Then Ardùvai ate and Te-Meriku drank, and the silence between them was now companionable, filled with the little sounds of night time: wind in the rowan leaves and running water, whispers in a tongue neither man could speak but each had known from his cradle. A flutter on the edge of seeing and a white owl drifted out of the dark on soundless wings, freezing the moment with its question, *Who will?*

Somewhere beyond the firelight some small creature screamed out the answer. Ardùvai took the flask and savoured the spirit on his tongue, letting it slide easy down his throat as mother's milk. The owl called again, *Will you?* and, in the stillness after, he asked, "What are you looking for, Te-Meriku, up here on the braes of the white glen?"

"Nothing at all. It's a deathwatch I keep, after a fashion. Word came today from Kistoru's hall that Ala his wife is dead."

The nightwatch was a man to whom words came easily, a quick retort, a laughing jest, and yet he kept his silence. His eyes flicked to the king's face, half hidden in the shadows. There had been some depth of feeling in his words but if it came of loss or love he could not tell. The king had spent his boyhood in Kistoru's hall, that much was common knowledge, and that such days were long gone. It would take a braver man than he to speak of them, or else a fool. He drank again, filling the moment with barleyspirit rather than an answer.

Te-Meriku pushed back his hair and said, "I'd watch the night beside her grave save she'd likely rise up and drive me off, berating me again for forgetting the distance between a bastard and a clansman. Years back she drove me from these hills. I was not then the king and there was little love between us, even before..." he let his voice tail off and held out his hand for the barleyspirit.

Ardùvai passed the flask without a word, knowing that tale as well as any in Lyikené. "Thodùhah bade me tell you there's a change in the wind," he said, by and by. "Edo Incithu's away with the tide."

"He knows what I want of him?" The king's tone was steady again. "Proof that the tale he told of Allocco's son is true."

"Aye, man. He knows the thing he's looking for, and thinks Habhain's the place to look for it. He had his ears open all the time he was in Felluria."

"An he does it he's worthy of his fee. The mercatkind can go unmarked where we cannot." He stretched, settling himself more comfortably against the wall. "I never saw the Later Lands save as hills in the distance, that time I hunted the captain of Ohmorah across the sea."

"Alas, I missed that sailing, being but a boy. I had to make do with the song. I had it by heart when I was eight and dreamed of glory." Ardùvai whistled the lay the piper had made of the king's deeds and the king's daring. He broke off as a thought struck him, linking one man of Ohmorah to another, a reason a man might leave his life behind. "Was he kin to Assiolo?"

"I do not know, I cannot say. We did not talk before I killed him. You think Assiolo will step out of the light and claim his blood of me?" Te-Meriku sounded almost amused. "He has no cause, no matter what their kinship. The man gave his word twicefold, to Hadùhai and to me, and broke it."

The nightwatch shook his head against such folly and took up his tune again.

"Enough, Ardùvai," the king said softly, "death is the end of all things." He raised the flask as in a toast. "He was a brave man for all he was a fool."

"Aye well, you'll find fools in any country, even in Lyikené."

Te-Meriku laughed hard and harsh in his throat. "Kistoru for certain, putting his faith in stories and in symbols."

"Yet the babe he reared became the king," Ardùvai countered. "That's a tale to prove Kistoru's foresight."

"So too it is, and I hope he finds comfort in the telling. There's none elsewhere." The quietness of the king's voice caused hairs to prick on Ardùvai's neck. He drew in his breath and held it, all jests forgotten in a moment. He was a man of Lyikené who dwelled in the king's hall: he knew as well as any 'twas when Te-Meriku spoke so soft he was most dangerous. "Thus far and no further, Ardùvai, for all you are my nightwatch. There's deep waters ahead and monsters 'neath the surface will drag you down and drown you."

Never before had he been unable to look Te-Meriku in the eye. Ardùvai held out his hands, acknowledging his fault, and willed them not to tremble. There were limits on the king's good temper he would let no man pass, no law in Lyikené but the king's will.

"Be easy, man," said Te-Meriku, " 'twas but a warning. My past is very close tonight and it's shortened my temper somewhat. I'm glad enough of your company and your liquor."

Ardùvai let out his breath, laughing. "I thought a moment you meant to keep my deathwatch too this night."

"Nay, you're safe enough. I needs must have a nightwatch, say the greyhairs in my hall, and I'd rather 'twere you than many another. I'll do you no harm, an you remember what's a tale to you is flesh and blood to me."

"There's a lesson to start me on the road to thinking."

"Have another drink instead," advised the king, "and I'll drink after you. What need for thought with spirit fine as this to hand?"

The nightwatch drank, and passed back the flask. "I spoke out of turn," he said, more seriously than was his wont, "but I'll keep my place beside you, Te-Meriku, until one of us is dead."

"Do you think I did not know it?"

The night was young no longer and the eight stars of the hawk hung high over the hills. The wind shivered across the brae and, behind them in the bothy, the fire had become a red eye, unblinking in the dark. " 'Tis midnight," said Ardùvai softly, marking the position of the hawk's head, "if it's a deathwatch you keep now's the time to mark her passing."

"What's fit for me to say?" Te-Meriku had flattened all feeling from his voice. "Ala hated me these twenty years and longer as only a woman can hate." But all the same the nightwatch saw the cold gleam of starlight upon his knifeblade and when Te-Meriku spoke again it was more gently, "She deserves more than that of me. When I was a babe, she suckled me and that's a debt I'll never now repay. But what I can, I'll do." A small movement of the knife and blood dripped slow and black as he held out his empty hands, palms down to the cold earth.

Ardùvai stood on the threshold of the bothy, no part of this for all he was the nightwatch. Te-Meriku's hands moved in a slow pattern as he called on land and sky to give shelter to the newly dead. Shreds of cloud wrapped the stars in a tattered cloak, deepening the dark. A shiver of white wafted across the blackened brae. *Who will?* an unearthly voice asked clearly. *Will you?*

Startled, Ardùvai gasped aloud, childhood tales suddenly recalled, childhood fears suddenly rekindled. The dead were dead and came not back but, at such a time, in such a place, that was a hard thing to remember. Such thoughts stretched out cold fingers and he drew back towards the glow of the dying fire, shivering though the night was mild and his cloak of heavy weaving. He was a man of Lyikené, putting his trust in his knife and his sword and his strong right arm, but here and now he was as afraid as any child of the dark pressing hard upon him.

The night was full of whispers and shifting shadows, sights unseen beyond the dark. Ardùvai looked to the king and saw a man he did not know, his flaming hair and blood-red cloak quenched by the night, eyes star-bright in the darkness, murmuring words not meant for living ears, an invocation, a confession, a lament for things that might have been and would never come to pass. For Ala, perhaps; for certain for another. He closed his eyes against the sight he had no right to see, his ears against the words he had no right to hear and curled his fingers in the sign against ill-fortune.

The wind blew and the moment passed. The stars shone bright and the whispers were no more than rowan leaves rustling above the stream. If the dead had been close by, they were no more; the only ghosts were in men's minds with no more than thought to give them substance. Te-Meriku sat back on his heels and spoke, level, steady, no trace of grief in face or voice, "That will have to do. She is dead and gone and in her grave, beyond my reach forever."

He sucked his finger to quench the bleeding while the nightwatch built up the fire to burn and burn and drive away the dark.

"I'll swear I thought myself a vole in the field margin when that owl called." Ardùvai laughed, himself again and proof against foolish fancies. "All I have is yours, Te-Meriku, if only you'll not tell my brother I was frighted by a bird."

"And you the nightwatch! Too good a tale by far to waste upon a single brother."

Ardùvai groaned to hear him, burying his face in his hands. The king grinned in the firelight and clapped him on the back. "Nay, your fate lies in my hands, man, and never you forget it. You can begin by sending me that firkin."

—+— —+—

The hunter's moon was waning from the sky, half past its fullness now and no longer drowning out the starlight. Too chilly at the end of autumn days to sit an evening in the garden. Assiolo sat on the windowseat, thrumming his lute, weaving snatches of music and memory into a song of summer to lighten the dark days ahead.

Marwy Ninek sat on the rug before the hearth, resting her chin upon her knees, finding the patterns in the fire, but often and often she turned to look at him and each time he felt her eyes upon him he looked up smiling.

The evening grew old and the fire burned low, falling into a heap of soft ash and glowing embers. At last Assiolo set aside the lute to yawn and stretch. "It grows late, love. Will you come to bed?"

She did not move except to hold out her hand to draw him down beside her.

"What's the matter?" He put his arm around her and she leaned her head against him. "You've scarce spoke a word tonight, love."

"I was thinking," she began. Her voice faltered and she flushed, crimson as any rose, and looked away, plaiting the fringes of her shawl about her fingers.

After a little time of silence, he prompted her, "What were you thinking?"

"Of things you've said and things you've done, our nights together. But over and again how much I love you." He brought her fingers to his lips and kissed them. All in a rush, as if she feared her resolution would desert her, she said, "I want you, Assiolo."

His hands closed fast on hers. Keeping his tone even, he asked, "Are you certain, sweet? No need to prove your love or courage."

"I thought you wanted me."

"Oh, I want you," he said, tightening his arms around her, wanting to hold her close and never let her go. "There are not words to tell how much I want you."

She looked into his face, gazing deeply into his eyes as if to find again the man she knew. He said, cupping her chin in his hand, "See, I am still Assiolo," and in a moment she smiled and laid her hand against his cheek. "Remember, love," he said, "I'll do nothing an you do not like it. Trust me."

"I trust you."

Assiolo kissed her lips and then her neck, moving slowly down to trace a trail of kisses across her breasts and belly. He breathed in the scents of her skin, lavender and rosewater tempered with the tang of salt, and bent his head between her legs. At once she tugged at his shoulders, pulling him back so she could see his face.

He paused a moment, looking down into her wide eyes. "Promise me, sweetheart, this is what you want."

She nodded, sliding her hands up his arms, across his breast. "But stay where I can see you."

Assiolo kissed her mouth again, teasing, tender kisses, each a feather touch against her skin. She laughed in delight, matching him, touch for touch, kiss for kiss, and he slipped his hand between her thighs, fingers circling, caressing, a languorous, gentle rhythm. When he heard her moan, he asked her, "Now?"

"Now," she answered.

Kneeling between her legs, he entered smoothly as he could. He looked into her face asking a wordless question and saw her answer in her eyes. "I love you," he said, "forever and for always." She put her arms around his neck and kissed him. Gently, carefully, he began to move. Soon she pressed her face into his shoulder, clinging to him, her breath coming in ragged gasps. His own need mounted but he held it at bay. Suddenly he felt her shivering and shuddering beneath him, crying out his name in wonder. He laughed aloud to feel her pleasure and quickened his pace to take his own at last.

"I did not know," she told him, later, as they rested, tangled still one into the other, "how could it be, to live so long and know so little?"

"Well, love," reluctantly he freed himself and lay again beside her, running his finger down the curve of her breast, "I think it was because I was not there."

"Oh, Assiolo." Her smile creased her eyes, quivering her mouth into a laugh.

"Did I not say that in the end it would be so very, very easy?"

In a little while she slept, curled in his arms, her head pillowed on his shoulder. Assiolo did not sleep but lay, cushioning her rest, entirely content, completely happy. He kissed her softly, whispering his love, and even in her sleep she heard him, her hand reaching blindly out in search of his to catch and cradle it against her cheek.

"So," said Yatta Tala next morning, passing by the garden as he swept dead leaves away, "you've passed the gate at last." Assiolo looked up, his face severe but for the little laughter in his eyes. "I've seen too many new-made wives across the years to miss that look."

"If I've told you once, mistress, I've told you a dozen times: I'll not speak to you of things that don't concern you."

"Oh, I'll not pry where I'm not welcome." The little laugh crept down to twitch the corners of his mouth. She sucked her teeth to see it, a crabbed old woman owning no man her equal. "Is it too much to ask that you'll sing an evening out of the minor? I've grown overtired of laments and dirges these last months."

And Assiolo grinned and touched his brow, acknowledging her mastery.

V, Lyikené: The mastery

Comfort for the comfortless
Aye and honey for the bee
Comfort for the comfortless
But there's nane but you for me.

The False Lover Won Back, *Traditional*

A hand thuds against the oaken door. He wakes all of a piece, lies in his bed considering who might disturb him so early in the day. Another thud, loud as the one that woke him, rattles the door and his question is answered by the voice calling through the lock.

He slides from between the sheepskins into the cold air and draws back the bolt. Until the year he turned twelve, they shared this attic, two boys together to fight and spar and play; then Imacah became a man, to bear by day the bronze sword forged for him when he was in his cradle and sleep by night in a fine chamber fitting to his rank. More nights than not, the past two years, he has slept there too, in Imacah's bed, at Imacah's side. But not this last sennight. Not since all was changed.

Imacah stands on the threshold, his eyes a-glitter in the grey morning light, his hair bound back into the clansman's knot. "Get your knife," he says, stepping into the room.

"Imacah!"

"I said, Get your knife!" Imacah's breath rasps of barleyspirit, but his narrowed eyes are steady and that part of him still sober knows well what he is doing. "My knife is waiting for your blood: you can face it with your own or empty-handed."

They have fought and played a hundred times, testing their strength and skill against each other, for a wager, for a jest, for the sheer joy of it. Now, as they circle each other across the wide attic floor, he realises he does not know Imacah's intent, the truth behind the seeming. Imacah is three parts drunk and reckless with it. Unless, of course, this is a feint. Cats play with mice. Easy enough for a sober man to play the drunkard and lull his foe to folly. Or is the drink because he has another, darker, purpose?

He continues his wide circles, watching this stranger with Imacah's face, feeling for a way to bring them both through this with skins intact.

Trying to get his measure, he watches him pace and feint and marks the hand holding the knife. Imacah fights with his knife in his right hand but shifts it always to the left before closing for the kill. He has oft intended to remind him of this trick, since a pattern plain to him is plain to others also. For the first time, he is glad it slipped his mind. His life may hang on knowing such a thing. He is but a naked man and, though Imacah has not put on his mail, the leather of his jerkin is thick enough to catch and turn a knife blade. A sennight ago he would have sworn on his life he knew all Imacah's moods and dealings but a sennight ago he was another man living another life. What does any know of another's heart? The only certain truth is the knife is still in his right hand.

Watching the knife, he dodges each sweep and jab, taking care not to be trapped against the wall. More than once, had this been another man, he could have slipped beneath his guard to slash and maim, perhaps to kill, but 'twas Imacah began this and so 'tis Imacah must make the ending. All he can do is wait and hope that, when that moment comes, he can reshape it to his own purpose. So he goes on as he began, dodge and parry, always defence, never attack, and watches the frustration mount in Imacah's eyes. Imacah can push him so far but no further and so, although this is Imacah's fight, it is he has the mastery. Almost he laughs to see it.

Almost. Not quite. Only a fool goads a man already drunk or desperate.

Frustration waxes at last into decision. Imacah leaps forward, intent blazing in his face, and, as he leaps, passes the knife to his left hand.

He twists sideways, rolling so Imacah's thrust meets only empty air, and sets down his knife. "I'll not fight your battles for you," he says, standing to face him empty-handed. "If you came here for a kill, I'll give you one. Strike and be done with it."

A flicker in Imacah's eyes. "You bastard whoreson."

He laughs. "So I have ever been, clansman."

"Coward!"

He smashes his fist into Imacah's gut. Imacah doubles up, grunting and gasping, and he follows with the other to his face. "I'll take that name from no man, not even you."

He steps back to give him room to recover his breath and wit, watching always the knife still held in his left hand. Slowly, awkwardly, Imacah stands, his face a confusion of thought and barleyspirit, his eyes dark and glittering in the hard morning light. Blood trickles down his cheek from brow to lip; his left eye will be black and swollen shut tomorrow, if either lives long enough to see it. Light plays along the bronze blade of the knife, a-tremble in a shaking hand.

"Te-Meriku."

In answer, he reaches out and closes his hand over Imacah's. Taking the knife from the slackened fingers, he sets it beside his own.

"So cold without you," Imacah whispers, "so alone."

"Let me hold you." Gently, carefully, he puts his arms around him, feeling him at first a stranger then slowly relax into the man he knows. "I am still myself. There's nothing need change between us."

Imacah cups his face between his hands, staring long and hard from overbright eyes until, perhaps, he sees what he wants and pulls him close for kissing. Imacah's mouth tastes of blood and salt and barleyspirit but his eyes are again the ones he knows. At that, his heart soars free into the sunlight because he has come back. "You and I," he says. He works his fingers through Imacah's black hair, untying the knot and tossing aside the scrap of grass-green silk. Wrapped in each other, they stumble and tumble onto the bed and, for a while, all is as it should be between them.

And yet, and yet, after the morning, everything is changed. He has had the mastery, and both know it. They speak, carefully, of little things: an arrow's flight into its mark, or a litter of hound pups. Never of ships or swords or the north country. Only of the present; never of the future.

Half a month slides by: quiet days, fierce nights. He lies on his back in the heather, staring into blue beyond blue, his thoughts drifting with the eagle across the afternoon, anywhere and nowhere. "The moon is dark tonight," says Imacah beside him.

"So too it is. What of it?"

"Apples," says Imacah, tossing his knife from hand to hand, "a reckoning with the king's men."

He rolls onto his side to look at him. The bruise about his eye has faded to a sickly yellow. "No."

"A month ago you were quite willing."

A month ago the world was a different place and he a different man. He shakes his head. "I cannot. Not now."

"To the edge of the world, you told me," Imacah says. "Now's the time to prove it."

He reaches out and Imacah's arms close round him, returning his embrace. Pressing his face into his shoulder, he hears Imacah's heart beat out the moments between the present and the future. Silence between them, a silence waiting for his answer but no words will come. He can do no more than hold him close and hope love is enough.

Imacah pulls roughly away to stand over him, his knife held in his left hand. At the look on Imacah's face, something breaks inside him and at last he screams aloud, a word, a sob, a cry into the tall air for his lost soul, "Imacah!"

No answer. There will never be an answer. Where Imacah has gone he cannot follow. He can only watch as he walks away across the heather into a future he cannot share. The eagle sweeps across the hillside, banks and stoops, drawn to some carrion, no doubt, out of sight beyond the ridge.

6: Banish misfortune

But he lay still, and sleepit sound,
Albeit the sun began to sheen,
She look'd atween her and the wa',
And dull and drowsie were his e'en.

Clerk Saunders, Traditional

The shortest day was withering into the longest night, the dark eye of the year. Outside the hall, darkness deepened; outside the hall, the gate was shut and barred, but in the hall people were gathering by ones and twos and threes. The hammerbeams were decked with holly, twisted about with ivy, studded with apples filled with cloves; the shutters were closed against the night, the stone walls were bright with lamplight and in each hearth an oaken log was set to burn until the morning. Last and late, Marwy Ninek came in, with Assiolo at her side, and then the door was locked behind them. All of the place were here, from the babe in arms to Yatta Tala. No need for any to come in or go out until the morning.

And if any of that company thought it strange that Marwy Ninek should choose to sit the long night through behind a locked door, when she had never done before, never since this hall was built, they need only look to Assiolo and let understanding come with the second thought.

When the hog was a pile of bones and the pudding a heap of crumbs and raisins, when the tables were set with beer and wine and barleyspirit, with trays of sweetmeats and savouries, with lamps to burn and burn and drive back all shadows and all darkness, it was time for music and for dancing. Marwy Ninek watched Assiolo move through the figures of a jig with Issa Baesina, her feet still light and nimble though her waist was six months swollen. Faster and faster sang the whistles, faster and faster beat the drum, faster and faster down the lines they went, spinning and twirling, stamping and clapping, until the musicians at last took pity on the dancers and called "Stay" that all might know this time through the tune would be the last. Their set complete, their pattern woven, Issa Baesina made her courtesy in answer to Assiolo's bow and they parted, flushed and laughing.

As he sank down beside her, Marwy Ninek poured Assiolo a cup of ale. He downed it and asked, "Will you dance, love?"

She looked around at the men of Felluria, at the butcher and the
blacksmith, at the creelers and the shepherds, and, blanching, told
him, "Assiolo, I cannot."

"No matter, sweet." He put his arm around her and hugged her
close. "It's enough that you are here, this year. But, sweetheart, here's
a warning," Assiolo's eyes danced, kindling his face into a smile,
"next year, I'll strip the willow with none but you." Marwy Ninek
twined her fingers into his and gave no answer. "Tell me true, love,"
he said after a moment, "this night a year ago, alone within your
chamber, did you think that you'd take a man to your bed or keep
company in the midwinter dark?" She shook her head, and lifted
up his hand to kiss it. "Then," he said, "next year I'll have you
dancing."

The laughter in her eyes near matched his own. "I'll tell no lies
and make no promises. *Perhaps* is all I'll say."

"Why, you're halfway there already. I'll have a pair of slippers
made for you of the finest red leather – I'll warrant you can kick up
your heels more neatly than even Issa Baesina."

Marwy Ninek smiled and blushed and said again, "Perhaps."
Then they sat awhile together, talking of little things of no matter
and much interest, two lovers contented in each other's company,
letting the world pass by without them. At length, whistle and drum
gave way to rebec, and Assiolo winced to hear so sweet an instrument
so barbarously abused. She felt his shudder and asked, "Will you
play?"

Assiolo signalled to the butcher's eldest boy, a tow-haired lad of
six or seven. "Go fetch my lute from by the middle hearth. Here's a
favour for your pains." He tossed him an apple of marchpane. The
boy grinned and caught it neatly, and skipped away across the hall.

"The lad has an ear for music," Assiolo said, "and, I think, a hand
for herbals. I must talk with his father about taking him as 'prentice.
Or think you he'd be set on having him follow in his trade?"

"His father has other sons, and like to have more still," answered
Marwy Ninek. "If the child's a taste for herbals and music, he'll not
stand in the way."

The butcher's boy brought up the lute and took the tray of
sweetmeats in payment, scuttling away to a clutch of children in a
corner before any could grab his collar and retrieve his prize. Assiolo
grinned, saluting his daring, then tried to frown when the boy threw
an applecore at the shepherd with the rebec to make him cease
his sawing. "Well, there's the proof of his ear," he said, against the
laughter in the hall, "but I must teach him courtesy an I take him as
'prentice. Now there's a space of silence, what should I play?"

"*Banish misfortune,*" she answered, softly, "as you played the first night I ever saw you."

He sketched the melody upon the lute, half a tune and half a thought. "I had not thought you listened, love, that night."

"Oh Assiolo, every word you've said, each note you've struck, is sealed fast in my memory." He looked up, smiling, music bubbling from beneath his fingers. "I knew you on that evening," Marwy Ninek said, quietly lest other ears than his heard her, "of all the men, in all the world, I knew you as my own. When you looked into my face, I wanted to run to you and say, *I'm here!* And I could not—I had never lain in a man's arms but once, and I would rather have thrown myself from the tower above the gate than know such things again." His eyes met hers but the lutesong never faltered, a paean of love and freedom, giving her the strength she needed to go on. "Assiolo, though I said no word, that night, and made no move, I think my heart would have withered and died had you gone your way upon the road next morning."

"For me, love, as for you that night," he said, "and, knowing that, how could I have a thought to leave you lonely? Now listen, love, and let my music tell you all I've ever wished for you, then and now and forever and for always."

At last he let the full tune come dancing out to fill the hall with music and drive sorrow and misery away into the dark. Some smiled to hear it, others danced, and even Yatta Tala tapped her toe upon the floor for all her face was scowling. Beyond the doors, beyond the walls, in the wind and rain, the year was turning but here, within the hall, was fellowship and laughter and company and dancing. The past was gone, the future not yet written; 'twas time to look ahead with light feet and bold hearts and smiling faces. Marwy Ninek leant upon the table, resting her head in her hands, and gazed at Assiolo, her happiness welling up inside her like a sweet spring on Cal Mora-side.

"The tune's the charm," she said, and Assiolo nodded, his eyes alight with love and merry laughter.

Yatta Tala came up sniffing. "That's pretty, lad, but that she's here tonight says there's more to you than music."

Marwy Ninek flushed and stiffened but Assiolo only bowed his head, full courteous but for the smile lurking at the edges of his lips. His fingers never ceased their movement 'cross the lutestrings, plucking and picking to conjure forth his melody. "That's between us two, mistress, but what I can, I'll show, if you've a mind to see it."

The old weaver sucked her teeth and settled herself into the chair beside him. For a little while, all was the same: Assiolo played, music rippled, men and women danced. Then, slowly, the light changed in the rafters, a soft glow as of sunrise in the summertime brightening the hall. Assiolo made no move, he said no word, but on all the ivy strands twined round the beams white roses grew, and on the holly boughs at every arch were other roses, red as blood. Music rippled, music swelled, and then the beams above their heads were beams no longer but branches of flowering trees, elder boughs laden with curd-white blossom and the hall was filled with the honey-heavy scent of summertime. Some stared to see such things, others laughed to find themselves a-dancing beneath the summer trees. Assiolo laid down his lute and drew Marwy Ninek onto his knee but still the air was full of music for a blackbird sat on the topmost twig, its yellow eyes shining in the sunlight, its yellow beak open in song, and the song it sang was *Banish misfortune.*

"A trick." Yatta Tala sniffed. "A foolish seeming."

"No seeming," said Marwy Ninek, "but the thing itself."

She twined her arms around her lover's neck and kissed him softly, cheek and chin. Then the blackbird sang the louder and Assiolo said, "I did but answer to your will, mistress. The tune is honest, and the thought likewise: what harm to deck it out in fancy?"

The weaver shook her head. "The world is as it is, lad, and fancy's but a step away from folly."

" 'Tis easy enough to put an end to fancy, an it displease you; the rest, being the truth, I will nowise hide."

The blackbird flew away into the shadows, sunlight faded into firelight, the branches were but beams bedecked with holly and with ivy, and men and women rubbed their eyes and thought, as memory slipped away into a haze of beer and wine and barleyspirit, *How foolish, how very foolish, to think there were roses flowering at midwinter.*

Yatta Tala scowled and went her way, to sup spiced wine and scold her granddaughter, though, often and often, her sharp eyes turned back to Assiolo and Marwy Ninek and, each time, her lips pinched tight, as if to hide her thought or keep her words unspoken. But Assiolo cupped his hand beneath his true love's chin and turned up her face to kiss her long and lovingly, and neither cared that all and any saw it.

So midwinter's night passed by, kept in good company. But after midwinter came the sallows, the sour days after the solstice, before the equinox, and the winter sickness fell heavy on Felluria. And first the winter sickness takes the old, and then it takes the young, and then all and any it can set its claws in. Beyond the walls, men delved in the frosty ground to hew out shallow graves. The shutters were closed against the night and Marwy Ninek sat by the fireside, working worn sheets into winding cloths. So too did many women within the stone walls of Felluria whilst others mixed cold clay to stop a mouth, lest dead tongues cried lamenting from the dark. She had lit all the lamps to keep the dark at bay, and candles too, each tongue of flame bending in the draught when Assiolo opened the door.

She put aside her work as Assiolo pulled off his boots and made space for him beside her on the settle. His face was grey and drawn with lack of sleep. "Is there wine? I need to drive away the day."

She stood up to fetch it, red wine from Escen with fire at its heart, spiced by the summer's sun. "The butcher's bairns?"

He took the cup and drained it. "All of the five. The eldest was the worst. Old enough to understand and be afraid." With sudden grimness, he muttered, "Yatta Tala may be glad of it. She'll have no more cause to complain of the baby's crying."

"Assiolo," she kissed his hair, "hush now. She's a kind heart under her sourness."

"She hides it well betimes."

She poured him another cup of wine. "I remember when she was young," she told him as he sipped it. "Bold she was, and beautiful. She made bad choices in her men, and her sons were like their fathers. They took up the youngest as a thief and hanged him in the marketplace in Ountrie. She grew old on the day that news came in."

"I'm sorry, love. I know full well her heart." He bent his face into his hands. "But, love, the sights I've seen today, the sounds I've heard. Of all the sounds in all the world the most pitiful is a mother weeping for her children."

Marwy Ninek pulled down his hands and kissed them. "What you can, you do."

"As much as any common leech or hedgewitch. I burn the herbs and say the words, I shake and shout and plead and still they slip away into the dark. It is not enough!" In a little while, he said, "Often and often these last weeks, I've wondered and, always, I've turned away. I've not life enough to save them all, and I'll not choose, deciding one shall live, another die. And so today I burned the herbs and said the words and watched them slip away into the dark. But if she knew, that poor, poor woman, how she would hate me." She shook her head against the thought but he said, "All the rest we can know together, love, but never that."

Never before had he said such a thing and his words caught at her heart. "Assiolo, do you wish—"

"No, sweetheart, no." He drew her down beside him. "What you are, you are, and what you are, I love. The rest is of no matter. And besides, tonight, watching her see them slip away, I found I'm glad to know I'll never suffer as she does; 'twas such a grief destroyed my father's heart."

Marwy Ninek put her arms around him, cradling his head against her breast, breathing in the bitter smell of burning clinging to his hair. She held him close, rocking him gently, soothing such thoughts away. "Hush, love, hush," she said. "You are tired, you are wretched. There is no remedy against the winter sickness – she knows that well as any."

He rubbed his hand across his eyes. "Pour me more wine, and then let's to bed. They are dead, and thinking on them will not bring them home."

–– ––

He woke naked between silken sheets in a room he did not know, flooded with sunlight and silence. He stood up from the bed and looked around. The room was richly furnished, its window wide open to a day so still, so calm, there was no breeze to flutter the leaves in the garden or stir the folds of curtain hanging in the casement. He found clothes within a kist and dressed himself. He found food and drink laid ready on a table. The wine was iced, the meat was hot. He looked at it but neither ate nor drank. Instead, he opened the door and walked out of that room.

–– ––

"Assiolo!"

He struggled into waking, cold pressing down on every limb, soft and heavy as snow upon the meadows. He looked up to see Marwy Ninek crouching beside him, pulling at his shoulder, crying in his ear. "Assiolo!" Panic cracking the edges of her voice. "Assiolo!"

Like a man three times his age, Assiolo dragged himself around to sit upon the bedside. He reached out his heavy hand to touch her cheek and could scarce feel its softness. She stroked back his hair, and kissed him, her eyes filled with her knowledge and her fear. His tongue was clumsy in his mouth but he forced it to his use. "Help me to stand. Keep me awake."

All the morning, she walked with him up and down the chamber, he leaning on her shoulder, she urging him on, talking of little things and pinching him until he answered. Up and down, ten slow steps from window to door and ten steps back again. Some time after noon his ungainliness made him too heavy and, with a long kiss and a hurried promise, she left him propped in the settle by the fireside. Assiolo fixed his eyes on the dull red of her ring upon his finger and held his hand close as could-be to the flames, yearning to burn the numbness away for her sake as for his. Yet, though he saw his

fingers redden and blister in the fire, even pain was too far away
to bind him to his flesh. Sense was slipping out of reach. Darkness
gathered, fluttering like a black crow's wing, at the edges of his eyes.
He shook his head and tried to stand, but pitched sideways onto the
hearth.

-+— —+-

He walked down long corridors and through great chambers. One
was a library, a round room rising to a great dome like a bee-hive
with light falling through the window at its high centre. For a long
time he searched through the books upon the shelves and tables
until he found the one he wanted. He tucked it beneath his arm and
carried it out into the garden, walking the smooth paths between the
trees and flowers. At the end of a path was a stone bench beneath
an apple tree and nearby, a little way across the grass, a rowan grew.
He sat himself down upon the bench, sometimes to read his book,
sometimes to watch the patterns of sunlight falling through the leaves.
All around was silence. No birds sang in the trees, there was no wind
to whisper through the leaves. He turned the pages of his book and,
when he found the place he needed, he read aloud.

-+— —+-

Within a very little time, Marwy Ninek returned with the blacksmith.
Without a word the man swung him up onto his feet, forcing him
to walk. Then up and down the room again, and a rough cuff from
the smith whenever his feet dragged or his eyes closed. And always
she was there beside him, holding his hand, drawing him on with
tender words. He clung to her, setting her face between himself and
darkness, making his thick tongue tell her of his love. After a while
he heard a dry voice muttering and smelled the astringency of bitter
herbs burning. His words slurred like a drunkard's, fumbling their
way out of his mouth. "You should not be here."

"No more than you should have been with those bairns yestreen.
You're five times the fool I am." Yatta Tala scowled at him, and
scattered another handful of dried stuff onto the fire, fanning it to
fill the room with smoke. "Don't fret yourself on my account. Death
itself's forgot me."

She turned away, muttering charms under her breath, and, though
he knew they had no meaning, he was glad that they were spoken.

On and on, across the floor and back again, curses from the smith
and blessings from his love, Yatta Tala at the fireside, her grey locks
tumbled all untidy from their bindings, gabbling misremembered
rhymes. The air was thick as water, his limbs heavy as lead and cold
crept onwards to his heart. His eyelids dropped and he had not the
strength to lift them.

–⊢— —⊢–

As he sat reading there, a man padded out between the trees. He was grey and thin, his feet made no sound upon the stone.

"I am called Thorn, my lord."

He marked his place with his finger in his book and looked up. "Thorn? Is that your name?"

"I have no name, my lord."

"If I ask, will you answer? And if you answer, will you tell the truth?"

"My answer to both questions is the same," Thorn replied, "I will do what I was bidden do. You are not my master."

"Why am I here?"

"To serve, my lord."

"And if I have no will to serve, being a free man brought here against my will?"

"That is of no matter. The past is the past. Here is now."

"Forever?"

"Forever, my lord."

He turned away and read a little more in his book. Then he shut it up and looked around at the shadows beneath the trees. "Tell me," he asked the grey man, "when does the sun set in this garden?"

"When the day is ended, my lord."

He smiled at such an answer. "When else indeed? You may go, Thorn; go tell whoever sent you these three things: I will not eat and drink, I will not serve, and, though I am Allocco's son, I am not Allocco."

"As you wish, my lord."

The grey figure padded away, vanishing into the space between the apple and the rowan tree. The sunlight did not fade and the silence pressed heavy on him. He sat still upon the stone reading his book. He had read it many times before in his father's house, long ago and far away, and had not thought to read it again. But, as he read, much he had once known came back to him.

–⊢— —⊢–

"Assiolo!"

Hearing her call what could he do but answer, *I am here*. But his mouth was stopped and no words would come. Suddenly he was choking, drowning in bitter smoke as the smith's rough hands forced his face close over the reeking fire. The struggle for breath brought him back into himself a little, enough to open his eyes and mumble thickly to Marwy Ninek, "I love you." 'Twas but the semblance of speech but she knew well his meaning and pressed her answer all across his face. And yet, he could scarce feel her kiss upon his lips and if he did not watch his feet shuffling across the floor he did not know that they were there.

At eventide, the smith gave up the task to a shepherd and, late in the night, the butcher took his place. Seeing the marks of grief about the man, the ribbons on his sleeve, tears ran down his face. *I'm sorry,* he tried to say, *I'm sorry.* But all speech was lost by now and his hand would not obey when he tried to grasp his arm. Marwy Ninek caught his hand and kissed it, pulling his arm around her neck to share the butcher's burden. The terror in her eyes was more than he could bear, that he should leave her alone and lonely. By force of will and the butcher's strength, he kept stumbling on but all the while the crow's wing fluttered at the edges of his eyes.

" 'Tis no good," he heard the butcher say, when he could no longer put one foot before the other, no longer flinched and gasped at the blows to make him, when even the choking smoke had no power left to shock him, "it's me that's doing all the work. He's not got the strength left to move a finger. Best lay him down. Pinch him, shout at him, keep him with you. If he sleeps now you'll not get him back."

He felt himself lugged 'cross the room and lifted to their bed. The butcher settled him gently against the pillow, as not so long ago he had himself set a dying child. He heard his footsteps and the creak of the door opening, heard him say, "There's some that do keep back the dark. Young men like him. You know that, Marwy Ninek. I'll warrant you've seen it happen, many times and many over the years."

Her voice, trembling on the edge between hope and despair, answered, "I have seen it. I'll see it again."

Yatta Tala, scowling and sniffing and brushing smoke out of her red eyes, leaned over him. "For shame, Assiolo, lying a-bed at noontime and you so braw and bonny." Her bony fingers pinched his cheek so hard he could almost feel it. "I met my match in you, lad. Don't you dare prove me a fool." Then her face bobbed out of sight and Marwy Ninek was there, lying beside him, pressing her body against his to warm him, cupping his face between her hands. "I am here, Assiolo, and I will not let you go."

He could not speak, not even to tell his love; he could not move, not even to kiss the strands of black hair falling across his mouth. All he could do was look up into her eyes, into her lovely face, and see in her fear the reflection of his own. All he could do was listen as she whispered and spoke and shouted and screamed at him. All he could do was struggle not to sleep, not to drift away into the dark. Black feathers brushed his cheek, soft and cold as snow upon the meadows.

—+— —+—

Another figure came out from between the trees, thin and silent as the first but brown where he had been grey.

Who might you be? he mused. Aloud he asked, "How are you called?" His words were swallowed up by the silence in the garden.

"Twig, my lord."

"If I ask, will you answer? And, if you answer, will you tell the truth?"

"All that I say is true."

"I have met few men who can make that boast."

"But I am not a man, my lord."

"I did not take you for one. Tell me why I am here."

"Because you are needed."

He laughed and shook his head. "Twig, Twig, you said you spoke the truth. Here there can be no need."

"My lord, I did not say that you were needed here. You are here because you are needed."

"So am I kept here until I am needed, like a horse within its stable? Or until I am made ready to be used?"

"Both, my lord."

He shut up his book and laid it down beside him on the stone. He stretched and set his back against the apple tree and looked at the brown figure before him. Though the sunlight shone very bright Twig cast no shadow across the garden.

He held up his hand to shield his eyes from the light, saying, "Go, Twig, and tell the one you serve three things: I will do only what is necessary, that of necessity I will be the judge, and, though I am Allocco's son, I am not Allocco."

"As you will, my lord."

The sun stood still above the garden. He read his book no longer. Instead he stared into the day that was no longer morning and never would be evening but was ever noontime at midsummer. It may have been a long, long time he sat on the stone beneath the tree but in the end he was only a man and the noonday sun was bright and dazzled him. So he took up his book and retraced his steps through the garden and the silent halls to the library.

—+— —+—

Marwy Ninek sat in lamplight at Assiolo's bedside. A week since he had taken the sickness, three days since he had known her. She had shaken him and pinched him, slapped and scolded him, shouted at him, caressed, cajoled and pleaded with him, but all to no avail: his brown eyes had closed and she had watched him slip away into cold sleep. Now she held his hand that still wore the ring she had given, and watched to bid farewell as he went into the dark. There was nothing else that she could do. She could not weep and, if she spoke her love and grief aloud, he would not hear. He would die, and she would live on, all alone and evermore would be so.

She bit her lip against the horror of such a future.

A rapping at the door, scarce louder than the rattle of wind at the window. She did not heed it, she did not turn her eyes from Assiolo's face lest she miss the moment when he left her. When the door opened, she glanced up in anger to see who dared disturb her.

It was a woman standing in the doorway, a woman she did not know, though she knew all the women of Felluria. The stranger wore a heavy cloak and hood against the night but the curves of her cheek and chin in the soft glow of lamplight were enough to show that she was beautiful.

"Who are you?" Marwy Ninek asked. "The gate is locked against strangers."

"So too it is. There are many ways to open a locked door but the simplest is to ask for it to be opened." The woman's voice lilted like a song, patterned with the rhythms of a foreign tongue. "I asked at the gate, as Assiolo did, and the porter let me in, as he did Assiolo."

Her words and the manner of her speaking were enough to make Marwy Ninek turn towards her; in such a way had Assiolo spoken, before the winter sickness stole all speech and sense from him. "You know Assiolo? You are of his country?"

"I knew his father, long ago. He was a man unlike all other men." The stranger put back her hood from her golden hair and stepped across the threshold to stand at the bedside. "I am not here too late? He is still living? 'Twould grieve me sore to know Allocco's son were dead."

Marwy Ninek bent over Assiolo, her black hair brushing across his cheek. "He lives—but that is my concern, not yours."

A gentle shake of a lovely head, a white hand reaching out to touch his face. "If Assiolo lives, then that is my concern. I have no hope for the dead, only for the living." This woman's eyes were blue as the midsummer sky, her smile bright and lovely as the sun at noontime. "I can heal your love and change one future to another."

"Once sense is lost, there is no healing from the winter sickness."

In such a time, many quacks had come peddling their remedies across the land—bundles of herbs cut at the moon's fullness, a white dog's foot, ambergris from Lyikené—all these and many other cures and miracles. All these, and many others, had failed. She would not again fall into false hope: that was the cruellest path of all to take.

"There are ways, my dear, did he not speak of them?" the stranger whispered. "If Assiolo dies tonight, surely he will go before his time."

That had been her only thought these seven days. Assiolo was her own, her dear, her very life. All she knew of love and hope and kindness came from him. He was a song among the roses, a promise in the night time, *I love you, forever and for always.* She clung to his hand and felt its chill against her skin, as if he were dead already.

The woman asked, "How old is he? Two score years?"

"Not even that," Marwy Ninek answered. She did not turn her gaze from Assiolo, lifting his head to settle it more easily upon his pillow though he was past all thought of ease and comfort. Resting her hand against his cheek, she silently cried out, "My love, my love."

"Too young then to die and leave you lonely, with empty arms within your empty bed, aching with your memories."

Marwy Ninek watched Assiolo lying in his sleep beyond sleep, silent and still but for the shallow rising of his chest, the little pulse beating slowly at his neck. The woman touched her arm with fingers warm as summer sunshine. "I can give him back to you, my dear, banishing misfortune for a while. I can give him forty years before the darkness takes him."

"That cannot be done!"

"Oh, but I can! Forty years I can give to him to make of what he will. Or I can leave you, I can go back into the night, and he will die."

Marwy Ninek cried out of her anguish, "You must not say such things.

"I can heal him, and I will!"

"You must not be cruel. It is not kind to say such things when they cannot be true."

Bending over Assiolo, Marwy Ninek cupped his face between her hands and kissed his clay-cold lips.

"All I say is true." The woman slipped her arm around her shoulders. Her embrace was warm and strong, comfort for the comfortless. Gently, she pulled Marwy Ninek away from Assiolo; gently, she turned her around to face her. "There are ways indeed, my dear. Assiolo would not use them but I will: I've life enough to save him. I've said three times I can heal him. Each time I spoke truly. The only end is death, and Assiolo is not yet dead." Staring into her eyes, the stranger whispered, "I can turn back the dark."

Marwy Ninek clutched at her, finding hope in the depths of those blue eyes when all other hopes had slipped away. "Then do so!"

The woman held her hands and told her, "But there is a price!"

"I will pay any price," said Marwy Ninek.

"For forty years of a man's life, the price will be a high one."

"For a year of this man's life I would give my own!"

"That is not the price I ask."

"What do you ask?"

"That tonight we make a bargain, you and I," the woman answered. "Tonight, I'll give you what you want if, when next we meet, you will give me what I want."

"What must I give?"

Red lips curved into a little smile. "That, I shall tell at the right time. That is not now, with his life slipping fast away. An you wish Assiolo to live, you must decide, and quickly. Which will you have, Marwy Ninek: life for your lover, or a dark watch into the morning and then to lie him in the stony ground beyond your walls?"

Marwy Ninek thought once, and she thought twice, she looked down at Assiolo and then she did not think again. What was the world to her without him in it? An he lived, an he came back to her, no price could be too high: no matter what this stranger wanted, she would give it, and gladly. She said, "You offer a choice that is no choice at all. I will take your bargain. And if you heal him and give him back to me, then you will have my love, and gratitude, and friendship all the years I am alive to give them."

The woman smiled. "It is enough for me that you keep to our bargain. Do that, and he will live. Have I your promise?"

"You have it."

Smiling, the golden stranger leaned towards Assiolo. She breathed into his nose, she opened his mouth and spat in it, she kissed him thrice, on his forehead, on his cheek, on his lips. As she sat back from him, Marwy Ninek saw a touch of brightness 'cross his face but surely that was only the lamp light reflected from the golden hair falling down around him. The woman sat beside him on the bed, taking his hands in hers and crooned a song, its tune a lullaby sung to a sleeping child but the words were like no lullaby sung in Felluria. Marwy Ninek listened, the hairs pricking on her neck. This lady and her song were full of life but there was no love to mellow it.

-+— —+-

A woman was waiting in the sunshine. Her eyes were green, her hair was red. Like Thorn, her step was silent. Like Twig, she cast no shadow.

"Shall I call you Leaf?" he asked, as he put his book back in its place upon the shelf.

"If that is your wish, my lord," she answered. "One word does as well as any other for one who has no name."

"If I ask —" he began, but she held up her hand, commanding him to silence.

"No, my lord. This time, I will ask and you will answer."

He took a book from the shelf and turned its pages. He put it down and tried another. Only when he had found the passage he sought for did he say, "You may ask, Leaf. But I am a man and, at this time and in this place, I do not feel bound to answer, or to answer with the truth."

She took a step towards him. "I am sent to ask three questions and carry back your answers."

He nodded, his face turned to the pages of the book. "Ask them."

"The first is this: *What gives you joy?*"

"That I love one that loves me."

She took another step towards him. "The second question, my lord: *What gives you sorrow?*"

"That I will leave her lonely."

Now she stood close by his side. She reached out to lay her hands upon his arm. "This is the last: *What do you regret?*"

He saw her hands lying upon his sleeve; he saw them long and shapely, brown as an autumn leaf; he saw them clear as daylight, but he could not feel her touch against his skin. She had no more substance than a dream but, as she turned her gaze to meet his eyes, he flinched from her.

He did not speak. A little time passed, and then a long time. All the time he did not speak, she showed no impatience for his answer. There was no need: all the time there ever was, was here. He closed his eyes and found himself alone in the dark. He counted out a hundred heartbeats, and a hundred more, and opened his eyes to look at her. "Your last I will not answer, Leaf. I made my choice freely: what she is, she is, and I will take what follows, the bitter and the sweet."

"That is answer enough, my lord," she said, and for the first time since waking he was sore afraid. "When you have read enough, lie down upon the bed. When you wake, you will find yourself again beneath your own sky."

—I— —I—

When her song was ended, the woman kissed Assiolo softly and stood up from the bed. "He will live to see the morning," she said, pulling up her hood to cover her shining hair, "and many other mornings after it. I wish you happy in your love. There are many men within the world but none like Assiolo. At midsummer, when it is time for you to honour our bargain, I shall return. Until such time, keep it close within your breast. Keep it close, and keep it secret."

"You did not say your name."

"Did I not? It is no secret." The woman paused in the open door, glancing back, her smile lovely on her curving lips. "I am Averla."

The name dropped into her mind like a stone into deep water and old tales from the east spread out in ripples from its fall. She cried out, "Wait!"

The door was shut, Averla gone away into the night, leaving behind the echo of her laughter and Assiolo stirring into life. He gasped for breath, as a man might do when he had been diving deep and come back to the surface. Marwy Ninek lay down beside him, holding him in her arms so, when he opened his eyes, he would see that she was there, waiting for him.

-⊢— —⊢-

He took a deep breath to calm himself. He watched Leaf walk away across the room, plain in the shadows, hidden by the light. He knew what she was and did not fear her, no more than he had feared Twig or Thorn. They were only spirits called out of the sunlight, taking shape awhile in a sleeping mind. But someone had had the strength to call and bind and send them, and so he was afraid. His father had been such a man; he did not like to think there was another. Such men were to be feared because they could not be bound by the laws of lesser men.

Because he was afraid, he sat a long time reading in the library. There was much he must know, much he must remember and all of it was here. He took up books as other men would take up weapons, arming himself against the time to come. For knowledge gained cannot be forgotten until the mind that holds it is broken or the flesh that carries it is dead. And all the time he read, the sunlight did not move and the wind did not blow and all around was silence. But, as he sat reading, memories stirred in the hidden places of his mind, beating against the cage he had made for them, fluttering up like birds into clear high sunlight. His father had been dead for half his life; he had found his freedom and desired no more than to spend his days quiet and safe within stone walls, to have a life well lived at his love's side and go easy into the dark when his years hung heavy on him. Now memory was free and he must choose again what manner of man he was. And so he shut up all the books and left the library, to lie down between the silken sheets, to wake in his own bed in his own chamber with his own true love at his side.

When he opened his eyes he saw that she was there, waiting for him.

VI, Felluria: Desire and vengeance

As I cam' in by Auchindoun on a May morning,
Auchindoun was in a bleeze, an hour before the dawning.
Crawing, crawing, for a' your crouse crawin'
Ye brunt your crop an' tint your wings an hour before the dawning.

The Burning of Auchindoun, *Traditional*

At the equinox the world is at its balance: between light and dark, between love and hatred, between desire and vengeance.

She sits in her place within her hall. A man, no man of Felluria, stands each side the door. Her hands are stained with the dark juice of lithia and bright strands of firestar are twisted in her hair. Beyond the door, a fire is burning. Flames leap and dance as a woman's soft flesh shrivels to blackened bone and the red king stands the whole light long, leaning on his sword, gazing into a distance only he can see.

Evening comes, setting the west aflame, turning the sea to blood. She sits in her place, captive between his captains, and looks the red king in the eye. He is only a man for all he has made himself a king.

Somewhere, not far away, the other side of the closed door, a child is screaming, on and on, a high, thin cry like a rabbit in a fox's jaws. There are no words left in that screaming; it is a mindless noise emptied of all but pain, a dreadful sound to hear even if she knew not what it was. The red king's hand moves in a hard, swift signal and the man before the door goes out. Between one heartbeat and the next, the screaming stops and she releases the breath she had not known she held. The man returns, wiping his knife, and takes up his place again, impassive as if he had never left it.

"Ketala Iitha is dead and gone," the red king says softly, quite sadly. "I know who you are and what you did; I know why you did it."

She could say the same of him. He has cast down her walls, cut the throats of old men on their knees for mercy, tumbled the beardless heads of boys across the court. Yet she has seen him cradle a woman in his arms, stroke back her tangled hair, lie her down upon the pyre and gently kiss her cheek, as if she did but sleep and he had no thought to wake her. The world is a dangerous place indeed if a man can love and still be a monster.

The moment lengthens into a memory, that same woman weeping beneath an apple tree, white petals falling soft as snow upon her black hair.

"Ketala Iitha is dead and gone," she echoes. She meets his gaze and sees the vein throb at his temple, his hands clench at his side. There are

many kinds of love and not all of them are gentle. "Death is the end of all things."

The red king asks, "Was it a girl child, or a boy?"

A beat of time before she answers. "A boy."

The red king asks, "What of my son?"

She thinks of its weight upon her arm, of its eyes looking up into her face. It is her kin but not her kind. She remembers the woman's tale of its beginning; a king hanging from an apple tree; children's blood spilled across the stone. She will give it its life but not a kingdom. In that at least she will keep faith with the dead. She says, "I cut his throat myself, and flung the body on the midden for the ravens and the crows, a tender morsel after the banquet you served them in Eulana."

For a long, long moment there is silence. The very air presses heavy in the hall, as on a summer's evening before the lightning and the thunder. Then the red king's anger breaks, crashing across the space between them like the stormwave against the shore. He steps towards her, clothed in bronze and blood.

A man of Felluria might go thus far, but no further. A man of Felluria might ack, red-faced, awkward, twisting his hat in his hands. A man of Felluria would not think to touch her an she were unwilling. But the men of Felluria are dead, lying in their blood among the tumbled stones, white bones beneath the trees. This is a man who sets no curb upon his own desire. Only a child could think to hold back the tide with a wall of sand. He tears the firestar from her hair and tramples the flowers beneath his feet.

"You set your will against me," the red king says, "and you shall bear the price of it. I have not got my heart's desire but I'll take what's left to me, and it will be enough." He pulls her from her chair and cups her chin in his great hand. "Today you were the Tion of Felluria," he says, "so will you be tomorrow. But tonight you are as any woman in this place and I will have the mastery."

Side by side, they walk together up the stair to darkness and do not look at each other's faces. "I'll not kill you," he tells her at the open door. "You'll live to see the morning, and many mornings after." Her breath comes quick and ragged. So might a hare pant in the heather as dogs bay and course across the hill. "But you will show before the morning," he says, smiling at her fear, "how great is your strength, how steady is your will."

Above the shore there stands a tower and in that tower there is a room. In that room there is a knife, and a noose, and a red fire burning. In that room there is a man and there is a woman and the night is black around them.

Later, later, after the morning, she takes up the little that is left and walks out of Felluria. She does not stop for the evening nor for the little stream across her path. The grass upon the further bank is soft beneath her feet;

the sky above her head is broken only by stars. Hope failed and love fell short but the taste of vengeance shall be sweet as apple on her tongue. She sets her burden down beside the stream and walks alone into the empty land, seeking an end to sense and self and memory.

Beneath this sky the liùthion whirl and swirl to the music of the stars and sea, singing the song of the wind upon the water. Pale-faced, dark-eyed, with their hair streaming around them like smoke upon the wind, they trace their patterns on the empty land and their dance has no beginning and no end.

She pays no heed to the dancers of the borderlands but sets her face towards a star and walks on steadily, looking neither left nor right. Behind her, the other side the water, all has fallen into ruin. Behind her, fires burn, women weep and the red king leans on his sword, to look about him on the desolation he has made, and laugh.

The firstborn tree grows upon a little hill above the sea. It stretches its branches out across the land, bent by the wind of the world and the wind not of the world, and its apples are pale and round in the starlight. So it has always grown; its growth marked the beginning and with its death will come the ending of all things.

At her back, her shadow clots into the likeness of a man whose ragged cloak swirls round him on the wind. His feet are bare, his eyes are black and he is crowned with stars. He holds up his hand and the liùthion slip from sight at the edges of her eyes. All that is left behind is silence, and the king beneath the tree.

His voice is the rising of the sea against the shore, the wind rustling in the leaves of the apple tree. "If you would eat, Thelis Ketala, you need but ask, and I will give its apples freely."

She can no more close her ears against him than silence the beating of her heart, and so she answers, "You know full well this fruit is not for me."

"An you do this, you cast aside many things that might have been within the waking world."

"The waking world is no concern of yours. It is not your place."

"No more than this is yours. There is another king beneath another sky better suited to your purposes."

"He is not my king!" she cries out. "I'll take nothing from him, not even vengeance."

In the borderlands there is no fear, no anger and no hatred, but these three things she has brought with her, carrying them in her heart across the empty land. The darkness in his eyes is her own darkness, the shadow she has brought from the sunlight into the borderlands. She thinks of many things beneath the other sky, of a fire and a flower and a locked door, a man's laughter in the night time.

The king takes her hands and draws her close. The wind blows his ragged cloak around her. She would flinch from the touch of any man but this king is not a man and there is no need to fear him. He is older than her world, the still centre that does not change when all and everything is altered. She puts her hands upon his breast and leans her head against his shoulder. He kisses her gently on her brow. And, at his cold touch, the thoughts and deeds of the waking world are far away; she can rest safe within the circle of his arms as the babe upon its mother's breast.

He offers an apple from the tree. "Eat, Thelis Ketala. Here is an ending to pain and grief and suffering, if you will but take it."

His eyes are blacker than night; she sees herself reflected there and, at that sight, steps back into her memories and purpose. She says, "You call me by a name that is not mine."

The king's smile is the ripple of starlight on the water. "I know all the names of all the men that live beneath your sky, and all the women's too."

"You are not a man, no more than I a woman."

"In your beginning, you were a woman; in your ending, you will be again a woman and this revenge you seek is a woman's revenge. A man used you to prove his strength and will, to you and all the world. Now you would use him for the same purpose. Think what it is you'd make of him: a heavy weight to press upon the world."

She reaches out and picks an apple: such a little thing within her hand and yet enough to turn one future to another. She looks at it, and smiles. "He brought my world to ruin. All that is his I'll take from him, and go gladly into the dark."

"Consider what it is that you desire." The king's voice is the gentle cold of snow upon the meadows. "There are seeds within that stolen fruit will grow astray beneath the sun and yield a harvest of bitter crabs. Others than you will reap it and eat what you have sown. The dead are dead, and nothing in that fruit can change it."

"Metius Estui died," she says, clenching her hand upon the stolen apple. "Ketala Iitha likewise. I did not die; I was left to live and to remember. I will not eat. Not here. Not now. I'll take this fruit and my revenge."

"As you desire." The king's voice is the ringing clash of stone on stone, the roll of thunder 'cross a darkened sky. "I am no man, Thelis Ketala, to force you to my will. I offered a choice and gave a warning. More I will not do."

7: We made a bargain

Au logis de mon père
Au bas-le Mont Quervaux
Il y a-t-un pommier doux et doux et doux
Il y a-t-un pommier doux.

Au logis de mon père, Traditional

The days slipped by and, as the sallows passed into springtime, the winter sickness let go its grip upon Felluria. And, as it did, so too did thoughts of her bargain fade from Marwy Ninek's mind. She kept it close, and kept it secret, and soon it seemed little more than a dream, no weight upon her heart, such was her joy that Assiolo lived. After a month, pale and thin, he got up from their bed, at first to do no more than sit by the fire, resting like an old man twice his age, but soon he grew strong enough to lean on her arm and venture out to see the buds swelling on the apple tree in his garden and take his place at dinner in the hall. Oftentimes, those days within their chamber, he would take up his lute but found his fingers had grown clumsy in his illness and, though he practiced long, he could not quite call back his former skill.

"You will have your own again," Marwy Ninek told him as, with a sigh one afternoon, he laid the instrument aside.

"In truth, I hope it," he said, turning his hands about and about before his face, trying to see how they had changed. "I feel some virtue has gone out of me and I am sorry for it, for my mother's sake. This lute was hers before it was mine."

Seeing his sadness, she said, "Tell me of your mother, Assiolo. That you loved her, I know, but you seldom speak of her."

"What's to say? I knew her too little and too late." She put her arm around his neck and lightly kissed him. He pulled her close to settle her upon his knee. "Would you have her story?"

"If you would tell it."

"Oh, it's little enough in the telling. She loved my father, and he, I think, loved her. But a man came—"

She drew in her breath and he said, quickly, "Not such as came here. A handsome, greedy wastrel with nothing worse than pleasure in his mind. He stole her future from her all the same. She was young and innocent, and did not know a man could smile and smile, and be a villain." Assiolo's eyes grew bright and Marwy Ninek put up her hand to his cheek, to offer comfort and brush his tear away.

"My father locked her in a house, so fine a place none seeing it would think it were a prison, setting wards upon the gates she could not even think to cross. The knots he tied loosened with his death but she had grown used to her captivity and never thought to pass the limits he had set on her." He sighed, a soft, sad look in his brown eyes, and said, "She was kind, my mother; I would I'd known her longer." She held him close and heard his bleak whisper, " 'Twas my fault I did not."

"Tell me of your homeland," she said, after a while of silence. "Not even the piper told me tales of further east than Escen."

"No, sweet? When he was there, he spoke of these shores often enough." She shook her head and Assiolo smiled, throwing off his melancholy. "I can do better than tell tales, love, not all my skill's gone with the music. I wonder I did not think of it before." Leading her to the casement, he said, "Look out of the window."

She looked, and her courtyard of grey walls was gone. Instead she could see great distance across the rooftops of a city to the sea. She saw pillared halls and houses built all of white stone, far greater and far finer than any in Eulana, set along wide streets and the people of the city walking to and fro about their business. Strange scents drifted on the breeze into her chamber, spices and perfumes of a foreign land. The sunlight shone upon the city and the sea and, faint and lovely in the far distance, bells rang out across the day.

"The White City of Ohmorah," he said, "the bells mark out the hour." He counted aloud, and told her, "The fourth hour of the second: 'tis noontime. See, there's the marketplace, with the Guildhall close by, and that square building's the Assembly," pointing out each place as he named them, "there, on the hilltop, is the hall where Allodola keeps her court."

"Oh," she breathed, "is it real?"

"Real enough in its own place, here but a seeming." Assiolo smiled at her delight, that smile she loved lighting his face and her whole life. "Would you see more?" he asked.

She nodded. He said no word, he made no move but, between one heartbeat and the next, the sight seen from her window changed. Now she looked into a white vaulted hall greater and far fairer than her own with streams of sunlight falling from high windows to pool upon the marble floor. In a moment, she heard music, pipe and drum and rebec, and men and women stepped from the sunlight and the shadows to weave the patterns of their dance across the many coloured stone. She heard the rustle of silk, the tap of feet against the beat of the music, a girl's laughter as she swung down the line of men, twisting between their curving fingers that never could quite catch her.

She could look and look and never have enough of looking, leaning on the windowsill in delight that such beauty could be in the world. Assiolo stood close at her side, his arm across her shoulder. At last, she turned from the vision; putting her hands upon his breast, she asked, "What are you, Assiolo, to do such things and turn your back on such a place?"

"Why, love, you were not there," he said, and so she laughed and kissed him. Beyond the window the light fell back into its proper places. She saw again the courtyard and her own stone walls, the children running and laughing in their games of ball, Issa Baesina sitting with her grandam with her summer-got babe at her breast. Pointing to the courtyard and the children, holding her snug in the crook of his arm, Assiolo said, smiling, "Here is the present I chose for myself. Your place is my place, forever and for always."

A pleasant place in springtime but nothing to match the wonders he had shown her. "It was so lovely, your homeland," she wondered in a while, "how could you bear to leave it all behind."

"If you'd know that," he told her, "there's one last sight to show you."

It was black night beyond the window. No moon or stars to light this darkness. She looked and looked and could see nothing. Then a word was spoken and there was light, a little light no brighter than a candleflame held on an old man's hand. He lit a lamp and then another, driving back the dark so he alone was illuminated, a tall man unbowed by age with a face like old ivory and eyes bright as the midsummer sky.

"My father," Assiolo said, and in his hard tones she heard his hatred and his fear, "I left my past behind, and he the reason."

The old man looked himself about, as a man does when he knows that he is watched, and turned his head to face her. Those fearsome eyes blazed into hers and all that she was was laid bare before him. His voice was dreadful in its clarity, *You have always been a fool, Assiolo, but what is she?*

She gasped and clutched at Assiolo's hand, whispering his name. His face was set and pale and the look in his eyes near matched his father's. She threw her arms around his neck, pulling his head down to kiss him and turn him back into the man she knew.

Outside, the courtyard was filled with spring sunlight and the laughter of children. Assiolo rubbed his hand across his eyes like a man waking from dreaming. "I'm sorry, love, I had no thought to frighten you. He is years dead, and I gone free of him. I'll not play these tricks again."

—+— —+—

The piper knelt in the leaf mould at Averla's feet, his hands scrabbling and clutching at her skirt. "An you do this, all will end in ruin. Even you."

Averla smiled, glorious in sunshine beneath the flowering trees. "I have the key to him. Assiolo's secret desire, his one regret, the little thing his love can never give him."

Many times he had begged for food and shelter along the way but never had his plea been uttered with such desperation. "And so you will hold him hostage against fortune! What can I do, what can I say to turn you from this path?"

"You can say nothing. You can do nothing. It was your hand that closed the gate. Assiolo lives in the world you made. So does Te-Meriku." Many times he had been turned away from gate or door or byre but no blow of stick or stone had fallen on him so hard as Averla's words. She smiled to see it. "So does that black-haired child. Almost, I pity her. A lover's heart is so easily broken, a lover's trust so easily betrayed. Do you ever ask yourself what she would have been, had you not left her alone to face Torùkotu? Perhaps she would have given me a different answer."

"The firstborn tree will live a long, long time beneath this sky. All that time is yours, to make of as you will."

"You offer me a life beneath this sky? I, who had all the time there is the other side of the sunrise!"

"Averla, if it's vengeance you seek, you may have my death!"

"Your death, my monster?" She laughed, raising him to his feet and brushing dried leaves from his coat. "Why would I want a thing that has no meaning? It lost that long ago, along with all the rest. Your life is all that's left to you and not enough to serve my purpose. You have been many things in your time but never the king."

He stared at his hands. His unspoken answer hung between them in the air, a whisper through the aspen leaves.

"Tell me, my dear," she asked, "if you had thought of me upon that longest day, would you still have shut the gate?"

"It was a day of fire and storm," he said, "the rowan tree was dead; the world was falling into ruin. I did what was necessary."

"That is not an answer." Averla's voice was gentle but she had no mercy in her, no more than fire has mercy for the fuel that feeds it. "Would you have shut the gate?"

The piper remembered all she was, he knew all she had lost, and all she desired again. He could not weep but the pity in his face was a dreadful thing to look upon, far greater than his pain. "Averla, I would not! But that day passed, that deed was done, and I cannot take it back."

"No, you cannot, for after Allocco's ruin you made a balance and set Tamarhak's son to keep it, king in the west with an apple in one hand and a bronze sword in the other. Te-Meriku holds that kingship now, guarding the tree beneath this sky." She held his hand and told him, "Te-Meriku is only a man. So too is Allocco's son. I shall bind him with ties of love and duty, shaping him to my purpose, and he will snap Te-Meriku like a dry twig and give me back my own."

He shook his head, opened his mouth to speak but she laid her finger gently 'cross his lips to silence them. "Aye, my monster, so would I have him do. Kill the king, and close a gate, and make a day last forever and for always, world without end this side the water."

"I will to Felluria," he found the strength to say. "I will tell Assiolo truth that he may arm himself against you."

In the sunlight beneath the trees she laughed at him. "The tongue that cannot lie! What will you say, my monster? That you sent him to Felluria to mend what you had broken and, in the mending, made him what he is. That it was you made Te-Meriku, of all the men in all Lyikené, the king. Oh, my monster, what a web you weave, tangling their fates together, one and two and three. That Assiolo has no cause to love Te-Meriku, I know as well as you. And if a man should kill a king, what does that make him?"

He flinched to catch her meaning. She leaned down and kissed him on the brow, red lips, soft and sweet as rose petals, brushing his skin, and said, "I do no more than take up the tools you give me and shape them to my hand. There cannot be two kings in one land."

"Averla, I made the balance, and will keep it. 'Gainst that, all the rest is nothing. Even love. But, please," he whispered, "please, have my death and let that be an end to it."

She laughed, and shook her head. "Ah, no, my dear, for you there will never be an end. Let you live, forever and for always, in the world Allocco's son will make for me."

He hid his face within his hands, shaking with grief and shame.

—⼁— —⼁—

Midsummer in Felluria. Tonight the fires would burn, the music play and women and men dance on all the slopes beneath Cal Mora. All that would come, but not quite yet. Now it was but three hours past noon, the sun still long from its setting, and Marwy Ninek sat quiet within stone walls and, beside her, sat Averla.

Averla's hair was the gold of a wheat field at harvest time, her eyes blue as cornflowers in the wheat. Her beauty glowed, ripe and rich and ready, bright as the sun at noontime, and Marwy Ninek felt herself a poor, weak thing beside her.

"Midsummer's come," Averla said, "and you must give me my desire, as I gave you yours. *I will pay any price*, you said: now is the time to prove it."

She sat up straight and met her eyes. "Tell me the price, and I will pay it."

"It is a night," Averla answered, smiling, "a night in Assiolo's bed. Tonight, I shall lie in his arms."

"No!" Marwy Ninek cried out, feeling the jaws of the trap close around her heart, "No!" Then, more calmly as reason returned, she said, "Even if you wish it, it is not for me to grant."

"Oh, but it is! Only you can grant it." Marwy Ninek stayed silent, knowing she had made a bargain. "One woman is not so unlike another in the dark, to a man who has drunk much at midsummer."

"Not to this man!"

"Then what need have you for fear?" Averla's voice flicked across the space between them and Marwy Ninek flinched as from the lash of a whip. "Enough of words. We made a bargain when he lay dying, you and I. I gave him forty years – in return you give me one night. You may break your word, but then mine will no longer bind me and he will be dead before the morning. Yours is the choice: does Assiolo live or die?"

She answered, cracked words through dry lips, "He lives."

"Then we are of one mind. It would be a grief to both of us for Allocco's son to die before his time." Marwy Ninek watched white fingers smoothing out folds of silk, red lips curving themselves into a lovely smile, and clenched her hands to fists. "This is what you do tonight – it is not much, my dear, no more than this: when he sleeps, open the door; you go out and I go in. And, at daybreak, he is yours again."

No little thing indeed! And yet, *I will pay any price!* She had given a promise and must keep it. She gripped Averla by the arms and looked up into her face. "Swear to me you will not hurt him!"

Averla laughed. "I gave him forty years of life – he's safe enough, unless you break your word. Do as I ask, keep your bargain and I'll be gone with the dawning. It is a short night, this one, the shortest in the year. There will not be much time for darkness in Felluria."

Marwy Ninek turned on her heel to leave Averla smiling in the sunlight.

The light slanted across Cal Mora, the sea was a shimmer of gold as the long day lingered and the evening rose up to meet it. Marwy Ninek sat on the windowseat within their bedchamber and felt her heart twist within her for all the smile upon her face. She turned away from his brown eyes, so tender and so loving. There was a question she must ask and could not while she looked at him.

"Assiolo, if you knew you were to die this night, could you go easy into the dark?"

"What question is that, love? My greatest sorrow is that I must leave you alone and lonely, time out of mind." Assiolo sat down beside her and cupped her face within his hand; he wound his fingers in her hair and pulled her close. "Only if I had seen you fall before me, could I go easy into the dark."

"You came so close to death in the sallows," she said, pressing her face into his shoulder.

"But, love, I did not die. I came back and saw you, beautiful in darkness, waiting for me, and knew I had come home." Gently, he turned her face so she must look at him as he gave her his promise. "Only death will keep me from you, love, from all else I will come back to you."

"I love you, Assiolo. For all that you have done, all that you are."

He kissed her tenderly, loving her above all else in the world, and so too did she kiss him. Yet even whilst she kissed him she could not forget her bargain. That, she could not tell, but she could ask, "Do you trust me, Assiolo?"

He stared that she should ask it. "A strange mood is on you tonight. Come to bed, love, and let me show you what my words are not enough to tell."

Between his kisses, she weighed her choices, balancing his fear against her own, wondering if some prices were too high, even for love. That thought she put quickly from her mind and then, in the time that followed, feeling his body around her and within her, she did not need to think at all.

The midsummer sun set and slowly, slowly midsummer's night settled itself across the land and sea. Assiolo slept, in her arms, at her breast. She held him close, watching the gentle rhythm of his breathing, and knew that if she chose he would slip quietly tonight from sleep to death within her arms, as he would have done in the sallows had she not turned back his fate. But she had made another choice and so she kissed him, and left him sleeping in their bed alone.

Outside the door Averla was waiting. She had let down her hair and it fell in golden light around her.

"One night," said Marwy Ninek. "To save his life, I made a bargain and I will keep it."

"One night," Averla answered, "is all I ask of you."

Marwy Ninek stood aside, Averla passed by and the door closed quietly behind her. Marwy Ninek reached out towards the door. It

had no lock, this door, to make a prisoner, nor bolt within to keep
the world at bay – the work of a moment to open it. She reached
out, but did not quite touch the wood. "One night," she told herself,
fighting back her wish to fling it wide, "one night. An I do this my
love will live."

Music rippled from beneath the door: Assiolo's lute but not his
touch upon the strings. She strained her ears and heard his voice,
sleepy and slow, speaking a tongue she did not know. Laughter,
sweet and thrilling as a lark in the high sunlight, wrapped itself into
the lutesong and then Assiolo spoke again, and the music ended as
Averla answered.

Marwy Ninek spread her hand against the oak. He was beyond,
her love, her life, and only an unlocked door between them. One
push and it would open; one step and she would stand 'twixt him
and Averla. And then? She flinched from the thought of what would
follow and turned away to keep her bargain, telling herself again,
"An I do this, my love will live."

Outside the walls, the music played. Outside the walls, many songs
were sung. Outside the walls, men and women laughed together,
dancing in the firelight upon Cal Mora. But within the stone walls of
Felluria all was quietness and shadow and Marwy Ninek sat alone,
her back against the stone and never did she move until the sunrise.

At the dawning, slowly, slowly, Averla opened the door and stood
laughing on the threshold. "I left him sleeping. He took no harm of
me, and – I think – much pleasure. He is a man, my dear, as other
men."

"You've had your night," Marwy Ninek hissed, through her rage
and shame. "Now get out, or I'll have you whipped from the gates
like the cur you are!"

"Oh, I'll go without a whipping." Averla's voice was smooth as
silk, soft and strong as cobweb. "I have had what I came for. Last
night, it was midsummer. After summertime, comes harvest. But you
must wait for news of the harvest that was sown last night until the
springtime – I'll send my sign to you, round about the equinox. Holly
I will send to you, or ivy." She stretched, lazy, lovely in the light of
sunrise, red lips curved in a mocking smile. "Know this, my dear,
my desire is Assiolo's too. Did you never think to ask if there was
aught he wished for? Or did you think yourself enough? Poor fool,
to love so well and see so little."

Marwy Ninek raised her hand and struck at her but Averla caught
her wrist and the blow did not reach its mark.

It was a sour day followed, that morning after midsummer when
things go oft awry, a day of spoiled milk and turned cream, of

snapped threads and broken pots, and thunder in the air. Their
chamber was heavy with the scents of musk and elderflowers. Marwy
Ninek opened the windows to let the wind from Cal Mora blow the
night away and lay down on the bed beside Assiolo, holding him
close, hearing his heart beat beneath her cheek.

He woke late in the morning. "Such dreams I've had," he whispered. "Light and terror, my heart plucked out and burned before
my eyes."

"Hush, love, hush," she told him, kissing him softly to drive the
night away. He was here, with her, a living man, and that was all
that mattered. "They were but dreams; they have no weight upon us
in the waking world."

Assiolo kept to their chamber for the few days that followed, feeling
sick and out of sorts. Marwy Ninek stayed close by, tender and
careful of his comfort, though, sometimes, when she thought he was
not looking, he would see a little shadow lurking behind her eyes.
But his sickness passed within a sennight and he rose up to work
the afternoon through in his garden, deadheading roses so there
might be a second flowering, pulling up tendrils of firestar, beautiful
and bitter, that choked any plant it grew on, but whilst he worked
he paused, often and often, to rest his hand upon the rowan tree's
grey bark or to watch the patterns of sun and shadow shift and play
across the afternoon. Longtimes he was ill at ease and knew not why
he should be: even from the edges of his eyes, he could see nothing
untoward in the day, nothing hiding in the light.

The day grew old, the light grew long and Marwy Ninek came
out to find him, wearing a gown the colour of the evening sky, and
his heart grew glad again to see her. "There is a rose on yonder tree,"
he said, laying down the trowel and pulling off his glove, "as fine a
flower as I have ever seen, sweet as love upon a summer's evening,
and you can have it if you kiss me."

Marwy Ninek stepped into his waiting arms and put up her face
to kiss him. With a hand stained by the dark sap of lithia, Assiolo
smoothed back her hair and tucked the rose above her ear, then
kissed her long and lovingly. But still he was uneasy, thinking of the
patterns in the light and the shadow behind her eyes. In the evening,
in their chamber, he took her hands again in his. "On midsummer's
night," he said, speaking softly, speaking low, "I had strange dreams."

He saw a flicker in her face like fear and felt her hands close tight
as if to hold him fast and never let him go. Assiolo drew her down
onto his lap, stroking her hair to soothe her. "Hush, love, hush," he
told her, feeling her tremble beneath his touch as in the first nights
he had known her. "I do not mean to speak of them; you told me

true, dreams have no weight upon the world. I want only to say midsummer is a time when all the world is out of balance, little darkness and much light. Light dazzles, sweet, light blinds but it cannot change the truth. And the truth is, I love you, forever and for always."

She laid her hand against his cheek. "For me too, as it is for you."

"What's the matter, sweetheart?"

She pulled the rose from her hair, a rose of a red so dusky its heart was almost black. "The piper gave me lithia," she said, "you a red, red rose. Roses are very sweet upon a summer's evening but roses wither, they decay. As with a rose, so with a man."

Assiolo caught in his breath, not knowing how to offer comfort against such a thought. It was the truth she told, slanting backwards from the future to blight even this time among the roses. Seeing her fear, Assiolo wished he could drive it from her, as he had driven all the rest away. Not all his love nor all his skill could do it.

She said, "There will be firestar upon the walls of Felluria when the roses have all fallen. There was a night, in the sallows. Oh, Assiolo " She broke off and kissed him.

He held her close and stroked her hair, whispering his love. When she could speak again, she told him, "I thought you'd die that night, and that thought I could not bear. More than my life, I love you."

"Hush, love, I'm here, hale and well and like to live as long as any other man. That night has passed – no need to speak of it."

"My love!" She pressed her face into his shoulder; after a long, long while, he felt, rather than heard, her halting whisper, a breath against his neck. "You'll get no child on me, Assiolo. Each of us is what the other is not."

He caught his breath as memory flickered, somewhere in the back of his mind. *What do you regret?* He closed his mind against the question: some thoughts he would not think. The world was as it was; the bitter and the sweet.

"Look at me, love," he said, and so she did. "I made my choices freely, and so much joy I've had of you that I'd never wish you other than you are."

Her arms twined round his neck, clinging close as lithia against stone, her lips brushed his cheek, soft and sweet as rose petals. Assiolo cupped her chin in his left hand and saw himself reflected in her eyes, answer for question, yearning for longing, love for love. "The future's not yet written but I'm here, sweet, will you take me while you can?"

At last a spark of laughter in her eyes, kindled from his own. "Forever and for always."

He bent his head and kissed her and, sweet and strong, she kissed him in return, her hands finding their way beneath his shirt to wander across his skin. Holding her close, his mouth against her mouth, Assiolo knew that this was what mattered, this was all that mattered, forever and for always, though the wind blew cold and chilled them, and the sun shone bright and dazzled them, and darkness took him from her. At last, without lifting his mouth from hers, he gathered her into his arms and carried her over to the bed.

He slept first and in a while she followed him, but before she slept she thought how sweet, how sweet the moment, lying cradled in his arms, hearing the slow rhythm of his heart beat out her lullaby. Lulled by his strength and sweetness, she watched him sleep, until at last she slept herself and sleeping slipped from his arms into a dream:

Three kings stood beneath the bone-bare tree. One wore red, and one wore green, the third wore black, and all their faces were the same. The air was full of music, for a blackbird sat on the topmost twig, its yellow eyes shining in the sunlight, its yellow beak open in song.

The red king held out his hand and in it was a sword.

The green king held out his hand and in it was a rose.

The black king held out his hands and both of them were empty.

They spoke with one voice, "What do you choose?"

She asked the red king, "What do you offer me?"

"I offer what I hold in my hand."

She looked at the sword. It was bright bronze with an edge like the north wind. She had seen the things a sword could do in a man's hands, but she was not a man and did not have the strength to use it.

She asked the green king, "And you – what do you offer me?"

As the red king had answered, so did the green. "I offer what I hold in my hand."

She looked at the rose. It was as perfect a flower as she had ever seen. Its petals were red and curving as a lover's lips; its scent was sweet as love. A woman might take such a rose as a pledge and a promise, but she was not a woman and must live on beyond the death of love.

She asked the black king, "What do you offer?"

He said, "My hands are empty. I can offer nothing."

All the while, the blackbird was still singing, a lovely, empty ripple filling the bright sunlight. Sadly, softly, the red king whispered her name; tears, shining like summer raindrops, ran down the green king's cheeks but she could not take the sword, she would not take the rose: one had too much weight upon the world, the other not enough. And that left her with nothing.

She held out her hands to the black king, who bent his head to kiss her lightly. His lips were soft and cold, gentle as snow upon the meadows. Then he led her back to where her love lay sleeping, and she lay down again beside him, to slip from dreaming into sleep and from sleep into the morning.

Assiolo woke early in the morning, feeling his love's soft warmth against his skin and her black hair tangled across his breast. The breeze blew through the open window and he could hear all the little sounds drifting on it as Felluria began the day.

"I dreamed," she whispered as she woke.

He propped himself on his elbow and smiled down at her. "Of me?"

She shook her head. "Of an old story, a tale told by the piper when I was a child, three kings beneath the tree."

He too had heard that story in his childhood. He laughed, and answered, "You've said it yourself, love, dreams have no weight upon the world."

She put her arms around his neck and pulled him close to kiss her.

A rustle and a whisper, a shimmer and a shiver, light flickering to form. Marwy Ninek started, looking over his shoulder to the bright sunshine falling through the window.

"What is it?" he asked.

"I saw, something."

Assiolo narrowed his eyes against the light, then turned back, shaking his head. "Nothing. A trick of the light."

Marwy Ninek rested her head against his breast, her arms around his neck. "I love you," Assiolo told her, in a while, thinking again of the shadow he had seen behind her eyes, "all that you are is my joy and my desire. So trust my love; know that I am yours my whole life long. Only death will take me from you."

"I trust you, Assiolo. Now, come here and let me kiss you."

And so he did, full willing, but later that same morning, thinking still of dreams and tales and shadows, of patterns in the sunlight, Assiolo went to Yatta Tala, saying, "Can you weave me a golden gown, mistress? I have a mind to see her wearing yellow, something soft and warm. I don't want her cold when the wind blows hard down Cal Mora."

—·— —·—

The mercatman had set up his stall in the strangers' place before the middle hearth. Others must make do with the tradesmen's booths behind the shore but Edo Incithu was a prince of mercatmen, known across half the world, and a man made welcome in the queen's court in Escen and the golden hall of Tarhn deserved no less than to be honoured in Lyikené. Or so the king said, when his helmsman raised his brows at a foreigner's presumption.

"The truth, Te-Meriku," Thodùhah said drily, "is in that gewgaw at your neck."

"A pretty thing, is it not?" The king touched the lacquered serpent twisting its way around his throat, blood-red but for its golden eyes. His own eyes narrowed, laughing. "To look at it, I'd judge it from the east but he found it in Escen, so he told me."

Thodùhah grinned. "And you believe him?"

"So I must, or else I'd have to kill him. He knew that when he gave it me."

The helmsman cast a glance across the hall to see Edo Incithu hold a lump of amber against the light to judge the clarity and mark the flaws. "A brave man, then, or else a fool?"

"A man who knows his value and my taste. And one who knows the boundaries – I marked he did not say 'twas wrought in Escen."

There were counting beads and tally-sticks cast all across the mercatman's table, counters marked with the signs for whalebone and ivory, wine and wheat and weaving; foxskin, red, white and silver, kidskin, sheepskin and sealfur; spices from Marihon, the sweet, the subtle and the savoury; agate and amber; gold from the mountains and copper from the mines; salt pork and codfish; heather beer and barleyspirit, tallow, beeswax, lamp oil; silk from Escen, linen from Lascatha and wool from Felluria; walnuts out of Cincern Dùn. At one end of the table stood three pairs of scales, each with two sets of weights, his own and the king's, lest any claim short measure, and beneath it a jar of wine, good red wine from Escen, to ease a trade and toast a deal. All the days his sailors worked like ants, moiling and toiling with barrels and bundles between the ship in the offing and the king's hall and, all the days and half the nights, the fat mercatman himself laughed and talked and jested, his nephew silent at his side, shaking out a bolt of cloth to tempt a woman, feeling the weight of fleeces offered by a hill lord's factor, or screwing up his eyes to judge the carving of an armring of northern ivory.

But it was not at his table in the hall that the king's main business with the mercatman was done. He had other men to think for him of ivory and wheat, amber and wine. Sure enough the king passed by, to drink a cup of wine and cast an eye about for trinkets, taking in the end a little thing of coral and of silver, a rattle for a child, but it was in the chamber next to the hall that he stretched out his legs to his applewood fire, wine and walnuts to his hand, and asked, "What news?"

The mercatman did not pretend not to understand, answering shortly, "He took the winter sickness."

"And died of it?" Thodùhah's question was quick with hope.

Edo Incithu's laugh was a glint of white teeth within his hennaed beard. "Assiolo did not die. He lay three days a-sleeping, and then woke to make his lover smile."

"Three days and then awaking?" the helmsman asked, his mouth downturned to know hope in a moment and see it dashed the next. "I've never heard of any returned after so long. You're sure this tale does not grow in the telling? If that's the truth I like it not."

The mercatman shook his head. "There's enough do turn back the dark," said the king slowly. "Young men. Strong men. It means nothing of itself. What of Eulana?"

"I got the truth a year back but not from him. I've never met a man so skilled in turning aside a question he does not wish to answer. You know, Te-Meriku, no matter what he is, I like the man. Other men would boast of such a deed."

"And such a bedding." The king tossed walnuts hand to hand, whistling a lay of Torùkotu learnt in his boyhood, " 'He hath taken her by the left shoulder, says, Dame where lies your lady?' " He broke off to say, "A sweet armful, if he can forget she drove a man to madness."

The mercatman shrugged. "Men can forget many things for a pretty face. And I've seen her thirty years and longer and never thought more than that she had a lovely face. I would as lief taken a stone between the sheets. But now," he sketched a shape upon the empty air and it was Thodùhah's turn to whistle, tuneless through his teeth, whilst the king's great laugh rang raucous out above it, "aye, Te-Meriku, 'tis true another man would boast of the bedding."

Crack went the walnut shells in the king's hand. " 'He hath taken her by the middle sae small, and oh but she grat sairly!' " He dropped them onto the table and picked out the nutmeats, tossing the shells into the fire. " 'And laid her down on the bonnie bed-sheets—' " He paused his song and asked, "you found the place?"

"I found the place." Edo Incithu nodded. "A riverbank near Habhain. He stuck in their minds clear enough for there to be no doubt, even a year later and longer: clothes like a beggar, speech like an outlandish lord and silver enough to stifle questions."

"And you are sure of what he did there?"

"Certain sure, Te-Meriku; since I knew you'd ask it, I lifted a stone and took a token. There are some sights I'd rather not remember but I can bear it, if I think on the price you promised me a year ago.

The piper's tales of his red hair are true." He took a leathern wallet from his pocket and pulled out a hank of hair, matted, fouled but here and there still light and bright as a fire's red heart. "I've seen none but yours, Te-Meriku, can match it."

The king took the hair between finger and thumb, holding it up against his own. "What think you, Thodùhah?"

The helmsman stared and sucked his teeth to see the likeness. "A match indeed," he grinned, and the king tossed the tangle into the fire to shrivel on the embers, "and you truly a prince of mercatman. I know not which to praise more, your stomach or your memory."

Edo Incithu spread out his hands and bowed. "An you give me my fee, I'll let your praises go."

"You shall be paid," the king promised lightly, "and I'll throw in a sop to soothe your stomach. Tell us where this thing is to be found."

"Assiolo took the long way through the mountains but 'tis best approached, as I did, from the eastern coast. You know it?" He took a charred stick from the fire and sketched a plan upon the hearth, a sandy shore within a bay, a rivermouth, a river curving through the wood. "I've earned my fee, I think," he said, seeing Thodùhah's nod of recognition, "and my time in Habhain was far from wasted. Those foxfurs pleased your lady well. A grey to match her eyes."

The helmsman sucked his teeth but could not quite hide his smile. "King's daughters have expensive tastes," he muttered, "and it's more than my life's worth to deny them. But those furs were not for her – she wanted them for our girl. Doesn't think that man of hers will keep her warm enough up in the north."

Whilst Thodùhah rattled on about his daughter, the child that was, the babe that would be, the king drank his wine and stared a little while at the scratchings on the hearthstones, shaping the seeing in his mind, a wooded shore, a river, a pile of stones.

A shimmer and a shiver, firelight flickering to form, a half-forgotten dream of mocking laughter. He cut through the talk to ask, "And of the piper?"

"Nothing, Te-Meriku. Not sight nor sound along that coast. I asked my brothers of the mercatkind and all say same as I did two years back: he was in Marac Bec and after that went eastwards and nothing and no one's seen him since."

"He's not a man," the king said, "and I was a fool to hope he'd act like one. He'll show his face when he wants to."

He looked again at the scratchings on the hearth, thinking of Allocco's son and considering his choices, and scuffed them over with his foot. The future was not written, nor were all dreams true:

the balestar had not risen, for all Allocco's son had killed a king and
woken from three days a-sleeping.

"You missed the tide, Te-Meriku," the helmsman said, late in the
evening when they were alone. "She'll not give him up now. It'll
mean a sack."

"You're likely right, if I had a mind to kill him."

Thodùhah poured the last of the wine into their cups. "You've
killed many men and many over the years. Why baulk at this one?"

"An he gives me a reason I'll kill him before the second thought.
But not because he is his father's son."

"He killed a king."

"And such a king. The stuff that songs are made of. Think you
they will sing such songs of me in half a thousand years?"

"Like enough, if you sack Felluria and kill Allocco's son."

Te-Meriku grinned and sang again of ships and swords, of fire
and flame and glory, of power and pride and victory, and Thodùhah
beat out his time upon the table. "'The smoke and the flames they
rose sae hie, the walls were blackened fairly, and the lady laid her
down on the green to die—'"

The song was not yet ended but, between one line and the next,
the king let it fall away to silence; he raised his cup but did not
drink. All laughter gone, he looked his helmsman in the eye and
saw him look away. "She did not die," he said. "She lived on after
the ruin."

With a flick of his wrist, he spilled the wine across the hearth, red
drops rolling and hissing in the fire, pooling dark as blood beside
his foot.

"He killed a king," Thodùhah said stubbornly.

"He killed a monster," said Te-Meriku. His eyes were hooded in
the firelight, hard as a stone, deep as the sea. "Whatever I am, I am
not that."

VII, Lyikené: The ebbing tide, the fading light

What's the life of a man, any more than a leaf?
A man has his seasons, why then should he grieve?
Although in this wide world he appears fine and gay
Like a leaf he shall wither and soon fade away.

The Life of a Man, *Traditional*

He sits alone a-drinking late into the night until, hearing the drag and shuffle of a twisting foot, he turns towards the door. Seeing that face, known only from old stories and bad dreams, he starts in fright before ever the dwarf opens his mouth. Wine spills from the smashed cup, red drops rolling like rowan berries 'cross the table to drip and pool upon the floor.

Imacah is not dead when they carry him across the hillside; not dead when they bear him over the threshold of Kistoru's hall upon a bier of heather and rowan branches, every berry shining in the lamplight bright as blood across green leaves; not dead when they set him down upon his bed and cut away the sodden shirt to show the ruin of his belly.

Not dead but dying. They are all men of Lyikené: they know a deathwound when they see it.

He stands before the open door, unable to pass it uninvited. Within, Ala, pale as her son, the same black hair, bends across the bed, her hands full of white linen that, as he watches, grows soiled and stained as with spilled wine.

Kistoru pushes past him. His eyes full of his son, he barks out, "What was done this night?"

He hears his own voice answer. "Haduhai's men on the stream side, as Imacah leapt from the further bank. He was over the boundary."

The tale he had from the ragged piper; the wonder is he should sound so steady.

Kistoru looks hard at him. Nothing of Imacah in his eyes. Father no father; heavy in his flesh, great only in his pride; a man, as other men. "And you were not?"

"I was not."

"You were not there?"

"I was not there."

Ala lifts her face and Imacah's eyes stare from it into his own.

He turns from those eyes as from the sun. He cannot look and not be dazzled by all that might have been, had he given another answer before the sunset. "Had you been there," those eyes say, "I would not lie dying. Had you been there," they say, "they would have stepped aside to let you pass. Had you been there," they say, *"the king would not have grudged an apple."*

Might have been will never be. All these things are true, and none of them. A broken oath cannot be mended; a broken bond cannot be rejoined; a broken trust cannot be regained. Even so, he whispers into the dark, *"Did I break faith with Imacah?"*

There is an answer in Ala's eyes and he clutches the doorframe so not to fall sobbing at her feet. *"You may come in, for sake of the love he bore you,"* she says, her voice thick with hatred and with grief, *"but in the morning get you gone. You are not welcome here, be you a hundred times the king."*

The hours drift slowly by, marked out by Kistoru's heavy feet pounding the chamber. He sits one side the bed, Ala the other, each careful to look only at Imacah and never at each other. Sometime in the cold, small hours, Kistoru asks, *"How runs the tide?"*

"It will ebb with the dawning."

Ala catches back her sob, stifling her grief behind her hands. The tiny part of his mind not filled with Imacah pities her.

Later, later, after the tide has ebbed and the day has dawned, when there is a lamentation from the women's side, when Kistoru is ranting and raging on the bloodprice with a winejar to his hand, when they are at last alone, he stretches himself upon the bed, lying beside Imacah as on so many mornings, holding him close for kissing whilst the wind throws rain hard against the window.

Imacah's hand opens, relaxing in death as before only in sleep, and the apple rolls onto the bed between them. A little thing, an apple, a man's life. Such a little weight upon his palm, holding within its golden skin all the things that might have been.

He puts the apple in his pocket. Later, much later, another day in another place, he tosses it into the fire and watches as it boils and bursts, shrivelling upon the embers until all is consumed. No burning ship for Imacah, no merging of fire and flame into the sunset, only cold clay to stop his mouth, a winding sheet in place of the king's red and the king's bronze.

"How does it feel," Imacah asks, from the shadows at his back, *"to know the time a man must die?"*

Noontime comes and he walks out of Kistoru's hall, alone and unaccustomed to his loneliness. Always there has been another to walk beside him, his other self, a shadow made flesh. His mind is filled with little things that do not matter: red wine spilled across the table, red rowan berries scattered across the threshold, a curlew probing sands uncovered by the ebbing tide.

He does not stop for the twilight nor for the little stream that runs across his path. When he stands upon the further bank the night is dark and deep. There is no trace of sunset over the low hills but all above the stars are very many, piercing the blackness of the night as sorrows prick a heart.

He knows where he is, of course. He does not look back across the stream but walks on into that endless night. Perhaps he walks an hour across the empty land, perhaps a day, perhaps a hundred years. It is of no matter: he walks, and his burden grows no less. Here he will never tire, never hunger or thirst, never be other than he is, a man alone and lonely in the dark. That thought grows within his mind until at last he stops and screams a name into the wind.

There is no answer. There will never be an answer. His scream soaks into the silence like water into sand. Behind his eyes he sees only spilled wine and rowan berries.

At his back, his shadow shifts and clots into the likeness of a man. He turns, hope speaking from his mouth. "Imacah?"

In the borderlands, as in the waking world, all hope is false. "He is not here. The price of a stolen apple is very high, beneath this sky and the other."

There is a pale-faced stranger at his side, almost like a man but for the stars tangled in his hair.

He knows who he is, of course. The king's face is the mirror of his own but for his eyes. His eyes are not the eyes of a man. They are filled with the darkness that came before the light and will outlast it.

The king says, "You will not find him though you search your whole life long. The dead are dead, and never come they back."

Slow tears run down his cheeks, though he is no stranger to death; he is, after all, a man of Lyikené who killed his first man at fifteen. There have been others since: each time it was no more than a game he played with Imacah when the moon was dark, a game that began in laughter and ended with the thrust of a bronze sword. They had not known death's meaning that dealt in it so easy and unthinking.

"Tell me," says the king, sitting down beside him 'neath the tree, and so he does. Except he finds he cannot tell what happened, only dreams and plans and might have been. He opens his mouth to speak of rowan berries, and instead tells tales of the north country he has never seen and the whales he has never hunted, of the ivory he has not cut.

He thinks to tell of wine spilled from a smashed cup, but recounts tales of his square-sailed ship, her grey gull's head and the long sweep of her black, folded wings, swift and low upon the water; of leaping from her neck onto the sands of an unknown shore; of his sword biting deep into the flesh of men he did not know and his arms drenched in red blood to the

*shoulder; of tumbled walls and weeping women and fires burning against a
lamentation.*

*Last and long, when all the rest is said, when the time comes to speak
of the ebbing tide, the fading light and the curlew calling at the water's
edge, of an apple's fall from a dead hand, he tells of his promise and his
beacon, of sailing forever and a day towards a star shining after the sunset
in the west beyond the west. All this he tells and each telling comes to life
in his mind, shaping itself from a thought into a memory.*

*And woven through every tale and thought and memory is Imacah, as
heavy in his flesh as any living man.*

"Can such tales be true?" he asks the king. "Did these things happen?"

*"Surely," says the king, his chin resting upon his hand, "had you not
said Yes! to Hadùhai."*

"So with a word I threw away my future!"

"With a word you changed it for another."

"And Imacah? Did I do so for him?"

*The king spreads wide his hands. "He is not here, and so you cannot
ask him." He looks into the king's black eyes. The darkness there is his
own darkness. "When Hadùhai asked, you answered, he gave you his
bronze sword and that was enough to turn you from a man into a king.
Now it is my turn to ask—will you take a gift from me?"*

*The king drops an apple into his hand. It lies on his palm, such a little
thing, pale and round in the starlight with one withered leaf still clinging
to its stalk.*

"What is in this fruit?"

*"As much as I can offer. Freedom if you will. An end to memory, to
self, to time itself, a dance upon the wind. Have you not been told, many
times in many tales, there is no life, no love or death in borderlands? Such
tales are true and in your hand you hold the reason."*

"Then I will eat and I will have my freedom."

"Forgetting all the world, all that you were, and are, and could be?"

"Even so."

*He raises the apple to his lips and bites. Its flesh is sharp and sweet
upon his tongue, the perfection of an apple eaten only in a dream. He
hears at last the song of star and stone and, from the edges of his eyes, he
sees the liùthion reaching out their hands to draw him to their dancing.
They have no flesh that can be maimed; they have no hearts that can be
broken; they know only the everlasting dream of borderlands.*

*"And Imacah?" The king's voice is the snap of branches in the frost,
the hiss of a falling star, the crack of a heart breaking. "All that is left of
him is memory."*

*Imacah! He gags, and chokes, and spits the fruit upon the barren
ground. The king smiles. "I did not think it. But an you say me no, then*

you must be king beneath the other sky, to stand by day beneath this tree and offer all that I cannot."

There is no hope in borderlands. The music is silent, the dancers are gone, his dream is shattered. To be the king is to know the time a man must die, to stand beneath the tree and hold the world in balance along the blade of a bronze sword. Bitterly he says, "Death is my only gift. Death is all I gave to Imacah."

The king is not gone but he no longer wears the likeness of the man. The sight is beautiful and dreadful as midwinter's night. "And did not Hadùhai give you a sword when he made you the king? Your world is as men make it."

He presses his face into his hands and sobs aloud because he is alone. Bare branches arch above him, shivering in the wind blowing across the empty land.

8: One green leaf and two red berries

He's ridden o'er the high, high hills
And he's down the dewy den,
And the noise that was in the Clyde water
Would have feared five hundred men.

Clyde's Water, Traditional

"It is time for me to ask and Assiolo to answer," Averla said. "Some women love their sons: I shall make mine into a weapon. See, my piper, I watched and I waited whilst you led your dance across the world. And, when the time was right, I stretched out my hand and took what I wanted. Here is my son, Assiolo's son that he thought never to be born. How do you wish him?"

The piper looked at the child sleeping at her feet. It was but a few hours old, wrapped in sheepskin in its basket of willow withies. A tiny thing, curled there like a seed with its life unlived within it, such a little weight upon the world. So many dangers all around, so many ways that it might meet its end in these first weeks of its life.

He shuddered at such thoughts and said, "Never that, Averla, never that! There are deeds I'll do, those I might wish to do, and those I will not even wish for." He bent down and placed his finger in its hand. Even in sleep the reflex tripped to curl its fingers tight. It gripped him, surely as it gripped its life. "You know what I am – you know as well what I am not. How could I wish your son anything but hope and health, blue sky above him and white flowers to delight him all the days of his life?"

He lifted the baby and cradled it in his arms. Averla watched, and her face was no longer mocking as she looked down at him. He did not see; he did not look at her, only at the sleeping child. She said, softly, "If you had been a man, how I could have loved you!"

"But I never was a man."

"Did you not wish?"

"Many times, Averla. But no longer. What I am, I am." He laid the baby back into its basket, straightened himself to look at her. "Maybe 'tis true, this child will give you the mastery. Assiolo could be many things, a man terrible and dreadful as his father, but this too is true: each time he's chosen love, though little love he'd known with Allocco as his father."

She shrugged. "Love has not served him well. Love gave me the mastery – the proof lies sleeping at your feet. For his sake, Assiolo will kill the king beneath this sky and give me back my own. But you, what will you do now, my dear?"

He drew a breath and told her, "All that is necessary to keep the tree beneath this sky."

Averla held his face between her hands. He gazed into her blue eyes and, as in his long past, the world was hidden behind their brightness. He closed his eyes but there was no hiding place, all the shadows were driven from him and her light shone in all the corners of his mind.

"Three times," she said, "you have broken faith with those you loved. Each time you called it necessity."

He swallowed once, he swallowed twice, and answered, "So I shall do again."

"Then go your way across the world, as I go mine, and we shall see which of us has the mastery." She kissed him thrice, his brow, his cheek, his mouth, though he was still as stone beneath her lips.

"I cannot turn you from your path, Averla," he said, as he stood up to leave her, "but remember this, an you set yourself against me: the kingship's more than a prize to be taken. If it were not so, any man could make himself a king."

She shrugged and lifted her baby to her breast. "So you say, my dear, but Allocco's son will break the pattern."

—+— —+—

Assiolo woke before dawn on the morning of the equinox. All in the room was as it should be, his love lay sleeping at his side, her black hair tangled across his breast, and everything was wrong. All the thoughts he did not wish to think ran round his mind like rats within a trap. He slid slowly from the warmth of their bed into the chill and looked himself about. All across the room, the light was too bright for such an hour upon the spring's grey morning.

Very quietly, lest he waken her, he asked, "Are you here?"

Thorn stepped out of the light falling through the open shutters. "I am here, my lord."

"Am I yet dreaming?"

"Perhaps, my lord. At some times, in some places, the line between a dream and waking is very thin. But such little things are of no matter. When you wake you will be in your proper place."

"My place is here, Thorn, at my love's side."

"My lord, no longer; you are needed elsewhere by another."

"I am to serve?"

"Yes, my lord."

Assiolo shook his head. "Go, Thorn, and tell the one who sent you these three things: that I am needed here, I will not serve another's will, and I will not be used against my own."

"My lord, you have never been my master and I do not serve your will. I am sent to say this: you have long been needed and soon you will be ready. You have eaten and you have drunk, my mistress is your mistress and you cannot tarry longer within these stone walls."

"And if I cross the water? I think you cannot follow."

"No, my lord. Not I, nor any other of my kind. But if you cross the water what will you do? Would you eat of the king's fruit and drink of the king's cup?" Assiolo did not answer, and the grey man smiled. "Beneath this sky, my lord, it is your part to finish what your father started."

He snapped out, "I am not Allocco."

"That is of no matter, my lord." The grey man turned away into the light. Before he slipped from sight, he said, "You are Allocco's son: that is enough."

Assiolo dressed and stood looking out of the window. Beyond the walls, dawn was but greyness and a bank of rain veiling Cal Mora. The morning after it was sullen-sour, clogged with mists and miserable with dampness: a day like many another in Felluria when the sun forgot to shine and noontime was no brighter than the morning or the evening. Assiolo had known many such days and grown well used to them. They served to sharpen the joy of summer sun. But he had eyes and he could see and, from the edges of his eyes, he saw the light was very bright. Such a light in such a place frightened him. This was light enough to drive away all shadows and secrets, light enough to make the hidden plain, light enough to change one future for another.

Assiolo! A rustle and a whisper, a shimmer and a shiver, light flickering to form. They were here, root and stem and branch, leaf and twig and thorn, hiding in the light. A word, a whisper, *Assiolo!*

He would not have it so. Assiolo turned his back upon the light; standing at the window, he stretched out his hands and said a word, then stood a little time watching the mists roll down the mountain to hide the world away. When they hung so thick about the walls he could not see his garden, he kissed Marwy Ninek as she lay sleeping, " 'Tis but a day, love. I shall be back after the evening," and walked out alone through the gates of Felluria into the grey morning.

There was no line to mark the edge where sea met sky. All alike was blank and empty, fog and cloud and mist and nothing more. Mud mired his boots and drizzle chilled his face but Assiolo pulled off his hat to bare his head and let the rain roll like cold tears down his face, and walked on into the mist. The grey walls of Felluria were behind him, the grey peak of Cal Mora above him, the grey lochside below him, but he could see neither keep nor mountain nor water, only the swirling, shifting patterns of the clouds moving around him as a cloak. If any sought, they could not see. No ray of sun could pierce this shroud. Wrapping himself in Cal Mora's fogs, Assiolo walked the whole day through between the mountains and the sea, a wraith slipping among the ghostly shapes of birken trees, through thickets of brambles and briars, beneath ash trees and bare rowans. When at last the grey light thickened into evening, he was wet through, bone cold and exultant because the sun had set, the equinox had passed, the light had faded, and he was where he wanted. His heart sang in his breast as he turned his face to home, following the path of the little burn that ran down Cal Mora-side to the sea.

He let the night wind quicken on the mountain and begin to blow the mists away. The wind blew rain hard into his face but he paid no heed; he could see the lights of Felluria shining below him. He pulled his hat down over his ears and hastened on towards his love. She would be waiting, with a smile, with a kiss and a caress, soft and warm and sweet. Hurrying, his mind filled with thoughts of her, Assiolo missed his footing in the dark and took a tumble into the water.

The water was deeper and colder than he had thought that stream could be. He had walked its banks a hundred times and known it always a little thing, running swift and shallow down the brae. Now he was tossed and tumbled in the bottomless flood, sometimes he sank, sometimes he swam, knowing neither up nor down but only cold, cold water that filled his eyes and ears and mouth, pressing breath and thought and life from him. In the last moments before sense was lost it came to him these were no more Cal Mora's waters.

Knowledge gave him the strength he needed. He would not die. Not here. Not now. Assiolo summoned his will, reached out his hands and found the bank and dragged himself heavy from the water to lie upon the grass. This side the stream, the sky was clear of clouds and moon. Low hills of grass stretched endlessly away and the wind blew cold into his face. A man was sitting at the water's edge, his knees drawn up to his chin, his head resting on his hands. As Assiolo sat up, the man turned his head to face him. His eyes were wide as the sky, black as the night, deep as the sea. Assiolo closed his eyes; he looked into the dark and saw the stars tangled in his hair.

"You spoke the truth last time we met," Assiolo said, "and now we meet your side of the water. But I had no thought to look for you today. This is not my place, and I will away from these borderlands."

The king's voice was starlight on the stone. "As you desire. I do not take the unwilling."

The stream was a ripple of silver no wider than a man could jump. Assiolo stood upon the bank, judging the distance, readying himself for the leap, but, at the very last, he looked, and saw the further bank was not the one he knew. His heart beat fast and he turned back towards the king.

The king's voice was the wind whispering through the grasses. "Flood waters carried you further than you know, Assiolo, Allocco's son of Ohmorah, and you've a long way yet to go, an you cross back over the stream. The place you left is not the place you'll come to. But you are here and I am here and you may eat the apples of the borderlands, if you wish it."

"The first time we met, I gave you my answer. It will not change, though you ask a hundred times."

The king's laughter was the splash and tumble of water 'neath the stars. "The first time we met, I asked another question. That has been answered."

The words echoed around the empty place beside him where his love should have been. Assiolo reached out his hands to grasp a shadow, to pull her close and hold her safe against all the harm the world would throw at her. She was not there and so he told the king, "Then I'll away across the water and hie me to my love's side. I gave her my promise and I'll keep it."

"Other ties bind you, other hands hold you, and promises are hard to keep. My sister now has the right to ask her question: if you will not eat, you must go to her to answer."

Assiolo paused a moment longer at the water's edge, then stood up and walked towards the king, seeing again a pale-faced man no greater than himself. Before him the stream wove a ribbon of starlight down to a silent sea, silent and still, a mirror to the stars. For this other sky was full of stars, all the stars of the waking world were here and many more besides whose names no man could know. Then Assiolo looked and saw that there was one thing more, an apple tree upon the hill stretching bare branches to the sky.

The king stood beneath the firstborn tree with darkness in his eyes and stars in his hair. He held out his right hand, offering an apple. His ragged cloak swung around him on the wind. "In borderlands is neither joy nor sorrow unless carried in a living heart. But joy and sorrow lie heavy on a heart and only the greatest can be brought so far. Ask your question, Assiolo, and I will answer."

Assiolo saw himself reflected in the king's black eyes and saw a man he did not know. He asked, "What am I to you?"

"The answer is to your hand." Assiolo held up his right hand to the halflight of the borderlands. Her ring upon his finger was a glimmer of silver and a black stone in the starlight. "I told you clear last time we met: you are the king beneath the bare tree."

The thought fell hard and heavy into Assiolo's mind as a stone falling to the sea. He cried out, "I am not the king!"

"Not here. Not now. But this is not your place."

The king led Assiolo to the firstborn tree. Its branches were leafless, empty as any tree in winter. "My sister has lived a long time beneath your sky. Beneath that sky, you killed a king." The king's voice was the soft cold of snow upon the meadows. "She knows as well as any there cannot be two kings in one land. In the end, an you meet the one whose face I wear, it will fall to you to make one future or another." Assiolo felt a cold hand on his shoulder and heard the king ask, "What do you seek?"

"To keep my promise to the one that loves me," he answered, quiet and desperate, "to live my life at her side and know all will be as it was."

"That life is ended. It ended in the sallows." The king's voice sounded in the silence of Assiolo's mind. He shut his eyes but still he saw the king; he pressed his hands across his ears but still he heard the king; and his heart broke within his breast as his future stretched away from him, vast and empty as these borderlands.

Behind his eyes, Assiolo saw a lovely face clouded with love and fear. He asked, "What happened in the sallows?"

"A light was lit to drive away the dark. Light burns. Light blinds." The king's voice was the rattle of dry branches in the wind. "Love is a little thing to set against it. When there should have been an ending, of love, of life, of everything that makes a man, she made a new beginning. Cross the water, and you will find out what was begun."

"And have my own again?"

"Never in the waking world does the road of a man's life run straight from morning into evening. My sister is all that I am not and walks beneath the sun and moon."

"You offer nothing!"

"I offer what I offer all and any who come into these borderlands. No more. No less."

"It is not enough!"

"You know what I am." The king's voice was the crack of branches in the frost. "The waking world is no concern of mine, and the desires of men are of no matter here. Here, there is no choice but the one: eat the offered apple and dance upon the wind, or else return across the water."

Assiolo looked into the king's black eyes and knew what he had always known. This king wore the likeness of a man but he had never been a man. He was the darkness before the light, a song of sea and stone and sky, beautiful and terrible as midwinter's night. He was not kind, he was not cruel. He knew neither pity nor malice. He knew only truth, and truth in his mouth was clear as water, hard as stone, sharp and shining as the blade of a knife.

A long while passed, or maybe it was no time at all. In this land, the sun would never rise, the stars would never set, there was no moon to wax and wane and raise a tide against the shore, and all the time there ever was, was here.

Assiolo opened his eyes; he saw the starlight on the empty sea and the king at his side and knew himself alone. But, in the borderlands where no flowers would ever grow, he remembered roses flowering at midsummer, a promise whispered in the night time, *Forever and for always*. He cried out, clinging to his love and promise as a drowning man does to a spar upon the surface, "What do you know of love that dares declare its ending? I cannot change the past but you know well as I the future is not yet written."

"Then hope is all you have to set against the past." The king's laughter was the ripple of the wind across the hillside. "Very well, Assiolo, I grant no boons and make no bargains but I will tell you true: when you stand in another land before another king, all that might be may be, if you are not blinded by the light."

—⊢— —⊣—

Marwy Ninek woke to find herself alone upon the morning of the equinox, that day of light and darkness. Assiolo's place in the bed was still half-warm beside her, his lute in its case in the corner, his book upon the shelf, but he himself was gone. She sought him first in the hall, and then in the garden, and at the last in Yatta Tala's chambers. He was not there, and none she asked had seen him. Only the porter, casting down his eyes, said he had slept overlong and woken after the dawning to find the locked door open. She turned away without a word to stand at her gate, her stone walls behind her and above her, and look beyond her threshold.

All around was silence. No breath of wind to lift the sea from its calm rest or raise the mists, slung low, shrouding Cal Mora in cloud that masked its bulk, hiding the braes, dimming the day to sullen halflight. All was quiet: no voice of bird or beast to break this hush. The bracken and heather were wrapped in swathes like silk; scree, granite, grass all sheltered from her curious eye and made invisible. The mists hung so low, so still lay the milk-white sea, she could not draw a line to mark the edge where one gave way to let the other start.

At her back was the noise and bustle of Felluria. Before her was mist and silence. She watched the mists drop ever lower, numbing the day to sleep, until it seemed there could be nothing more beyond the gate than grey cloud and emptiness, forever and for always. Perhaps there was a world beyond the mist: she did not know, she could not tell. All she knew was that Assiolo was not in his place beside her.

Somewhere, nearby, out of sight, a seabird called to its mate; sweet its call on two notes, high and higher, rising to the sky that domed unseen in azure beyond the mist. Her heart beat, her ears strained for the answer. None came. Once, twice and again, the bird called; each time the same two notes, long, drawn out, so lonely she thought her heart would break to hear them, perfect, unexpected beauty tearing her heart and leaving it desolate. Each time the silence ate the sound and the cry fell back and vanished as if it had never been.

A long, long time she stood there, noon, afternoon and evening merging into one, muffled by mist, wrapped in watered silk, until at last she heard wings beating their way into the distance. At last, when the bird was out of hearing and all around was silence, she retraced her steps to the garden: where Assiolo had gone she could not follow. She must wait for his return.

Longtimes Marwy Ninek walked to and fro between the rowan and the apple tree, though the night was dreich and the garden made of no more than brown sticks and promises. In summertime, there were roses here, and lavender; in summertime, swifts skimmed the grass by day and, by night, bats flickered, shrilling on the edge of hearing; in summertime, she stretched out at Assiolo's side, her head in his lap, listening as he sang in a sweet, strange tongue she did not know but loved no less for his sake. But summertime was far away and the apple and the rowan tree were both as bare as last year's bones. The sour wind from Cal Mora rattled their branches and threw rain hard into her face. She pulled her coat tight round her and crouched beneath the rowan, bending her head to feel its rough bark against her brow. She put her hands onto its trunk, as any woman might to ask protection for her man against the storm and the future.

She crouched a long time beneath the rowan, hiding from the world and from herself in the dark behind closed eyes. Then she stood to face the world again and, when she turned, saw the future in a sprig of holly bound to the grey bough of the apple tree. After that, though she pressed her back against the rowan's trunk, she knew it was only a tree and could give no solace. It could offer no protection and no hope. That tree had died long ago, the world was as it was, clotted with hatred and fear, and Felluria again become a place where all hope was false.

Marwy Ninek broke the thread of golden hair binding the holly sprig to the apple branch. One green leaf and two red berries lying in the palm of her hand, a little thing in all but its meaning. She cast it down and crushed it with her foot. It made no difference. Averla's laughter rang inside her head. *Holly I will send to you!* No other hand but hers had shaped her future.

There was no trace of him upon the mountainside or on the moorland. But a shepherd, gathering the hillsheep to the shieling, found a sodden clot of black at the burnside on Cal Mora and, picking it up to see what it might be, found it was a man's woollen hat lying in the mud. Then he looked again, and read the tracks that ended on the bank, the scrape and scrabble where a falling man had clutched at a bog myrtle bush to save himself and dragged half of it in with him.

"He must have misstepped in the mist," the shepherd told her. "It's a fair drop and the water runs swift beneath it with the snow-melt from the mountain. Surely the stream caught him and carried him down into the sea."

He had thought to say some word of comfort. But she raised her face to stare at him and, when he saw her eyes, he could not speak, and left her.

Marwy Ninek laid the black hat out before her on the table, reshaping it into its own likeness. This was his hat indeed, and surely the shepherd's tale was told in good belief. But she knew Assiolo was not drowned; she knew he did not roll in the streams of Cal Mora or sink in the salt, cold sea. She knew where he had gone, and why. Memory must be her comfort, and his promise: *Only death will take me from you.*

He was not dead but he was gone and the hope he had left behind was not enough to lighten her darkness, nor his memory enough to keep her warm in the night time or stand betwixt her and the wind, and her grief was a shadow cast across Felluria, a quiet dark grief that spoke no word and knew no comfort.

The days that followed were mired in mud and rain. Marwy Ninek sat beside her window staring into the damp garden when she heard a knock upon the door. She did not answer and, when the door opened, she turned to see who dared disturb her solitude.

"Why do you come to me, Yatta Tala?" she asked. "I did not send for you."

"If you'd sent, I'd not have answered," said the weaver in a tone near as empty as her own. She came into the room and laid a bundle of white linen on the bed. "Another asked me, and I'll keep better faith with him than you did. You're not the only one within these walls sore-hearted since his leaving."

Marwy Ninek stared to be spoken to in such a way. "You forget yourself," she snapped. "What was he to you?"

Yatta Tala busied herself with the swathes of linen, unwinding them across the bed. Marwy Ninek turned from her. She pulled her shawl tight and looked from her window into Assiolo's garden. No trace of green there yet, the buds still tight and small upon the apple and the rowan, no more to the roses than twig and thorn.

"I'm an old woman now," the weaver said, "my fires burned out long ago and I'll go no more a-dancing on midsummer's night. All the men I kissed are gone and none of them was worth the love and tears I gave them. To each her own folly."

The wind cast rain against the window. Marwy Ninek pressed her brow to the pane while, at her back, the weaver's dry voice went on, "Count yourself fortunate I had grown old before Assiolo came to Felluria. I was greedy when I was young, I took what I wanted, and I'd have wanted him. But it was you he loved, and he staked his life to win you. The rest of us were left to gnash our teeth and wish in vain that he might look once at us as oftentimes he looked at you."

Marwy Ninek's answer was bleak and bitter as the rain beyond her window. "He is gone. The rest is no concern of yours or any other in Felluria."

The weaver snorted, her hands busy, her eyes downturned towards her work. "Always he looked at you as if he could never look his fill, so fond and tender he could scarce bear the wind to blow on you. If he left you, it must be of your doing!"

Marwy Ninek blanched bone-white, her eyes great pits of grief. Her hand stretched out to steady herself against the wall. *He lives*, she told herself, *Assiolo lives. His life is worth the price.*

"And what have you done but creep in shadows since?" muttered Yatta Tala, all the while unwrapping folds of linen. "If ever I'd had a man like Assiolo, I'd have followed him to the ends of the earth in my nightgown, and woe betide any who stood betwixt us."

Marwy Ninek kept her eyes fixed on the rowan tree below her in the garden, but her mind was filled with thoughts of holly, of one green leaf and two red berries. At her back, the weaver ranted on. She paid no heed, no more than to the rain. There was nothing Yatta Tala said she had not thought already. Only when the weaver called out her name did she swing around to bid her be silent and saw her shake out a golden gown, rich and warm as summertime, scattered all over with red roses.

"This is the gift he left for you." The old woman's voice was hard and harsh as the wind whistling down the mountain. "*Make it warm and soft, he told me. I don't want her to be cold when the wind blows from Cal Mora.*" She sniffed, wiping her hand across her eyes. "At the time I thought he spoke as any man in love might speak. But Assiolo knew more of the world than other men, and now I think he had another purpose. Well, here it is and I never made a finer. He deserved the best, did Assiolo, and the best is what I gave him."

Marwy Ninek took five paces from the window and reached out to touch the gown, gathering it into her arms. The wool was soft as thistlesilk against her cheek, light and warm in her hands as eiderdown. She could not weep but she sank down beside the bed to clutch the gown and sob aloud, great, dry, gasping sobs that once begun would not come to an end. "Assiolo, oh my love, my love."

Yatta Tala watched for a time, unmoved. She was no stranger to grief, nor to shame, nor disappointment. She had lived long enough to know that in the end all comfort is false, all hope in vain. At last, Marwy Ninek's sobbing ceased. She sat back on her heels, forcing herself to silence and to calm. He was not there. What purpose then to call on him?

The weaver set a kettle of water to boil upon the hearth. When it was singing, she looked through the cupboard until she found what she needed and set it steeping in hot water. She gave a cup to Marwy Ninek and took one for herself. "Feverfew," she told her, sourly. "Good against the headache. I'll warrant your head's sore enough after that greetin'. So drink up, and when you're calm again we'll talk of Assiolo."

Marwy Ninek took a sip of her tea. "What would you speak about with me? Would you talk of the future? It stretches out ahead of me, an empty, lonely place where I must live watching all I know die around me." Again she drank; again she spoke, "Would you speak of the present? I gave my love into another's hands and she'll not treat him kindly." A third time she raised the cup to drink, and then she asked the weaver, "Would you talk of the past? I stole an apple and became an empty vessel, hatred reflecting madness." Marwy Ninek set down the empty cup. "Torùkotu left a ruin behind him. Assiolo sought to mend what he had broken. Now he is gone."

"Then follow him, you little fool!"

Marwy Ninek stiffened. Then she swallowed down her first retort and said, flattening all feeling from her voice, "Where he's gone, I cannot follow. There's a stronger wall than mine around him now."

Yatta Tala shook her head, muttering under her breath of love and Assiolo, and Marwy Ninek pressed her face into her hands. "You think you see," she said, "you think you know, but you are blind and you know nothing."

The old woman picked up the dress from the bed and smoothed out the creases, holding it up a long moment to look at it before folding it away within a kist.

"Oh, I have eyes and I can see. I see a wretch who bleats of love but waits and cowers and trembles. If once I'd had a man like him,

I'd not have let him go. I'd have held him tight though the wind blew on me and the sun shrivelled me and the fire burned me."

Anger, fierce and strong as wildfire 'cross the heather, set Marwy Ninek's heart a-blazing. "I love him well," she said, standing to face the weaver. "As much as ever woman loved her man, so do I love Assiolo. Hold him tight?" she asked, "Not let him go?" She looked into the old woman's face, and this time Yatta Tala could not meet her eyes. "When he lay a-dying in the sallows, you burned the herbs and said the words but I made a bargain with Averla and kept him from the dark."

"That golden witch!" The weaver sucked in her breath. "And on midsummer's night, when you sat alone beneath the wall?"

No tremble in her voice, no hesitation. "I kept my bargain."

"A pretty trick to serve him." Yatta Tala crooked her fingers 'gainst misfortune.

"He lives; Assiolo lives! Now I must wait and I must hope his love is stronger than Averla's desire." Her anger had burnt out quick as wildfire, leaving behind a wasteland of sorrow. She sank back into the windowseat, pulling her shawl round her shoulders. "Assiolo came here to escape the shadow of his father, to forget the things he learned from him. Did you think him a man like other men?"

"I'll soon think him as much a fool as other men, if you go on this way. I've neither time nor words to waste on you." The weaver sniffed and turned away, saying at the door, "If I were you, I'd set the blacksmith's boy to tend that garden. Shame to let it run to weeds because he is not here."

—+— —+—

The fat mercatman had not crossed the sea this year, preferring to linger in Felluria. He sent his nephew in his stead, a man much like to him in face and not at all in form, saying 'twas time he set his own stamp upon their trade. He sent gifts too, to ease his nephew's entry into the king's good favour: the pelt of some spotted beast, very like a cat's save in its size; a silken robe bedecked with, at the first glance, glass-green gems and, at the second, the shining shells of beetles; a knife with an obsidian blade. Te-Meriku wondered at the skin and laughed at the robe and cut his hand upon the knife blade and gave Silus Danatu a welcome, after a fashion. So it was a young man, and a nervous one, who faced the king across his counter in the sheds behind the harbour and said, "Assiolo is gone from Felluria."

"Gone! How can he be gone?"

"The how and the why I cannot tell. Only the simple truth: he is not there."

"Tell me," said the king, and his quiet words trickled like cold water across the space between them, "tell me all the truth you know."

The young mercatman swallowed and stammered. "I can tell no more than an old woman told my uncle: six months ago, or a little longer, he was gone between the night and morn."

"Dead in a ditch, perhaps?" suggested Thodùhah. "Had he an enemy?"

"It's possible, I grant you." Silus Danatu shook his head. "All things are possible. But 'tis clear Marwy Ninek does not think him dead, for all she walks like a widow through her days. I've never seen such grief."

The king remarked, quite lightly, "Seems strange he'd leave her when he'd done so much to win her." His face was mild, his voice was quiet but there was a storm brewing in his eyes.

"Who can say what goes on between the sheets," Thodùhah said.

The king leaned close across the table, asking, "You think it a lovers' quarrel?"

The mercatman shrank back, pale beneath his beard, spreading out his empty hands. "Te-Meriku, I think nothing, I know nothing beyond the fact that she woke one morning and found him gone."

"And no news of the piper."

"No news at all."

"What will you do, Te-Meriku?" the helmsman asked later as the king sat a-drinking by the fire.

"Allocco's son within stone walls was well enough; without them he's another thing entirely. Ready my ship for sea – we're to Felluria quick as can be to have the truth from Marwy Ninek."

–+— —+–

The ship came out of the west following the path laid by the rising sun across the sea, its passage 'cross the water beautiful and dreadful as a hawk's flight across the empty air. A lovely sight to look upon, sleek lines low in the water, red and gold and bronze bright in the sunlight, an eagle's head at its prow and its square sail bellied full of air; a lovely sight indeed, for one who could not read the meaning and the purpose written into every line and curve.

One ship, Marwy Ninek thought, looking from the wall towards the loch mouth, *fifty men*. But fifty men who feared nothing and no one and would go laughing into the dark, for sake of a snatch of song sung when they were dead. All this she remembered. All this she had seen before.

Behind her, standing between her daughter and her grand-daughter, Yatta Tala muttered, "Here's a beginning I did not look for."

The great gates of Felluria stayed shut fast that morning. By ones and twos and threes, its folk gathered in the hall. None of them had ever seen a ship of Lyikené but they were the men and women of Felluria and the old tales ran in their blood. A fisherman began to speak, "We're not cowards, here in Felluria. We will go out and fight, and they will find our iron knives bite as fierce as any bronze."

"And when you're dead, my brave hero?" the weaver cut him off. "When you've made your stand with your iron knife and died at the thrust of a bronze spear, what happens then?"

He flushed, and did not answer.

Marwy Ninek looked around the hall and saw fear in Felluria. She leant her back against her wall but the cold stone brought no comfort. There were mattocks here, there were scythes and sickles, there were shepherds with their shears; the blacksmith had his hammers, the fishermen their gutting knives and the butcher his cleavers. Here and there, among the throng, a man in middle age stood straight in mail, an iron sword at his hip, a buckler on his arm. A dozen years ago and longer, across the Inner Sea, the queen of Escen had made her war, drawing young men to her fight with a promise of land and silver. Few had returned – the queen had kept her promises when she won her peace – only those heartsick for the west, who yearned to see the hawk's eight stars hanging above Cal Mora on a summer's evening, not evermore reflected in the wide, slow waters of the Eus.

"One ship alone," the whispers ran around the hall, people thinking of the past, seeking to reassure themselves against the future. "It is not war. There is no need for fear. We have kept the covenant here in Felluria."

The blacksmith's boy who had been set as lookout on the gatehouse tower came into the hall. "Three eagles on the sail," he said, breathless with his news, "and a green branch at the mast-top."

And, in the silence afterwards, some fool cried out what all there knew, "It is the king!" and that was an end to silence.

A man banged his hands upon a table top and, when he was not heeded, clambered up, stamping his foot to make himself heard about the thrum and fright. He was none of Felluria, though all there knew his face, Edo Incithu, the fat mercatman of Cincern Dùn, come this year as in many before it with a shipload of wine and spices, trading for weaving and barleyspirit and hillfleeces from Cal Mora. "It is not war," he said, in the voice of one who knows the world and all the people in it. "That branch is the mark of parley. Te-Meriku comes to talk and not to fight."

"Whenever did the king of the Sea People speak with any in the Later Lands?" Yatta Tala asked. "He did not speak with the fishermen of Ittachar before he killed them. It is a trap to lull us into folly."

"That king is dead, two hundred years and longer; this one makes no use of tricks and subterfuge," replied the mercatman. "Te-Meriku wears but a single face."

Marwy Ninek said nothing. The sailors of Ittachar had broken the covenant and paid the price of it. None in Felluria had ever dared such folly, but still the wind had blown and the tide had risen, and, after the ruin, all that had been left behind was firestar, blazing red and gold across broken walls.

"Even the Sea People grow tired of salted cod and roasted mutton," the mercatman said, "they crave red wine, and wheatenflour, and walnuts out of Cincern Dùn. Because they crave such things, I have had dealings in Lyikené, even in the king's hall. My nephew's there now in my stead whilst I weigh up your oats and barley."

"You have not thought to mention this before, Edo Incithu," said Yatta Tala, drily, "though we've known you longtimes in Felluria."

"I was hardly like to mention it, in Felluria," he answered in a tone to match her, "but my kind follow our fortunes, even into the west. There's many a woman in the Later Lands wishes for a skein of amber beads to hang around her neck or a white seal's fur to wrap her 'gainst the cold. The mercatkind will go where others won't, and are welcomed where others aren't." He let his gaze wander over the weaver's attire to the bunch of lace at her chin set with a long pin of gold and mussel pearls. "That trinket, mistress, at your neck was wrought in the west and, six years back, you had a cap of white sealskin of me. Those seals don't pup without there's ice and snow. The whalemen must take them before the sea-ice melts." He shrugged his shoulders 'gainst her scowl, as if these were little things of no matter.

From the corner of his eye, he saw Marwy Ninek put up her head and throw back her shoulders, as a woman does bracing herself against the wind. He did not turn towards her, he spoke as if to all or any in that place, but still his words were meant for her. "He's all you think he is, Te-Meriku, there's none cross him and live, but still he's passing honest. There's rich men in the Later Lands give their word and break it – I'll take the red king over them."

The mercatman looked around the faces in the hall, the blacksmith, the fishermen, the armsmen and the weaver, at Marwy Ninek white-faced beside the wall. "You've known me thirty years and longer, and none here's had short weight of me. I'll go to the wall and ask his will on your account, if it seems good to you."

Silence.

Marwy Ninek took three steps into the room and, when the mercatman next turned to her, she met his eyes and nodded, very slightly. "If it does not seem good to you," he said, lightly enough for it to be a jest, though in his pocket he crooked his fingers in the sign to avoid ill fortune, "then I'm to the wall on my account to ask safe conduct out."

There was a ragged laugh that fell away to nothing.

The blacksmith nodded first and, after him, the fishermen by one and two and three; the women thought longer than the men but in the end consented and, last of all, even Yatta Tala bowed her head, though still she scowled. The mercatman smiled and bowed. "Then by your leave, I'll do what is necessary." When he looked again, Marwy Ninek had slipped away. Beneath his breath he muttered, "And by my life, I hope I'm right," though none there chose to hear him.

The king stood before the great gate though it was locked against him. His hair was red, his sword was bronze, and he as fair a sight upon the world as the sunset and the morning. He cried out so all within might hear, "Marwy Ninek, Marwy Ninek, let me come in!"

The mercatman stood upon the tower above the gate and looked upon the king. He called down so all without might hear, "Te-Meriku, I am sent to speak for the men and women of Felluria. They bid me say this: *The king of Lyikené is not welcome here. And if you come for fight there is cold iron within these walls to match your bright bronze.*"

The king's voice was light with laughter. "It was not for fight I came into Felluria, Edo Incithu, nor even to play a game of fox and goose with you and drink red wine across the evening. The fight and the game and the wine will keep for other days. Today, I would talk with Marwy Ninek."

Shaking his head, the mercatman said, "She'll not talk to you, Te-Meriku, within these walls of stone, nor yet aboard your ship upon the open sea, not even if you stand upon the tideline with empty hands betwixt the land and water. I am bid tell you: *This is not your place—be gone back into the west.*"

"Tell Marwy Ninek that I will speak with her. Tell her," said the king, and now only his mouth was smiling, "that I am a patient man. I shall wait outside her gate until she speaks to me, be that a twelvemonth and a day. I'll not come in unless I am invited but nor shall any that are in go out. It would be a shame," the king said, all trace of laughter gone from face and voice, "if sheep should go astray, and the grain be left unthreshed, and the fishermen's catches rot upon the beach and there be want and hunger in Felluria because the gate is shut."

Between the first gate and the second, under the eyes of the blacksmith with his hammer and the butcher with his cleaver, the king stripped to his skin, combed out his flaming hair and put on the shirt and britches tossed down to him. On the wall, men watched, shepherds with stones ready in their slings and another with an arrow nocked on the bowstring. As Marwy Ninek waited she saw at the edges of her court the armsmen who had fought in Escen, poised like dancers before the music begins, falchions drawn, eyes a-glint and a-glitter beneath the shadow of their helms. But, though he must have seen and must have heard, the king of Lyikené walked barefoot through that place easy as a man at summertime beneath the flowering trees.

He walked towards her, his empty hands outstretched, and, in the moment of terrible clarity before the merciful dark rose up to swallow her, she knew Assiolo a liar: Torùkotu was not dead. He was here within her own stone walls, a man again, red-haired and smiling, her past, her nightmare of flesh and pain and terror.

Strong hands caught her as she fell and laid her, not ungently, down upon the grass.

Faces swam in the light above her and around her. Someone, a woman, Baesina Yatta, held a cup to her lips. Marwy Ninek sipped the water, keeping her face turned down, but from the edges of her eyes she saw the king still there, standing not ten feet away between the butcher and the blacksmith. With Baesina Yatta's arm around her, she took him in in glances, trying to calm the thunder of her heart.

Knowing he was watched, the king turned his head to stare and, for the first time, she saw his eyes. His eyes were all his own. He was too far to judge their colour – grey, perhaps, or else dark green or blue – but the look in them had never been in that other man's eyes. He waited patiently for her to be ready. At last, she put off Baesina Yatta's arms, rose up and took two steps towards him.

He did likewise and the women drew back from her, the men from him, so they were alone within a little space and but five feet of green grass between them.

"Why are you here, Te-Meriku? What do you want of me?"

"An answer to a question: where is Assiolo mor Allocco?"

To hear that name come from that mouth was near as much as she could bear. She stared and stared and did not answer.

The king laughed, a hard, harsh laugh that had no kindness to it. "Not so long ago, a new tale was carried to the west, one that ended happily with two lovers together in a garden of red roses. It told of an outlandish lord who walked into the woods to slay a beast and set his lady free. How far this tale was true, Marwy Ninek, you know far better than I. Here and now," he said, "I see the garden, not the man – where is Assiolo?"

Her answer was a sullen whisper. "He is not here."

Again, a short, hard laugh. "That I knew already. Half a year since he got up from your bed and left you. But he is Allocco's son and so I ask again, where is Assiolo?"

"You can ask, Te-Meriku, but I think I am not bound to answer."

She saw again the past king in the present, her vision doubling across the years: the same tumble of red hair, light and bright as a fire's heart; the same straight nose; the same wide mouth; the same white-skinned, easy arrogance, a pride beyond all measure.

"It seems to me most strange," he said, slowly, carefully, measuring out his words, "that a man should do so much for you, should kill a king, drink of your cup and lie in your bed, and you not send a search for him across your moors and mountains. That must mean one thing of two: either he is dead or else you know to whence he's gone. If he's dead, say but the word and I'll away again into the west."

"He is not dead, my love, my life," she whispered. "Even now, I'd know if he were dead."

"Then where?"

His eyes were steady, pushing her towards an answer. "He is gone to Averla."

He stared and started at the name. "Averla?"

"Aye, Averla!" Her words had been months unspoken and tumbled in a flood. "She stole him from me with a midsummer bargain, left me alone and lonely, and yet I cannot quite hate her. She gave him life, Te-Meriku; gave him back to me, a living man. If your love lay dying in your bed would you not do likewise?"

His smile was gone, his face hard as a stone. "Marwy Ninek, before ever I heard Assiolo had come into Felluria, I dreamed Averla named him as her own. A dreadful dream of light and fire, the long-haired star rising to shine 'cross land and sea. I put it out of mind – I'm not a man to put much faith in dreams and portents. But I remember. And now," the king said, quietly, terribly, "I would know if it were a true dreaming."

"A dream! A dream has no weight upon the world."

"I did not cross the sea to bandy words. I ask, and you will answer. Now, tell me all."

His command flicked like the lash of a whip and she could not help but tell him. He listened to her halting tale in grim-faced silence, a dreadful figure in the sunshine, his hair flickering about his face like flame.

When she had done, the king laughed, short and bitter in his throat. "Easy to forget in these Later Lands, that, always, since the gates of morning closed, Averla has walked beneath the flowering trees. Easy to forget all that was hers she'll have again, if I cannot keep my place this side the water. Tell me, Marwy Ninek," he asked, and fear trickled like cold water down her neck to hear him speak so soft and dangerous, "if a man should kill a king what does that make him?"

Her first thought rose as answer to her mouth and she swallowed hard upon it. No need for words to lend substance to the thought. She said instead, "Those tales were old when I was a child. Who but the piper can know if they are true?"

She might not have spoken for all the heed he gave her. "No man wakes after three days a-sleeping of the winter sickness, and this was Allocco's son. I am blind I did not see. I am a fool I did not guess." He spoke as to himself, a man seeing plain the hidden pattern. His face curved into a grimace. "I missed the tide indeed. Averla asked, and you gave her what she needed: the means to bind him to her will."

"Assiolo lives – he breathes!" Her cry hung a long time on the wind, a seagull's scream upon the empty air. For that life and that breath she had kept her bargain.

The king's tone was cold, his answer quick, "That is of no matter, if a man's wit and will are not his own."

Within the court two wagtails hopped, pied grey and white, a flutter of wings and tail. They had no weight at all upon the world, knowing neither past nor future, and neither men's words nor women's deeds were of concern to them. She watched the birds foraging across the grass a little while until she found the words to answer. Her voice rough with rage and grief, she said, "Assiolo sought to mend what had been broken. He did not know a man could die and nothing that he broke be mended."

"No more, it seems, than you remembered a man could live and still be lost. Torùkotu lived and breathed for many years after you drove him from his hall!"

"Do you dare name that name to me, Te-Meriku, here within the walls of Felluria?"

"I speak as I will, Marwy Ninek."

Old laughter echoed out of a remembered night, mocking her across the years. She shut her mind against the memory and counted out her heartbeats, forcing her breathing to slowness. That had been another man, in another time. This king was taller than that man had been; leaner too, with several days' growth of beard blurring the hard outlines of his face.

Staring at his face to keep these differences firm in her mind, she asked, "What would you have me do, Te-Meriku—fall at your feet and beg for mercy?"

The king shrugged. "Mercy is not my gift. If your death would undo your deeds, I'd strike you down before the second thought." Again that mirthless smile. "Alas for both of us, killing you will not bring an ending."

She shivered in the sunshine, the golden gown no proof against the chill wind blowing down Cal Mora. The king met her eyes, she saw herself reflected there and turned away in shame. He took a step across the space between them, reaching out towards her.

She shrank away, blanched with her fear, sickened by the thought of his hand upon her skin. The king's hands were empty, he had left his spear, his sword and knife behind him in the ship waiting two arrowflights beyond the shore, but he was a man, and a man of the Sea People, and she had no strength to match him. She scarce heard the blacksmith's shout, "No further, barbarian!" nor yet the rattle of mail as armed men stepped forward, their iron swords raised and ready.

"Nay, I have only words to cast at you," said the king, stepping away and turning slowly round to show his empty hands. Armed men stepped back, swords lowered, their eyes fixed still upon him. "It is your deeds that should put you to fright today, not mine. Tonight, Marwy Ninek, and every night after, when the light fades and the stars grow bright, look to the east. There is a star not there that will be."

She let out the breath she had not known she held. He was but one man and they were many in Felluria. One word from her, one cry, one signal from her hand and he would die: there was no need to fear him. Keeping such thoughts hard in her mind, she clenched her hands within her sleeves, raised her face to his and told him, "That star marks out the death of kings! It will not rise for me. Are you afraid, Te-Meriku? Do you flee your fate across the sea, like a boy in fear of whipping? What is your death to me? All men must die, and few in these Later Lands will shed tears for the deaths of any of the Sea People."

The king was alone within the stone walls of his enemies, barefoot in an ungirt shirt and ill-fitting britches, but she could not long meet his eyes. Those eyes were deep as the sea and full as dangerous.

"That star marks out Averla's will. Should I die and the west fall into fire," he said in a voice that reached every corner of Felluria, and thrice a hundred hearts beat fast to hear him, "should the sun stop still at noontime, should the gates of evening close and the firstborn tree grow no more beneath this sky, should Averla have her own again, all in these Later Lands will shed a river of tears, weeping that they are not the Sea People dead and gone into the dark, beyond all pain and fear and suffering."

She was within her own stone walls but, even so, the sky was high and empty above her and there was no shelter from the wind blowing down Cal Mora. Her past was very close, the long past and the near, and out of one had come the other. She closed her eyes and said aloud her own love's name, knowing full well he was not there to answer. It had been half a year and longer since he had been at her side, his arm around her shoulders, standing between her and the wind.

"I know what Averla is, I know what she wants," the king said, almost gently. "I said her, *No!* but, now she has Assiolo at her side, I do not know if even I have the strength to stand against her."

"You are wrong," she answered in a halting whisper, unable to see Assiolo in the man reflected from his eyes, "he is no monster. He is only Assiolo." The man she knew had a tender mouth for kisses and gentle hands for caresses; he was a gardener who coaxed flowers out of the stony earth; a healer who knew much of herbs and simples; a singer of lovesongs and lullabies.

The king shook his head. "He is fire and sunlight, Allocco's son, a heavy weight upon the world with all his father's skill and strength. All that he put aside to love you – all that Averla will use for her own purpose. The long-haired star will be the pledge of it."

They stood a long time in silence, in seeming a man in a ragged shirt and a woman in a golden gown, making the sight in many eyes, watching, waiting for one of them to say a word or make an ending. Marwy Ninek looked all around, at the butcher and the blacksmith, at armed men below the walls, at the flutter of Baesina Yatta's blue scarf, but Te-Meriku never looked except at her. And when she had looked everywhere else – at the swallows' nests beneath the eaves, at the firestar clinging to the walls, at the clouds scudding across the sky above the stone walls of Felluria – at last she looked him in the face and saw the question there, one she had seen many times before, in the blacksmith's eyes testing the weight of iron, or in the butcher's, pausing as he whet his blades to consider the edge, or in Yatta Tala's, feeling the strength and smoothness of a thread, or even in Assiolo's as he found the tuning for his lute.

And, stranger still, behind the question was a touch of something else, perhaps the last thing she would have looked for in a man of his country.

"Watch the sky, Marwy Ninek," he said, "and wait. If Assiolo returns, let him bide within these stone walls – I'll keep my peace and my distance. But," he said, "if the long-haired star shines in the east, 'tis I shall come to you. Averla must not have her own again; the world must not fall into fire and ruin. It is my part to keep the balance." The king held out his empty hands towards her. "If that star rises, strange times are like to come. I would have you beside me when they do."

"Strange times indeed. Never before did Lyikené call upon the later lands for help. And it is a call that is like to go unanswered."

"It is you I ask, and you alone. I think you'll answer, for love of Assiolo." He stooped and picked a harebell from the grass beside his foot, a little thing, delicate in his great hand. For a moment she thought he would offer it but he threaded it into the laces of his shirt. "Or else from hatred of Averla, twisting a good man out of his proper shape."

"And what am I against Averla?"

A spark of laughter in his eyes. "Against Averla, you are nothing. But for Assiolo you were everything, so I would have you at my side to stand between them."

"You are afraid," she said, amazed, "and ask this because you fear to lose your kingdom. You seek to use my love against my lover." She met his eyes and told him, "My desire is not your desire, Te-Meriku."

He shrugged and smiled. "You desire to twine Assiolo from Averla. So too do I. You desire to keep what you love safe. So too do I. And I – I ask this of you because you love him, and perhaps that is enough to balance all the rest."

She shook her head and he said, almost as if he pitied her, "Your stone walls did not keep you safe: Torùkotu cast down those walls, Averla spoke softly and the gatekeeper let her in. It does not matter how high the wall is built, how thick, the weight of iron beneath each threshold – none of it is enough to keep out those that wish to be within. But, if you stand with me, there is a chance that you will have your own again. Or are you yet so sore afraid that you would rather let the world fall into ruin than pass beyond your gate?"

Of course she was afraid! He was brightness and terror come out of the west, a fair-faced man of Lyikené, red-haired and ruthless. She knew what such men could do, even when they set aside their spears and swords and knives, even when their hands were empty.

Shivering in her golden gown, she told him, "I never heard the Sea People brought any end but one, Te-Meriku."

"That is the truth, after a fashion," he answered, a flash of laughter in his face that turned him from one man to another, "but we have kept the tree safe in the west since the long day ended. Remember that, Marwy Ninek, and answer when I ask."

The day was blue above her, pale and delicate as a harebell, and the east wind blew cold down the slopes of Cal Mora. She watched as he walked away towards the gate, watched as the gate closed behind him and, though she stood within her own stone walls, there was no shelter from the wind.

Three blood-red eagles on the sail, their talons outstretched to rip the world asunder. The nightwatch slept, curled in his sheepskins against the curve of the hull, easy as a shepherd beneath a tree at noontime. "Well?" asked Thodùhah, guiding the ship out into the sound beyond Loch Mora's narrow mouth.

The king scowled. "A poor, trembling creature. Your daughter had more courage at ten years old."

The helmsman laughed. "Easy to be brave when you know nothing of the world."

"She was afraid of me."

Thodùhah's blue eyes glinted in the sunlight as his face creased into a smile. "And aren't we all a-feared of you, Te-Meriku? You could kill any of us between two heartbeats."

"If you're afraid of me, you hide it well. Likewise your lady." The king rubbed at the stubble on his chin. "Not in that way. As a woman fears a man who's hurt her. She swooned when first she saw me and I'll swear she called me Torùkotu in that moment."

"Doubtless one red-haired barbarian looks much like another."

Te-Meriku nodded, his attempts to scratch his shoulder baffled by the leather of his jerkin. He swore beneath his breath, a curse upon the Later Lands and all who lived in them. "What's the matter?" asked Thodùhah. "You've been twisting and squirming since we took you back."

"That shirt they made me wear – it had a flea in it. I tell you, Thodùhah, I've a mind to sack the place just for that."

Then Thodùhah proved with his laughter just how strong his fear was of the king.

─┼─ ─┼─

Midwinter. The king walked through the wood, snow on the branches, frost on the trees. The darkness parted itself around him, the splinters of frost shining bright as the stars in the sky. He walked in silence through the night and left no mark upon the snow. Tonight, as he walked out of the wild wood into the world, there were no boundaries between a dream and waking.

The king stood between the earth and sky. When he spoke, the world fell quiet to listen. "If you are there, show yourself."

The meadows were full of shapes and shadows. Light and lovely as the falling snow, the liùthion danced around him, existing only at the edge of vision, in the world and out of it. Their dance span and wove its patterns across the meadows as snowflakes span across the sky but the king was the still centre, the fixed point, more solid than any flesh, more real than any dream. The world was ever changing but he endured forever and for always.

He spoke again, his voice the gentle cold of falling snow, "Come out of the dark." He held his hand out to a darker shadow beneath the shadows of a bone-bare tree.

The piper stepped from beneath a birken tree, its pale branches hung all about with ice, bleak and beautiful as hope. "Only in borderlands can we meet, between your lands and mine."

"Are you come to beg an apple?" The words rang out into the night, the clear cold of broken ice skimming across a frozen loch.

"I cannot eat that fruit, beneath this sky or the other."

The king raised his hand. The music died away to a memory of sweetness and loss, the liùthion were gone; nothing was left to break the emptiness of snow and frost. All that remained was the wind upon the meadows, the soft and silent fall of snow upon the night. The piper shivered in the silence and the cold, because he was afraid, as he had never before been afraid, even on that longest day when the sun burned fierce and still above him.

The king bowed his head. His cloak was ragged and his feet bare but there were stars tangled in his hair. His voice was the wind rattling the birken tree. "As you desire. I do not take the unwilling. But, if you did not come to eat, why come here at midwinter when I cross the water to walk in the wild wood?"

"You know all the ways of all the men that ever walked beneath the sky. You know why I came to you." The piper held out his hands. The king took them in his own, cold hands and turned the palms face up that he might study them.

"Ask and I will answer." The king's voice was the snap of twigs upon a winter's night. "But think before you speak: remember that I make no promises, I offer no hope, I grant no boons and I make no bargains. What I am, I am."

The piper let out a long breath. His life hung before him, white mist in the black night. He asked, "What is left to me?"

"You live and breathe, you walk beneath the sun and moon."

"Why can I not come to my rest? The dead are dead. All else that lived to the long day's evening found peace in Ohmorah. But I? I lost my way, my hope, my name and still it is not enough!"

"For all things there is a price. That is the one you pay, piper from the gates of morning."

"I saw the rowan die; I saw the sun stand still at noontime, a red moon rising and fiery dancers setting the very wind to flame." The piper looked up into the king's pale face but could not meet his gaze and shut his eyes against it. Behind the blackness of closed eyes, he saw a flicker of sunlight across the green leaves of a rowan tree, a fall of golden hair. He heard a well-remembered song, rich and sweet as honeycomb on midsummer's day. He closed his mind against the memory and cried out, "After fire burned and water drowned, I made a balance this side of the sunset. All that I did that day was necessary."

The answer came back quick and hard. "Who are you to judge necessity? A balance made along the edge of a sword is no balance at all."

The piper's face twisted with anger or regret. "The lives and deaths of those in the waking world are no concern of yours!"

"You came to me to ask your questions, and I have answered. The truth is all I have to offer you."

"Then there is no hope left to me."

"You live and breathe, you walk upon the earth. All this is left to you and it must be enough."

"It is but half a life, walking across the years towards an unkind death."

"Yours is the only hand that shaped your fate." The king bent his head to study the hands he still held within his own. "You chose, and know the penalty of choice."

The piper snatched back his hands. He was never good to look upon but now he wore the face of a monster: hate sat on his brow and shame upon his cheek. He cried out, his anger spilling like steam from a boiling pot, "Allodola found peace, the Liùthion found love and Allocco is dead! I would trade all my freedom and my choices for any of these three."

The king said only, "Yet, even now, you seek to shape the future to one of your own choosing." His face was quiet and still, free from anger, and from love.

The piper bowed his head, his anger gone, his sorrow left to him. He thought and he remembered, and he said, "An I do not, all I have done before I did in vain. One choice leads on to others, and there never is an end."

"Death is the end of all things beneath your sky, piper from the gates of morning." The king turned away and his ragged cloak swung around him on the wind of the world and the wind not of the world. "Enough and more than enough of words. I am to my dancing and all who choose may join me."

He spread wide his hands. The sky around him was jewelled with starlight; the wind and the land and the empty air filled again with music and shadows. He danced and the kindred of the borderlands danced with him in the long night, and there were no boundaries between a dream and waking.

The piper watched, and let old memories rise through the years to the surface of his mind. Here and now, he knew how much he had feared and how greatly he had failed. Above his head, the winter trees, white and clean as last year's bones, stretched out their branches to the stars. A long, long while passed by before he turned away, limping back into the shadows towards the company of men.

VIII, Felluria: What purpose a beginning?

There was blood in the kitchen,
There was blood in the hall
There was blood in the parlour
Where my lady did fall.

Long Lankin, *Traditional*

The king has had his hunting and, in two great hearths, the midwinter fires burn and burn and drive back the dark. The doors are locked against the night, against the world and the wind; by torchlight and by firelight, the king of Eulana feasts, and his lords and captains feast with him. Between the fires, the blind harper plays the song he has made, a song of the king's strength and the king's will and of the beauty of Ketala Iitha for whose sake he made a devastation.

The door is locked; no one may come in this night, no one go out. Beyond is darkness, within is light. It was ever thus at midwinter: it is a night unlike all other nights. The pattern formed before this king.

But patterns unravel, patterns can be broken. There is a knock upon the wooden door.

The harper falls silent between two grace notes.

Another knock.

Men look, one to another, uncertain and uneasy.

The king stands up in his place.

Another knock.

Patterns shift and twist, flowing from one form into another.

Another knock, louder than all the ones before, and the king calls out, "Open the door!"

And, at his words, the pattern is broken.

The wind blows out of the night through the open door. Torches gutter, smoke swirls from the fires, men cough and splutter but the king stands straight, looking to the door and the figure standing in the doorway.

Her hair is black, her dress is torn, her feet are bare: she is a little ragged thing of no more moment than any woman in Eulana. As she steps forward and the door closes behind her, she puts back her hair from her face and, for a heartbeat, only for a heartbeat, the king sees a dead woman walking in his hall. He cries out, and if it is with joy or horror no man there can tell.

The moment passes, and he laughs, holding out his cup to toast the living. Men clap and whistle, knowing their king's dealings in Felluria, and a man who has drunk more than most blows a kiss as she passes. She walks down the length of the hall between the tables looking neither right nor left but only straight and level towards the king sitting in his place at the high table.

She stands before him. From beneath the rags of her cloak she pulls a net of apples and lets them spill across the table.

"A gift to you," she says, "from the orchards of Eulana."

The king picks an apple from the table. It is small in his great hand, its skin rosy in the torchlight. "There was a poor harvest from the orchards of Eulana."

"Surely a man of Lyikené does not forget that apple trees live on when many other things die and are lost from the world forever?"

He looks from the apple to her face. The captain beside him pulls at his sleeve. "My lord, you cannot trust her."

The king settles back into his seat, drinks his red wine. "Who spoke of trust? Seven years since, at the equinox, she set herself against me. That night I had the mastery."

The apple lies in the palm of his hand, sweet and ripe to eat. He strokes its smooth skin with his finger and offers it, smiling. She flinches from his hand. He tosses it to her, laughing to see she remembers all he taught her. "Eat!"

She eats the apple to its pips, her eyes never looking up into his face. "See," he says to his captain, "it is only an apple. Do you think I am afraid of a woman and an apple, here in my hall with armed men about me?"

There is a second apple lying on the table, a little golden apple shining in the light. The captain pulls at his sleeve again as the king reaches out to take it. "My lord, she is not a woman."

"She's shaped like a woman, and one full young and tender. I'll deal with her tonight as I did once at the equinox." Again, men's laughter rolls around the hall. The king calls out, "Is the door locked?"

A man calls back, "My lord, the door is locked and barred."

He says to her, "The door is locked." He says, "Tonight it will be as it was last time we were together. Midwinter's night," he says, smiling, "is very long."

She gasps and steps away. He laughs, and bites into the apple. Its flesh is sharp and sweet upon his tongue, very good to eat in that winter dark.

She has not smiled before but now a smile flickers across her face, bright as a little flame that strengthens as the light dies from his eyes.

The king blunders around his hall like a moth around a light and the darkness in his eyes is terrible to see, if only he had left her with pity enough to see it. But pity was not one of the things he taught her: she looks and laughs to see him so. Her laughter has no kindness in it, and much mockery. So had he laughed one grey morning as he unlocked a door to let her leave him. She laughs, and then she turns away towards the oaken door, but the door is locked and she does not have the key. The captain seizes her arm, a strong, hard grip she cannot break, and swings her round to face him.

"What did you do?"

She does not answer.

The captain strikes her hard across the face. "What did you do?"

She looks up, her cheek bleeding from the ring upon his finger, her lips bleeding where the blow mashed them against her teeth, and does not answer. He hits her again, harder than before. Only his hand holding her arm keeps her on her feet. She looks beyond him to the ruin she has made.

An apple rolls slowly 'cross the table. The captain puts out his hand to catch it; such a little thing, ripe and round and rosy. What could be sweeter than an apple in the winter's dark, or more innocent?

The captain has never walked beneath the other sky nor stood beneath the tree before the other king but he had his beginning in Lyikené and drank in tales of borderlands with his mother's milk. He says, "It was the apple."

The door is locked against the night, midwinter's night, the dark eye of the year. Without is darkness and softly falling snow; within is clamour and confusion, firelight falling on men's faces, reflected, shining, from their eyes; without is silence, within is madness. All that makes a man has been stripped away: his name, his self, his memory. Only the shell remains and soon it will be shattered. Men stand to face the monster, bronze swords ready in their hands. The captain draws in a long breath, sick and shaking that such things are possible, he who has spilled children's blood across the broken stones of Felluria and looked on unmoved as a man led a woman up a stair to darkness.

His hand reaches for his sword but never finds it. His king takes him, rending him with tooth and claw, ripping the soft flesh of his neck. His grip loosens on her arm as his blood washes over her, warm and red and reeking. He falls, cast aside like a broken puppet. She looks up into the face of a monster and sees again the man she knew.

Somewhere, behind him, out of sight, a man is screaming. So had a child screamed seven years since, wordless, empty, in the rain beyond the door. With a roar, he turns towards the screaming to finish what he has begun.

The men within the hall have knives and swords, but swords and knives do not serve them well. They have words and wits, but wits and words are nothing set against his blind desire. They have fear, and fear is their undoing. He strikes them down by one and two and three until he paddles ankledeep in blood about the hall. Blood on the walls, blood on the floor, blood spilling like wine across the table, blood pooling like water before the *fire. Even she, who has seen Felluria fall into ruin, has not thought there could be so much blood within the world. The world and the night are red, and that is all.*

He has sloughed his clothes as a snake its scales and wears no more than other men's blood over his skin. His face is wet, his teeth crusted, his red hair several shades darker than before. He is not a man, he is not a beast: there is no word for what he is except abomination. She stares into his yellow eyes, breathes in the reek of his bloody breath and waits, in an ecstasy of pain and rage, for him to kill her, a welcome, wanted end now she has had her vengeance.

And waits, and waits, until at last she realises what this waiting means, and laughs because she cannot weep, peal after peal of dreadful, ringing laughter, looking into the future she has made, from hatred and from vengeance, in place of all the things that might have been: the sweet taste of apple on her tongue, the song of stone and star, the quiet king's cold embrace, the neverending dream of borderlands.

Later, later, in the time before the morning, the only screaming in the hall is hers. All other tongues are silent; all other eyes stare and stare and do not see. No tales will be told of this night, no songs be sung. She twists and struggles, her nails and teeth of as much moment against his thrusts as scratches torn by briars. What purpose all her strength and all her will when thrice she has set herself against him and thrice he has had the mastery?

Midwinter's night is very long, much darkness, little light. Sated with death, satisfied by flesh, he pads the hall. The floor is slick and shiny, dark pools in the shadows, bright as spilled wine in the lamplight. The door is old oak, locked and barred. The key lies nearby, fallen from a dead man's hand, red with a dead man's blood. A man might ask for a door to be opened or else set key to lock. He is a man no longer. Neither flesh nor oak has strength to stand against him—as well keep back the tide with a wall of sand. He smashes it, easy as a child trampling a castle on the shore, and slips away into midwinter's night. For a little while his footsteps are a pattern pressed in frost, tracing the way into the dark. But not for long. Soon all that is left is silence, the softly falling snow.

She sits hunched in her pain before the dying fire, sticky and stinking with dead men's blood. She has not thought of life beyond this night. This was the end, as far as thought could think: an apple sweet upon the tongue with oblivion seeded at its core. For this night, she crossed into the borderlands; for this night, she stole an apple; for this night, she said the quiet king, No! All this were done to make an ending: what purpose a beginning? The weight of the future presses upon her, cold and heavy as clay upon a corpse.

There are knives a-plenty scattered 'cross the floor. She balances a dagger in her hand and tries its point against her throat. Death is only darkness and silence: no thought, no pain, no memory. So much harder to live, to turn her face to the sunrise and know the day will come, and another after it, and another, and another, that all the days the dead will never see are hers to live and to remember. She is not old, not even in the reckoning of women, but she has seen death many times: red petals floating on a dark drink, red blood dripping from a bronze sword, red flames flowering on a ruin. Each time it has passed her by and left her desolate.

Her hand trembles, firelight playing along the edge of the bronze blade. In a little while she sets it down upon the hearthstone. She does not have the strength to drive it home. What she is, she is, and what she is, he showed her. She presses her hands across her eyes and the cracks of colour spread and shatter her darkness, bright as firestar upon a stone wall.

9: A white-haired boy

She sho'd me a cup o' the good red gowd,
Well set wi' jewels sae fair to see;
Says, "Gin ye will be my lemman sae true
This gudely gift I will you gie."

Alison Gross, Traditional

Assiolo woke, naked between silken sheets, in a room he did not know. The room was flooded with sunlight and, beyond the open window, a blackbird was singing in the garden. He sat up and stared all around him, he held out his hand to touch the hangings of the bed and the panelled wood upon the wall, then lay back in despair because all he saw was real and none of it Felluria.

In a while he heard a bell in the distance tolling out the time. He listened, counting, and found it was the first hour of the second. A little time again and the door opened. A voice he did not know said, in a tongue he had not heard spoken, "Good morning, my lord. My name is Gru. I am come to make you ready for the day."

"How long has it been?" he asked in the same language.

"In the world beyond the walls?" Assiolo nodded. "Five years, my lord, or thereabouts."

"This is not my place."

"Yet you are here, my lord, and I am sent to make you ready," said Gru. "I will obey my order."

He sat up so he could stare across the room at the man. "I am in a place I do not know, Gru, brought to it without consultation or consent. I am in no mood to be treated as a child. If I ask, will you answer?"

"No, my lord. It is not my place or part to answer." Gru set pitchers of hot water and cold upon the marble table and laid out a pair of razors and a dish of soft soap beside them. He took clean towels from a chest and chose clothes from the wardrobe and spread them close to hand. "Rise now, my lord, and let me make you ready."

"Whose servant are you?"

Gru did not answer. He stood waiting near the bed. In the flesh of his right arm there was a brand and the device of the brand was the sun and the moon. Seeing this, Assiolo made no more protest. He got up out of the bed and let Gru drape a robe around him. He let himself be washed and shaved, he let himself be dressed in linen and in silk, and all the time he searched back through his mind for the means to make sense of what he saw. For this was a place that echoed Ohmorah but was not Ohmorah, this was a place where men were slaves yet had faces like to the First People, who had fled their foundering land the day the gates of morning closed.

When he was dressed, Assiolo held out his hand. "Give me my ring, Gru."

"I know no ring, my lord."

"My ring with the cornelian seal."

"I know no ring, my lord."

"If I am here, then so too is my ring. I want it back." He heard his words ring out lordliwise and arrogant. He would not have spoken so to any man in Felluria but this was not Felluria. There were other rules here, and he must be another man. Gru gave no further answer. He only stepped away to open the door and wait patiently until Assiolo was ready to follow where he led.

Assiolo followed Gru down hallways laid with carpets. He passed pictures and statues, saw how doors and windows were set to display a view of gardens and of flowers. There was nothing in Felluria to match this place for beauty or for luxury. Here was dressed stone and polished wood; here, he saw, a room might be decorated to display a single perfect piece of pottery or glass. He had been brought up in rooms like these, in houses built in the east by exiles lonely for their lost land.

There were many people here, men and women about their tasks within these walls. All were young and strong, all fair, all with the sun and the moon burned into their arms; all turned their heads or bowed their eyes as he walked by that they might not be seen to look at him and those that were closest drew away so his shadow would not fall upon them.

Gru led him through a great domed library lined with rising rings of books and ladders that slid along the shelves to reach them. When he had been a boy in Ohmorah, Assiolo had known such places, and the books within them. That was long ago and far away. He had become a man, and come out of the east, and left such things behind. Since then, he had learnt many things, of the world and of himself, but none of them from books. There was no library filled with the writings of a vanished world within the stone walls of Felluria. But Gru did not let him linger in the library. He led him on and out into the morning air, down paths of fine hewn stone beneath the flowering trees.

A woman waited in a garden of white roses. She wore a gown the colour of the summer sky and her golden hair flowed free, lapping her in a shining mantle.

"Eat, drink and be welcome, Assiolo, Allocco's son of Ohmorah. You will find in Faranon all that you desire." She held out her hands, offering wine within a silver cup and bread upon a silver platter.

Assiolo shook his head, wise to such a trap. "Madam," he said, "I will not eat, I will not drink, and I will take no welcome of you."

He looked at the roses, he looked down at the green grass and up towards the sky but he would not look at her. The woman gave the cup and plate to Gru who took them and stood aside to wait until he should be needed.

"Oh, Assiolo, Assiolo, did not your father teach you courtesy?" Her voice was light and laughing, a teasing caress upon his ear. "You might look on me even as you refuse me."

He flushed like a child rebuked. Against his judgement, he looked her in the face and caught his breath in a hard gasp to feel the lightning strike. Desirable in every way, this lady, warm and ripe as summertime. Assiolo flushed again rose-red, a man this time, and stepped back in confusion, his heart a-thunder, his blood pounding in his ears, ashamed that flesh should be so weak before her smiling gaze. He called his own true love to mind, conjuring her sweetness and her trust, the promises he had made her.

The woman waited, lovely in her garden, until such time as he stilled his blood and calmed his breathing.

Recovering his poise, he told her, "Madam, I know not your name. But by your deeds I know you. You have taken me from my home and from my love, brought me as I must think great distance across the sea to a place that reeks of an accurséd land. So, though I do not know your name, I know enough to have no trust in your fair face or your fair welcome."

Her red lips curved into a smile, lighting her face as sunrise lights the eastern sky. "The time will come, Assiolo, when you take what is offered you. Then you will eat and you will drink and you will take your welcome."

"From your hand, madam?"

"Perhaps from my hand, perhaps from another. Time will show." She bent towards a rose tree. The trees were without a thorn, the roses they bore were white as snow, perfect as any flower can be but that they had no scent. Such roses had grown in his father's garden when he was a boy. She picked a rose and tucked it in her hair. "As to my name, it is told easily enough. I am Averla. There is no secret to it; use it as you will, Assiolo."

That was the answer to make sense of all he saw. He turned away, saying, "Knowing your name, madam, gives me no more trust in you than I had in my ignorance. Let you know this: I am Allocco's son – in that I had no choice. But in all else I have a choice, and so I say this clearly: I will not serve your purpose for all Allocco was my father. You'll not use me as you used him."

Assiolo walked away across the garden. It was a lovely place to wander on a summer's morning, full of rare trees and flowers to delight his eyes and many birds to sing in all the branches. He found pools of clear water and saw golden fish swimming beneath waterlilies. None of this could gladden him. It was to him not so fair a sight as the heather moor beneath Cal Mora and not a flower in it could match a single harebell on those slopes. He searched a long while for a gate but, though he found the wall around the place, and followed it the circuit round, he did not come to any gate nor could he climb the wall.

Beneath an apple tree, Assiolo cried out his true love's name, calling out across the distance and the years. His cry slipped away into the sunlight. She was not there to answer and he could not pass these walls to keep his promise.

At last he retraced his way along those paths and found again the garden of white roses where Averla waited, smiling.

"All that is here, is mine," she told him. "Why do you think you should be different from the rest?"

Assiolo thought, *What gives you joy?* His love was strong in him as he answered, "I gave myself to another. There is nothing left for you."

He did not know why she should smile, why she should laugh, but laugh she did, most merrily, and her laughter blew away on the breeze across the garden.

"Let me tell you what she is, your black-haired love." Averla placed her hand upon his arm to draw him down beside her. "She is the Tion of Felluria."

"That I knew before I knew her."

"Did you, Assiolo? There are no Tions in Ohmorah. She has a woman's face, she has a woman's body but she is no woman. She cannot weep, she cannot age, she cannot give a hope of harvest – you sow your seed on barren ground."

"Madam, tell me a thing I do not know and I shall stay to listen. She is the beginning and the end of all my desires."

"Oh, Assiolo, Assiolo, did you think you knew her?" Smiling, Averla asked, "Did she not tell you what she did, your own true love? Tell me, Assiolo, when you woke that morning in the sallows, when you found yourself the only man to have got his sense back from the winter sickness, did you think it was a white dog's foot beneath your pillow or a bundle of moon herbs burned in your chamber brought you back to her?"

He remembered a voice asking, *What brings you sorrow?* His blood pounded out the answer. The sunlight swirled and darkened; the chitter of birdsong was dull and distant. The world shrank down to two blue eyes and one red mouth that asked him, "She did not say that she had made a bargain? I gave you back your life that night and in return she gave me what I wanted. She was so afraid of losing you to death, your black-haired love, she did not stop to think that you could live, and still be lost to her.

"She knew it later, and yet she kept her bargain. There was a night, Assiolo – surely you can remember – when she slipped from your bed to let me slip into the space she'd left beside you."

He cried out, "That cannot be true!" but even as he spoke, he remembered a dream of honeyed wine and the scent of elderflowers, of golden hair and strange, sweet caresses.

"Marwy Ninek knew what she did, she knew what I wanted, and yet she gave you to me. That night was only the beginning." Averla's voice was soft and honeysweet, a whisper in his ear. "The third question, Assiolo: you need know regret no longer. Here you will find your heart's desire."

He fled from her. As he passed through the halls and chambers, he glimpsed, never full on, only from the edges of his eyes, the armsmen clad in blue and steel, their swords naked in their hands. Back in the bedchamber, he shut the window and closed up the shutters to keep the sunlight from him. He turned to the door and found it had no lock. It was of no matter. A lock would keep no one out that wanted to come in. He lay down upon the bed to sleep but, when he woke, he was still there, alone.

Assiolo stripped himself and sat naked in the dark. He would not move; he did not speak. Three times each day, Gru came with food and drink; three times each day, Gru carried the untouched plates away. The days were long and the nights were terrible, crazed by dreams that did not fade on waking. Often he sobbed aloud, crying like a child afraid of the dark; often he pressed his hands across his eyes that they would not see, over his ears that they would not hear.

On the evening of the third day, Assiolo lay down upon the bed, being now so weak and silly with thirst he could neither stand nor sit. The dreams pressed down upon him but they were no longer terrible. He could hear distant voices calling him away into the dark and held out his hands that they might come closer.

He woke from fever-dreams to Gru's touch upon his shoulder. The man held a wooden cup to his mouth.

Assiolo turned away, cracked lips gasping out his whisper. "I will not eat, I will not drink and I will not be bound."

"The cup is rowan wood," Gru whispered, his words so faint they were no more than a flutter of breath against his ear. "I filled it from a running stream. If you drink it will not bind you."

Assiolo moved his lips against the cup and Gru let a trickle of water run into his mouth. "Little now," he warned, "more later."

When he had drunk half the cup, Assiolo lay back against the sheets. "Will you suffer for this?"

"If I do, it is of no matter, my lord."

Water, and the thought behind the hand that offered it, drove back his death enough that he could think. He thought but thinking changed nothing, and still he would not eat. He would not let himself be bound; better to toss away this life Averla had given like the worthless thing it was.

In the morning, Gru came to him with the cup refilled. When Assiolo had drunk, he said, "Water is good but it is not enough. You must eat."

"Why do you care if I live?"

"Because you are needed."

"I am not a bird to live on rowan berries. All else that is here, is hers." Assiolo turned his face to the wall. "I am her captive but I do not choose to make myself her slave."

He heard the door close, leaving him alone with his thoughts and memories until, in the evening, Gru came again with the cup. This time, when he had drunk, he said, "There is a way, my lord, if you will trust me."

Assiolo raised his head and looked at him. He trusted no one in this place, though Gru had brought water in a cup of rowan wood and given him a little time to think in freedom. He had not asked if it had been Gru's mind behind that act, and Gru had not told.

"I'll do only what is necessary. Tell me your way. If it seems good to me I'll follow it – trust is of no matter."

"Very well, my lord. You must wash yourself and dress, and come with me."

He tried to stand but had to hold the bedpost to keep upright. Like a child, he let Gru wash and dress him. Then, leaning on his arm, he walked slowly along the corridors of Averla's house past the half-seen armsmen. This time Gru led him up wide stairs and down hallways painted with a parade of animals. All the creatures that walked or ran or crept upon the land were there, and many more besides. Gru stopped before a doorway.

"Will you go in, my lord?"

"In such a place as this, only when the door is opened, and I've seen what lies within, can I answer such a question."

Gru smiled and opened the door. Across the floor was a litter of toys and clothes, of wooden bears and building blocks and painted carts; a rocking horse stood by one wall, its mane and tail tangled with coloured ribbons, and a perfect little playhouse against another. A second room opened from the first, divided from it by an arch, and there a white-haired boy sat at supper with his nurse. Each stared to see the men standing in the doorway.

"Will you go in, my lord?" asked Gru. "You cannot fear a woman and a child."

The child stood up from the table and walked towards him, curious and unafraid. "Who are you?"

Assiolo saw brown eyes beneath pale hair looking up into his face and clutched at Gru, whose arm held him firm and steady. He knew the child's face well. A face like this had looked out from a portrait in his father's house, a painting of a child who had died in flame or wave long before he had been born. All the love and hope his father had had in him died with him on that day – there had been none left for any of the sons born in his exile.

"Who are you?" the child demanded. "Who is this, Gru? Does my mother know him?"

Assiolo said, "I am your father." But he could say no more before the darkness sucked him in and only Gru's strength kept him from pitching headlong to lie at his son's feet.

When he woke, he found himself lying on the child's narrow bed and the boy seated on the floor beside him.

"Why did you fall down?" he asked.

Assiolo answered, "Because I have not eaten in the days since I came here."

"Oca!" his son called out, lordliwise, and his nurse looked round. "Oca, bring food for my father!"

She looked at what was on the table. There was roast duck, creamed turnip and peas cooked in their pods. She shook her head at it, seeing Assiolo lying pale and wan, still too weak to stand unaided, and instead filled a bowl with junket and poured out a cup of milk. The boy took them from her and sat down on the bed beside him. "Will you eat this?"

He was far from his home and his love had betrayed him. Even his life was not his own. Assiolo looked at the boy beside him and the third question echoed in his mind, *What do you regret?* Then he took what was offered him, and ate.

There was a light step in the room, a rustle of silken skirts. "Mother!" cried the boy and ran towards Averla. She lifted him, and blue eyes and brown looked smiling down at Assiolo. "Did I not say that you would eat, and you would drink? Welcome to Faranon, Assiolo."

Assiolo did not answer. He set down the spoon and empty bowl upon the floor and looked beyond her to Gru who stood in the shadow by the door and would not meet his eye. Then he forced himself to stand and face her. "I am bound, madam, but not to you. I took food and drink from my son's hand, and from him I'll take my welcome."

-⼗— —⼗-

Marwy Ninek sat, wrapped in her dark grief. She did not smile, she could not weep and she knew no comfort. Four times midwinter had come, four times it had passed and this was the fifth year she had sat each night at supper with an empty place beside her. Yet little else had changed because a man was gone: the music played, the fires burned and lamps were lit against the dark while all around her in her hall made merry on midwinter's night.

She did not hear the music, the food was ashes in her mouth and the wine sour in her cup. All around were many men's faces in the lamplight, some were old and some were young, some were fair and some were foul and none was Assiolo's. She sat and watched the night go by, she spoke when she was spoken to, and elsewise she was silent.

Beyond the hall, the wind blew hard and, out of the wildness of midwinter's night, came the rap-rapping of a hand upon the door. She started up with a wild cry as the great oak door opened to let the cold wind of midwinter blow in. Between one heartbeat and the next, every lamp within the hall was quenched, and each fire was dead in its hearth, and cold starlight shone upon the stone. The hall stood empty, her door wide open to the night, and a man waited at the threshold, a pale-faced stranger in a ragged cloak holding out his empty hands.

"What is it?" Baesina Yatta's fingers clutched her arm, drawing her back into the warmth and firelight.

Marwy Ninek looked right, and she saw the flames dancing in the hearths; she looked left, and saw the folk of Felluria laughing in the lamplight; she looked straight ahead and saw the door was locked. As surely as the hall was full of light and warmth and song and fellowship was the door locked.

"Nothing," she answered, sitting down again in her place, shaking her head against such foolishness. "A trick of the light."

She lifted her cup of wine to drink and drive such sights away. A shepherd played his pipe, another beat out the rhythm on his bodhrán, singing a song made so long ago its words had shed their meaning. Her thoughts slid away into the past: another midwinter and Assiolo in the musician's place before the middle hearth, the sweet tumble of notes falling from his lute, his brown eyes smiling as he sang.

Again, the rap-rap upon the door. Marwy Ninek put down her wine. The wind blew wild, the door blew open. She stood and looked neither right nor left but only straight ahead to see the open door, the starlight on the stone and the quiet king waiting on the threshold. And, at that sight, she rose up from her seat and walked towards him.

"Is it true," she asked, "tonight all lands are borderlands?"

His whisper was the rustle of wind through the bracken on the hillside. "For those that have the ears to hear or the eyes to see. I cannot come in, Thelis Ketala. Will you come out, or are you yet afraid?"

What need had he to ask it? All the years since Torùkotu came out of the west she had been afraid. She was afraid of her past and of her future, she was haunted by all she had done and all she had left undone, but him she did not fear. She stepped lightly across her threshold; she put her hand into the king's and together they walked in the frost and the starlight in borderlands between Felluria and the sea.

"The tree is bare," he told her, offering an apple, "the harvest has been gathered and the leaves blew away on the wind. Will you take me for your king and dance with me, and forget your loves and sorrows in your dancing?"

Even in the borderlands love and sorrow weighed heavy on her heart. But, though she cried out for Assiolo with all her love and breath and life, her shout was a little thing that died away to nothing in the silent night. He was not there; another stood in his place beside her. She reached out, seeking an end to sorrow in the sweet taste of apple. The liùthion gathered at the edges of her eyes, whirling and swirling on the edge of vision, their hair tossing like smoke upon the wind. They danced upon the empty air, free of time and flesh and memory. They had no more substance than a dream; neither love nor hatred bound them to the waking world. As they were, so could she be. But, even as she took the apple from the king, she remembered a song sung at midsummer in a garden of red roses.

She opened her hand and let the apple fall upon the frozen ground. Though her sorrows tore like rosethorns at her heart, she would not give them up: some things should never be forgotten. "I'll take nothing from you, not even an end to sorrow," she cried out to the wind and starlight. "Assiolo would not dance with you, and nor will I."

The liùthion were gone away into a dream; the king's voice was
the snap and crack of ice beneath her feet. "The choice you made
is the choice you must live with. An you do not join me, you must
dance to another's music beneath another sky. There are others there
to dance with you – three kings to weave the pattern of the future."

She had no care for kings. Her mind was filled only by Assiolo,
his smile, his touch, his love. She asked, "Will I have my love again?"

His laughter was the ripple of water against the empty shore, the
starlight falling on the sea. "How your dance will end I cannot tell: I
do not call the tunes in the waking world and so I'll tell no lies and
make no promises. *Perhaps* is all I'll say." He bowed his head and
kissed her brow with his cold lips. "Go carefully, Thelis Ketala: I do
not ask three times and so we will not meet again. If you cross the
water, you'll not find me waiting 'neath the tree."

Memory lapped at her mind. "Beneath that tree, you gave me a
warning."

"Beneath that tree, I told you many things. All of them were true.
So too is this true: there is but one end beneath your sky."

She clenched her hands within her sleeves. What need had he to
tell her this? All she had ever done came from that bitter knowledge.
She asked, "Why did you come to me?"

The king was not gone but he no longer wore the likeness of a
man. He spoke out of the silence of midwinter's night, hard as the
stone, cold as the frost, terrible as the darkness after the light, "I
came to ask what I have asked and say what I have said. Now I am
to my dancing."

—+— —+—

Since he had eaten he was become a part of this place. Still Assiolo
took great care he should eat only with his son and take nothing
from Averla's hand. He would not be bound to her more tightly than
he must be. Yet every day and every night he woke and ate and
slept within her walls and so, though he was not yet a slave like Gru,
with the sun and the moon burned into his flesh, he was no longer
free. He could walk for hours within the gardens and never find the
gate. He could try every door in this great and lovely house and,
though none was locked to him, none led outside unless it was into
that garden. But, within these limits that she set on him, he could
do as he pleased and so mostly he spent his days within the library,
where each book he read he made him more his father's son.

Once, this thought was too strong in his mind and he put down
the books and paced the circle of the library and tried to think only
of Marwy Ninek, her smile, her touch, her love. And yet – he stared
blindly into the light falling from the window high above – even as

she kissed him she had kept her secret. Then Assiolo opened up the books again and sat reading late into the night. All his hope of freedom lay between their pages and so he read, filling his mind with others' words until the time that he could find his own.

Some days, he carried books into the garden. On such a day, he stretched out in the shade beneath a beech tree, puzzling out the meaning of a text written in a dead tongue. He heard a step on stone and looked up to see Averla walking with her son towards him. He stood, ready and wary, at the sight. This was no chance meeting – no deed of Averla's was ever left to chance.

"You eat beside Alcedo at his table, Assiolo, you take your food from his plate and drink from out his cup," Averla said. "But that aside, you say no word to him nor yet seek him out except to serve yourself."

"Madam, what should I say? He is a fine boy; the only thing I've seen in all your house that does you credit." Assiolo stared into her eyes and hated her. Each time they met a wild desire rose up in him to set himself against her and now he had found a means by which to do it. He said, "I do not like the name you gave him, madam, and I will have it changed to one of my choosing."

"He was named to honour you," Averla answered, and he knew she mocked him. "Alcedo is an old name of your family – your own brother's name."

Assiolo looked at the boy. In truth, he had not thought before this moment of the naming of a son of whose birth he had not known nor wanted. Even now, he only held in his mind the knowledge that here was a small victory to be won. He said, "Madam, it is for the father to name a son. I do not like your choice and so my son shall bear another name. He will be Imacah."

"Imacah!" Averla spat back the word, and he smiled that she was angry.

"It is a name of great renown and glory. The day the gates of morning closed, Imacah mor Tamarhak bore willingly the weight laid on him after the fire and the flood."

To his surprise, he felt the boy put his small hand in his and heard him whisper, but not so soft his mother could not hear, "I want to be Imacah."

Assiolo drew the boy to his side and the pair of them faced her together. "You made me a father, madam, and I say my son shall be named for the man who kept his word that day, when all the world came close to ruin."

She stared that they should defy her. Assiolo watched, seeing her consider them and choose her battles. She said at last, "It is a little thing, Assiolo, one word rather than another: let it be so."

The boy called out, "Mother!" as she turned to leave them. Averla paid no heed, striding away towards the house. The child moved against Assiolo's arm to follow her and he let him go, thinking the boy ashamed because he had set himself against her. He had no desire to keep him against his will.

Assiolo sat down on the stone rim of the fishpond and watched the fishes circling round and round. He dabbled his hands in the water but they would not come to him. He thought over and again of what he had done; each time the memory pleased him and, more than that, that he had had the mastery of Averla, even within her own walls. What he could do once, he could do again.

In a little while he heard quick footsteps on the path towards him. The boy flung himself hard into his arms and clung to him so that he must hold him, awkward and unaccustomed, whilst he sobbed against his chest.

When he could speak, the boy said, "She is very angry."

"Very angry," he agreed, setting the boy beside him and wiping his face with the corner of his shirt, "but with me far more than with you. She loves you, and she does not love me."

His son looked up at him with great hurt eyes. "She sent me away! She would not answer me!"

Ashamed, Assiolo said, "I am sorry. It was wrong of me to use you in this way. I was angry but you should not have to suffer for my anger. If you wish to please her, she shall have her way and you shall be still Alcedo."

The boy shook his head. "I like your choice better."

"In truth, if you are certain, I think it is the better name. No doubt I shall suffer for it later but I think it worth the price."

They sat in silence. After a while, because he could think of nothing else to say and wished to be alone, Assiolo made a boat of a twig and two leaves and gave it to the boy to sail upon the fishpond. He picked up his book again but felt the boy's hand pull at his sleeve. "Will you tell me the story of my name?"

And in the sunlight of Faranon, in the garden of his enemy, Assiolo told the tale of Imacah mor Tamarhak, who had given up his love, and his hope, and all his future, to be the king and keep the balance and guard the firstborn tree beneath this sky. When he was done, he did not think to take up his book again.

They made two fleets of ships to sail across the pond. Then laughing, each whipped up the water into waves so that his own would sail and the other's sink. At the evening they walked back along the path together, each much stained with mud and pond water and each well pleased with the other's company.

But at the door, Averla waited, lovely in the sunlight. She held out her hands and Assiolo watched as the boy ran into them and saw her smiling as she kissed the pale, bright hair.

Here, every day was like the one before and always it was midsummer. The sun rose in the morning, and the sun set at night, and the light lingered long after its setting until the full moon rose to pass over the garden and all the pools and paths were bright with reflected light. All the days were like Averla herself, shining and lovely, an eternal summer. Always, there were white roses flowering in her garden; each day, the wind blew through the leaves of rowan, and of apple trees, whose fruit was set though never ripe. But there were strawberries aplenty, ripe and red and ready.

Assiolo sat in the shade of the beech tree and, nearby, his son was playing hopscotch in the garden. He had made a gardener mark out a ladder on one of the stone paths and now cast stones to see where he must hop. As he played, Assiolo heard him chant in rhythm to his jumping,

> "Three kings beneath the tree are seen,
> Of day and night and might have been.
> But day and night fill dark and light
> There is no time for might have been."

"What is that song?" he asked.

The boy skipped and jumped and answered, "Oca sang it when I was a baby." He went back to his game.

> "The red king, black king and the green
> Say was, was not and might have been.
> I know what's what, I know what's not
> I'll never know what might have been.

> "Three kings beneath the bone-bare tree
> Say will, will not and it might be!
> If I do what another will not
> Can you tell me what might have been?"

Assiolo picked up his book and walked back towards the house. When he had been a child he had played that game and sung that song, giving it no more thought than his son did now. Now his neck pricked with its meaning.

Next time Assiolo met Averla within her garden of white roses, she smiled at him and pinned a flower to his coat. He plucked it off at once, dropping it upon the path to crush it with his foot, and asked, "Why did you bring me here?"

"Because I wanted you, Assiolo. What I want, I take. Your son is the proof of it." Averla took his hand and, at that touch, his body remembered her. He flushed with shame and cast down his eyes; laughing, soft and sweet as a breeze on a summer's day, she told him, "Anytime I want you, Assiolo, I have only to hold out my hand."

Assiolo made no move, he said no word but the air between them snapped like lightning and thunder. Sparks crackled in her golden hair and Averla stepped back as if he had struck her. "Not quite, madam," he told her. "In Felluria, I was only Assiolo and undefended. Here I am become again Allocco's son and can arm myself against you."

"Assiolo, not Imacah mor Tamarhak himself could arm himself against me. Do not think, because you have not drunk from my cup nor eaten at my table, that you are free. In my beginning I was light, and fire, and air, the sun that never set." She leaned, smiling, towards him. "Oh, Assiolo, Assiolo, did you believe it was for no more than a night time's pleasure and a bright-haired boy I drove your death from you?"

"What reason, then?"

"You're not a fool, Assiolo, do not behave like one," she chided. "Only a man can cross the water, only a man can be the king beneath the tree, only a man can close the gates of evening." Averla's laughter was the flicker of sunlight through the leaves. "I am many things, Assiolo, but I am not a man."

His mouth twisted into a little smile. "And I am many things, madam, but I am not a king."

She smiled, indulgently, as if he were a foolish child. "Surely you remember what my brother told you? *He who kills the king is the king.* In the west, Assiolo, as in Eulana."

Memory gripped his heart, cold words in a cold wood. The quiet king was all Averla was not; his the tongue that could not lie.

Averla said, echoing the tales told in his boyhood, "The piper made the king in the west to hold the world in balance, a man of bronze and blood and fire with an apple in one hand and a sword in the other." For a moment there was silence in the garden. "But a balance," said Averla, smiling and lovely in the midst of white roses, "can be broken. It has been said many times before, Assiolo: all men must die."

"Save I, madam, it seems, since it pleased you to give me back my life."

She leaned in close and stroked his face, almost as if she loved him. "You may die, Assiolo, if you wish, when you have done what I ask of you, when you have closed the gates of evening to make a day last forever, finishing what your father started. You may choose death but what need for death in such a world? I will make little darkness and much light, world without end this side of the sunset."

Assiolo shook his head. Better to hang himself from the branches of the firstborn tree than be a man such as his father. Averla saw his answer in his face and drew him down beside her. She said, gently, holding his hands as if he was a child, "There was so much you could have done, so much you might have been. But you took Marwy Ninek to your heart, and she gave you to me. You killed one king for her sake; you'll kill another for mine."

Assiolo counted out a hundred heartbeats, putting a little space of time between them. "I killed a monster but you'd make me a murderer, and that I will not be. I have no quarrel with Te-Meriku." He looked up, meeting her blue eyes. Their light dazzled him but he would not this time turn away. He measured out his words, shaping them in his mind and mouth into strong, hard stones to build his future. "My will, madam, is all my own, for all I live the life you gave me, and I care not one whit for your desire. I am not my father and I will not serve. All I desire lies within the stone walls of Felluria."

A ripple of laughter sweet as summer breezes. "Then why do you linger in this place?"

"Because I cannot find the door!"

"And you your father's son!" Averla laughed. "When you've made your choice you'll find the door, Assiolo, easily enough. Which will it be, your lover or your son?"

Loud and clear he gave his answer, to let his words give substance to the thought, "I love Marwy Ninek before all else in the world, madam, and far above this son I neither knew nor wanted."

"Do you, Assiolo? But what do you regret?" Averla smiled, and, with that smile, his little strength was gone; he could no more close his eyes against this smile than his ear against her words. His eyes saw the woman standing in the garden but, behind his eyes, the light burned and burned and blinded him. "I have watched you, Assiolo," she whispered, "far longer than you know. Your heart is tender for all your learning and your will. I've given you your heart's desire, plucked from the realm of might have been: your son that you thought never would be born. He gave you water, and you drank; he gave you food and you ate, turning back into the world for sake of him."

"A son no son! That is a child that should never have been born!"

"When you were asked, *What gives you joy?* you answered; when asked, *What gives you sorrow?* again you answered, without a pause or doubt. But the third you would not answer. Why was that, Assiolo? What did you regret so much you would not name it, even to yourself?"

That was the thought he would not think, the question he would not answer. Assiolo bowed his head, and slipped away into the sunlight of the garden. And yet, although he walked the wall thrice round, still he could not find the gate.

-+— —+-

"The piper's found his way back into the haunts of men," said the fat mercatman. The king looked up from his wine, his question on his face. "I came on him in Anach, his back against the mercatstone and his hat set out for ludgings, playing that pipe as if he were no more than any other beggar."

"How'd he look?" growled Thodùhah.

"In face and form just as he's always looked. Well, save for his eyes. Were he a man, I'd say he had bad dreams." Edo Incithu paused to drink, as Thodùhah spat into the fire. "He'd a message for you, Te-Meriku," he said, after a moment, "and a gift."

From his pocket he pulled two slips of birken bark bound together with a strand of blue wool and laid it on the table before the king. Te-Meriku unwound the thread and lifted the upper slip away to reveal a single dried flower. Its colour had long faded, vanished like the spark of life itself, but the five-petalled shape of lithia could not be mistaken for any other kind.

"And the message?" asked the king, laying the flower in its bark bed aside very gently. So old a thing, so fragile and so delicate, would fall to pieces at a careless touch.

"Only a question: *What is Marwy Ninek to you?*"

The king stared and then he laughed, short and hard. "Nothing at all for her own sake. Does he think me Assiolo to find charm in a trembling glance and a quivering look? But I'll use her 'gainst Averla if I can – even if it means using one lover's heart against the other."

"Four years I've seen her since he left," said the mercatman, "and always she asks if I've had news along the way. Often and often, seeing her face, I've wished I had some tale might offer comfort."

"Where Assiolo is she knows full well," Te-Meriku said grimly. "And that he lives. From that knowledge she can take her comfort. There's none elsewhere."

"If you'd shape her to your hand," said Thodùhah, his eyes fixed on the flower, "best teach her first the difference between the dead king and the living. If she thinks you Torùkotu come again, she's scarce like to take your part against her lover, no matter what Averla's made of him."

"Oh, what I can, I'll do," Te-Meriku answered. "I'll show her a riverbank near Habhain. An end and a beginning." He drank up his wine and pushed back his chair. "I'll bid you both goodnight. It's a fair, fine evening and I'm away to clear my head upon the hillside."

Ardùvai fell in beside him as he stepped from his hall into the gloaming.

"I've known limpets with a looser grip than yours," the king said, taking the path along the shore. "I suppose, if I say you're not needed, you'll answer that you're my nightwatch."

Ardùvai's laughter rang out into the evening. "And so I will, Te-Meriku. So save your breath for walking."

For a while their path followed the top of the shore and small stones rattled 'neath their feet. The breeze was full of the clean smell of saltwater, tempered with the tang of seaweed at the highwatermark. Far down the shore, the little waves of a retreating tide brushed and whispered against the shingle, slapping the sides of dragonships. Seabirds called and whistled in the halflight and Ardùvai paused a little time to watch an oystercatcher flying fast and low along the tideline, thrilling to hear it call out, sweet and plaintive, to its mate. A rush of wings and a second bird followed, disappearing into the distance and the dark.

But if the king marked such sights he showed no sign of it. He walked on with even pace as the evening thickened around him. Near the humpbacked rock, where the ground rose softly from the beach and a little stream ran down from the hill, he turned inland to walk beside the water across turf cropped short by rabbits and by sheep. The nightwatch quickened his step to catch him and the two went on together. Behind them the indigo of the eastern sky was patterned bright and, even in the west, the stars were pricking into life in the time after the sunset.

"When we were boys," said the king, quietly, "Imacah and I, we dreamed of sailing forever and a day into the west beyond the west."

Ardùvai's surprise was clear in his sidelong glance towards Te-Meriku. "When we were boys, Almecu and I," he answered, lightly, "we thought of little more than besting each other in any way we could. Near seven years, I've had the upper hand and now you've gone and given him a place beneath your sail and there's all again to play for."

The king laughed softly and continued on his way. After a while, the grass beneath their feet gave way to heather. Te-Meriku looked neither right towards the stream nor left towards his nightwatch but only ahead towards the western stars, the hawk rising to hang above the hillside, and neither spoke again, either of the past or of the present.

They had walked an hour, perhaps a little less, beside the stream, their eyes accustomed to the night and their ears filled with the sound of running water, when Te-Meriku stopped beside a tangled patch of briar and bramble. "Thus far and no further, Ardùvai. Go back; take a girl to bed or drink a man under the table. I'll come to no harm the other side the water."

Stubbornly, Ardùvai shook his head. "I gave my word by land and sea. That does not change because it is the equinox."

"Bide here then, if you must," Te-Meriku conceded, "but I'll have this night alone, unwatched."

He unbuckled his sword and laid it down upon the bank, setting his knives beside it, and leapt across the water, then walked up the hill towards the firstborn tree. Ardùvai watched him go, hunching himself down in the heather, the folds of his cloak pulled tight against the wind. "One is one, and all alone," he said quietly to himself, as the king shaded into the shadows on the further bank, "and ever more must be so." He laughed softly in the dark. "Not all the old songs are true. I can wait as well as watch, Te-Meriku."

Upon the hill, beneath the tree, Te-Meriku stretched himself out, green grass for his pillow, the wind in the leaves whispering a lullaby, a song with words he did not know. Only on the very edge of sleep did he remember: this was the song he had sung before he was born.

He woke to starlight. All above the sea the stars were very bright and very many. All the stars he knew were there, and others too among them, whose names he did not know. He leaned his back against the tree and looked into the night, the sea a mirror to the sky. He asked the starlight and the silence, "Am I yet dreaming?"

The answer was the rustle of the leaves above his head. "At some times and in some places, the line between a dream and waking is very thin."

The king stepped out of the shadow of the tree, at the first sight almost like a man. His feet were bare, his cloak was tattered but there were stars tangled in his hair. Quietly, he sat down beside Te-Meriku, resting his chin upon his knees.

They sat together in silence for a while, looking across the empty land down to the sunless sea. Te-Meriku spoke first, "There is a star not there that will be."

The king shook his head, and the wind whispered through the apple tree. "In your sky, Te-Meriku, not in mine. Look and you will see: all the stars there are, are here."

Te-Meriku turned to him. So strange to see his own face looking back: his very self and yet a man he did not know. "There cannot be two kings within one land."

The king's smile was a silver ripple across the surface of the sea. "Yet you are here, and I am here."

His turn to laugh. "Beneath the other sky, I am the king; here, only a man." His laughter was a little sound against the vastness of the borderlands and soon fell away to nothing. In a voice that was not quite his own, he asked, "What does it say of Allocco's son you wear my face still?"

Here, as in the waking world, all hope was false. "I have worn many men's faces in my time. Perhaps I shall wear his a little while. The future is not yet written and many things are possible. Even that."

Te-Meriku thought a little time, considering the future, remembering the past; thinking of an old man at the tideline; of grey eyes staring, unblinking, into the light; of an end and a beginning.

"When I asked, *How will I know?* Hadùhai told me: *The king knows the king.* I've seen many men since that day but never a king among them, and so I've wondered, often and often across the years, is the kingship a gift to be given or a prize to be taken?"

The king's touch was the smooth cold of starlight on his arm. "Both, beneath your sky."

IX, Lyikené: What's left behind

"Come and get warm, lad."

He looks up, stupid with grief and cold and hunger, into the face of the king's man. Above him, the branches of the apple tree reach into the evening sky, the leaves just touched by the turning season and the fruit flushed to gold.

He makes no answer; he looks, and then he looks away.

The helmsman kneels beside him, puts his hand upon his shoulder. "Hadùhai told me where I'd find you. It's been three days now you've sat here. It's a tree, lad—it'll not bring him back however long you sit beneath it."

He cups an apple in his hand to feel the ripe, round weight of it. Beneath this sky, if tales be true, it offers understanding and a new beginning, but it is not his to pick, not yet, and so he lets his hand drop back empty. "Three days," he says, "only three days. It seems so much longer."

"Seems, not was," the helmsman answers. "He knows what's due to Hadùhai and would not keep you, save that you were willing."

The king's man can give him twenty years or more but it is he that stumbles down the hillside, leaning heavy on his arm. All the thoughts he does not wish to think flood back into his mind, now he is no more alone. "Where are you taking me, Thodùhah?"

"To the hall. You can bide there awhile, out of the wind. It's close by the king for all the times he wants you. There's much that you need know, and little time enough to learn it."

They walk on a little way. The evening thickens around them, the light draining from the day like water into sand. Memories stir: spilled wine, spilled blood, the hole left by a wolfspear in a man's side, cold fingers slipping from his grasp. He shakes off the man's arm and straightens his back against the wind.

"I know love," he says, "and loss. I know what's left behind when the man within is gone." His voice is quiet and calm and empty as the surface of the sea.

The helmsman makes no answer but his breath quickens a little.

He says, reaching for his knife, "I know all the ways to kill a man. Tell me, Thodùhah, what is there left for me to learn?"

He holds his knife in his right hand and looks the helmsman in the face. "The dead are dead," he says, "and never come they back again. They have no need of vengeance: revenge is for the living. I am alive, but one I loved is not."

He sees in the helmsman's eyes that he is afraid. Of course he is afraid—only a fool would not be, and this man has never been a fool. He has good cause for fear: there are many ways to kill a man and not all of them are quick.

The helmsman says, holding his voice low and careful, "If there is aught you would know of Imacah, ask and I will answer, I or any of the king's company."

"I know the price of a stolen apple," he says, slipping the knife back into its sheath. "I will not speak of Imacah, to you, or any of that company."

He has but one question and that no living man can answer. He had not asked, and now it is too late. They walk in silence down the hill and do not look at each other's faces.

The weeks slip slowly into the sallows, the sour days after midwinter, before the equinox, into a night, for him a night as many in that year. Another night he would find oblivion in wine but, in the morning, he is bound to Hadùhai and so needs must find another means of driving back the dark. He looks around, glimpses a woman across the king's hall; her face means nothing of itself except that it is in every point unlike the one that haunts him. As men's voices raise themselves in song, he seeks her out in the shadows behind the harpsong, turns up her face and kisses her. Her mouth is still beneath his, closed against his probing tongue, her body stiff beneath his roving hands.

"Is this what you want?" she asks when draws breath. Her voice is a thread, vibrating like a harpstring stretched to breaking point. "Soon you will be the king—all that is here, is yours. Will you take it?"

She is so light and brittle between his hands, her wrists no thicker than twigs to snap between his fingers. He looks down into her face. Her eyes make him think of water running through his fingers, the ebbing tide, the fading light. He is afraid to be alone, she to be alone with him. Desire slips away into the space between them. To take her would be no more than to exchange one darkness for another.

He opens his hands and lets her walk away, clasping her wrist between her fingers.

"You frightened her." The voice comes, high and piping, accusatory. "You should have asked before you kissed her."

He shrugs. "She's taken no harm of me—I did no more than kiss her."

"She did not like it. Perhaps she thought you were like Torùkotu."

He looks down into the child's accusing gaze. "Who," he demands, "has been telling you tales of Torùkotu?" He has forgotten that, when he was a boy, he had all those tales by heart; that he longed for nothing but a star to rise and lead him to destruction and to glory.

He knows who she is, of course. There are those in this hall would whip her if she were their own; she is too pert, they say, and forward for a child of nine. They do not say such things before the king. His son died, and his son's son; this child and her mother are all he has left to call his own.

She says, "If you kissed me, I would not be afraid."

He pours a cup of wine. "You're over young for kisses."

"No." She shakes her head as if such a thought were of no matter. "Look," she says, "here's why."

"That's a pretty toy."

She flashes up, "It's not a toy!"

No more it is. Almost with reverence, he takes it when she offers, feels the perfect weight of it, the ivory carved to fit the hollows of a man's hand. Even the knives made for him in the king's armoury are not a match to this lovely, deadly thing.

He slides it back into its sheath. "Do you know how to keep an edge to it? How to use the blade and the point?" She shakes her head and holds out her hand for her treasure. "Come to me and I'll show you how to use it."

"To kill a man?"

"If that's what you want. Do you think you'll have a need to kill a man?"

It is her turn to shrug and turn the question. She asks, "Why did you kiss her?"

She is only a child and it does not matter what he says to her. He drinks before he answers, says, "Because I could," drinks again and says, "Because I was alone and lonely." He finishes the cup and says, hoping he frightens her, "Because your grandsire's order killed a man."

10: The long-haired star

I went to my love's bedroom door
Where I had been many times before
I could not sleep nor yet get in
The pleasant bed my love lay in.

The Handweaver and the Factory Maid, Traditional

Armed men, bronze mail above their leather, bronze helms acap
their hair, paced and circled on the ground before the hall. Ardùvai
lounged in the sun near the door, eyes half hooded 'gainst the light,
with a sprig of gay gold broom tucked in the lacings of his shirt and
his sword beside him on the grass. Perhaps he watched the cut and
thrust of practice, perhaps he only drowsed the day away, a young
man taking his ease on a bright, spring morning.

The king came out of the hall, clad in his mail, and strode into
their midst, pulling his sword from out of its sheath. He cast a glance
around. "Who'll take me on?"

A jostling clamour. Te-Meriku's eyes swept over them. In a
moment, he pointed to a clansman with a flash of yellow silk knotted
in his hair. "You, Kestai mor Iùthu, let's see what they taught you in
your grandsire's hills."

The man stepped forward as the rest fell back. Ardùvai sat
straight; if he had drowsed, he did no longer. The armsmen paced
and padded on the stone, two swords' lengths and a half apart.
They played and parried a while, circling and weaving around each
other, their blades ringing like bronze bells as thrust was repulsed by
counterthrust. *Watch the eyes*, thought Ardùvai, *you'll see his thought
before the move.* He saw the king probing, testing the man's skill,
finding his weaknesses. He saw the clansman move across the stone,
each footstep light as dancing; saw the laughter in his face as he
slashed and parried; saw the sunlight's bright flicker on the bronze
blades, a pretty pattern shaping itself across the morning.

The pattern twisted out of true. Te-Meriku lunged forwards and,
as the clansman parried, knocked back his sword with his shield in
a buffet that jarred the man's arm to his shoulder. The man leapt
backwards out of reach, his breath coming in hard pants. The king
pressed forward his attack, driving the clansman round to where the
sun shone full in his eyes, back towards the wall to where he had no
space to move. Ardùvai watched his strikes grow wilder faced with
this onslaught, all rhythm gone, all thought.

Suddenly the king struck low, slicing at the clansman's left leg; a slash, had it been in earnest, to cut the tendon at the knee and leave a man hamstrung on the ground. The man gasped, his eyes flicking to the trickle of blood dripping down his leg. In that moment of surprise, the king wheeled on his heel and brought the edge of his shield up and across, hard against the man's face to knock him down. All there heard the jangling clash as bronze hit stone. The clansman lay, blood pouring from his nose, his mouth opening and shutting like a fish on the streamside, his dropped sword by his side, the king's blade at his throat.

The king stepped forward and said something, too low for other ears to hear. The young man bit his lip and nodded. Te-Meriku turned away. He looked himself about a moment, then tossed down his helm on the grass beside the hall as he took a place next to his nightwatch.

"What need for that?" asked Ardùvai. "He's a-courting a fisher's girl along the shore. She'll not thank you for mashing his nose and spoiling his beauty."

Te-Meriku shrugged at such a little thing. "He fought as if it were a game we played. Next time he'll do better, and so will all the rest that watched it."

"What's the matter?" The king said nothing, running his finger along the blade of his sword, squinting down the edge to look for dents or flaws. "Te-Meriku, what's amiss? You've been jumpy as a cat since the piper sent that message."

"It's not a game, Ardùvai!" the king burst out. "It will come: that's been certain since the piper closed the gates of morning. And, whether it comes tomorrow or in a hundred years, we must be ready."

"Aye, man, and all of us with a place beneath those eagles know it." Ardùvai paused, staring through half-closed eyes into the light. In a little time he said, quietly, "But it's a lot to put on a green boy fresh from the mountains."

"I've no use for grass-green lads. Any fool can use a swordblade; I need men who know its meaning."

"Whenever did a man think who did not have to?" the nightwatch countered. "You play well enough as fox, Te-Meriku, but you'll never pass middling with geese. You've kept yourself too long alone to think as many."

The king shook his head, impatient at such thoughts, and took up his complaint again. "It's the waiting drives me to distraction. Waiting for a gate to open, waiting for a star to rise, waiting for the piper to show himself monster or musician. And I can do naught but wait until another calls me to the dance. Wait and watch for that damned star. Five years, man, five years and longer – what does Averla do with him that it must take five years?"

A little light laugh from the nightwatch. "Well, old tales say she's wondrous fair. He's a man as other men. Maybe he'd rather lie tangled in her golden hair than face you and your bronze sword."

"Aye," spat out the king, "Averla's wondrous fair. But there's something foul about her too. A man who'd lie with her is a man besmirched forever."

Ardùvai looked sidelong at him, raising a brow. "You speak as if you knew her."

The king turned away, too late to hide the flush staining his skin. "Dreams and tales, Ardùvai, dreams and tales. They've only the weight we care to give them." He stood, balancing his sword in his right hand. "Will you give me a bout? I'm sick of sucklings and half-taught boys."

"I thought you had no mind for games?" Lazily, Ardùvai looked him up and down, measuring with his glance the difference between the king's bronze and leather and his own linen shirt and finespun britches. "Can't you see I dressed with other sports in mind? The sword's only for show."

"Speed against substance, then?" At last, a spark of laughter in the king's eyes. "I'll leave off helm and shield but it's for you to guard your beauty."

"Aye well, if it'll turn your mood." Ardùvai grinned and pushed himself to his feet. "To the first blood, and loser pays the forfeit."

Quick as a snake he struck from stillness, but the king had leapt aside and his thrust met only empty air. Ardùvai laughed aloud as the world drew back and all that remained was the moment: the clash of bronze on bronze, the glint of a man's eyes, the blood singing in his ears.

+— —+

In her house of Faranon, Assiolo knew, Averla had the mastery, all that was here, was hers, and yet he found there was an hour that was his, if he could wake and take it. An hour, when the moon had set and the sun had not yet risen, when he could watch the stars in the sky and, by their small changes night on night, know time passed beyond the walls Averla had built to keep time out.

One night it was not Gru who brought hot water and clean towels or laid a laundered nightshirt out upon the bed. Assiolo returned to his bedchamber after another evening spent late within the library but, when the door opened, a woman came in. Quiet and neat, she set out the cans of water and turned down the sheets.

"Where is Gru?" he asked her as she worked.

"I do not know, my lord. I was sent tonight in his place." Her voice was soft and calm, very pleasing to his ear.

Assiolo sat upon the windowseat half hidden behind the curtain. Often his eyes slid from his book to watch her move around the room. She was pleasing to look at and all she did was done with supple grace. He saw the swell of her breasts beneath her gown, her slender waist and her round arms.

"What is your name?"

"Casarca, my lord."

Then, again, Assiolo tried to read but he could not long keep his eyes from her. She had not looked at him except when she paused in her tasks to answer his questions, but he knew she was as much aware of him as he of her. Why else would she be there? It burned within his mind he had but to hold out his hand, had but to say one word and she was his.

When the room was ready for the night, she paused before the door. She kept her eyes turned down to the floor and said, "If you are lonely, my lord, I can stay with you a little while."

He did not answer but he laid his book aside and stared at her. The curve of her cheek was smooth and lovely; her hair was dark, cut curling to the nape of her neck. He did not dare reach out his hand: if he passed the space between them, he would not be able to draw back. The silence was counted out in his heartbeats. At last she raised her face and smiled. His breath came ragged as she met his eyes; looking at him without fear or doubt, she took a step towards him. He looked away from her, measuring out his breaths to drag back some semblance of calm. He wanted her – as surely as he was a man he wanted her.

He heard her ask again, a touch of laughter in her voice, "My lord, shall I stay?"

She had asked, now he must answer, but all his words were lost within the moment, pressed from him as by the thickness of a dream. Smiling, she crossed the room and knelt before him. Still he could not move, he did not speak. He did not want her for herself – only for that sweet, brief oblivion that would free him a moment from the past and the future. Clever fingers pulled at his laces, warm hands caressed him, a willing mouth enveloped him. Assiolo gasped and spasmed, his hands closing tight on the stiff velvet of the curtain.

She sat back on her heels and looked up. "I can offer more, my lord, an it pleases you."

It would be so very, very easy. No need for any words. A night, and nothing more. She reached up, her sleeve fell back and he saw the sun and the moon burned into her arm.

At that sight his heart stood still. What had he become to welcome such embraces? All that he had given to his love, forever and for always. This was corruption clad in comely flesh. Another snare. Another binding. Averla's laughter echoed 'cross his thoughts: *Any time I want you, I have but to hold out my hand.*

Assiolo cried out, "No!" and all the light within the room gathered itself about him, waiting for his word. All the time there was stretched out into a moment, his to do with as he willed.

She cowered before his rage, not moving, scarce breathing; the only sound the thunder of her heart. Nothing left now in her face but fear. The words his father taught him rose blazing to his mouth. Let her be scorched by the fire. Let her be blinded by the light. He drew in his breath to make it so.

At his feet, Casarca gasped, a wordless plea for mercy. So small a sound, and yet enough to make him pause. He looked down and saw himself reflected in her eyes, a man of light and fire. The sight shocked him to his senses: he would not be that man! She was Averla's creature, not Averla, and had done no more than she was bidden do. To strike at her changed nothing. The light drew back into its proper place as Assiolo let out his breath in silence, himself again, his father's words fading from his tongue.

Shaking, shamed, he told her, "You may go, Casarca; go tell your mistress I have no desire for company. And say this also: should there be another time when Gru is needed elsewhere, I shall make myself ready for the night without assistance."

All that is here, is mine, Averla had told him, and now he knew the truth of it. As Oca nursed her son, as Gru was eyes and ears, so had he his purpose in her life with his allotted task. He pressed his hands across his mouth that his scream of anguish should not ring out into the night of Faranon.

Later, later, Assiolo opened the casement. All through the night he had burned with shame, to know himself a man as other men. In the first nights here, he had ached with his longing for his love, for the touch of her skin, for her kiss and her embrace; now he wept that memory was so fugitive within this place, and flesh so weak, words lost their meanings and promises their virtue. And yet, when he was done weeping, he saw beyond the window it was again that hour between the moon and the sun when only stars stood between darkness and the garden. Even Averla could not change the common stars within the sky and, with that thought, hope pricked in his mind. Like the stars, it would not outlast the night but it was cold and true for all that. He gazed up to find the north star, then looked to the west and the eight stars of the hawk.

"Bela, Belata," he whispered, "Morigu, Te-Ata, Yatta, Issa, Tascu, Ku."

Each shone a little brighter as he named it; no weight upon the world, free of the past and of the future, beyond the purposes and meanings men made for themselves, as cold and true above the wall of Averla's garden as above Cal Mora.

The moon had set; the sun had not yet risen; for a little while, he could walk unwatched beneath the stars and so, silent, he slipped from the silent house. A scent, elusive as memory, sweet as the things that might have been, floated out of the night garden. Assiolo walked barefoot down stone paths and across damp grass until he found the tree whereon red roses grew. Their petals were quenched to black by starlight, their scent was sweet and each stem sharp with thorns.

The sky was free of sun and moon, and so was he to think of the past and consider the future. First he was angry with his love that she had betrayed him. For a while, he believed her less than he had thought. He put such thoughts aside; so, too, had he failed; so, too, this night, had he fallen short. Now, all he felt was pity, because her fear had been so much greater than his. For a while, even pity cast a shadow over his memories of love; for a while, the flower was cankered; for a while the jewel was flawed. Then Assiolo held out his hand to the rose upon the tree and remembered the moment when he knew she loved him — remembered her in sunlight in his garden with a rose in her black hair. There was nothing could touch that memory. It stood entire, and whole, and perfect, forever and for always; not even knowledge could tarnish it.

He held the red rose in his hand and wept, and cherished every tear, for every tear he shed proved that he was yet himself.

The sky was free of sun and moon, and so was he. By morning, when the stars had faded, he knew what he would do. He did not try to sleep again, but early, very early, went to his son's rooms. He stood at the child's bedside, staring down to watch him sleep while sunrise crept across the floor towards him. The sight did not change his mind. He knew the price, and he would pay it. He kissed the boy gently, one kiss upon his brow. It was all the farewell he would give him — it was more than his father had given him.

He left the room, and at the door, with downcast eyes, Oca stood aside to let him pass. Then, for the first time, he sought out Averla of his own will. "Madam, I have made my choice. I am not your creature: I will not serve — I will go free this morning."

"Do you have strength enough to stand against me, Assiolo?"

"Aye, madam, strength enough today," he answered. "You've shown me the way of it. I'll hold out my hand for what I want and not count the cost."

"And your son, your greatest longing, your deepest regret?"

"Your son, madam." Assiolo made his voice cold as his father's. "I leave him to your kindness and your conscience. I made a promise to Marwy Ninek before his beginning, and I will keep it."

"She feared and she failed, Assiolo. Do you think she is your hope of safety?" Averla held out a rose. Once, it had been red; perhaps, once, it had been lovely. In her hand, it was withered and decayed, a brown thing, and ugly. "Would you take her to your bed again, knowing now all her secrets?"

"All she did, she did for love of me. I would she had not done it but I gave myself to her freely. I'll not turn my back on her though the storm wind blew her astray. She has waited overlong for me already." Averla dropped the rose upon the grass, a broken thing of no value. "Love is bitter, madam, as well as sweet but that you cannot know – never having loved!"

Assiolo saw her blue eyes grow dark as stormclouds on a summer's evening and gathered himself to face her anger. He knew that he could match her. She had no hold upon him but the boy.

The storm did not come. Averla held out her empty hand to him as in friendship and in parting. "Then go your way across the world, Assiolo, and I'll go mine."

He did not take her hand. Baffled, he watched her walk away across the garden and, baffled, he walked through the halls of Faranon.

He could see plainly now: all that had been hidden was made visible, no longer hiding in the light. He walked down the long hall towards the oaken door. Armsmen stood on either side, sunlight catching on the silver of their steel, dazzling with reflected gold. Only their eyes moved in their still faces, watching as he passed by. Soon Gru fell into step beside him

"Would you come with me, Gru?" he asked. "Beyond the door you could be free."

Gru shook his head. "I made my choice, my lord, the day the sun and the moon stood still together in the sky at noontime," Gru told him, as they walked between the lines of armsmen, slaves with the faces of the First People. "So did we all that dwell here. There is no freedom anymore; not here, and not beyond the door."

"Surely, Gru, you would rather walk again beneath the sun and stars, and feel the salt wind on your face."

"That is of no matter. Here is now."

"Forever?"

"For me, forever. But you, my lord, are needed."

"Yes, Gru, in Felluria."

"There is one here that needs you. You have a son, my lord." Gru put his hand on Assiolo's arm and, when he stopped, surprised by such a touch, said, low and urgent, "He does not have forever, he has only you."

Assiolo shook his head. "He is Averla's son. The little of me she needed to make him she took by a foul trick. He has had his life of me, and his name. He shall have no more."

"No child can choose who sires him, nor yet the manner of his siring – and surely you cannot forget it, you that were born Allocco's son!"

Assiolo paused to stare at him, a slave with the sun and the moon burnt into his arm. He saw the shadow of the man he had once been upon his face; he heard the echo of that man in his voice.

He shook his head against such thoughts. *Let the world be as it is.* He would not see. He would not hear. He would go home, to where red roses grew within the shelter of stone walls and his love was waiting for him to keep his promise.

"Here is the door, my lord." Gru's voice was quiet and colourless again. The shadow and the echo had fled away into the sunlight. Gru opened the door and the wind blew in to fill the hall of Faranon with the tang of saltwater. Silently, Assiolo put on the black coat Gru gave him; he took the hat and gloves from him with a nod of thanks.

"Ivory and silver, my lord," Gru said, "enough to carry you to Felluria, and bring you food and shelter on the way."

At the second thought, Assiolo took the purse as well.

"Your ring, my lord, with the cornelian seal."

He felt it hard and heavy on his palm. He saw the chipped stone, the king beneath the tree. It was his ring, cold and true, a whisper and a promise, but, when he slipped it to its place upon his finger, it twisted round, as if it had grown larger or else his hand had shrunk.

Two sets of footsteps ran down the hall towards him. Assiolo saw Oca, with a leathern bag slung across her shoulder, and the boy trotting at her side, dressed for the road in a blue coat and stout boots.

"I am coming with you," the boy said, with the certainty of a child used to his own way. "Oca told me so at breakfast. She said you needed me."

Oca held out the bag. Assiolo shook his head and said to his son, "This is your place, Alcedo —"

The boy snapped out, "I am Imacah – you called me Imacah!"

Assiolo did not heed him; as if he had not spoken, he went on, "Your place is at your mother's side. A month ago you did not know me; you'll forget me soon enough."

He had no more to say. The door had been opened and he could go out. He stepped across the threshold and felt the wind blowing in his face. Now the walls of Faranon were behind him, he saw his love's face clear within his mind with its look of hope and trust. The road stretched out ahead. Far down that road, across the sea, was Felluria, and Marwy Ninek, and all the future he wanted and needed.

Assiolo took seven paces down the road, and then seven more. Behind him was the open door and, at that door, his son, with two slaves at his back, stood screaming into the wind, "Take me with you!"

He tried to close his ears against that scream, to put one foot before the other and walk away. He could no more do so than he could close his mind to the memory of another boy standing on the quayside as a white-sailed ship slipped away, the piper on her deck, staring ahead into the west with never a backward glance. *Take me with you!* A child's piping cry, louder than any gull, whipped up into the wind and blown away forever. *Please, you must not leave me with my father.*

There had been no answer; the ship had sailed, and all his life had followed from that silence. Remembering the agony of that betrayal, Assiolo paused upon the road; he took another step, then turned back to his son, bending and catching him up in his arms when the boy ran to him, lugging the bag behind him.

"How long can you give me, Gru?" Assiolo asked. Another question burned on his tongue, *Whose will is done this day?* He could not ask, for Gru would be no more free to answer than he was to cross the threshold and walk out into the morning. Instead, Assiolo looked at his son, who smiled at him, and his heart sank to see the trust in those brown eyes, a boy he had neither known nor wanted but was his son, for all that.

Gru shrugged. "Perhaps an hour. No more than that."

"Very well, Imacah," Assiolo said, "we will go together."

He walked along the road, away from Faranon, his son's hand held in his own, conjuring the while the memory of love amidst the roses. In the evening, he saw a new star rising in the east, a long-haired star whose yellow light cast all the rest to nothing. When he remembered what was written of such stars in his father's books, the fate that they foretold, Assiolo crooked his fingers 'gainst misfortune, then laughed aloud at his own folly. Maybe that star told truth; maybe, in the west, the king would die, but such things were of no concern to him, whatever others called him: he had made his choice and was going home, to live his life within stone walls, his son's father, never his father's son, with his own true love beside him.

All was in order, the ship stowed and ready; arms and gear and men, chosen, counted, tested. Nothing to do but wait for the morning and the tide. Te-Meriku stood afore his open window, looking out across his country, twilight on the water, sunset on the hill. Some evenings, he could see the tree in the distance, outlined against the sky the other side of the water. Some evenings. Not this one. He could see the stream twisting in a golden ribbon down the brae, the gentle rise of the hill beyond it, and nothing more. And, though he would not look at it, he knew that, behind him in the east, the long-haired star was rising, a streak of sulphur in the indigo sky, and the common stars were quenched beside it.

But, for all that, it was a fine, fair evening, with bats flickering about the eaves and a blackbird on the weathervane singing out to all and any of its strength and love and courage. And, harsh and raucous 'gainst the blackbird, men's voices spilled from the hall, raised in a song of deeds and daring he had known his whole life long.

A rap-rapping on his door.

"I'm here," he called out, "and ready."

He picked the red snake from the litter of gewgaws on the table and fastened it around his throat, feeling the cool weight warm against his skin. The door opened and he turned around to face it, expecting Ardùvai or Almecu or any of his company come to fetch him to the drinking. None of these. Instead a woman stood at his threshold.

"Liùthánwy." Impossible to keep surprise out of his voice, impossible not to stare.

There were many women might think to seek him in his chambers but he would have thought this one as like to do so as the sun to rise in the west.

She bowed her head, a touch of her mother's cold courtesy. "Te-Meriku."

"Does your mother know you're here?" She shook her head. "Your father?"

A half-smile crossed her face, quick as a flicker of light 'cross the surface of the sea. "My father is with the children, feeding them sugarplums and telling tall tales to make them scream and beg for more. Easy enough to slip away at such a time."

She stepped into the room and closed the door behind her, stood facing him across his table; still a little thing, slight and brown in her grey cloak and kirtle.

"Why are you here?"

He had known – how could he not know, with Thodùhah his helmsman? – she had come back from the north country, and why, but he had glimpsed her only in the distance, walking on the seashore whilst her daughters played between the tides.

She met his eyes as easily as the old king her grandsire. "Ardùvai told me you were alone. I wanted to see you before you sailed. A word, Te-Meriku, and nothing more."

He raised his brow, thinking of words they could have said, one to the other, seven years ago and longer. No answer in her face to say what she remembered. She laid a dagger on the table 'twixt an armring of whale ivory and a slip of birken bark twined about with blue. "My father says you are away to Felluria with the tide. When you are there, give this to Marwy Ninek."

Strange how close the past could seem, conjured out of the dark by a bronze knife. He drew it from its sheath of red leather, feeling again its perfect weight in his right hand. It was a pretty thing with a hilt of ivory and gold, almost like a toy, if he looked not at the blade. The business of that blade was death, edges keen as the north wind, a point to bite out a man's life, cruel and clean as winter frost.

Liùthánwy bowed her head and turned away towards the door. He looked up, surprised. "Is that all you wished to say to me?"

"No more than that, Te-Meriku. I'll bid you good night, and hope for a fair wind in the morning."

So quiet her voice, so colourless; so subdued her manner. She seemed no more than a wraith with the face of a woman he once had known. He thought of water slipping through his fingers, slow rain falling down upon a silent sea. Had she loved him after all, that whaleman out of the north she married 'gainst her father's wish? She had never told, and there were things he could not ask, for all he was the king. He said, letting the evening light play along the edges of the knife, "I remember teaching you to use this. *Show me how to kill a man,* you asked, and so I did."

His words held her back, though her hand was already lifting the latch. She swung around to face him, grey eyes deep with memory. "The only time I tried, I failed." At last, some hint of feeling in her voice; a throbbing note, half a laugh and half a sob.

Strange to laugh at such a thing, but laugh he did. "That, too, I remember."

He sheathed the blade and set it back upon the table, took five quick paces across the room to stand looking down at her. "It's been a long time, Liùthánwy, since we were together." Her eyes were yet the colour of the sea when rain was falling. Too bright, those eyes, glittering in the lamplight. The years slipped away between them and he reached out to the tear upon her cheek.

A gasping breath, a ragged whisper. "Please, Te-Meriku, don't touch me."

Quick as if she had spat at him, he dropped his hand down to his side. "Are you afraid of me? You never were before."

"No," she whispered, her eyes fixed on his face, "no."

Relieved, confused, he turned away, choosing an armring to give her time to gather her composure. He considered gold, weighed up the merits of ivory, and tried to call the whaleman's face to mind. Seven years he had had of her. She must have loved him. Why else take him against her father's wish and go away into the north?

After a little time, he heard her light tread across the room, saw her hand stretch out across the table, a slender finger pointing. "This one. My grandsire wore it when I was a child."

A heavy weight within his hands, red gold from the mountains chased around with running hares. He turned it between his fingers. "All I have, was his."

"You are the king. Who else will wear it if you will not?" She laughed, soft in her throat, as he slipped the ring to its place upon his arm. Her laughter turned her from a grey stranger into the woman he remembered.

"Liùthánwy!" He reached out across the space between them but she stepped away, slipping like water through his fingers.

"I should go," she said, pulling her cloak tightly round her. "The children must go to bed or my father will be no use to you in the morning."

He made his voice as quiet and colourless as hers. "Ardùvai will walk with you to your father's house."

She shook her head. "No need for that. I came alone."

"I've no mind to make excuse to Thodùhah because some fool laid hands upon his daughter. There's deep drinking in the hall tonight."

"I still remember all you taught me." Her grey eyes met his, coolly level. "I have another knife."

"So does every man within this place," he told her, half in jest, resolved in such a little thing to have the mastery. "They're good lads, sober, and I'll not spare one so you can prove how much you remember."

Her face flickered in a half-smile but she did no more than bow her head. He opened the door and beckoned to the nightwatch. In the last moment before she stepped out, he asked, "What is Marwy Ninek to you that you'd give her Hadùhai's knife?"

"If you do not know, I cannot tell," she answered, softly. "But, Te-Meriku, go gently with her. She will be afraid to sail with you upon the open sea."

—⊢— —⊢—

Night by night, the long-haired star rose out of the east; night by night, it climbed the sky; slowly, slowly rose it up until it hung above Cal Mora, a sickly yellow light that drove the common stars to dimness; night by night, Marwy Ninek watched it from her walls. Its rising marked the death of kings, the fall of kingdoms, bones in the meadows and blood in the trees. She watched the west and waited, and, too soon, saw the sight she looked for: a square sail in the distance.

In the evening in her chamber, Marwy Ninek sat in the window-seat, silent and thinking, while rumour and whispers rustled around her hall. She had not sat an hour alone, an hour but barely three, when Yatta Tala came in, asking no leave as she sat down in Assiolo's place beside the fire.

"They say the red king goes in search of Assiolo," she said. "They say he asks you to go with him. They say that star means Averla is like to have her own again. So, Marwy Ninek, what will you do?"

"I will not go." Marwy Ninek reached up to close her shutters against the evening that she might not see the tail of the yellow star hanging above Cal Mora. "Assiolo gave me his love; I know he'll come back to me. He pulled me back into the light; I'll trust his word over any other man's, and far above the red king of Lyikené. I'll stay within my walls."

She had thought to end discussion but her voice cracked at the edges. Hearing the tremble, a lutestring out of true, Yatta Tala sucked her cheeks into a bitter smile. "Pulled you back into the light? What did you give in return? Your fear, Averla's desire, and now the red king's hunting!"

"Averla did what I could not," Marwy Ninek flung back. "He was dying and all my love and all my life were not enough to save him."

"You gave him to that golden witch and now you are afraid!" Yatta Tala spat into the fire. "And what of us, if you refuse? Have you thought of us who dwell within these walls? Do you think that king will wait outside the gate or break it down?"

Other women's tongues, long silenced, whispered down the years, *Open the gate. Let him have his own*, and after them the jeering echo of men's shouts beneath the walls, the deadening thud-thumping of a bronze-clad ram against an oaken door.

Unseen within her fists, her nails drove into her palms. She forced herself to think of Assiolo, of his kindness and his promise. The weaver went on, "You broke faith once with Felluria – you'll not do so again. You are one and we are many – if you say no, we shall put you outside the gate ourselves."

Her tongue was thick within her mouth. "You would not dare!"

Yatta Tala said, slyly, drily, "Five years I've had to find the words. If I ask, I think there are some here that will answer. If not tomorrow, then in a month, when hunger bites in their bairns' bellies because the gate is shut. One night, I'll give you, and then, if you're still shivering here in the morning, I'll hie me to the hall and say what must be said."

"Yatta Tala, I will wait for Assiolo," said Marwy Ninek, "wait here for him."

Stronger now, that roughness in her voice, a cracking and a shaking. She flushed to hear it, and closed her mind against that night; against the crash of stone and roar of flames; against the screaming; against the red king's laughter. To calm herself, she picked up Assiolo's book from its place upon the shelf and traced a finger over the embroidered flowers, lavender and roses, rosemary and thyme; all these he had planted in her garden; all these grew there still, for all he was not there to see them.

"Wait? With the red king at our gate, there's many of us like to go into the dark while you are waiting." The weaver's laugh was bitter as the night wind off the mountain, her eyes hard as two flecks of granite. "Tell me it is not so!"

Marwy Ninek thought of Torùkotu, smiling in the time before the ruin, of Te-Meriku laughing beneath her walls, *I am a patient man!* and shook her head.

"And if you'll not think of us," the weaver said, pressing her advantage, pointing at the lute case in the corner, "then think of Assiolo. When he's done here, the red king's going hunting – what price Assiolo's life if he meets him along the way?" She pinched Marwy Ninek's chin between bony fingers and turned it up, holding her firmly so she must look up into her crabbed face. "The Sea People never brought any end but one."

What need had she to tell her that? Marwy Ninek closed her eyes as the weaver hissed into her darkness, "I look to see a lover, who gave her word to the best man ever to step within these walls. Instead I see a coward and a fool, who brought Felluria to ruin and played the bawd for Assiolo."

Marwy Ninek pulled herself from the old woman's grasp and stood to face her. "I'll not be judged upon the long ago," she said, her hands clenched on the book, "but you know, Yatta Tala, that Assiolo never said a word he did not mean, nor gave a promise he would not keep. He will come back to me."

The weaver's eyes widened but she swallowed her surprise. "Then I've but one question and that is do you love him?"

Marwy Ninek remembered a midsummer's morning, Assiolo tucking a red rose into her hair; the long months afterwards when, with infinite tenderness and infinite patience, he taught her a man's touch against her skin could bring pleasure and not pain. Aching with her memories, she answered, "More than my life."

"Then go stand between him and that king." A strange note in Yatta Tala's voice, hungry, yearning. "Five years since I'd have gone after him, had he been to me what you say he is to you."

Again Marwy Ninek shook her head, thinking of Assiolo. "He will come back," she said, conjuring his dear face out of her mind's darkness. "He will come back to me. And I'll wait here 'til he does, full forty years I'll wait, and longer."

"Forty years is like to drive Te-Meriku past patience! Like to starve us all to husks." The old woman leaned forwards, her sharp eyes glittering in the firelight. "That's fear talking, not love. Love would dare anything to have her own again – even the red king's sword. You're afraid to pass the gate but there's many afraid of what'll pass if you will not. Te-Meriku will have you in the end and all here know it." Marwy Ninek began to speak but Yatta Tala cut across her, jabbing at the air with her finger to drive her meaning home, "No doubt Assiolo was afraid to walk beneath the bare trees at midwinter but still he walked there, because he loved you. You! A clinging weed that takes and waits and trembles!"

Marwy Ninek's eyes blazed from a face suddenly bleached white. "You know nothing of what there is between us."

"I know men," Yatta Tala snapped, "and I know Assiolo."

A pause as each stared into the other's face, then Marwy Ninek reached out, her eyes full of sad pity. "Yatta Tala —"

The weaver shook off her hand as if it burned her. "Did you think, because I have grown old, I could not love him? Aye, and I do – better than you, I'll warrant! You little fool who lives so long and knows so little. I'd not have served him as you did."

Marwy Ninek said quietly, "Better he lives than lies rotting in his grave."

Yatta Tala caught in her breath. After a moment she muttered, "Aye, I'll give you that."

A little time of silence as each conjured thoughts of Assiolo. Then the weaver's face hardened again. "Maybe I'll say a word in the morning, maybe I won't – still the red king's at the gate." She walked towards the door, but paused a moment at the threshold to say, "The time for waiting's passed."

After she had gone, Marwy Ninek sat a long, long time in the seat beneath the window, tracing her finger along a stem of lavender, across the petals of an embroidered rose. *I am yours*, her love had said but, over and again, another thought ran through her mind, *The red king's at the gate*. So, long ago, had another king come calling; she had said him no, and all had ended in fire and flame, in a tumble of stone walls and a lamentation in the night time. Full five years she had been waiting. Now, as she turned the pages of a book she could not read, she wondered what weight against the future had a promise given by a man who was not there.

The fire burned low, the room grew chill. In the grey hour before the dawning, she set her shoulders 'gainst the wall, sitting straight with Assiolo's book in her lap. All she had seen before, she would not see again.

—+— —+—

Assiolo walked slowly down the road towards the harbour town. As he walked through the gates, the watchmen's eyes swept over him; looking at him with idle interest, they saw his clothes were fine and that he carried a leathern bag and very little else, besides the boy. Inside the gates, he stood a little while beside the road, watching the people of the place. Then he walked the streets an hour or more, studying each inn or sailors' lodging house he passed. At last he walked back to one he had considered twice already and bought a night's food and lodging for himself and the boy. The landlady's questions died on her lips before his stare. His eyes were brown and mild but hard to meet. He carried his silence with him like the child clinging around his neck.

In the room, he laid his son down upon the bed and sat holding his hand until he slept. Then he stood before the window watching the light die behind the hill and the sea darken. Soon the moon would rise, close to its fullness. When the watch called the fifth hour of the third, there was a knock upon the door. Assiolo opened it and took the tray of food from the maid with a single word of thanks. He laid the tray upon the table and lit the lamp. Then he locked the door and barred the shutters across the window. They rattled a little in the wind.

Assiolo spoke one word aloud and the rattle of the shutters stopped. He waited a few minutes to listen at the window but all around was silence so he crossed the room to kneel beside the child.

"Imacah," he said, touching the child upon his shoulder, "wake now, Imacah." He spoke quietly but, in that muffled room, his words seemed loud in his own ears.

The boy stirred. "Where are we?"

"At the harbour of Cincern Dùn. You grow heavy, lad—my arm yet aches that carried you. Next time, you must carry me." He ruffled the boy's hair.

The boy smiled. He said, "I'm hungry."

"I chose this place for thick, stone walls and oak shutters on its windows." Assiolo pointed to the table. "There's food there, of a sort. Do what you can with it, and I'll take your leavings."

The boy took a seat at the table and peered into the dishes, used to far better fare. "What is it?" he whispered, not liking what he saw.

Assiolo looked and prodded with a knife at something that fell to pieces at the touch. "It was fish once, I think; what it is now, I cannot say. This brown stuff was perhaps green at its beginning – maybe it is cabbage, maybe it is not. But even I cannot bear to do more than look at it and so we'll never know for certain." He smiled, as he took a package from his bag and gave it to the boy. "Eat the bread, lad, and the cheese. That can't have suffered at our cook's hands. Here's something to sweeten it."

The child opened it to find sweetmeats of marchpane and candied fruits. Comforted by the thought of sweets to come, he took up the bread and ate it hungrily, and even nibbled at a bit of cheese to please his father, though it was not much to his liking. Assiolo took a cup and poured wine for himself, filled another one, well-watered, for his son. He waited until the boy had eaten the bread and sat picking crumbs of sugar from the rinds of oranges. Then, slowly, not looking at his son, he said, "Imacah, it's not too late. You don't have to come with me across the sea. I can leave you here – tell the landlady who you are and she'll keep you safe, for ivory and silver if for no better reason. Once I'm gone, your mother will find you within a day. You can go home, and forget me, and be again Alcedo."

The boy cried out through his mouthful, "I do not want my mother! I do not want to be Alcedo!"

"That is the safer choice!"

The boy said, quite quietly, "I thought you wanted me." His face screwed up. "Oca said you needed me." He was willing himself not to cry but fat tears broke through the struggle.

Assiolo quickly rose to stand behind the boy and stooped to put his arms around him. "Imacah, of course I want you. You are my son, and I want you, more —" he checked himself. He had been about to say, *more than all else.* That was not quite true and so he would not say it, not even to give comfort; he had promised himself he would only tell the truth to the boy and so, if the truth were not kind, he must be silent. He said, holding his son close, "You're not six years old, the world is a very dangerous place, and I do not know if I can keep you safe." He did not say, *love is not enough*, but he knew that it was true.

The boy said, "I want to be with you." His eyes looked up into his face. It was a strange look, Assiolo thought, for a boy of five, both pleading and commanding, the look of a child who has seen more than he should of things he had not understood. He met it steadily but his heart beat fast.

He put his hands over his son's, and their fingers locked their hands together. "Very well, Imacah. I shall not ask you that again. We will stay together, and try to keep each other safe."

When each had eaten what he could, Assiolo set the tray outside the door and locked it. He stood before the door to say what he had said earlier to the wind rattling the shutter. Then he poured himself another cup of wine and asked his son, "How shall we spend the evening?"

They found a battered game of fox and geese within a cupboard. Two of the geese were missing but they made do with bits of twig and played three games. Twice, the boy took fox and Assiolo's geese danced round it on the board, tantalisingly out of reach, until at last he took pity and let them stray into range. But the third game, Assiolo played fox and, this time, he had no mercy but wreaked carnage in a few sure moves.

"I've had near thirty years more practice," he said in excuse, seeing his son's face. "I played this with my father when I was a boy. Fox or geese – he always won."

The boy's face lit up. "I beat you twice!"

"True enough, lad – but I am not my father."

"What was he like?"

He did not answer at once. He reached out to the lamp and turned it down very low to leave only a tiny flame that burned clear and steady in the dark. He poured out wine but did not drink. Only then, out of the shadows, did Assiolo tell his son, "An old man who knew the world too well to love it. He did great harm, to many and to me." The boy sat silent and stared, wide-eyed and fearful. To break that silence, Assiolo said, forcing a lighter tone, "Now you must sleep again. I'll need you before the morning."

"To listen?"

"Yes, lad, tonight as on the others."

"Will you light the fire?"

He shook his head. "We're playing geese to Averla's fox; fire is one of her tools. You'll be warm enough asleep beneath the blankets."

The boy settled into bed and Assiolo sat at the table, drinking his wine and playing fox and goose against himself. Long after he had thought the child asleep, he heard him ask, "Are we going to Felluria?"

Assiolo started, knowing he had not named the place. "To Felluria?"

"Back to your home."

"Yes, Imacah, to Felluria."

The boy asked no more questions. Assiolo sat silent, turning his ring upon his finger, thinking of Felluria and of Marwy Ninek as the night grew old around him. Almost, he lost time and place within his thoughts but, each time he heard the wind rattle the shutter, he remembered where he was and said one word and then the wind was silent. At last, he could not sit waking longer and woke his son.

"Listen, Imacah," he told him, wrapping him in a blanket, "sit quiet until the morning, and listen. If you hear any step, however light, if you hear any whisper, however faint, or any song, however sweet: do not give an answer. Wake me. Wake me before you draw your next breath!"

Then he lay down and slept at once while the boy sat curled between his father and the wall to listen as the night slipped past and the rattle of the wind at the window grew louder. But the only voice he heard was his father's, crying out against his dreams, and, though he was afraid, he did not think to wake him.

And in the early morning, Assiolo woke, confused and terrified by dreaming, to see his son dozing beside him. He stood up from the bed, to splash cold water on his face and draw comfort from the knowledge it was no more than a dream and she safe within her stone walls with her people all around her.

X, Felluria: The dried flower and the ruined pipe

A beggar, a beggar come o'er the lea,
He was askin' ludgins for charity,
He was askin' ludgins for charity.
"Wad ye lo'e a beggar man O?
Lassie wi' my tow-row-ray."

The Beggarman, *Traditional*

It is said, by men, there is a ghost among the ruins. The women do not speak of ghosts, but the women never speak of Felluria at all, or of what happened there. They leave their gifts upon a stone as evening falls. Once the stone had been a lintol but the wall it had been set in tumbled long ago, the day the gate was breached. It is little enough the women leave on the stone, for there is very little they have to spare: a bowl of milk, a loaf of bread, sometimes a honeycomb and, when times are hardest, they leave nothing but a promise.

No woman walks into the ruins. They are not fools, whatever their menfolk call them. But, in the early days, men walked there, in daylight, for fear if they did not they would be thought afraid. Until once, only once, three young men, bold as young men are, foolish as young men are, fell a-drinking on a summer's night and thought to spend the night amidst the ruins and lay the ghost to rest. Their fathers found them in the morning. Two were stretched full length in the shadow of the tower, cold and hard as the stones that smashed their skulls. The third lived out his days but to no good purpose for his wits had fallen out through the hole in his head and all he ever did afterwards was rock to and fro, jammering out his fear of a ghost in the night time.

After that, not even the men dare walk among the fallen stones, not even in the brightness of the summer sun. Still the women leave their little gifts upon the stone and do not speak of them to their fathers or their brothers. For women know the things that men do not, they remember what men forget and then they think the thoughts that not even the best of men can understand. Women know the world is a crooked place for all that men try to make its ways run straight.

The time comes when the fallen stones are bare no longer but skimmed with grass. Summertime decks them in wildflowers, sea pinks and campion, meadowsweet and harebells, celandine and violets in the damp shade, sea holly where the salt wind blows. Brambles and briars stretch out a tangle of thorn and flower across the sunwarmed rocks, and birds sing in the thickets. There is a scrub of trees, silver birch mostly but rowan beside the streams. They cannot grow tall and straight towards the sky but must bend against the wind. In the short summers, when Cal Mora is clad in green and purple, the ruins are less bleak and a stranger might almost think it a pretty place to ramble in the afternoon among the grassy mounds where harebells dance in the wind.

Winter shatters such illusions; then the broken walls stand sharp-toothed against the grey sky. Winter shows the place for what it is, a burial ground for hope. In the rain and the dark there is no more desolate place along the western shore.

A beggar comes there on a winter's morning, unasked as beggars do. A stunted, twisted creature, with a face out of a half-forgotten tale, limping along the path that runs below Cal Mora, and why he should think it wise to walk this way no man can guess, for pickings are poor at any time in Felluria and worst of all in winter. There is barely enough in these sour sallows, after the solstice, before the equinox, for the people of the place and nothing at all to spare for a beggar, however merry his music, however sweet his tongue. He tries door after door but each is set firm against him and on the road out of the village he is as empty as on the road in.

Before nightfall he comes to the ruins. Rain lashes over them; heavy, peppered with hailstones. He pulls his ragged coat tight but it cannot keep out the night. He stops and thinks awhile, looking left and right about him, then walks into the ruins: there is nowhere else where he can go if he does not choose to walk out the night in the rain. He halts before the black tower, still standing though all the rest was tumbled long ago. The door has rotted on its hinges and the twisting staircase is blocked with rubble but it is shelter, after a fashion.

He makes a fire of sticks and driftwood that burns blue with salt. Since he cannot eat, he sits cross-legged before the fire, his back to the stone wall, and plays his wooden pipe for himself and the wind and the rain.

The night falls down upon that dreadful place. The wind howls around the tower and the rain spits at it. Half-sleeping, the beggar raises his head from his knees. Surely he has heard a noise that is not the wind or the rain. He says to the dark beyond the doorway, "If you are there, show yourself."

There is no answer. The beggar looks into the night, giving his eyes time to forget the firelight and see beyond the dark. He sees birken trees tossing in the wind, he sees rushes bending in the rain but he sees nothing else. He says, "I could not come sooner."

There is no answer. The only living things moving in the night are the trees and the rushes but he is sure that he is not alone.

Quietly, he goes back into the tower and builds up his fire. That night he sleeps, but never long enough to let the fire burn low. Each time he sleeps, he does not dream and, at every waking, he knows that he is watched.

In the morning, in the daylight, the beggar rises to put his pack together. Then he sees the proof that in the night he had not been alone. His wooden pipe lies in the fire and half of it has burned away to ashes. As he stoops to it, he finds a single flower lying on a flat stone beside it. He picks it up very gently and sits a little time, staring. The colour has faded, the petals are withered but he knows it as well as he knows his own hand. He sits a long time in the cold morning beside the ashes of his fire, holding the dried flower and the ruined pipe. At last he lays the pipe down beside the ashes, tucks the flower carefully in the pocket of his shirt and makes up his pack.

Before he leaves that place he says to the silence, "I am not a man. There is nothing I can give you."

There is no answer. He no longer expects an answer. He takes up his pack and walks away from the tower, heavy with the weight of memory. At the fallen lintol, half buried now by briars, he pauses and says, "Maybe one day a man will do what I cannot." Then he goes on his way, back along the path below Cal Mora and does not look behind him.

Time passes. The black tower stands above the shore, between Cal Mora and the sea. Firestar climbs its walls, pushes twisting, seeking tendrils into the cracks between the stones and all the summers long the tower burns with the false fire of lithia. The sun shines on the tower and bakes the stones; the rain falls on the tower and seeps into the spaces between the stones; cold freezes in the cracks of the tower and cores of ice lie between the stones. And, slowly, slowly, year after year after year, the sun and the rain and the ice and the firestar do what a man did not and at last the tower tumbles to the ground, stones upon stones, ruin upon ruins.

She walks out of the ruins on the day the tower falls. Her feet are bare, her dress is rags but on her black hair she wears a crown of firestar burning in the noonday sun. She walks into the village and the women give her what she needs, as they have given what she needed over all the years that have gone by. The women know who she is, they know what she is, they know what happened, though it was long years before their grandmothers' great-grandmothers were born. They bring warm water and wash her; they bring food for her; they comb out her hair; they dress her in clean linen and warm clothes.

All this was ready for her; it has always been ready, for the women of Felluria have not forgotten. The men forgot her long ago, but the men only died the day Felluria fell into ruin. One by one the women kiss her, each seeing herself reflected in her eyes. She kisses each in return and then together they go to find the men, to tell them there is work that must be done and walls that must be built.

11: The dead king and the living

"O what's your will wi' me, Sir Knight?
O what's your will wi' me?
You're the likest to my ae brither
That ever I did see."

Proud Lady Margaret, Traditional

In the dawning, on the seashore, with the weaver's grim smile at her back, Marwy Ninek had been stronger than her fear but the open sea was the domain of the Sea People. She stood beneath the square sail with its belly full of wind and watched the grey walls of Felluria, then even Cal Mora itself, grow small behind her. There was empty sky above her; cold sea beneath her; the fighting men of Lyikené around her. Upon the sail, three red eagles screamed their silent scream into the morning. She heard it, and trembled. A dead man stood beside the mast and laughed, his red hair blowing on the wind, the sunlight gleaming on his swordhilt. She turned her back on him but he was there amongst his kindred, in the flash of sun on bronze, in the length of a bronze spear. Assiolo's smile was long ago and far away, slipping from her memory into the sunlight.

Late in the morning, the king came to stand beside her. If she stepped away from him she must step closer to his men and so she did not move. She shivered to have him so close by, and had pride enough left in her to hope he thought it was only with the wind.

"Why are you afraid?" he asked, and she had no need to speak. He could read her answer on her face, and in the grip of her hands pulling her coat close around her. "Will you not trust me, upon the open sea?"

The sea stretched away, vast and empty. Cal Mora was but a shadow against the sky; all that was hers was far away and long ago.

The king signalled to a boy, who put aside the helm he was burnishing, and brought food, smoked fish and twice-baked bread, some kind of cheese. He gave a cup of small beer to the king, who drank a little and offered it.

Her fear was greater than her thirst; she bowed her head and did not drink.

Te-Meriku took a piece of bread from the platter and broke it in two. He held half out to her, saying, "The past cannot be changed, the future has not been written, but I swear no harm will come to you upon the open sea."

Mute with her fear, she shook her head. A herring gull mewed above them on the wind, crying out to take what she would not.

"Marwy Ninek, I never made a promise I did not keep. Nor did I call you out of Felluria to take what is not mine. I am the king of Lyikené; I hold by day all the other king holds in his everlasting night." The wind blew his cloak around him, the wind blew his words towards her. "You must drink and you must eat, for you'll need strength in the time to come. Love and hope are not enough."

Again, she shook her head, and he tossed the bread to the grey gull.

"It will take a long time for you to die," he said, after a while, as she gripped her left hand with her right, bone and sinew set against him in the only way left to her, staring at the great peak of Cal Mora falling back into the distance, "even if you will not eat, even if you will not drink. You are not a woman to slip easily away into the dark."

He was too close, too bright and strong and certain in the wind and light. There was but a step between them, a little space he could cross by stretching out his hand. His cloak flapped against her side and she set her teeth, stifling the panic rising from her past.

The king unbound a dagger in a sheath of fine red leather from his forearm. "Take this, Marwy Ninek." He closed her hand upon the knifehilt, a handspan of ivory ridged with gold. She felt it hard and warm as flesh, a thing made by men to serve their purpose. "If you'll not trust me, trust its edge; if you'll not believe me, believe its point."

The knife slipped from its sheath easily as a hand from a glove, a lovely, deadly thing. Each edge of its bronze blade was sharp as winter sunlight and the gold wire tooled around its hilt of whale ivory formed the figure of a branching tree. It fitted her grasp as if no other hand had ever held it, as if it had been waiting for her over all the years since it was wrought in Lyikené. Its balance gave her balance on the swaying deck; its weight gave her back her weight upon the world.

At last, holding the bare knife in her right hand, she had resolve enough to look him in the face. "Why give you this to me?"

He answered lightly, "I thought you might sleep easier beside me with that dagger to your hand. It's an old blade, that one, a wise one. It's killed many men in its time, even a king of Lyikené."

Though she looked long at him, she could not read his face nor even judge the colour of his eyes: they seemed neither green nor grey nor blue but, like the surface of the sea, restless and changeable.

"What do you seek?" she asked.

"No more than I have sought before: to keep the balance and the tree that are my charge. I am not Torùkotu to remake the world around his own desire."

His pride was written on his face, the pride of a king who lived by his word and by his sword and knew that both were true.

"Then it matters not one whit whether I trust you or no," she said. "I seek Assiolo to bring him from Averla's grasp to safety. Since you seek him too, our paths lie together for a little while and, in that time, I will eat and I will drink with you."

"I am glad," he said, unsmiling. "We've a way to go together, you and I. We'll to Lyikené, soon enough, but first we must go, as Assiolo did, to Habhain. I've heard the tales of what he did there and I've a mind to see for myself if they are true. After all," he tossed another piece of bread to the gull, "if a man should kill a king, what does that make him?"

She caught her breath, swallowing back her first quick words. It changed nothing to deny the truth.

One day north, they sailed, and two days east, their course set through the Skerries by the sunstone and the stars. Three nights Marwy Ninek lay down, in the last place before the curving hull, beneath an awning of sealskin, with the king wrapped in his red cloak beside her, his great sword laid down naked between them, her bronze knife cradled at her breast in its sheath of red leather, and let the waves rock her to sleep. By the first evening, she knew the boy who served the king was Renùku, thirteen come the midsummer moon, counting Te-Meriku his father since his own died in his service; that two lint-haired men, alike as self and mirror image, were brothers who had drawn lots as to which should go a-courting, and when the girl they drew for heard the tale she would have none of them, not the winner nor the loser; that the quartermaster had bet an acre of ground against a handspan of ivory that the boatswain's seventh child would be another daughter.

The man who told her these, and many other, tales was Thodùhah, who had been helmsman to Hadùhai, the old king, and fired the ship that carried him into the west. He had looked with contempt upon her coat and called out to Renùku to bring his pack. Now she bore the bronze knife on her forearm, as he had shown her, and wore the clothes of any man of Lyikené, and no longer shivered when the wind blew hard. Late into the evening, she sat at his side whilst he told of his own country, of the fishing fleet that went north each year after the herring and the codfish, each ship's sail dyed in the colour of its clan, out of sight of land for weeks on end that there might be salt fish in the winter; of the salmon that rushed up the rivers in the springtime and leapt the waterfalls until at last they spawned and died; of the grey whales that came each summer into the west to sing in the deep sea, their voices like drowned bells shaking the ships in the water. Softly in the night, the north star held at his left hand, he told her how no man of Lyikené could die easy in his bed until the tide was at its ebb. Late and last, he told her of the curlew that calls three times to bring the dying forth, that they might go with the smell of saltwater in their mouths, as it was when they were born.

This was his last sailing, Thodùhah said as the second day gave way to sunset, when he had given the tiller to the nighthelm and they took their places with those whose turn it was to eat; he had grown old, the salt had stiffened his joints and his wife had forced him to a promise that he would rest beside the fire and let another take his place. "She was born a king's daughter," he said, "I would not lightly cross her. But when the king asked," he told her, an old man speaking quietly in the dark, "I could not help but answer. Before I was anything else, I was the king's man."

Her eyes slipped sideways to the king, laughing with the night-watch over a game of knucklebones, and she shivered at the sight.

The third evening, as she sat with Thodùhah, the nightwatch came to sit with them. The helmsman nodded as he sat down. "Ardùvai."

The young man laughed. "You can do better than that, Thodùhah. 'Twould be courteous of you to make my introduction, clansman to king's guest." He pulled a flask of horn and silver from his pocket and held it up to show the helmsman. "When you're done, we can drink to friendship."

He snapped his fingers and the boy came up bringing three cups, each of wood and rimmed with silver. The nightwatch set them in a row before him and poured a dram in each; looking again to Thodùhah, he sighed. "Alas that I left courtesy behind me in my grandsire's hills to live among fishermen and shorefolk."

"For sake of your liquor, I'll do it." The helmsman reached out to take the nightwatch's hand in his right and hers in his left and touched their fingertips together. "This black-eyed chancer, Marwy Ninek, is Ardùvai mor Ardùvai, the smoothest rogue in all Lyikené."

She looked up into his pale face, fine cut and handsome, blackened by a sennight's growth of beard upon his chin, into the smile in his dark eyes, and pulled her hand away, a fraction too soon for courtesy.

"Oh, Thodùhah, you sell me short, and deny my forefathers their glory." The nightwatch bowed his head to her, gracious as any lord, but mocking laughter glinted in his eyes. "Marwy Ninek, I am

Ardùvai mor Ardùvai mor Morigu mor Inistai mor Ardùvai mor
Thorinah—"

"He has a glib tongue and a laughing smile," continued Thodùhah,
"and a thousand years of clan's blood running through his veins,
but don't think to play him, fox or goose, however sweet he asks it.
He'll have the silver from out your purse and the gold from off your
fingers before the first cup's empty."

Ardùvai's black brows arched in shocked surprise. "I'd never
take advantage of a guest and a stranger." Thodùhah sucked his
teeth and shook his head at such a bare-faced lie but took the
cup Ardùvai held out. "Nay, here's a hint," the nightwatch said, "if
you've a liking for a win: set yourself as fox against Te-Meriku. Even
Thodùhah can take him when he's playing geese—nay, I'll tell you
worse than that, Marwy Ninek: I've known my brother do it." He
spread his hands wide, his face dancing with laughter. "My brother's
that sandy-headed lump yonder. Ask him his name and he'll stumble
past Morigu, but he answers to Almecu. He got his father's brawn
and our mother's sweetness; I, her wits and quickness."

He offered her a cup, so gracefully she could not help but take it.
"And from your father?"

"I got my name, Marwy Ninek, and that's more than enough for
any man." An edge, sharp as a bronze blade, showed itself a moment
behind the silk. He raised his cup. "A toast to friendship!"

She sipped and felt smooth warmth caress her tongue, another
thing entirely from the firewater of Felluria. The sunset faded from
the sea and there was cloud enough in the east to hide the long-tailed
star. All across the ship, little lanterns shone out, their lights catching
on the clear colours in the clansmen's hair, on the king's blood-red
cloak and flame-red hair. Someone started to sing the song of the sea's
daughter, beating out his rhythm on a little drum. Thodùhah and
Ardùvai drank and talked, and, as she drank and listened, Marwy
Ninek thought how strange it was, how strange, to sit afloat beneath
the stars with men of the Sea People. She had seen, long ago, such
men, hard-handed, hard-hearted, their arms drenched to the shoulders in the red blood of Felluria, monsters after the likeness of their
king. Yet old Thodùhah would tell tales of his granddaughters as long
as there was anyone to hear them, and Ardùvai's jests, though sharp
enough, had no real malice to them. But the king—though he had
given his word and made no move to break it; though by day he left
her to Thodùhah's company; though by night he never passed a hairs-
breadth beyond the sword blade, not even with his eyes—was another
thing entirely. Each time she looked at him, by sun or star, she caught
her breath, seeing past horror in his living flesh. And yet, she could
not help but look at him, fascinated as a woodmouse by a weasel.

Perhaps Ardùvai saw her eyes sliding often to Te-Meriku for, in a while, he asked, "Did you never hear the tale of his beginning?"

"Never," she said. He lifted a questioning brow. "We have our own stories in Felluria," she said, cold as she could against the challenge in his eyes, "that fit our fancy better. Enough to know there is a king without speaking of him too."

"Even so," he answered, "that one's worthy of the piper, in any country."

"Aye well," grunted Thodùhah, wiping his mouth, "men are not so quick to tell it in these days, even in Lyikené. He's been twenty years and more the king, and that wipes out all the rest. But Hadùhai stirred a hornets' nest, the day he gave him his sword."

"Why so?" she asked.

"They're a proud lot, the clanlords of Lyikené, stiff-necked, stiff-kneed, measuring a man's worth by his generations." The nightwatch grinned, and Thodùhah sighed and shook his head. "Look there, Marwy Ninek," he said, pointing at Ardùvai, "and tell me if there's wit or wisdom in such a measure."

Ardùvai spread out his slender hands, a man sorely affronted, and muttered darkly of shorefolk and of courtesy, but the look in his black eyes invited laughter. She bit her lip and turned to Thodùhah.

"No man's born to the kingship; the king asks, a man answers. But," Thodùhah said drily, " 'tis passing strange, how, often and often, of all the men in all Lyikené, the king has asked some clanlord's son, his own as like as any. But Hadùhai broke that pattern, and set over them a green lad of just eighteen who could not tell his father's name, nor yet his mother's either, not if you set a knifeblade to his throat to ask it."

"And my grandsire's hair turned white the day he did it," Ardùvai cut in. Thodùhah snorted into his drink, and the nightwatch's roguish smile flashed out. She bent her head to hide her own. "Oh, that's the truth I tell you—white as a tuft of cotton grass, between the sunset and the morning." With a sidelong glance towards his brother, he said, "After that, nothing had power to shock him, not even Almecu." He laughed, seeing her caught between curiosity and disdain. "Tell it from its beginning, Thodùhah. You were the king's man when the king was Hadùhai."

"Aye, man, I will, far as is fitting." Thodùhah stretched and settled himself more comfortably against the hull, and held out his cup to Ardùvai for filling.

"Imagine a night," the helmsman said, "a dreich night in springtime, maybe a sennight after the equinox. A shepherd in the lambing pens finds a bundle of stained sheepskin tucked in beside a ewe is not a lamb at all but a red-haired baby with the natal string still on him, bawling his lights out to find himself alone." He paused and spat to avert ill luck. "I'd not do it myself but such a thing is not unknown, in Lyikené; a mouth too many, or the mother dead at its birthing. One thing to make an ending, another to let it take its chances all alone. But what's quite unknown, and what makes this shepherd take this babe up to the hall of Kistoru his lord, are the feathers tucked with the child into the sheepskin." He pointed to the sail with its blazoned eagles. "Three feathers, Marwy Ninek, and each plucked from a sea eagle's wing.

"That's how he found his name. Since there was none else to give him, Kistoru called him *Te-Meriku* for that eagle, and gave him to his wife to rear with his own boy. He gave out later that she would have it so, because the winter sickness took her baby." Thodùhah spat again. "Whenever was a woman's heart eased to nurse another's brat when her own is dead? Ala hated him, then and ever after. It was the eagle's feathers saved him, and Kistoru's fear. Kistoru reasoned that somebody had left those feathers with the child, and so there was somebody standing back beyond the day, watching its fate. Well, Kistoru soon thought himself a fool; if somebody was watching, he never showed his face and those feathers were all Te-Meriku ever had of him."

"Except his life," said Ardùvai, filling up the cups.

"Except his life," Thodùhah agreed. "Well, those two boys grew up to be the wildest lads in all Lyikené, and that's a deal to tell. Imacah had the pride of any lord's son that's taught to think no man his master, and Te-Meriku a bastard's pride that must have his own great deeds to boast of since he cannot of his father's. Closer than brothers they were, and neither cared a whit that one had all and the other nothing. When they fought – and oftentimes they fought, slipping by night across the boundaries to goad the young men of one clan, or another – it was ever back to back so that none else could slip a knife between them; like one wild beast they were, with two heads to watch a foe, and two bright swords to strike him down."

He grinned, and the nightwatch took up his laughter. "Barbarians, you call us in your Later Lands," he said, watching her face to see if she would flinch, "and all your tales are true. Our only law is the king's will."

Strange to laugh at such a thing but laugh she did. Perhaps it was the knowledge of the knife upon her arm or the warmth of the barleyspirit rising to her head showed her the way. She drained her cup and let Ardùvai refill it while she waited for the rest.

"The best that can be said of those days," Thodùhah went on, "is they did nothing drunk they'd not stand by sober. When Hadùhai called him to the kingship, it was said, and none so quietly, the old man had lost his wits." A third time, Thodùhah spat. "Hadùhai killed the man who said that in his hearing, and then all the rest were silent."

She glanced again towards the king, lounging against the hull, gambling with the quartermaster and two clansmen, and marvelled that such a man, so certain in his pride, could have had so uncertain a beginning. Thodùhah beside her supped his drink and, in a while, she asked him, "But why should Hadùhai choose Te-Meriku over all the men in Lyikené?"

"Some said it was because of those eagle's feathers; others because he was weary of the clanlords and their rivalries and sought to humble them," Ardùvai shook his head, laughing at such a thought, and the azure silk knotted in his hair flashed bright as a kingfisher's wing, "and some said it was for love of his red hair."

"And you, Thodùhah, what do you say?"

Sharp eyes met hers. "I, Marwy Ninek? I say that Hadùhai was the king, and one king knows another when he sees him. He saw in Te-Meriku all that was needed, and went easy into the dark." He too looked to the king and said, more quietly, "And Te-Meriku put aside his wildness when he took the king's sword in his hands; after Imacah died, he seemed a while as old as Hadùhai."

Laughter from the dice game. A rattle of dice and a click-clicking of counters; the king betting high, "A five of ivory upon the red," and throwing six; a clansman matching him upon the black; the quartermaster throwing three upon the green and bemoaning his bad luck.

She began, "How did Imacah—" but, as she spoke, Ardùvai snapped round, his right hand moving in a sharp, curt gesture that bid her to silence clearer than any word. He cast a quick glance towards Te-Meriku, another at the helmsman. But Thodùhah only rubbed his face, an old man puzzled by an old mystery.

"Often and often I've wondered it," he said, more to himself than in answer to her question, "why they were not together that last night? Imacah was three years the older—since he could stand on his two legs and toddle after him, Te-Meriku had followed every place he led. But not that night. 'Twould have changed one thing to another had he been there."

He tossed back the last of the barleyspirit and pushed himself to his feet. "Tell her what you will, Ardùvai. That fool at the helm'll miss his mark if I don't put him straight."

His going changed the mood. Ardùvai's eyes, all laughter gone, steady and unblinking, were fixed on the king. Marwy Ninek pulled her borrowed cloak around her, muffling herself in its heavy folds, uneasy to see what was not meant for her and yet ashamed to look away. But the nightwatch sat, silent and still, his brightness quenched. For a moment he had forgotten her, else he would not have let his heart show so clear upon his face.

"Aye well, Imacah," Ardùvai said at last. "What I know I'll tell, though I was a bairn in those days and my lump of a brother not even born. But I love my life as much as any other man and it would take a braver tongue than mine to speak on his end, an Te-Meriku could hear me."

Her head felt thick and heavy, the spirit sour in her mouth. She set down her cup, dizzied by the lights rising and falling in queasy motion as the ship turned against the wind.

"For all they were so close," Ardùvai said, leaning near and speaking quiet, "not a month after Hadùhai gave Te-Meriku his sword, Imacah went alone a-seeking apples across the water. No man picks that fruit without it's the king's will. Hadùhai had set his company to guard the tree, and all Imacah got was a wolfspear stuck in his belly as payment for his daring."

Te-Meriku's harsh laugh rang out above the other noises of the ship. "Another six! Luck runs my way tonight."

"Hadùhai made him a king but he's still a man, as other men. Imacah died," said Ardùvai softly, "and what there was between them died not with his death. Seven years I've watched his door; I've seen him open it to many and to many, but Te-Meriku's lived alone and lonely for all that."

The stars swung above her, very bright and very many, or perhaps 'twas but the lanterns of the Sea People. She did not know; she could not tell; her mind was clouded by barleyspirit. She looked up into a pale face, black eyes beneath black hair, and, for a moment, it was not the nightwatch looking back at her. She whispered, "The price of a stolen apple is very high, beneath this sky or the other."

Those three days upon the sea the wind blew something of her fear away but, on the shore, fear came back to stalk her. Fear stepped into the woods behind her with a tread heard only in her mind and was not there when she span around to face it. Fear was a face across the clearing; a man beneath a tree; a snatch of song; the flash of sun on steel. Here, in the wild woods of Eulana, she was out of her own place, away from her stone walls, and the sun was a golden eye watching her from morning into evening.

Often and often, that long summer's day, in the morning on the shore, where the ship rested like a beached whale across the highwatermark, after noon beneath the trees, where men made camp under the quartermaster's direction, she glimpsed movement from the edges of her eyes, as of the swirl of a man's blue cloak. Always at such times, her hand felt for the knife. Once, she asked Ardùvai, "What man is that?" but, when he looked where she pointed, he laughed, for it was only Renùku with his hood pulled down around his face. She did not share his laughter; it had not been the boy she saw across the glade but a man whose face she did not know. And that could not be, for now she knew all the faces of the king's company; aye, and could tell a shoreman from a clansman by the braid hanging down his back, and a man of the fisherfolk from either by the stormy petrel's breastbone pinning back his hair. Late in the evening she said to Thodùhah, in the quiet, in the dark, as he bade her good night, "There is a stranger here."

He shook his head. "That cannot be. Not in this place. We have eyes and see nothing; we have ears and hear nothing. It is the wind in the trees, and the shadows after the brightness of the open sea."

But she too had eyes to see, and she knew that she had seen him, sidelong where the light was bright and dazzled her; she too had ears to hear, and she had heard him, whispering her name no louder than the rustle of aspen leaves above her head.

They had given her a sealhide tent to sleep in. The king lay before its flap, wrapped in his red cloak; the nightwatch sat not ten feet away, his drawn sword 'cross his knee. The sun had set, and clouds covered the moon. He was not there, not now, the unseen stranger. She slipped into sleep, cushioned on sheepskin with her knife in her hands.

She struggled and twisted in the red king's grasp but his strength was the greater. He pressed her down, his mouth mauling her breasts, and she had not breath enough in her crushed throat for screaming as strong hands pinioned her upon the sheet and strong legs pushed her own apart.

A tearing pain, a hot whisper in her ear, *The first taste is e'er the sweetest.* His laughter was the reek of wine against her face. He tangled his fingers in her hair and thrust over and again, smiling to take his pleasure.

Warm fingers clasped her hand and pulled her from one night to another.

Marwy Ninek sat up, uncertain of the line between reality and dreaming. In the first moments after waking, her mind was yet filled with the crashing rhythm of the ram against the gate, with the red king's flesh battering into her own. A shadow moved, and he was there beside her, his very self for all the night time drew the colour from his hair. She gasped out, "What you want, I'll do but don't hurt me. Please, don't hurt me."

The red king did not move towards her, he did not move away. He knelt beside her, holding her hand, quite lightly, in his own, and another man's voice spoke from his mouth, "He is not here. Only I am here."

"Te-Meriku." She pulled away, heavy still with the weight of dreaming. "Did I cry out? I had no thought to wake you."

"It's of no matter. I know what it is to have bad dreams," he said, softer than by day. "I too sleep easier upon the sea where the wind can blow my dreams away. But, on land and sea, you can lie safe at my side as sister is by brother."

She tried to speak, to say, "It was a dream, only a dream!"

Nothing she said had meaning; her broken words fell away to silence and she could only stare down at his hand, so unexpected gentle. Te-Meriku picked her sheathed dagger from the sheepskin and offered it. "But, if you do not trust me, remember that you have this blade."

She took the knife and, slowly, her racing heart regained its rhythm; slowly, her fear curled itself back into its nest within her breast. Te-Meriku stood, bending his head against the ridgepole, and looked down at her, his eyes unreadable in darkness. "Tomorrow, we'll to the riverbank and you can look beneath the stones. An end, perhaps, to such dreamings."

For a moment she saw him at the threshold, silhouetted against the stars. Then he let the tent flaps fall and left her, lying alone and lonely in the dark.

"Assiolo," she whispered, conjuring his face behind her eyes, "Assiolo."

He was not there to answer. Another man had answered in his place, and that knowledge kicked hard as the nightmare against her heart.

—+— —+—

Not long after noon, Assiolo and Imacah walked down into the harbour. The boy looked all around in wonder but Assiolo searched out the captain of the *Sandpiper* that was set to Escen on the morning tide. He spent a long time sitting with him at a table in a tavern on the quayside, standing him drinks and negotiating the price of passage for himself and the boy, haggling over the extra that he must pay for the use of his own cabin that they need not sleep amongst the sailors in the common berths. The boy grew quickly bored listening to such talk and found a length of fishing line. Soon he had begged a hook and a lump of bait from a sailor and spent the afternoon lying on his stomach on the pier fishing for the crabs that lived beneath it, finding they were greedy enough to take the bait and wise enough to let it go each time he pulled it above the surface.

Once the deal was struck, and they had shaken hands upon it, the captain counted up his fee and Assiolo and his son went aboard to sleep the night. Yet early in the morning, just as the ship was set to sail, Assiolo took up his bag and his son's hand and the two of them went again ashore, to leave the *Sandpiper* and the harbour behind them. The boy pulled at Assiolo's sleeve to question him but he put his finger to his lips to silence him. When they were beyond the gate, and the ship out of the harbour, he looked down at last. "Well, Imacah?"

"They did not see us go. We walked past them, and yet they did not look at us."

"That's the trick to it. We walk quietly, and they do not see clearly that we are there at all." He smiled with satisfaction. "I made sure enough people knew that we were on that ship and bound across the Inner Sea for Escen. They'll swear to it if questioned, and it will take even Averla a while to send across the sea and find it is not true. Tomorrow, we'll go another way. Air and fire are her elements – earth and water will baffle her awhile."

‡— —‡

At dawn, three men went a-hunting along the shore for waterfowl, taking Renùku along to learn to use his bow upon a lesser target than a man. Others went into the wood in hope of boar or deer. Fish in all its forms was well enough upon the sea but men on land craved meat. Those who walked beneath the trees came back at noon with empty hands for nothing had crossed their path that was worth the killing, not even a rabbit. The quartermaster laughed at them that walked so loud to give the wild things warning, and held up a net of shining fish to show he had had better luck.

"Come with me," Te-Meriku bade Marwy Ninek, when their meal of grilled mackerel was eaten. "There is something you must see within the wood."

He spoke as the king, a command that must be obeyed, and so she followed him. She did not like to walk alone with him beneath the trees and stayed always three paces behind, her bronze knife naked in her hand. An hour or more they walked, keeping always to the shadows between the trees, avoiding the sunlight pooled in the glades. At last they reached a riverbank tangled all across with brambles and sweetbriar bonny in its blooming.

"What do you see across the river?" he asked.

"More trees," she said, "more of the wood that we have walked together."

"It is so today," he told her, "but it is not always so. There are times and there are places where the borderlands are but a step away, even in these Later Lands. This is the place but not the time, and what you must see lies on the nearer bank."

The king walked a little further, keeping to the riverbank until he found the thing he sought for: a pile of stones, longer than a man and maybe half as high. A crabtree grew beside it, its branches reaching out towards the further bank and twisted all about by briars. Somewhere, nearby within the wood, a blackbird was singing, mixing its song with the ripple of water and the rustle of leaves.

"What do you fear?"

She looked, and saw, and then she understood and shrank back into the shelter of the trees.

Te-Meriku started to pull stones from one end of the pile, stacking each neatly at its side. While he worked, she sat beneath an aspen tree, her knees drawn up to her chin, her face pressed into her hands and her blood pounding in her ears.

It was an hour or more before the king called to her, "Come, Marwy Ninek, and face your fear."

She could not move. The wind stirred the aspen branches and leaves rattled and rustled, speaking in a whisper she could not understand. Te-Meriku waited beside the crabtree, his cloak caught on a strand of sweetbriar. His face was hard and harsh in the shadows of the wood. She met his eyes and knew his will was stronger than hers and, in the end, he would have the mastery. She heard him say, "There is no need for haste, all the time you need is here, but you will see what lies beneath the stone before we leave this place."

She opened her mouth to answer but he turned his head to look into the wood and held up his hand for silence. A moment passed, and then another. They were alone, surely they were alone save for the blackbird, but the king said quietly, "If you are there, show yourself."

The song fell silent as he spoke. She heard a scuffling sound in the undergrowth that might have been a bird turning over last year's leaves, then a sound of dragging footsteps through the litter that surely was no bird; she saw a ragged coat that had once been blue, and the twisted creature wearing it, a countenance from a twicetold tale.

"It's good to see you, lass," the piper said. "It's been a weight of days since we walked together on Cal Mora-side." At that face and at that greeting, the memory of the roses and the music in that far off summer, long ago before the ruin, rose up to choke her. "The world's a wider place by far than the stone walls of Felluria," he said. "Now you are here, and I am here; so too the dead king and the living, in the place where Allocco's son changed one future to another."

The aspen tree was solid at her back, the bronze knife solid in her hand, steadying her against the future. "For love of me, Assiolo came here; for love of me, he faced a monster." At first she could manage little better than a whisper but to speak of Assiolo strengthened her. "For love of him, I left my stone walls behind to walk beside the king."

The dwarf's smile was little better than a grimace, but his voice soft and sweet as she remembered. "Aye, lass, I do not doubt it. But here, all ways go crookedly." He turned and bowed his head to the king. "Te-Meriku. You're far from Lyikené, and the wild wood is not the open sea. This is not your place, within this wood, beneath these trees."

Te-Meriku laughed beneath the crabtree and freed himself from the briar's thorns, plucking a spray to tuck in the clasp of his red cloak. The blackbird sang again, telling the wild wood of its strength and its will. He said, "I take it's not by chance we meet here, piper from the gates of morning?"

"No chance at all," said Kenu Vanithu. "Our ways lie together for a while."

Te-Meriku's laughter had dried up. "So you too are bound into the west?"

"Even so." The piper's tone was steady. "I made the balance and I seek to keep it."

"No more than that?"

"No more than that."

Their eyes met and the hairs pricked on her neck to look from one face to the other.

"In the west," growled Te-Meriku, his hand resting on his sword-hilt, "I am the king and guard the tree beneath this sky. Any that set themselves against me will live long enough to rue it, but no longer. Remember it, Kenu Vanithu."

"No need to bid me to remember – 'twas I gave Imacah mor Tamarhak the kingship. He kept the balance that I made, and so too have all the kings who followed after. Bronze swords have served well enough across the years. Against fools and fisherman, leastways. Against Averla —" The piper shrugged and left the thought unspoken. "But what of you, Marwy Ninek?" he asked, looking to her across the stones. "I knew you must come here in the end but I'd thought it would be sooner."

She fumbled for her answer. "I did not know the place until Te-Meriku showed me."

"Well, you're here now, so look well. This is what Assiolo did for love of you. Look well and think on what it means."

The sunlight filled the wood with green and gold, kindling the king's hair to flame. Slowly she rose up, her fingers curled around the dagger. The knowledge of the knife gave her courage enough to stand. Its hilt was smooth and certain to her grasp, its blade could cut, its point could stab. She took a step towards the pile of stones, and another and another, and, at each step, the distance between the present and the past grew less, and fear rose up like bile within her throat. Another step, and she no longer saw Te-Meriku; she no longer saw the piper; all she saw was Torùkotu, laughing across the years. She closed her eyes against the sight but there he was, set at the heart of her own darkness, as in all the time since Felluria fell into ruin.

"It means more things than one," said Te-Meriku, softly. "Because the past was terrible does not mean the future must be. Open your eyes and look at him."

The long light slanted through the leaves and, when at last she opened her eyes to look at what lay at her feet, she saw sunlight fall onto his face. That was no more his face, fair and hateful, but only shreds of skin across a skull. Stones had baulked the wolves and crows of a meal but little things that could creep and crawl and squirm between the stones had gnawed and nibbled and left a husk behind.

She turned from the thing beneath the stones towards Te-Meriku. The moment stretched out into another, and another. She could not move, she could not speak, she could scarce even breathe.

"The dead are dead," he said, stooping to take one stone from the pile, "and never come they back. Dead men have no weight upon the world, for good or ill."

He dropped the stone to crush the skull to pieces. At the crack of old bones breaking, she looked up and saw the king beneath the flowering tree, a sprig of sweetbriar at his throat, holding out his hand. And somewhere, nearby within the wood, caring nothing for any deed of men, the blackbird poured its ripple of sweet notes into the evening, a liquid, fluent song meaning everything and nothing.

When they returned to the shore, the Sea People were waiting. Thodùhah stood to greet Te-Meriku and scowled at the piper limping at his heel. The dwarf smiled to see it, and greeted him by name, then turned away to stow his gear in a hollow tree, paying no heed to staring men. More than one made the handsign to ward off ill-fortune.

"Not a word, Thodùhah, from you or any other," Te-Meriku warned. "Remember what he was, and what he did."

"And so I do, and like him less each time I remember." The helmsman flung up his arm to block the blow Te-Meriku aimed at him, only half in jest. "Aye, I'll remember too you're the king and doubtless know what you're doing. I'll say no more than that, and nor will any other."

"Any who do will answer to me. He's—"

But what the king would say was never said, for then the boy, with tears blinding his eyes, came running from the seashore to the king, to clutch at his cloak with scrabbling hands and sob that he must, "Come! Come now!" but gave no reason why. So the king went out with him and men stood about, uneasy, waiting, until Thodùhah lashed them with his tongue, reminding them of what they were.

In a little time, the king walked slowly into the camp and the hunters followed him with broken bows in their hands and fear upon their faces. Te-Meriku held a great bird in his arms, cradling it in his cloak tenderly as if it had been a fallen comrade. He laid it down and all came to stand in silence around the blood-red cloth to see the golden wings that spanned a man, the dreadful talons, the dead, dull eyes that in its life had outstared the sun.

"How came this to happen?" asked Thodùhah.

"It was a goose," one of the hunters said. "We heard it first, and then we saw it." Another echoed him, "A grey goose, flying from the sea low towards the shore." The third man said, "By my life – it was a goose I shot! I saw my arrow reach its mark. Then a curlew called three times and it fell to earth an eagle."

Renùku asked the king, his voice choked with grief or fear, "How can it be? To shoot a goose, and kill the sea eagle?"

"It matters not how it happened," said Te-Meriku, his hand on the boy's shoulder. "That it has happened is enough – we must deal with the world as it is, lad, not as we wish it to be. Keep these for me until I return."

He gave his sword and knives to Renùku and walked alone along the shore carrying the eagle. The nightwatch started after him but Thodùhah held him back with a touch on his arm and a shake of his head, so no man followed as the king walked away, not even with his eyes.

Marwy Ninek watched them from a distance, the men of Lyikené, sitting silently beneath an aspen tree with the piper at her side. Almost, from the edges of her eyes, she saw the stranger standing close by her, sunlight glinting on his steel. His laughter rippled across the afternoon. He was there, sure and certain he was there, this unseen stranger, daring to mock the sorrow of the Sea People, to

scorn the king that must walk alone with his namesake in his arms.
Yet, everywhere she looked, she saw no man at all, only the light
flickering as aspen leaves tossed in the breeze. She gripped the bronze
knife in her right hand, and his laughter died away.

—┼— —┼—

Their mark sat in the lee of a crabtree, wrapped in his black coat
with his leathern bag beside him, the boy curled sleeping at his side,
his head resting on his knee. They had seen him as he came ashore,
a stranger with a child as his companion and none to greet him on
the quayside. They had watched him all the day, as he walked from
Ountrie harbour out onto the shore; seen him stand longtimes at the
highwatermark whilst the boy ran and played with seaweed on the
spread of sand, chasing the tide across the beach. They had seen
the flash of silver in his purse and the ring upon his finger, seen
he wore no knife in his belt and yet, when the child grew tired, sat
down beneath the tree easy as if strong walls encircled them. A fool,
a foreigner, an easy prize: theirs for the taking.

He barely started at the touch of the blade against his neck. They
watched his eyes widen as he saw them there beside him. He did
not move, he did not cry out; he sat quiet, waiting for what would
happen next. At his side, the boy slept on, not knowing what men
did in silence in the sunlight.

Old Handy knelt with his knife in his right hand, his finger at his
lips in warning. Young Handy pulled the bag from by his side. It was
not heavy. There was bread there and a quarterweight of honeycake,
a parcel of ham, a withy box of strawberries; more to his taste, he
found his purse with ivory counters and silver pieces, but, beyond
that, only a change of linen, spare clothes for the boy and a book he
could not read. He tossed the book aside and pushed the purse into
his pocket.

"Are you afraid?" Old Handy asked, sitting back on his haunches.
His eyes were wary, the knife was ready. Their victim's eyes flicked
sideways to the child then back towards the knife. He did not move,
he did not speak. "Wise man," grinned Old Handy to his son. Young
Handy reached out, taking the man's hand to draw the ring from
his finger. The boy woke at the movement and cried out to see the
strangers and the knife.

Young Handy jumped as a hand closed on his own. Old Handy's
knife gleamed in the sunlight, moving towards the man's throat.
Then there was a smell of burning in the air, the stench of seared
flesh. Old Handy screamed in pain, clutching at his hand burned
blistered and raw. The knife fell down upon the grass and, for a
dozen heartbeats, all heard the hiss as it cooled on the damp ground.

Young Handy swore, and fell backwards to find he could not stand again. Their victim, a victim no longer, shining and terrible, pulled the boy close into his side, speaking quickly in some outlandish tongue to comfort him.

"Did you think I could not keep what is mine because I have no knife?" Assiolo asked, reaching out his hand to the knife. It did not burn him. He offered it to the old thief, who would not take it, and, with a shrug and a smile, drove the blade into the turf and left it there.

He pulled the purse of silver and ivory from the young thief's pocket and put it in his own. He folded the linen and put that too away; he smoothed the pages of his book and laid it atop the linen. Brightness faded as he did these things, leaving behind only the play of sunlight through the branches of the crabtree. Then Assiolo looked at the old man, who moaned and swore, cradling his blistered palm in the other.

"There's a stream yonder," he told him, "hold your hand a long while in running water and it will soothe the pain." He held out his left hand with its old, white scar across the palm. "See – it will fade, in time. In the end, everything fades."

He touched him gently on the shoulder, and the old thief cursed him again beneath his breath; he nodded to the young thief sprawled upon his back, and the man found he could move again. They fled from him, from the stare of his brown eyes, the smile upon his face and the fire within his flesh.

Assiolo watched them go. He told his son, "Fools and rogues will see what honest men do not. It's all trickery, Imacah, in the end, and theft."

The boy looked at his father, and did not understand why he should be so sad. He thought it wonderful that he could do such things, and had no need to fear a knife or any man that walked beneath the sun or moon.

"Will you teach me?"

Assiolo's face grew grim. He looked down at the boy and thought again of all that he had sworn he would not do. And yet, one by one, he had taken up the tools his father had given him and each time their use came to him more easily. He said, "No, Imacah, I will not. I learned a great deal from my father I do not choose to teach you. I took you from your mother so she should not set you on that path."

He was tangled in Averla's nets and for what purpose? For sake of a brown-eyed boy that should never have been born.

He shook his head to clear it of such thoughts. Assiolo picked up his bag and gave his hand to his son. "Come, Imacah. There's a boat waiting at the harbour, for us and for the tide. They say in Tarhn there's a king lives in a golden hall – in a threnight, we'll find out if such tales are true."

—┼— —┼—

The king walked along the shore, the sea eagle, his other self, his namesake, in his arms. It was more than half his life since last he wept but, now, away from the company of men, he let his tears run down his cheeks, warm as blood and salty as the sea. In a hollow of the dunes, he built a pyre of driftwood and watched it burn whilst all he had lost came back to haunt him. It was not until the fire had fallen into a heap of bones and ashes that he saw he was not alone. There was a woman sitting in the marram grass atop the dune, her hands clasped around her knees. Slowly, slowly, as the king stood to face her, she rose up and walked down the slope towards him.

In her hand she held a little bunch of pink sea thrift from the clumps that grew here and there among the marram. She put back her hood, letting her golden hair fall free, and dropped the thrift into the ashes.

"You crossed the tideline," Averla said, as the flowers shrivelled and burned. "You walked beneath the trees, and now the sea eagle is dead. This is not your place, Te-Meriku."

"It was not I began this," he answered. "I had no thought to be your enemy until you set your will against me."

"You make all the world your enemy – you and all the kings before you in the west."

"I guard that tree, Averla. There was a covenant made when the long day ended. I have kept that covenant, I and all the kings before me, since the piper closed the gates of morning. And I am yet the king: not even you can take that kingship from me."

"Assiolo killed a king. What does that make him?" She put back her hair, shining and bright as the sun across the water. "You know as well as I there cannot be two kings within one land."

"And if he sets himself against me he will die. He's but a man, for all he is Allocco's son. But you, Averla – did you think I would do nothing more than wait for him, like a lamb tethered at the shambles? Now, you are here, and I am here: kill me if you can."

Averla laughed. "Te-Meriku, Te-Meriku, both of us know that that would have no meaning. This is not the time, this is not the place."

"Perhaps I shall kill you. I've killed many in my time."

Blue eyes stared, merciless as the noontime sun, and Te-Meriku shivered to see himself reflected there. In all the days of his kingship, he had feared no man but now fear trickled like cold water down his spine. Very quietly, Averla spoke and, at each word, the king felt the noose tighten round his neck. "Do you think yourself my equal, Te-Meriku? You know you cannot kill me, not now and certainly not upon midsummer's day. If you could so much as touch me, you'd not waste breath in speaking."

Averla's eyes burned bright as the flame within a lantern. He flinched and turned away, blinded as by the sun. No man could bear that light for long, not even the king of Lyikené who held the world in balance with his swordblade and his will.

He cried out, "Think you that you have bound Assiolo as you did his father?"

The wind blew across the shore, rustling the grey-green leaves of the marram. Above the dunes, a sea gull drifted by, its raucous scream a lament for its lost soul. Averla turned from the king to watch the bird sweep out of sight into the empty evening and the light dimmed, as when a cloud passes across the sun. "Assiolo loves me not. He is not his father." Her voice was flat and level, her fire damped and hidden in her flesh. "But I have bound him all the same, setting a tie upon his heart he will not even think to break." Averla smiled and took his arm. "Look yonder to the tideline."

He looked and, though she made no move and said no word, he saw there was a child upon the shore, a laughing boy with sunlight in his hair, splashing barefoot in the sea.

Te-Meriku drew in his breath. "Is it the truth you show me?"

"Real enough in his own place, here but a seeming."

"He is a child that should never have been born."

"He is the child that turned one future into another. The price is very high, to gain my heart's desire, but I think it worth the paying."

"Alas that others must pay the price of your desire."

Te-Meriku turned and watched the boy; saw him fling up a hand to wave across the beach to a black-clad man standing at the highwatermark, who raised his own hand in return. A long, long time, the king stood in silence, watching the boy playing at the water's edge; he watched him weave his patterns of footprints across the sand; he watched him dance with the wind in his face, a ribbon of seaweed trailing from his outstretched hand.

"Look well at him, Te-Meriku," whispered Averla, her hand upon his arm. "He is the future you will not see, another Imacah to take his place among the tales men tell, my hold upon his father's heart."

The king let out a short, sharp gasp but said only, "You have Assiolo; I, Marwy Ninek. All he gave her, he gave freely. When she asks, I think that he will answer."

"Do you think love enough?" Red lips curved into a smile, white fingers gripped his arm and turned him around to face her. He twisted in her grip but had not strength enough to break it. "Do you think she will come to trust you?" Averla asked. "That would be passing strange, given what you are."

"In many ways," said Te-Meriku, "but not in all. She came out from her stone walls to sail with me. That is no little thing, Averla. The future is not yet written, not even you can tell it true."

She knelt beside the fire and rummaged through the ashes. They were yet red hot but her hand took no harm of them and, in a little time, she found the thing she searched for amid the hollow, blackened bones. She held it out upon her palm, an arrowhead of bronze cast in the king's own armoury.

"You are out of your own place," Averla said, "and the world is very dangerous beneath the sun and moon. The days wax long, the moon is full: that you will not die upon this shore, that Marwy Ninek is at your side, does not mean that you are safe or she is safe."

"I have my sword, and my strength, and men of the Sea People about me."

"What are swords and men against Allocco's son? Look there, Te-Meriku, your death is written 'cross the sky." He looked to where she pointed. The sun had stooped beneath the west but, in the east, the long-haired star was rising, casting a sickly yellow light across the land and sea. "I've shaped Assiolo to my hand and he'll give me back my own. And Marwy Ninek – what use is she to you?" Averla asked, smiling as the star's light settled on her hair. On her outstretched hand, the arrowhead burned bright as the balestar. "She's not a woman, but she has no more strength than any woman. Her flesh is as soft, her blood as red: she can suffer in all the ways that women suffer. She learned that long ago. Such lessons are not easily forgotten. Assiolo loved her; as much as ever man loved woman, he loved her. In return she gave him to me, and what I gave runs yonder on the strand."

"I know he loved her; I know she loves him still."

"What does the sea eagle know of love?"

"You killed the sea eagle." A rueful smile, an honest answer, and a flicker of surprise in Averla's face. "I am only a man, Averla. Of love, I know as much as any man, the bitter and the sweet." Te-Meriku stood straight in his red cloak and met her eyes. "The sea eagle is dead, Averla, I am not. Next time we meet, it will be in my own kingdom, and there, I swear, by land and sea and by the empty air," he moved his hands through the pattern of the oath, "I shall not meekly play the part assigned to me. That star is a false seeming, full as much as you!" He stamped hard upon the ashes of the fire, and cried out, "Let the world be as it is!"

There was no child upon the shore, no man at the watermark, no woman at his side. He stood alone among the ashes, the balestar's light full in his eyes, and listened to the wind, a rustle and a whisper through the stiff leaves of the marram.

How does it feel, Imacah asked from the shadows at his back, *to know the time a man must die?*

Holding the answer in his mind, Te-Meriku piled sand atop the ashes before walking slowly back towards the company of men.

XI, Lyikené: I came to keep you company

Well, it's doun intae yon grass-green field, Hey doun hey derrie day
Well, it's doun intae yon grass-green field, Hey doun
Well, it's doun intae yon grass-green field,
There lies a knight that's newly killed. And sing la do an la do a day.

Three Ravens, *Traditional*

He stands beneath the tree, unable to bear longer the company of men. Here, he can be alone. He hunkers down, setting his back against its trunk, and screams his question to the wind. "Did I break faith with Imacah?"

The wind blows hard and cold, whipping his hair into his face, but there is no answer. There will never be an answer. Looking out across his country, he sees the world and the sea are grey, and that is all.

A blackbird's rattle tells him, sometime in the afternoon, he is no more alone. Without lifting his head from his knees, he says, "If you are there, show yourself."

The child steps into sight, her cloak caught up across her arm to stop it trailing across the ground. From its colour it must once have been her grandsire's; even patched and faded it is a splash of brightness against the grey day, wine red, rowan red.

She bows her head, thinking perhaps to borrow a touch of her mother's courtesy. "Te-Meriku."

A prettier child would have looked charming, a maiden out of a story with her basket on her arm, going out to face the world with nothing but her wits and her innocence to defend her. She is too much like her grandsire ever to be pretty; here and now, in so overlarge a garment, she is merely ridiculous, aping her elders' style without any of their substance.

He meets her stare until she looks away. Only then does he deign to return her greeting. "Liùthánwy."

"I thought you would be hungry." She sits down on the grass before him, just too far away to touch, and lays the contents of her basket out between them, bread, cheese, a piece of honeycomb.

"Does your mother know you're here?" She shakes her head. "Your father?"

She shakes her head again. "My father is with the king."

"Why are you here?"

"You said that you were lonely. I came to keep you company."

He helps himself to bread and cheese. She breaks a bit from the honeycomb and eats in silence, licking the sweet stickiness from her fingers.

When she is done, she says, looking down at the broken bread between them, "Kistoru is called today before the king."

He checks his first impulse to strike her hard across the face, forces himself to chew slowly and to swallow, not to shake her until her neck snaps, not to break her like a green stick between his hands. She goes on, with just a hint of a tremble in her voice, enough to show him both her fear and her control of her fear, enough to show she is indeed Hadùhai's blood and Hadùhai's bone, "They will make a settlement."

"Kistoru must take what he is offered, since Imacah was over the boundary."

"Four whalehorns, eight bars of bronze, twelve ewes in lamb and the spear that killed him," she says, reciting the words someone has taught her. "The king set out the price."

He leans his back against the tree, feeling it hard and cold behind him, and makes his voice as empty as he is able. "A price fitting a hill lord's only son. Perhaps Kistoru will be satisfied."

The child crouches forwards and puts her thin hand on his arm. "I brought you an apple. My mother stores the best of them."

It is a little thing within his hand, its golden skin withered but the flesh within still sound. He bends his head to smell it, the scent of sunshine and autumn. Such a little thing, an apple, a man's life.

"Did your grandsire send you, child? To do what he could not."

He leaves those words unspoken but, perhaps, she understands, for she looks up into his face. "Eat it, Te-Meriku," she whispers, "please." Her eyes are the colour of the sea when rain is falling. "A new beginning."

He cannot eat. The very thought of apples sickens him. He throws it hard as far from him as he can. Slow tears run down her face.

"The child is of my blood," the king says, an evening not long after, as they sit together beside the fire of applewood, drinking red wine from Escen, cracking walnuts out of Cincern Dùn. "My son is dead, my son's son died in his cradle, but she is my own heart's blood. I think, had she been a boy, had she been older, I'd have asked of her what I asked of you."

Might have been flickers in the fire, might have been lingers in the shadows, just out of sight, just out of reach, the echo of a word not spoken.

"She is a child."

"Children grow. Alas, I will not see that one become a woman." The king sighs, refills his cup and sits, silent in his thoughts, staring into the fire. "You know, I think, something of women, despite Kistoru's son."

"As much as any other man."

Perhaps a little more than most, these months in the king's hall. Never the same too often; never a lie and never a promise; a night and nothing more. Men's eyes too slide sideways towards him, thinking perhaps, like the women, to offer him what they would not another man. But Imacah is dead and his taste now runs only to women: he can caress their round breasts, let himself sink into their soft flesh, so unlike his in form and feel, and thrust himself into that moment of oblivion when he is free of thought and flesh and memory.

"There are many will come easily to the king's bed. No need to take the unwilling."

So he had seen, the old eagle still longsighted in his hall. Or, he wonders, had it been the child, speaking of what was not her concern?

Hadùhai says, "There is no law in Lyikené but the king's strength and the king's will." He, unwilling, listens, knowing it for truth. "No one will set their back to the door and say, to the king, thus far and no further."

"So I must set a curb upon my own desires when I am king."

"When you are king, you must follow your own star. Your will be done, as mine is done." Hadùhai pauses, sets his hand upon his shoulder, saying softly, "But look ever to the living, lad. Dead men have no weight upon the world," the king spits into the fire to burn ill luck away, "for all that a young fool, selfish and silly as his father, must needs take a wolfspear in his belly rather than sit at the king's left hand."

He opens his mouth to answer, to say it was not so but the king cuts across him, "Oh, words are good and words are true but if you'd have the measure of a man look to his deeds."

"There is no other man beneath this sky could say such things to me, and live," he grinds out. "I'll not speak of Imacah, even to you!" Their eyes meet and he says, more quietly, "He died, and half my heart died with him."

"Words, lad, words. You are alive and lusty, and that says more of you than any words."

"There are high crags and deep waters and sharp swords in Lyikené."

" 'Tis true enough," Hadùhai says, "there are many ways for a man to die before his time. The king must avoid all of them."

He drinks his wine and keeps his silence, thinking of rowan berries tumbled 'cross the floor, of beads of blood scattered 'cross green leaves.

"You gave up that right the day you said me, Yea! Do you understand, Te-Meriku?"

Hadùhai has not raised his voice but, suddenly, he is terrible, the king who can do all the things another man cannot, can see what other men cannot, and his tone makes clear this question must be answered.

"I understand!" he says, slamming down his cup. Drops of wine roll and dance across the table, red as rowan berries, red as spilled blood.

Silence between them, broken only by the snap of logs within the flames. At last, the king sighs and stretches, no longer dreadful, no longer terrible, only an old man sitting close to the fire, wrapped in his cloak against the draught whispering through the cracks in the shutters. "*No harm in taking comfort where it's offered.*"

"*You have not done so.*" *He knows as well as any other in Lyikené the king has slept these twenty years alone; that each year, when spring is just beginning, he lays the first sprig of appleblossom on a cold grave below the hill.*

"*You're young, lad. Young hearts heal as old do not.*"

He cries out, because this is not true, not for him, "*I know as much of love at seventeen as you do at seventy!*"

"*And why not say the child at ten? Oh, I wish she were but five years older. She's what you need, Te-Meriku, she sees you clear as I do, but by the time she's ready it'll be too late for you.*" *He shakes his head, unable to think of such a thing. The king says quietly,* "*There's many kinds of love, Te-Meriku. And when you are seventy, sitting by this fire with some young stripling, you'll know it.*"

Summer comes, and he walks the shore, sometimes with the king, sometimes with the child tagging at his heel. He has grown used to her, these months, and taught her what he was taught years ago in the space before Kistoru's hall, what all boys are taught when they have first a knife. She is quick on her feet as any boy despite the hindrance of her skirts. Today, when he tires of the game, he sets his path towards the great humpbacked rock that straddles the tideline, grey granite bedaubed with yellow lichen. Even at the highest spring tide its top stays dry; once or twice he has sat there all alone, from one tide to the next, watching the waters rise and fall around him. They climb in silence, he with his longer reach pulling her up behind him when she cannot get a grip on the smooth sides, and sit together looking out across the bay.

"*Look there!*" *she cries out, pointing to the sky.* "*Look there!*"

The great bird cannot be mistaken. It is a shadow against the light, sweeping easy as a dream across the empty sky. The wind whips up his hair and she pulls her ribbon from her own to tie it back so she can see his face.

"*Red and gold and bronze,*" *she says,* "*so beautiful. I wish I were beautiful.*"

He laughs at her. "*You're the king's grandchild. Hadùhai's blood will serve you better than any beauty. I would I had such a birthright.*"

"*You have the feathers.*"

"*And so I do. And a tale that gains each time of telling.*" *Over and over, since the apples set on the tree: a highborn babe snatched from its cradle, dropped into Kistoru's waiting arms to raise as his own son. A drunken tale for a man to cling to when his future has been ripped away, when his wife denies his bed in grief, when a bastard whelp is lifted up to glory.* "*Don't believe everything a man says, even if that man be a clanlord of Lyikené. He told other stories when I was a boy with neither name nor future that are as likely to be true."*

The summer sun beats down upon them, the eagle wheels above them, drifting away across the heather hills. He lies back on the rock, letting the sunlight dazzle him and drive away the future and the past. She rests her chin on her knees, biting her lip. "I love you."

"Do you, Liùthánwy?" Her words have little weight upon the world and none at all upon his heart. "I'd thought you over young to play such games."

"It's not a game! When I am grown, will you love me, Te-Meriku?"

"Don't wish for the moon, child. When you are grown, you'll find a better man than me to love you."

Her face bleaches bone-white and he knows, too late, how much he has hurt her. Who would have thought a child of ten could know love? She bites her lip again, swallowing down words or tears. He sits up and puts his arm around her shoulders; feels her stiffen against his touch, unyielding as a figure carved in wood.

"What I can, I'll give you," he says. He holds out his empty hands, one turned up and one turned down. "I swear to you, by land and sea and by the empty air, I'll stand your friend forever."

He moves his hands through the pattern of the oath but she holds out her knife. Shrugging, he offers his wrist and she scores it lightly. A line of blood wells up, as from the scratch of a briar. "See," he says, "you have my word and my blood."

She turns the knife to her own thin wrist. "By land and sea and sky," she says, between clenched teeth, "I'll love none but you."

Her blood runs out, too much, too fast, dripping warm and red across the stone.

"Little fool, you cut too deep." Seizing the knife, he rips a length from his shirt to press hard upon the wound, makes her hold it there as he ties another tightly above her elbow. "No man's worth such folly, child."

Though grey lips, she asks, "Not even Imacah?"

He hears his laugh ring out, so hard and harsh it sounds like a stranger's. "How could he be? I am alive!"

He laughs and laughs and cannot stop because, when he is done laughing, there can be nothing left but tears.

12: Men must fight and men must die

Then the blood was shed on every side
'Til I got her from among them
So come, all young men, would you do likewise?
Fight on until you win them.

I Dreamed Last Night of my True Love, Traditional

Late in the evening, when the king returned, his hands were empty and his face very tired, as if he had walked a long, long way. Silently, he took his place among the Sea People and did not eat, he did not drink, but sat beneath an oak tree with eyes that stared and stared and did not see.

The world beneath the trees was black and silver. The moon was full and far too bright, a wide eye in the sky to watch when the sun had passed away into the evening. It quenched the common stars to dimness, only the balestar's yellow light could stand against it. Marwy Ninek lay awake, alone with her fear in the king's tent. The king's place before the flaps was empty; he had not lain down to rest but sat longtimes beneath the oak, wrapped in his cloak and a space of silence no man dared cross, staring ever eastwards to the long-haired star. She had not known she had learnt to match her sleep to his until he was not there.

She lay awake and watched the chinks of moonlight slide across the ground. There was no wind to stir the leather flap but, as she watched, the gap grew wide to let the light pour in and pool beside her.

"Are you afraid?"

Close by her side the shadows clotted into a man. Fear wrapped itself around her throat, choking her with a ribbon of moonlight. He laughed to hear her gasp. "Did Assiolo never show you the trick to it? Walk quietly, hide in the light and no honest man will see."

The bronze knife lay to her hand, waiting for her to be ready. It knew what must be done and would do its part, if she had strength enough for hers.

"Are you afraid?" the stranger asked again. His breath whispered against her face, his weight pressed heavy on her, his roving hands slid over her, before, behind, above, between, below. "I was sent to ask three questions and carry back the answers. That was the first, to ask and to be answered."

Her fingers closed upon the hilt.

Mocking laughter in the moonlight. His left hand pulled up her shift, his right hand undid his laces, his knees pushed her legs apart. All this she had known before. She would not know it again. The knife was firm within her grasp. He whispered in her ear, his breath hot against her cheek, "My second is, *What do you trust?*"

"I trust this knife," she said, and struck at him. Quick and sharp, the blade went home, slipping between his ribs. She twisted the knife and he arched in agony. Blood spilled warm and sticky over her until, with all her strength, she pushed him away, crying out to Te-Meriku.

The stranger lay where he had fallen. He turned his head to look at her and, though his death was very close, she saw him smile, as if he had indeed the mastery. The man reached out, catching her hair to pull her down towards him and whisper, "This is my third: *Do you think love enough to give you back your own?*"

The moonlight on the floor waned small; the king was at the threshold, the nightwatch at his back. Te-Meriku knocked the man away: no time left to him to have his answer. She heard the snap as his neck broke, saw the king toss him aside, a puppet with its strings broken. Together they looked at the corpse in the moonlight. Both saw the sun and the moon burned into its arm. Both knew their meaning.

"I am the king," Te-Meriku said, "and yet I did not see, I did not hear."

The dead man's eyes stared empty into hers. She told the king, and her own words startled her, "I think it is because you are an honest man!" Then she laughed, a bitter jest against the world. "So was Assiolo an honest man. There is no place of safety for honest men in the world the piper made."

Shaking, stained with a dead man's blood, she crouched with the knife in her hand, laughing because she could not weep until Te-Meriku put out his hand to steady her. She flinched from his touch but he knelt beside her, showing her his empty hands. "Marwy Ninek, I am not your enemy."

His speaking calmed her. She remembered the look in his eyes as he stood beneath the crabtree and that, tonight, when her fear was at its strongest, she had called out and he had answered. She dropped the knife and turned to him, pressing her face against his jerkin. It smelled of salt and sweat, of the oil used to dress the leather, but behind this, faint as a memory of long ago, was the dry aromatic scent of mountain thyme.

"Will you trust me?" he asked, as he had the first morning of their sailing. She answered, looking only at him that she might not see the dead man beside them, "As I trust the knife you gave me."

Te-Meriku wiped the knife and gave it back to her. He wrapped her in his red cloak, quenched now to blackness by the moonlight, and scooped her up into his arms. As he passed him by, he said to the nightwatch, "Do what is necessary here. And, Ardùvai, do it quickly."

The king carried her to a tent where a dozen men were armed and waiting, for all had woken to her shout. "Stay, Thodùhah. The rest of you, out now! Break up the camp – get the ship fast beneath the tideline." To Marwy Ninek, still cradled in his arms, he said, "You'll be safe with me upon the open sea. Averla cannot reach you there, no matter that the sun shines or the moon is bright."

He set her down by Thodùhah who took one look at the blood drenching her shift and matting her hair and asked, "What happened, Marwy Ninek? Where are you hurt?"

She could not answer. There were too many men about her, clattering with their goods and gear. She held her knife in her right hand and shrank trembling against the king.

"Te-Meriku," the helmsman's voice was grim, "if any of this company has raised a hand against a guest then death's too kind a fate."

"Not her blood," Te-Meriku told Thodùhah, shortly, his arm close and strong around her, "nor any of Lyikené. The rest I'll tell another time – give her a drink to steady her."

The old man handed her a cup with barleyspirit. She was still shaking too much to hold it steady and it slopped and spilled until Te-Meriku took it from her and held it to her lips. Greedily she drank, and soon the liquor set some distance between her and the things she had seen and done that night.

"What of that twisted creature?" Thodùhah asked. "Things go awry when he is near. I set three men to watch him ere he slept. Say but the word."

"He's what he's always been," said the king. "He neither slew the sea eagle nor came a-creeping through the moonlight. Wherefore shall I kill him?" The helmsman began an answer but the king raised his hand for silence. "No, Thodùhah! He's not a man. He stands outside the laws of men; it was ever so, since the days of Imacah mor Tamarhak."

"Imacah called him monster!"

"And so he is. But it is not all he is," Te-Meriku told him. "Enough, man. Bid Renùku bring Marwy Ninek her gear, and bid him be quick. I want us gone with the daylight."

The night was growing old; at last the moon set, all and around the darkness thinned into morning. The nightwatch had stripped the corpse and hung it by its ankle from a branch that the ravens might eat its liver and the crows peck out its eyes. It swung slowly round and round while spots of blood fell down, pattering upon dried leaves like drops of rain.

Men must fight and men must die but the sun still rises and fills the wood with green and gold. The armed men came with the sunrise. The sentries had not slept at their posts, neither had they grown unwary at night's ending. Perhaps a man of Eulana would have heard the silence press heavy on the wood, perhaps a man of Eulana would have known that birds do not cease to sing because the sun has risen, but the sentries were not men of Eulana. They were of the Sea People. They knew the patterns of the tide across the shore and the stars across the sky, they could read the purpose in the grey gull's flight and hear the meaning in the curlew's call, but they knew no more than the child at its nurse's breast of what was hiding in the light beneath these trees of oak and ash and aspen. Paths run straight in Lyikené and a man can see great distance. Here, all ways must twist and turn about the trees and oftentimes were blocked with brambles and with briars.

Six men stood as sentry as the camp was broken up and five of them were dead before the last saw movement from the corner of his eye; unthinking, he twisted sideways so the blow missed its mark and gave him the time he needed to call warning before he died.

"So it begins," said the piper to himself, hunkering down in his blue coat in the hollow of the oak tree. The hanging man swung slowly to and fro above him, its eyes staring blindly, its ears deaf to the clash of bronze on iron and the cries of men, as they fought, as they died.

The piper had lived a long, long time; he was not deaf, he was not blind, there was nothing he did not know of the ways one man can break another with a sword, with a spear, with his own bare hands. He watched, and nothing that he saw was new to him. He saw a man die cleanly, his head near cut from his shoulders; he saw another scrabble to keep his guts within his belly; he saw two brothers, the nightwatch and the day, fight back to back, until one had his head smashed by a swinging mace as if a man's skull were no more than an eggshell; he saw Te-Meriku the king ever where the press was greatest and that, though the iron blades, the maces and the spears, thrust merciless at any other of the Sea People, no blow was ever struck against him. *Not here*, thought the piper, *not now. Yours is a different fate.*

All this he saw, and all this could be seen by any of the Sea People, had they the time to stand and stare. Yet more than this he saw, that was still hidden by the light from the eyes of men. He saw a woman standing on the edge of darkness between the clearing and the forest, a golden-haired woman who smiled and smiled at what was done, and did not turn away.

Renùku crashed down beside the tree. The boy had lost his sword, his strength not yet equal to his courage. The ragged slash across his face from ear to chin would mar his looks forever, if he lived long enough to heal it. "Can you walk, lad?" asked the piper. The boy nodded. "Get to the ship, if you want to live. It's beneath the tideline."

Renùku did not move, but only stared out at the fray, blank with pain and fear. The piper shook his shoulder. "The dead are dead, lad, makes no sense to join them. Run."

The boy ran, his face wet with blood and tears.

The last tents were all aflame and Marwy Ninek stumbled past, Thodùhah beside her, his drawn sword ready in his hand. Her face was a mask, all thought and feeling driven out by terror. *She has seen this before*, the piper thought. *This is the thing that shaped her.*

Armed men sprang towards her. The quartermaster took one, his sword biting deep; then the king was there, his arms red to the shoulder with other men's blood, and cut down the rest, easy as a farmer in the cornfield. He said something to Marwy Ninek the piper could not hear. She made no answer; she was not looking at Te-Meriku but beyond him towards the wood.

The light was too bright and dazzled her. The piper, whose eyes no light could blind, saw her put up her hands that she might see clearly. The moment passed, the light died. No one was there in truth or seeming, only the sunlight falling between the trees to windflowers on the mossy grass.

Te-Meriku's shout rang out, pitched to carry above the clang and clamour of the day, "To the ship! To the ship!"

Those that could run did, Thodùhah dragging Marwy Ninek with him. Te-Meriku stood his ground but, at his cry, his enemies melted back into the sunlight. One alone remained, his hair as bright as hoarfrost on a winter's morning. He held an iron mace and Te-Meriku brought up his sword to parry it. The man laughed, poising light as a dancer before the music starts, easy as a cat before its pounce, terrible as a hawk before its strike from the clear air, and swung with all his weight. The king's bronze sword snapped under the weight of iron. Then this man too was gone, leaving his laughter behind him, and the king alone with the dying and the dead.

From the hollow of the oak tree, the piper watched the king pick up the pieces of his sword and kneel beside the nightwatch, his bloody hand upon his shoulder. "Time to go, Ardùvai. You'll live, man, to this day's ending and many others after it."

"Almecu?"

"He's gone." Te-Meriku's fingers tightened on Ardùvai's shoulder, pulling him back. "I'll sit a deathwatch with you, aye and speak for him myself, but our first duty's to the living."

Ardùvai shook off the king's hand and bent back to his brother, holding him in his arms. Around and about, the Sea People gathered up their wounded comrades, tender and careful as mothers with their children. The dead were left beneath the trees where they had fallen, having no more need of kindness or of succour.

An edge of roughness in the king's voice. "Ardùvai, we must away."

"A moment." The nightwatch cut a lock of his brother's sandy hair and kissed his ruined face good-bye. He took his brother's cloak, stained as it was with blood and brain, and covered him with his own, then stood up from the corpse, swaying a little. The king reached out to steady him. "I gave a promise to our mother I'd bring him home again," Ardùvai whispered, black eyes a-burning in his bone-white face. "There'll be a reckoning for this, I swear it."

"Sometimes there are promises we cannot keep," the king said, his arm around his shoulder, "now come away."

That's true enough, the piper thought, as he followed them down to the shore. *One thing to make a promise, another thing to keep it.*

The quartermaster passed a sheathed sword to the king as Thodùhah took his place at the helm. At his word, the oars cut into the water to take the ship out into the bay. The piper found himself a place beside the gunwale and stowed his gear beneath a rowing bench. That place was empty, the man being dead beneath an aspen tree. When the ship had left the lee of the land behind and slipped out into the sunlight the oars were shipped and the sail with its three red eagles unfurled to catch the wind. The nightwatch sank into his brother's place, his brother's cloak around his shoulders, his hands still wet with his brother's blood, staring back towards the shore with blazing eyes. Those men as were unhurt saw to their comrades after the quartermaster's direction, he knowing much of leechcraft.

"A dozen dead within the wood," he told the king as soon as he had time, "and three more like to die before the evening. The rest will live if their wills be set on it."

Marwy Ninek had curled herself near Thodùhah. Now and then he glanced down or set his hand upon her shoulder, a touch of comfort she was glad to feel. She gripped her knifehilt and tried to drive her memories away: a vision of Averla watching as men fought and died in the space between them. Halfway through the morning, the boy came up with food and wine, his face stitched and salved.

He tried to eat but, wincing, set the plate aside. "I ran," he whispered in the end, and could not check his tears.

"So too did I," said Thodùhah, between mouthfuls. "So did Marwy Ninek."

"At the king's command. 'Twas the piper bid me."

"And that's the best I've ever heard of him. Lad, had Te-Meriku known what was in that wood, or I, we'd not have let you set your foot one step above the tideline."

One man died quickly before the noontime; another lingered into the afternoon, falling first asleep and then quietly into the dark. The third one had a hard time of it for all the quartermaster's poppy. At last, he cried out for the king. All the rest drew back to let him through, making a space and a silence in the time before the evening. Te-Meriku took the man in his arms, stroking back his matted hair.

"Kestai, what do you seek?"

"Darkness," he gasped, his eyes steady on the king's face, "and silence." His hand fumbled at his side until he found the knife he no longer had the strength to lift.

"Are you certain?" asked the king, taking the knife in his own sure grip to hold it where the man could see.

Kestai nodded. "Please," he mouthed, "before the sunset."

"That I can grant," Te-Meriku said. He bent close and kissed him thrice, on the forehead as a father, on the cheek as a brother, on the mouth as a lover, and drove the knife hard home. He laid the body down and set the knife in its right hand. "Give the dead to the sea," he said to his company. "Let the sun set on the living."

Marwy Ninek felt Thodùhah's hand tighten on her shoulder. "It is not a little thing to be a king," he said, quiet enough for the boy not to hear. She nodded. Te-Meriku had turned his attention to the sword the quartermaster had given him. Its hilt was two handspans of whalebone, as plain and unadorned as the scabbard round the blade. He drew it from the sheath and hefted it, squinting along each edge for any flaw, taking a minute to find the balance of its weight in his hands.

The piper stood up from his place, as if he wished to speak. Te-Meriku nodded slightly to his helmsman; Thodùhah jerked his head in answer, then whispered to the boy. The dwarf had not taken a step towards the king, a step but barely three, when Renùku put out his hand and caught at his sleeve. Perhaps the boy asked for a tune as the price of passage, for, in a moment, he sat down again, pulled out his pipe and began to play. Then the nightwatch called Renùku to him, bidding him bring oil and a whetstone for his knives which had, he said, grown dull upon the land.

Marwy Ninek had not thought that she could sleep but sleep she did, the short night through, wrapped in her cloak in her place against the hull, her arm across her face to shield it from the moonlight because men had better things to do than raise an awning. When she woke, she sat again near Thodùhah and looked out across the water. The morning light splintered on the sea and, dazzled, she raised her hand to shade her eyes.

"In the wood, beneath the trees," she asked him, "what did you see?"

"I saw nothing," said Thodùhah from the helm, "beyond my comrades and my enemies."

"Nay, lass," said the dwarf, "none on this ship saw aught but the light." She looked hard at him, and then she turned away. "There is no need to say it," he said, "I know your thought. You wonder what it says of me that I saw what honest men did not."

"You are not a man; perhaps it says no more of you than that."

"Perhaps no more than that," he agreed. "But you saw too, many times and many, a man the king did not. What does it say of you that you can see those hiding in the light?"

And so she had, but it had not been a man watching yestermorn beneath the trees. "You saw her too?"

"Oh, I saw Averla watching in the wood," he answered. "My eyes are not dazzled and, even in the sunlight, I see clearly. She has her plan, she has her purpose, and she has the means to come to her desire."

She remembered, and it was an ill thought to make her shiver in the sunshine. She asked, sharply, "Is that the truth?"

"All that I say is true." The dwarf smiled, and never had his smile seemed so much like a grimace. "Averla gave him what you could not. If Assiolo is forced to a choice, which will he choose?"

"I love him, and he loves me."

"I do not doubt it. Yet you and Averla, between you, changed his future."

She turned away and did not answer. The dwarf pulled out his pipe and played a lovesong. Many times, sitting in the evening light among the roses, she had heard Assiolo sing that song and now her heart clenched at the memory.

She could not bear such sweetness, each note a memory of love betrayed. "Enough!" she cried out to break the music, and the king came quickly to her side. The piper shook his head when Te-Meriku looked at him, his question in his face.

"How soon until Lyikené," she asked, for sake of saying something to break the silence.

"Seven days," the helmsman said, "unless the wind changes its course."

"What chance of that, Thodùhah?" asked the king. "You know the sea and all its rules and reaches better than any other."

The old man held his finger to the wind. "No chance at all."

"Alas that I am no more than a man." Te-Meriku spread out his open hands, laughing. "Men I can command, but not the wind. The wind blows where it will and no king beneath this sky can turn it."

"King of the Sea People," the piper jested, "but not king of the sea."

"What I am, I am, and it is enough," answered Te-Meriku, certain and smiling.

"Are you so sure? Do you know why Tamarhak's son named me *Monster*?"

"Tell me."

"Because I see what men cannot. My eyes are neither dazzled by the light nor blinded in the dark. As Averla has her plan, so do I have mine. Yesternoon, I told you true: I will keep the balance I made. Remember it, Te-Meriku; remember too I've lived a long time in the world and in that time there have been many kings in Lyikené. Not one of them had the strength to stand against Averla. Now look me in the eye and say again, *It is enough!*"

"Enough indeed!" said the king, very softly. "Find a place and keep to it. We have had enough of words."

The piper bowed his head and turned, finding his way over rowing benches to the prow. Men drew back as he passed them, and any that his shadow touched crooked his fingers in the sign against ill-fortune. The king's eyes followed him, resting longtimes upon him. Perhaps the piper noted this, perhaps he did not. He sat cross-legged 'gainst the hull, chewing dried fish and twice-baked bread, drinking small beer from the common store. Shadows shortened across the morning. At last he pulled out his pipe and made a melody rise up into the day, light and dancing as the ship's passage 'cross the water. Suddenly Te-Meriku cast off his cloak and his jerkin and laid the sword in its scabbard down upon them, set down with it the knives from his sleeve and his belt. He barked an order to his men, bidding them pull out the benches and clear a little space, then, in his shirtsleeves, turned to her. "Marwy Ninek, let me show you how to use that knife."

"It served me well enough in the moonlight," she answered. The king's mood had darkened, the laughter gone from his eyes and the distance yawned again between them.

"The blow was fortunate," he said drily, "a wonder you did not hit a rib. As well he came to frighten you and not to kill. Next time it might be otherwise."

Still she hung back.

"You trusted me in the moonlight," he said, "and walked alone with me beneath the trees."

He showed her, as he might have shown the boy, all the places where a man's life lies close to the surface and the ways she might use the blade against them; made her practice, over and over, drawing the knife from its sheath within her sleeve, smoothly and unseen, using her hand without her eye to guide it. Then he challenged her, "Kill me if you can."

She hesitated, the blade naked in her hand. "You have no knife."

He laughed. "I do not need a knife to kill you. That one redresses the balance a little."

After an hour he told her, as she sat rubbing her bruises, "I am bigger than you, Marwy Ninek, I am stronger. If you pit your strength against mine, you will lose. So do not try to fight as if you were my equal. Your hope lies in that blade. Keep it safe, keep it secret, then use it as I showed you. A moment is all you will have. A moment is enough."

Again she tried, again she failed. The next time, when he came at her, she twisted to let his weight unbalance him so that they fell together and brought her knife up to press its point against his throat. She stared into his eyes, exultant.

"Very good," he said, a smile glinting in his eyes, "but look down." She looked and saw he held a second knife just above her belly. "You'd have followed me into the dark, with a slower death than the one you offered me. The knife was there but you did not see because you were not watching."

Thodùhah called out, "An old trick, Marwy Ninek."

"That is not fair," she said pulling away, somewhere between rage and laughter. "I did not know you had another knife."

Te-Meriku sat up laughing. "It's not a game to kill a man. You love your life and so does he. The only rule is this: better your enemy dies than you. The past is gone, the future may never happen – the moment is all that is left to you. Remember that." He put the knife away and held out his hands. "Let us try again."

She did not move. The past swirled around her like the strands of his red hair. "There was a knife within the room. I thought that I could use it." Her voice was hard with hatred. "Late in the night, he slept and I took it from the table."

The king lounged beside her, easy in the sunlight, as if she spoke to him of little things that did not matter.

The sunlight faded against the memory: herself, naked, bleeding; firelight shining on the bright bronze edge as it swept down towards the monster, towards the pulse beating at his throat.

"He was not asleep," she said, flat as she could manage. "It was a game he played, over and again, to offer hope and then, laughing, snatch it away. Like you, he was bigger than I am; like you, he was stronger."

A hand twisting hard around her wrist; the knife clattering upon the floor; herself pleading for mercy; the red king pushing her down again into the dark. Memory clenched itself about her heart; she looked at her bronze blade and asked, "Could I have killed Torùkotu that night?"

He shook his head, no trace of laughter left in his face. "Not if you dealt with him as with me today. The balance lies with strength and knowledge."

"You're very like to him, Te-Meriku."

"Am I? Are you quite sure?"

"You are the king; your will the law. No one says to you, *No further.* Your only limits are the ones you choose. Only the very brave or the very foolish would think to set themselves against you."

She knew it was the truth she spoke and yet, beneath his steady gaze, it was truth blurring into falsehood. He had given her a knife and shown her how to use it; he had answered when she called to him; he had pulled her from the nightmare. She swallowed hard and forced herself to speak. "The men of Felluria were dead and I had set myself against him, denying him his love, denying him his son. He locked the door and told me all that he would do before the morning unless, unless..."

All around them the day moved on, in the unhurried movements of the Sea People, in the roll and sway of the ship upon the water, in a grey gull's scream as it quarrelled with another of its kind. And all the while, the piper played, little tunes known to each man there in his cradle. Te-Meriku lounged in the sunlight, listening, waiting.

"I kicked away the chair," she said at last in a dry whisper, hugging her arms around her knees, "and even that was not enough. He let me choke and cut me down and kept all his promises before the morning."

She looked again at the king, who sat so close beside her, his hair flickering on the wind like strands of flame, but could not read the thoughts within his eyes, nor even tell for true their colour; they were not grey, nor green, nor blue but each and none in turn as one moment passed into another, like the surface of the sea itself as the patterns of light and shadow shifted across the afternoon.

"There's many in this world a-feared of me, and with good reason," Te-Meriku said. "I've killed many and many in my time, and doubtless will kill more before the end; how it will go with

Assiolo, I do not know, but I can tell you this: such horrors in the night are no part of me."

She nodded. *Passing honest*, Edo Incithu had said of him. *He wears no face but one.* His face was like that monster's but behind it was another mind entirely. There was a strange, hard comfort in that thought.

"And so you sought revenge," he said, after a little time of silence, "stealing an apple and a man's wits."

"A broken vengeance all among the ruins." Memories of blood swam beneath the surface of her mind. She forced them back into the dark. "Not the end I sought."

"Death is the only end. Assiolo knew it." Te-Meriku shrugged and picked up her knife. "I've killed men for less than was in Felluria and, if I have bad dreams, 'tis not for sake of them."

She held up her hands, so small beside his, pointing at the bruises on her wrists where he had caught them to throw her down upon the planks. Strange to laugh at such a time but laugh she did, a bitter laugh with no humour to it. "You have your skill, Te-Meriku; you have your strength and your kingship and your company; you know all the ways to kill a man. I had no strength to kill him, a king with armed men all about him. I thought, if I showed him as a monster, his own kind would bring him down in his own hall, as the pack turns on a rabid wolf. But, even mad and mindless, his strength and will were greater than all the rest."

"The apples of the borderlands are not the apples of Lyikené. There was another king better suited to your purpose."

Idly, with one finger, Te-Meriku traced the pattern of branches twisting around the ivory hilt of her knife. Now, in the sunshine, she saw the tiny golden apples growing on that tree. Always, they had been there, but she had never looked close enough to see them; always, it had been the blade she thought of, never the hilt. Such a little thing, an apple, to change one future to another. She had been a fool, she thought, looking at Te-Meriku, never before to see that, in Lyikené, the bronze blade and the apple tree were one.

"It was Assiolo brought me hope, a new beginning," she burst out. "I could not give him up. So when Averla offered me his life —" She remembered brown eyes staring out of the winter sickness, begging her, beseeching her, *Don't let me sleep!* "I cannot regret that choice, Te-Meriku, though the world fall into ruin."

"Aye, I know it," he said softly. "Love's bitter full as much as sweet and oftentimes our choices twist themselves into another's purpose. Assiolo had strength and will enough to kill a monster and yet Averla's held him fast full five years and longer. What he is now, neither you nor I can know."

She could only whisper, "He is Assiolo, my love forever and for always."

The king set down the knife and turned to her, meeting her eyes a moment in the bright sunlight, then went to talk with the nightwatch, who sat, grim-faced, honing his sword upon a whetstone, wrapped in his brother's cloak.

As he had done before Eulana, the nightwatch slept the light away, all through the morning and far past noontime, to wake only when the sunlight, slanting from the west, slipped beneath the sealskin awning and shone full onto his face. But now, when he woke, he sat always in his brother's place, though he no longer wore his brother's cloak and no longer honed his knives. They were sharp as could be; blades bitter with regret, sharp as sorrow, edged with ill intent. Come the evenings, in the hours before his duty, he would call out for a game of fox and geese. Ruthless with fox, baffling with geese, he played with all his skill and none of his jesting; played any who would take him, aye, and beat them too, nine times out of the ten – the boatswain and the quartermaster, a clansman with a broken sword-arm, the boy if he could find no other – his black eyes glittering within his pale, cold face, pocketing their tally-sticks and promises to be redeemed upon the shore.

The fifth night, the piper took the challenge; sitting down to play, he shook his head at Ardùvai's offered stake. "I'm but a beggar, lad. I've neither gold from the mountains nor ivory out of the northern seas."

The nightwatch's mouth stretched itself into a wide grin. "I'll play for love of playing with my friends, Kenu Vanithu. You were not among them last time I made count. My stake is there – set down one to match it or else give way to one who can."

The dwarf's smile was no more mirthful than the man's as he laid his pipe beside the board. "Is this playing high enough to tempt you? I'll set my livelihood against your promise."

"What promise?"

"That you will answer when I ask, and do what I require."

"What would you have me do?"

"If I told you that where be the gamble? So will you play?"

Ardùvai's eyes were chips of jet, glinting beneath black brows. "Aye, I'll play – but you must take me fox and geese to win this wager. Less than that and I'll have four fingers from your right hand to mar your livelihood forever." He set a knife beside the pipe and sat back, lounging against his brother's gear. His smile was thin and wolfish. "You have the geese."

The piper stretched out his hand, turning it this way and that before his face. A fair hand it was for one so twisted, fine-fingered and graceful, with neither line nor scar to mark its age. A moment's pause, then, with a shrug, he reached down and moved the first goose.

Ardùvai's fox was lithe and nimble, snapping at the edges of the flock as the geese waddled across the board. One goose was down, and another, and another, but it was the piper's face filled with mocking laughter as he moved another into the fox's path.

"You know that you must take it," he said, against the nightwatch's hesitation.

"And when I do you close the trap." Ardùvai made the move, then swept the pieces from the board. "It seems you'll have fingers left enough to play the second of the pair."

Then Ardùvai set up the board and they played again. A long, defensive game this one, the geese clustering tight to give no entry to the fox, pushing it towards the edges and the margin. And yet, and yet, slowly, slowly, the fox crept round, nipping and nibbling at the flock, sliding, slippery as any fish, through the traps sent to catch it, until at last it slunk behind the line to wreak carnage at its leisure.

"It seems," the dwarf said, smiling, "I'll keep my fingers to play another day. Your promise binds you, Ardùvai."

"Kenu Vanithu," said Ardùvai, through gritted teeth, "I know all the old tales; I know who you are and what you did. You beat me fair, and I'll keep my wager if I can, but I was the king's man before I met you. I'll not act 'gainst him in any way, for any reason. And if that means I am foresworn, sobeit."

"Nay, lad, that was not the wager." The dwarf picked up his pipe and slipped it back into his pocket. "We did not speak of ifs and buts and maybes. When I ask, you will answer." He nodded to the nightwatch and stepped away, leaving Ardùvai cursing behind him.

And since Eulana, Marwy Ninek thought, looking around her at the Sea People, much had changed. Thodùhah was yet the same, sitting at the helm or near it, setting the ship's swift course across the water, but there were spaces on the benches, dead men's gear set carefully astern, men nursing broken bones and swordcuts, looking sidelong at the piper, fingers crooked against ill-fortune. On the sixth day, another died despite the quartermaster's leechcraft. They gave his body to the sea, wrapped in his sea-green cloak, a plait of his children's hair bound tight around his wrist. Standing beside Thodùhah, Marwy Ninek watched without a word, her hood pulled down across her face. Nothing she could say could give meaning to the moment.

"Men die, lass," Thodùhah muttered, "and many go before their time. The world is as it is."

"I know," she said, shivering for all the mildness of the morning. "And yet I wish it were not so."

That afternoon, a squall blew up, the sea grew choppy and a shoreman, carrying a pan of fishscraps to cast over the side, stumbled as he passed her. The contents of his bowl tipped over her, a noisome mess of blood and guts and scales. She looked up, her first thought that 'twas no more than mischance, and flinched from the anger in his face, heard his hissed words in shocked surprise. "Treacherous whore!"

Her blood thundered in her ears as she looked beyond him, this way and that, seeking out the king's red hair, saw him at last, far forward at the prow beneath the eagle's head, his back towards the company, his face towards the west. She opened her mouth to call to him but the shoreman cursed again, leaning over her, looming and terrible, his breath hot on her face, his hands outstretched.

Her right hand crept towards her knife. The next breath, the nightwatch was beside her, catching her wrist with a shake of his head, hurrying her aft and shouting to the boy for a bucket of saltwater and a rag, cursing the great oaf's clumsiness to any with the ears to hear it. In that same moment, Thodùhah beckoned from the helm and the boatswain took his place. The old man stretched and came forward, took the shoreman by the arm, staying his protest with a sharp word, bidding him sit and be silent, lest a bad beginning become a worse end. Men shifted position, clustering close upon the rowing bench to screen them with their bodies. Soon, a game of knuckle bones began, lively and loud, but, oft and again, watchful eyes flicked forward to the king. Nothing in his manner showed that he had seen or heard. The quartermaster joined him at the prow and what he spoke of none could hear but that it caught the king's good humour all could see.

"What did Kalanu say to you?" Ardùvai muttered 'neath his breath.

"No need to make great cry of it," she answered, plunging the rag into the water and wiping fishguts from her face and hair. "His cousin died today."

"So did a dozen more beneath the trees." His voice was grim, his eyes hard as obsidian. In the black depths of those eyes she glimpsed a ghost, a man who was not there. "What's that to anything? He's sworn an oath, he and every man aboard, that cuts across all kith and kin, to take the king's enemies as his own, and the king's friends likewise. And if he'll not remember for himself, another man must do it for him."

"Not on my account." She remembered the women of Felluria, long ago, in the autumn of the ruin; their stony eyes, their bitter words. "Ardùvai, let it go."

He was a fine-made man, slender and graceful, more lightly built than many of his comrades, but she had seen him fight and knew his strength and quickness, wielding a sword as if it were a part of him. Not an easy matter to set her will against his. Even so, she shook her head. "The insult was to me. Let it pass."

His eyes met hers and this time there was no silken sheath around the blade. "Nay, it cannot pass – such affront to the king's own guest. Te-Meriku will spill his blood across the deck an he hears of it."

"Don't you think blood enough's been spilt already!"

"After you and I drank to friendship together?" He raised a mocking brow. "No need to trouble the king – he'll face my knife before the day is done. Any that slights you, slights me, and I've no mind to wear a stain upon my honour. No little thing, among the Sea People." A little light laugh against her gasp but then something of the hardness went from his eyes and he said, "Oh, don't fret on it; it's not become a killing matter, not yet, and I'll make certain that it doesn't. Te-Meriku'll keep his back turned, since I can claim the insult for myself."

Marwy Ninek sighed with relief to catch his meaning and gave her mind to washing. There were fishes' scales and fishes' blood trickling down inside her shirt. She undid its laces, trying to wash and keep her modesty. Ardùvai turned his back, standing between her and other men's eyes, and, at the second thought, she shrugged and pulled off the shirt, crouching between the benches in her shift to cup saltwater over arms and neck. Ardùvai eyed her fouled shirt with distaste, then pulled off his own and dropped it on the bench beside him.

"Clean two days since," he said, "better than that stinking mess. I'll wear my brother's last. I'd give it you save that you'd be lost within it. A great, clumsy, careless lump, Almecu..."

He could not hold his tone quite steady and it faltered on the name. She paused her washing and looked up. She remembered a-drinking with him beneath the stars, his careless laughter and his easy pride. Now, had she been a woman, she could have wept for the change in him. She sat back on her heels, saying softly, "Ardùvai."

He turned around and she saw the vivid bruises on his arms and chest where mail had turned an edge aside; a thin scar, healed but still red, across the ribs of his left side, marring the whiteness of his skin. A lover might have traced such marks with pride, reading his prowess written there, or else with trembling fingers, knowing that, though this time death had passed him by, next time it might be otherwise. But she was not his lover and his body was of no concern to her; only that cracked note mattered, speaking of a pain that ached harder than bruises, cut deeper than a swordblade. His eyes, glittering and dangerous, dared her to speak but grief she knew in all its forms, and grief she read in the hollows of his cheeks and the purple stains beneath his eyes. "It was true enough," she said quietly, standing to face him, "all that Kalanu said. Had it not been for me, you'd not have been beneath those trees and, had you not, the dead would still be living."

"Might have been will never be."

"Ardùvai —"

"The worst moment's yet to come," he interrupted, his voice low and throbbing, "my mother's face when she sees he is not there. He ever was her favourite. Her youngest, her lastborn, the child of her good fortune."

And, for the aching desolation in his words and the sorrow in his eyes, she would have stepped in and held him close, comfort for the comfortless, for all he was a man, and near a stranger, one of the Sea People. Only the fishguts stayed her. Perhaps he saw her sympathy, for his face twisted into a rueful grin. "Here's a time to speak of it, me half-naked and you reeking of fish. Almecu died afore his time, I'll grant you, but you had little enough to do with it – Averla's toying with Te-Meriku, and so's the piper too, I reckon. The rest of us are just the geese, no matter in ourselves, easy pickings when we break the flock. But," and, for a moment, his eyes danced with something of their former jesting, "the geese together can baffle the wiliest of foxes. That's something to remember, and that's the lesson I'll knock into Kalanu's thick skull."

Fishguts or no, she took his hand in hers. "Your brother died before his time, and in some measure that is due to me. I'll not forget this, Ardùvai, and, when the time comes, what I can, I'll do."

"I'll hold you to that promise," he answered, master of his grief. "There's many and many that will die, if Te-Meriku cannot keep his own, and those that live on will rue it. He'll need us both upon that day."

"No chance then," she asked, "nor even courtesy, that you should offer me your barleyspirit?"

A flash of his old smile, bright as sunlight through black clouds. "No chance at all, but something of courtesy. I've neither your years nor Te-Meriku's but I drank in old stories with my mother's milk. Since the piper closed the gates of morning, there's been a reckoning due. Te-Meriku wants you aside him when it happens, and I'm the king's man. I'll keep you safe and get you there, anyway I can, but if we're friends along the way so much the better, for his sake as well as ours."

She nodded and stooped again to washing. After a while, he poured the filthy water over the side and hauled up another bucketful. "You'll smell of herring 'til this journey's end," a sidelong glance, his roguish smile, "ah well, so too do the fishwives. Their menfolk like them all the same."

"Ardùvai." Half a laugh and half a warning.

"Nay, herring was never to my taste. Eel now, long and —"

"Ardùvai!" Impossible not to let her laugh ring out, though men's heads turned around towards it. She bowed her head and busied herself with rinsing off the rest of the fish. When she had done what she could, her hair was dripping wet but clean of blood and slime; her face and arms likewise, though here and there silver scales still clung tight to her skin. She pulled on his shirt. It was finer than the one she had had before and smelled faintly of salt and ambergris.

Ardùvai looked her up and down and his grin brought out her own. "It suits you fine, being you're dark as I. Now, go talk to Thodùhah. No doubt some wonder of those bairns has slipped his mind until this moment. I'll keep that reckoning with Kalanu, and then I've more of that barleyspirit if you'll join us in the drinking afterward. He'll own himself a fool, soon as his blood's cooled. When he begs your pardon, give it at the second asking – that's the proper way among the Sea People." He turned away, then said over his shoulder, "And, mind, if Te-Meriku asks 'twas but ill-chance. No doubt you'll conjure memories – he's smelt fish in the night time often enough, herring as well as eel."

She had meant to thank him, but her laughter swallowed up her words and before she caught them back he was gone away over the benches, tossing a knife from hand to hand, calling out to Kalanu for satisfaction.

All that afternoon, the king stood beneath the carved head of the sea eagle, watching the empty sea and the empty sky, his hand resting on the hilt of the worn bronze sword and the piper's tunes ringing in his ears. Not until late in the evening did he turn back towards his company and even then he sat apart with Thodùhah to eat and drink.

"That knife," said Thodùhah, nodding to where Marwy Ninek sat with Ardùvai, "I knew it well, twenty years ago and longer. Then it hung at Hadùhai's side."

"Even so," said the king, slicing their meat with his own knife.

"I know the one Hadùhai gave it to, before ever you were king." The helmsman took the portion he was offered and broke hardbread for the king. With his mouth full, he said, "It was not you, Te-Meriku."

"That's also true."

"How came you by that knife?"

"There's no mystery to it. Hadùhai gave it to your daughter before he died and she to me before we sailed."

Thodùhah chewed and thought awhile. His eyes slipped sideways once or twice towards Marwy Ninek and each time after to the king, perhaps to catch him unawares. But Te-Meriku ate and drank, resting his back against his hull, at his ease upon the open sea as another man might be beneath a tree at noontime. He spoke briefly of little things and Thodùhah gave back broken answers, his mind across the water.

At last the helmsman spoke his thought. "She came back to us with the bairns after her man died. He missed his mark and the whale's blow shattered the boat to driftwood."

"They say you freeze before you drown, in those northern seas, even in the summertime." Yet the king's mind wandered too, slipping away across the water and the years, soaring as a grey gull might to the shores of Lyikené, to a night as no other in that year. Beneath the mast the piper played, his tune a thread tying that night to this. Behind the music, Te-Meriku heard an echo of women stamping out the beat; behind his eyes he saw her, spinning down the line of men, with silver bells like apples ringing in her hair.

He drank until his cup was empty to silence the ringing of those bells. "That news I heard, a twomonth since."

"Did you, Te-Meriku? You did not speak of it."

"What's to say?" He shrugged and beckoned, holding up his empty cup. Renùku brought them more wine. The king nodded his thanks, and turned the boy's face towards the light to see how it was healing. Satisfied, he sent him to his rest. "Men die," he said to his helmsman, "and speaking of them will not bring them back. I did not think you mourned him overmuch."

"No more I did. When she told me what she'd do, I asked her, *Why?* Why him when she could have any man in Lyikené? Seeing her face as she looked at him, I thought he was a fool. The truth was written plain enough." Thodùhah rubbed his hand across his face. "He gave me bronze and ivory enough to wed a dozen daughters. A good bargain, on the face of it." He drank again and muttered, "He had red hair."

"Did he?" asked the king. "I cannot now remember. Only that I too thought he was a fool. How many years did he have of her?"

"Seven years." Thodùhah's mouth snapped shut as if he grudged them, every one.

"So many? She seemed so much the same an I saw her again."

The piper played and all across the ship men fell quiet to listen.

"What was there between you?" Thodùhah asked. "Before she went away with him into the north?"

"Very little," said Te-Meriku. "She said me *Yes* one night, and so I stayed and kissed her; she said me *No* another, and I went unkissed away."

He shut his mind against an evening on the further bank, light on the water, buds bursting on the tree, his hands outstretched, certain of his welcome. Her answer, halfway between tears and laughter, *When apples grow on an orange tree, when the seas run dry, when you want me for myself, I'll kiss you again, Te-Meriku.*

"No more than that?"

"No more than that."

"Yet she gave you that knife."

"Even so." He looked sidelong, reading the expression on his helmsman's face. Thodùhah supped his wine in silence. Lightly, he asked, "Would you speak more of it?"

"Te-Meriku, I'm only her father and she long old enough to make her own choices. But you cannot blame a man for thinking of the things that might have been, when one is his daughter and the other the king."

"I'd not take her unwilling; not her, nor any other."

Thodùhah said drily, "What need of that? All you could desire is offered you – I should think by now you've kissed every woman in Lyikené, and half the men besides."

The king's harsh laugh rang out across the ship. "I had not kept count – nor knew you did so for me!"

"Well, 'tis of no matter. The women for forgetfulness, no doubt; the men to conjure memory. But, often and often, I've thought it: she'd have loved you for yourself, if only you'd have let her." The helmsman's voice was steady as his blue eyes but yet the king started, as if he probed a half-healed wound. Wine spilt between them, red drops like rowan berries rolling across the wood in a pattern neither man could read. "Imacah betrayed you with his death and you've made certain that no other can do likewise. She's no more a fool than I am, my Liùthánwy."

When at last Te-Meriku answered, his tone was low and dangerous. "Enough, Thodùhah, no further. I'll not speak of Imacah." Very quietly he spoke, but the piper, whose ears could hear a bat's squeak on a summer's evening, turned his strange eyes first to Marwy Ninek, and then to Te-Meriku, and played another tune made, long ago, upon another evening, the day a man died in the utmost east.

With those golden eyes upon him, other, older memories welled up from the shadows of the king's mind: red rowan berries scattered over heather, the ebbing tide, the fading light. The dead slipped away on the evening tide; they cared not that they left the living behind with empty hands and aching hearts. It was all one to them, the silence and the dark. But love was love for all that, and died not with the dead.

—┼— —┼—

At noontime, Assiolo came ashore. The boy was sorry and sulky to leave the sailors who had made a pet of him, and sorrier still to leave the monkey that chattered from the rigging in answer to his cries of farewell. He looked about and thought Eulana a poor, plain place after the wonders of Anach, where a conjuring woman had dazzled him with doves and pulled silk scarves and ivory counters from places none had been before, or after the king's hall in Tarhn, where the king sat on a golden chair, and ate from golden plates, and held, so it was said, though his father laughed to hear it, the life of the land in his two hands. He looked around him, seeing a whitewashed village set about its harbour, and dragged his feet on the road behind his father.

"There," said Assiolo after an hour or more, pointing towards grey walls in the distance, tiny beneath the mountain's bulk. "Felluria. Our journey's end."

The boy shrugged; he was tired of travelling. These last nights on the tossing boat he had wept for Oca in the dark and taken no comfort from his father. "My feet hurt."

"I'll not carry you this time," Assiolo answered. "Sit down and rest. We are in no hurry here."

They sat down, sheltering from the wind beneath a rowan tree. Somewhere nearby a blackbird was singing. He gave the boy honey cake, hoping to sweeten him before he must walk on. The branches rattled in the breeze. "My lord?" He span round, seeing a shadow move from the corner of his eye. "My lord Assiolo?"

The boy had seen nothing, he had heard nothing – he sat eating slowly, licking his sticky fingers after each bite.

"Wait here, Imacah," Assiolo said. "I want to stretch my legs upon the hillside."

The boy was sulky still and let him walk away without an answer. Assiolo walked up the hill a little way. A man was standing beside a tangle of briars, plain in the shadow, hidden in the light. He saw, with sadness and without surprise, that it was Gru and walked forward until he stood close enough to touch him if he but reached out his hands.

Gru's tongue spoke words that were not his own. "Since it is not you, it must be your son. I've come to take him to his mother."

Looking him in the eye, Assiolo said quietly, "I killed a man once, Gru. I do not want to kill another."

"Then give Averla back her own."

"You told me I was needed," Assiolo said, hoping against all hope that Gru would see the world for what it was, "you told me my son needed me."

Gru's eyes were clear and empty. "I do not remember."

Very sadly, Assiolo answered, "There are many things you do not remember." The salt wind blowing in the night time, the rise and sway of a ship's deck beneath his feet, the freedom to choose his own way across the world. All these had been Gru's birthright; all these he had put aside; all these he would never know again. This he said so that Averla, who watched behind Gru's eyes, listened with his ears and spoke out of his mouth, might hear. But then Assiolo held out his empty hands, he spoke very softly in another, younger tongue and, speaking, spoke to Gru alone.

"Gru," he said, pleading to the shadow he had seen behind Gru's eyes in Faranon, "Gru, it need not end this way. You've been near my friend. You gave me water in a cup of rowan wood, you opened the door, you gave my son to me. Remember what you were, before the fire, before the flood—"

"Gru!"

Assiolo swung around towards the shout and a padding of feet behind him in the heather. His son had followed after all and cast himself towards Gru, shouting, "Gru, I've missed you. Is Oca with you too? She promised. Such things I've got to tell you! A monkey in—"

Gru's hands reached out, Gru's voice said softly, "Come, Alcedo, I'll take you to your mother and your home."

"No!" cried Assiolo, and set his son behind him. "He's yet a child and does not know the world. When he is grown he can make his own choices—until then, I am his father and I will stand between him and those that would seek to use him for their own purposes."

Gru shook his head. He did not heed the warning in Assiolo's voice. He did not look at the wide sky or the flowers upon the briar, nor did he look at the green bracken or at the sea. He held out his hand; in that hand he held a knife and he looked only at the sunlight rippling on the blade. The boy caught his breath to see it; Assiolo saw him look between them and felt the world shatter into pieces.

"This I was bid," said Gru, "*Take back the life I gave him, and the boy.* As I was bid, my lord, so will I do."

"Imacah," said Assiolo, "turn away. Walk down the path towards the sea. Go to the shore and wait for me below the tideline. Do not look back."

"Will you come after me?"

"I will come after you," Assiolo promised. "Only death will take me from you." He had made that promise before, in another time and place, and he had not yet kept it. But he would do all that was necessary to keep his promises, though the cost be very high. "Go now, Imacah. Wait for me upon the shore."

He heard footsteps fade away behind him, the boy crying and a seagull screaming on the wind. Then he heard Gru's voice, "A man must die today."

"So says Averla. But she is not here, Gru, only we are here. There is no need for either of us to die."

There was no answer. He looked into Gru's eyes and saw there could never be an answer. Gru's words had been lost long ago, with his future and his freedom and all that made him a man. He stepped towards him with the knife and Assiolo held out his empty hands in answer.

Light upon the hillside, a light of the sun and a light not of the sun. Light upon the sea; light through the leaves of the briar; light glancing off the steel blade of the knife. A cloud passed over the face of the sun and, for a little time, the sunlight dimmed but there was no less light upon the hill. Soon, soon, the cloud blew by; soon, soon, the sun shone again upon the hillside, shining upon the man and upon the thing that had been a man, lying on the grass where it had fallen, the knife beside its open hand, its empty eyes open to the sky.

The day was calm, the air was still; no wind to rustle the leaves of the briar bush; even the blackbird was silent. Assiolo put his hand upon the prickly branch of the briar and asked the sunlight and the tree, "Are you here?"

The grey man stepped out from the shadows beside the bush. "I am here, my lord."

"Go, Thorn, go now to Averla and tell her these three things: so will end all who lay hands upon my son, there are none can command my will, and I will keep my promises."

"My lord, you have never been my master and I do not serve your will. You have long been needed and now you are ready."

Assiolo said, very quietly, "I will not serve." The light gathered itself around him and Thorn stood out, sharp against shadows. "Go, Thorn. This is not your place. Yonder lies Felluria where my love is waiting. I'll make of those walls a barrier Averla cannot pass, though she blow wild as the hurricane upon the gate or ask sweet as honey through the lock."

At the snap of Thorn's fingers, the light fell back into the day. "I have never been a man, my lord, and I am proof against your tricks. I have said what I was bid to say. When the time comes, our mistress will ask and you will answer."

Assiolo cried to the sunlight and the silence, "I am not Allocco!"

"That is no matter, my lord." The grey man turned away from him into the light. Before he slipped from sight he said, "It is enough you are Allocco's son."

Alone, Assiolo sank shivering beside Gru's corpse, holding a dead hand in his own. The first lesson his father had taught him, and the last, was that all things were possible, if you did not mark the cost. And Assiolo wept on the hillside in sight of the stone walls of Felluria because, between the man he was and the man he wished to be, there stood a bright-haired boy.

XII, Felluria: Deeper than the sea, stronger than the stone

> *Oh the willow tree will twist,*
> *And the willow tree will twine,*
> *And I wish I was in that young man's arms,*
> *That stole away this heart of mine.*

The Seeds of Love, *Traditional*

The mistress of Felluria no longer steps through her days like a shadow in the sunlight. She has put aside her dark, plain gowns of grey and black and indigo and sits the evenings clad in red, dusky as a damask rose in summertime, or in the green of birken leaves in spring, or in a gown purple as the heather upon the braes of Cal Mora. She has let down her closebound hair and it sweeps around her in a heavy ripple of black silk. Often she wears flowers in her hair. Never now lithia, for all the firestar is her banner. Instead she wears the wildflowers of Felluria: a garland of tormentil, a nosegay of violet and primrose, a white crown of windflowers or, in the weeks around midsummer, a single red rose.

Now she has come to life, men's eyes slip sidelong in the evenings. Always, she has been beautiful but always her beauty has been quenched as the moon behind grey cloud, always she has been a hard, cold thing like a stone upon Cal Mora, admired but not desired. Now she is lovely as the new moon shining; now all men can see she is beautiful. Their eyes slide sideways—covetous, greedy, longing—but if she sees she pays no heed. She looks only at one man, the outlander with his smooth chin and tender mouth whose brown eyes look smiling into hers.

Men see this and say, maudlin in their cups at evenings' ends, "He would be nothing without her."

The weaver smiles, and says nothing.

Men say, "All that he has, she gave to him."

The weaver laughs; this is true, but it is not all the truth.

Men say, "He shaves his beard! What make of man is he, content to be taken for a eunuch or a stripling!"

The weaver stares at this and mutters beneath her breath, "What man of Felluria walked into the wild wood at midwinter?"

By day the weaver watches the outlander, levelly, approving. She sees a quiet man who keeps the garden he has made in the stony soil. She hears a voice lifted in song when he thinks he is alone. She sees, always, when he walks with his love on the hillside he puts himself between her and the wind.

It is said, though none will say who said it, he comes of the First People.
It is said and, again, no one can trace the first teller of the tale, he can
make a light in darkness shine out of his bare hands. It is whispered he is
a prince in exile because another stole his kingdom.

These tellings, and others, flicker around the hall as the evenings darken.
Sometime after the equinox, before the solstice, the weaver seeks him out.
She is old and has learnt much of men in her time. Three men have lain
in her bed and she has outlived her love for all of them; the sons they gave
her are long away, across the Inner Sea to Escen, dead in the mercatplace
in Ountrie.

None of her men and none of her sons, the sailor, the soldier, the thief,
would she have found as she finds him, sorting dried flowers and herbs and
scratching lists on tablets of white birch bark with oak apple ink.

The weaver is old and has won her warm place by the hearth by virtue
of her skill at her craft and her sharp tongue. She counts no man her equal,
no man the equal of any woman in Felluria. So, when he looks up from
his work and sees her standing there, she is surprised to find she cannot
meet his eyes. Old tales told to a girl in winter rise up through her mind:
the hunter and the hunted in the wild wood, red blood and white snow
and the far bank of a frozen river. A shiver prickles down her back. Then
she remembers her pride and tells herself he is only a man, even if he is an
outlandish prince, and asks her questions.

He smiles and answers fairly. To the first question, he says, "My father
came of that people. I have neither that honour nor that life." His speech
is easy, fluent but this is not his mother tongue; his speaking lilts with the
rhythms of another land.

In answer to her second, he holds out his left hand. An old, white scar
runs across its palm; he tells her, "Only a fool holds fire in his hand."

At the third, he smiles. "There are no princes left in the east. In these
later days the kings are in the west." Again misplaced tales swirl through
her mind: a pale king at midwinter, starlight on the snow. She drops her
eyes, confused.

He picks up a handful of dried feverfew flowers and wraps them, pressing
his ring into the wax that seals the packet. "Good against the headache,"
he tells the weaver, turning back to his herbals. "It's close work, weaving,
hard on eyes as these northern nights grow long."

Her nearsight has been sharpened by years of patterning. She sees plain
the device stamped in the wax, and looks up at him. His face wears a look
she has not seen before.

"All those tales were true," he says, "but now that king is dead."

Not long after midsummer, he comes to the weaver and says, "I'd like to
see my dear love wearing yellow, warm and bright as the gorse flowers on
the hill. That would cheer me through the dreary days when the rainclouds

round Cal Mora hide the sun for weeks on end. Can you weave me a
golden gown, mistress?"

"Hard to find the dye for it," she answers shortly, proof against his
smile.

"Saffron," says he, handing her a packet wrapped in silk and sealed with
wax, "from the crocus fields of Marihon. I had it from the fat mercatman
of Cincern Dùn."

"Costly stuff." She thinks of pinching out a few threads to colour
a custard; baulks at the extravagance needed to dye a golden gown.
"Mercatmen from Cincern Dùn do not grow fat on rosewater and feverfew."

"Do you think I used her name against my debts? Perhaps if I was a
prince, I would have done; for sure if I was a prince, he would have let
me." He spreads out his empty hands and looks her laughing in the eye.
"Alas, here I am only a man and a stranger and yet to prove my credit in
a mercatman's eyes."

"No doubt he cheated you," she says to show she is not charmed. Her
youngest son had a way with him, a smile in his eyes to charm a woman
to his will, but her youngest son was a liar and a thief. She learned her
lesson well in the days before he left her; she will not be fooled again.

"No doubt he did," he agrees. "I hope you'll not do the same." He
meets her eyes and she looks down at the packet in her hands. "I've seen
your skill these last months in Felluria. If you turn me down, I'll ask no
other. Will you do it?"

"What of the yarn?"

"That choice I give to you, mistress. You have your craft as I have
mine. Let it be something soft and warm. I don't want her cold when the
wind blows hard down Cal Mora. She was too long without a shelter from
the wind," he says, and her heart melts towards him. Three sons she's
had and three men to father them but not one ever looked like this when
speaking of a woman.

"I know the yarn. The hill sheep on Cal Mora—the underfleece is all
that you can wish for, soft as thistledown and white as seafoam." Her
heart is softened but not her voice. She tells him, harsh and brisk, "It'll
cost you, and the weaving too, but I'll see you done by fairly."

"Thank you," he says, holding out his hand to her, courteous as if he
were indeed a prince.

He pauses at the weaver's door to watch as the golden wool is stretched
across the loom. It is a place of women, these rooms where she works her
webs. There were men here once, lovers, brothers, sons. The men are gone,
to death or across the sea, and now only the women remain. There are
three of them, alike in all but years. The old weaver stands to her work.
She sings and on each beat she sends the shuttle flying across the warp.
Her daughter sits by the fireside spinning golden thread, tapping her feet

to spin the wheel to match her mother's rhythm, and her granddaughter, her hair plaited through with crimson silk, sits in the seat beneath the window and cuts the wool she needs to sew the figures in her tapestry, her six-month child sleeping in its nest of sheepskin at her feet.

The babe stirs from sleep and he asks, looking tenderly towards it, "What is its name?"

Its mother answers, "She has no name, not yet." Seeing his surprise, she tells him, "When spring is come, when a year and a day have gone by since I bore her, then I'll name her. Until then, she is mine alone."

"What of her father?"

She laughs, and tells him, "Midsummer, Assiolo. Surely even in your land you keep midsummer?"

He flushes, confused by her answer. "Then shame on him who left you to pay the price alone."

She stares and answers shortly, "No shame to bear, no price to pay."

He says, finding his words slowly, "When I was a boy in my own country, one old enough to know it told me this: the world is very large and cares not that we are in it; our lives are very short and, when they are done, there is nothing else. No dreams within the darkness. But at midsummer, life calls out to life." He stoops and picks up the baby, lulling it back to sleep in the crook of his arm. Looking down at it, he asks, "Surely the songs sung at midsummer call out for more than a night's desire that falls with the fires to ashes in the morning?"

The child rests heavy in his arms, a soft, warm weight smelling sweetly of milk and lavender. He thinks of that other child that had so little weight within his hands and none at all upon the world. As he cradles the baby, he wishes for it all the other will never know: spring rain to wash it, tall trees to shelter it, green grass beneath it and blue sky above it. Softly, he says to its mother, "I believe, as this life all we have, the only hope we have of safety is that life does indeed reach out to life, that our hearts become as white flowers that grow for us and not red fire that burns all it touches."

The young woman tosses her head and turns back to her woolwork; her mother laughs, hard in her throat, as if he spoke in jest.

"Fine words, fine words," the old weaver tells him, and does not miss a beat in the rhythm of her work, "but here the flowers faded when the fires burned. The men died and we remember, we women of Felluria, what happened to the women left behind when they went safely into the dark."

The look on the young woman's face matches her grandam. She says, "I took what I wanted and went my way alone.

He shudders at her speaking. He says, mildly as he can, "So did my father. So, no doubt, did Torùkotu."

There is a sudden silence at the loom; the spinning wheel jerks to a halt as the yarn snaps; a needle full of thread is held high. Three women stare to hear that name spoken aloud within the stone walls of Felluria. He says, softly, very sadly, "Alas that others must pay the price of their desires."

That day he sits for a long time with the baby in his arms singing a lullaby in his own tongue whilst the women do their work. Often and often the weaver glances sidelong at him that she might carry his face within her mind all the time he is not there, this brown-haired stranger out of the east. The world is a bitter place; she has built stone walls about her heart to keep it safe, and taught her daughter and her daughter's daughter to do likewise. He is only a man but a man like no man of Felluria; a man whose hands were strong enough to drive back the dark, tender enough to bring joy where there was only fear.

Her heart twists in her breast to look at him and she wishes more than half her life away. He is a man met too late; a man who broke down the walls around her heart with no more than a word and a look that is half a smile and half a frown; a man she wants and cannot have. She has grown old, her beauty faded long ago and he will never see her as she was, as she still is in the secret places of her mind. She must weave the golden cloth for another to wear, another who will never wear her age upon her flesh and face. She throws her shuttle to and fro and remembers her daughter's father, a man met at midsummer. Sometimes a night lengthens into a lifetime: more often it does not.

"You'd have made a good father," she says out of her jealousy and bitterness. Her words make a sudden silence in the room as his song breaks.

She sees his face and anger falls from her. She presses her hands across her mouth but is too late: words spoken can never be called back. In his face she sees again there always is a price, even for love itself. His love runs deeper than the sea, stronger than the stone, but the one he loves is not a woman: she has more life than any woman but it is hers alone, never to be shared, never given to another. She is her own posterity.

Gently, carefully, he returns the child to its mother and leaves them without a word.

Next time he seeks the weaver out he finds the spinning wheel still and the tapestry frame standing empty beside the wall. Only the weaver is at her work; the others have gone out to fill the baby up with sunshine on this rare day of winter sun. She sits and weaves the golden cloth and, as she weaves, he sings, a song made by the piper long ago.

"There are three things I fain would see
A rose, a king, an apple tree
Then all that might have been could be.
But might have been is never seen
Though snow falls white and leaves grow green.

"*A red rose growing on the tree*
No fairer flower I'll ever see
To catch the light and scent the night
And drive the nightmare out of sight.

"*A king again where king should be*
To stand beneath the apple tree
And walk the light and hold the night
And drive the nightmare out of sight.

"*A song beside the flowering tree*
A song to set the caged heart free
To love the light and share the night
And drive the nightmare out of sight.

"*The rose is blighted by the sea*
The king hangs swinging from the tree
The music's but a memory
And might have been is never seen
Though snow falls white and leaves grow green."

When his song is done and he has set aside the lute, she turns to him and says slyly, "We put aside our hope and set our trust in no man. Have you not proved that we were foolish, we women of Felluria?"

"What I could, I did," he answers. "Only time will show if it was enough. Oftentimes I think it is; then I hear her dreams and know again that it was not."

He looks out across his garden, while a disquiet settles on his heart. Last night, between the sunset and the morning, he again bore witness to the weight of the past upon his love, dark and heavy as rainclouds over Cal Mora.

He turns towards the loom. "It must be ready for when the days are wet and sour, a golden dress to keep her warm when the wind blows from the east."

"It will be ready by midwinter," the weaver gives her promise.

"Then I'll pay you at midwinter when the work is done," says he, "but keep it close until it is needed."

At last the golden gown is finished. She spreads it out before him. He stares amazed. He had thought it would be one surface but she has woven a song into the weft and warp. He sees the pattern twist in the winter sunlight and that the roses broidered over it are red and lovely as the roses he brought from Eulana. He reaches out to feel its silky softness.

"Tell me your price," he says to her, when he has had enough of staring. "I do not think it could be too high; I never saw such work as this."

"*Pay me for the wool,*" *she answers brusquely,* "*and for the red silk my granddaughter used to sew the roses.*"

"*But for the weaving?*"

"*Love made the gown,*" *she says, scowling up at him.* "*Who am I to put a price on love?*"

13: No man can choose who sires him

She's taen out her wee penknife
All alone and a-lonely
And twined the sweet babe o' its life
Down by the greenwoodside-y.

The Cruel Mother, Traditional

"She is not here," said Yatta Tala, smaller, more bent than Assiolo remembered, but her sharp eyes the same.

He had come to her when he found their chamber dark, its shutters closed and fastened, his book upon the shelf and his lute in its own corner, Marwy Ninek's red shawl discarded on the windowseat, her comb and brush and polished mirror gone from the dresser, the kist that held her clothes half empty. Yatta Tala had taken one look at him, another at the boy clinging to his hand, and bid them to sit them down and rest their feet, sending her granddaughter to the kitchens for food and wine, for dainties to tempt the child and make him smile. And when he had, and come out from his father's shadow to look about, she bid a girlchild, a little bigger than himself, take him away to play with him, being sure to mind the well, and stay clear of the forge, and not get underfoot within the hall, and to be back before the sunset.

"Enwy Issa, my granddaughter's daughter," she told Assiolo, in answer to his question. "You used to sing her lullabies." He remembered a babe wrapped up in sheepskin, and the years he had not lived yawned between the past and present. "And now you've got one of your own," the weaver said, "and he was not born yesterday. How'd you manage that, Assiolo?"

"Midsummer, mistress," he kept his face steady and even managed a wry smile, "surely in these lands you keep midsummer."

Age had withered her but her eyes were sharp yet, and the mind behind those eyes. She sucked her teeth and shook her head, moving her fingers in a charm to avert ill-luck. "So that's how it was, that night."

"That's how it was. Not by my choice but no less my son to love and to look after. And now I am here, and he is here, and yet all is not well. I came back to keep my promise to my love and cannot, since she is not here. And so, mistress, the only question is," he asked what could not be asked before the children, flattening his voice to hide his heart, "since she is not here, what harm has come to her?"

"None I know of," the weaver said, though she looked at him only sidelong. "She went out to find you, not ten days since. How could she know, lad, you'd come walking down that road today when, five years and longer, there'd been no word of you, not even that you lived?"

"I gave her my promise and she loved me well enough to trust that I would keep it. Only death could keep me from her, though I be thrice five years delayed upon the road."

"Then it's mischance, Assiolo, and I'm sorry for it, but no use ranting on the things that might have been."

She turned away, busying herself finding clean sheets in her linen press to make up a bed for the boy. Assiolo bent his head into his hands. *She is not here!* The thought beat through his mind, over and again, as it had from the moment he stood at the threshold of their silent, empty room. *She is not here!* He felt a hollow where his heart should be. He looked up and all about: this was her place, these her stone walls – how could she not be here to fill it? And yet, and yet, *She is not here!*

"There's a tale untold behind your words," said Assiolo slowly. "I'd hear it, mistress, from your lips. I've been longtimes away from home and lonely. Where exactly did she go to find me?"

"A sixmonth after you were gone, the king came out of the west." The old weaver's words came as a rush, as the floodtide surging up the shore. "That time he did but speak with her; days since, he returned and took her away with him upon his ship."

Shock jerked him forward in his chair and set his heart a-thunder. "Took?" The word burst from his mouth. "Tell me the manner of this taking! There is no mark of fire upon the gate nor wounded men about the place – are you all turned cowards in Felluria that not one who lives within her walls or eats at her table chose to stand between her and that king?"

Bad dreams rose to his mind like the vomit to his throat: dying men beneath green trees; her screams as she was dragged away towards the ship; a red-haired man with bloody hands dealing out death with his bronze sword. No dream but a true seeing. He pressed his hands against his mouth, retching, swallowing back sickness whilst blood pounded in his ears and the room swam all around him.

Yatta Tala wrung out a cloth in water and passed it to him that he might wipe clean his face and hands. "He had the apple bough upon his mast and came ashore alone with empty hands."

Assiolo wiped his mouth and cast the cloth aside. "What matter that his hands were empty? That he was alone? That makes him scarce less dangerous."

"We made him strip between the gates. We looked to see a monster but saw only a man." She could not help her smile at that memory, though she tried hard to at his frown. Taking pity on his distress, she laid her hand upon his sleeve, comfort for the comfortless. "There's no woman here counts her as other than a sister or a daughter. We'd not leave her alone, Assiolo, not with any stranger and least of all with him. Each time the king stood before her, he tried no trick or game. I heard every word he said, and so too did half a dozen more."

He could not yet speak but shook his head. She met his eyes, uneasy, but said only, "Te-Meriku asked, and she answered."

"He did no more than ask her?"

"That is all that happened here: the long-tailed star rose in the east, the Sea People came from the west. When the king asked, Marwy Ninek went with him of her own will. He offered hope of finding you, Assiolo, saying you too were bound for Lyikené."

Though he knew full well the answer, he asked, "When did that star rise?"

"Three sennight and a day ago, on the night of the moon's darkness."

That night he had passed the door of Faranon and set his foot towards Felluria. The pattern stood complete and other eyes than his could read it; in the west, as in the east, men knew its meaning, one man above all others.

"Hope!" Assiolo laughed to think of it, a hollow laughter that was close to tears, dark thoughts of his dreamings running through his mind. He had read of such stars in his father's books and knew well their meaning. "I'll warrant you Te-Meriku came here hoping. He came because he read his own death writ across the firmament and thought, since he must die, to make certain he is longtimes remembered. You have grown foolish, you and all Felluria: so too did Torùkotu make himself remembered."

The old weaver, not knowing why he should laugh so, stared and stared and, in the end, she slapped his face to shock him to his senses.

After the weaver's blow, Assiolo was himself once more and could think clearly but he was no nearer to belief. His love was gone, and he would follow, but still the weaver's words beat through his mind: *She went of her own will.* Slowly, he said, "I am away quick as can be to bring her home. Te-Meriku will die for this and, by my life, he'll not go easy into the dark. But," he said, and hairs prickled on her neck to hear him, for all he spoke so quiet, "there is much here I do not understand. First and last, it passes all my understanding to hear you say she went freely with the king."

"He was looking for you, lad, and seeing hope she took it." Her answer came quicker than her wont. She had known many men across her years, aye, and faced their anger too, but never had she seen rage like this, so calm and yet so dangerous. "The king said he knew you were bound to Lyikené and that he'd take her to you." She drained her cup and said, in something more like her usual, dry manner, "Longtimes she'd waited, full five years and longer. That's too long to lie alone and lonely. She loves you, Assiolo, what else would she do but seek you?"

Her fingers were like dry twigs against his skin. Like the walls around him, she had seen many years and yet offered no strength or shelter from the storm.

"She would wait within her walls!" he cried, shaking her hand from his arm. "What is five years to the Tion of Felluria? She would have waited forty!" He stood up to pace the room a while, six steps from wall to wall and back, over and again. "So, she is not here," he said at last, "but there must be more than this. She'd not have gone with that man of her own will. Do not forget, mistress, I know her, even if I have been five years away. I know her better than any in the world." He cast his words over his shoulder at her, but all the answer she could give was to shake her head, tight-lipped.

Assiolo paused his pacing to look closely at the weaver. "She loved me, she trusted me and yet, even with me to walk at her side and shield her from the wind, she scarcely dared pass the gate." Standing over her, he said, "Of all the men in all the world, Te-Meriku is the last Marwy Ninek is like to have followed. If he took her not by force, then it must have been by treachery."

She shook her head. "No treachery. You should think better of her, Assiolo. Love gave her courage in the end."

He poured more wine and sipped it slowly, his gaze fixed on the weaver. Yatta Tala's eyes flicked up and then away. A new disquiet settled on his heart to see again that unease in her manner. It was a little thing enough, hardly enough to notice, but strange in her that was wont to be so sure and certain.

"There's something still unsaid. I shall have the truth, be it a great or little thing."

The weaver kept her silence, but she would no longer meet his eyes.

Assiolo looked and looked and saw, beneath his stare, unease ripen slowly into fear. "You've lived a long time, mistress, and I've counted you my friend since first I came to Felluria but this tale passes all believing," he told her, and heard her breathing quicken. "I know what happened the night Torùkotu took Felluria; I know everything he did behind that locked door."

He found that he must pause a while to find the words and lifted his cup to his mouth with shaking hands. When he could speak again, he said, "It keeps a man awake at night to know such things are possible; the wonder of it is she could bear to have me touch her. So I'll not believe this story, mistress, though it is you who tells it, not if all Felluria stands beside you and swears by land and sea and sky, swears on their mothers' graves and their children's lives, that it is true."

She shook her head again, standing up to leave him. "I've told you thrice what happened," she said, "now I'm away to find my grandchild and the bairns. We'll keep the boy safe if you're away into the west."

"Sit down!" Assiolo's voice flicked like a whip. She collapsed back into her chair, shaking. "I will ask and ask," he said, "until I have the answer."

Quietly, calmly, knowing full well what he did, Assiolo locked the door. When he dropped the key upon the table, the rattle of iron was too loud in the silence and Yatta Tala started in her seat, a sharp, quick gasp escaping her lips before she gathered her composure and straightened her back to look him, scornful, in the eyes.

"You've changed across the years," she told him, "and not for the better."

"I am a man," Assiolo said, sitting down to face her, "but I know things no man should know, I've done things no man should do: there is no law of men can bind me, an I do not wish it."

She looked up and saw a man she did not know curving his face into a bitter smile that did not reach his eyes. All the light within the room wrapped itself around him in a golden cloak so only he was illuminated.

"Longtimes I set a curb upon my will," he said, each word a stone dropped into the silence, "content to live as others live but, for my love, I will forsake all limits. That is the only warning I shall give you. Marwy Ninek is gone, and I will have the reason."

"Assiolo, lad," Yatta Tala whispered, "Assiolo, why will you not let it rest?"

"When I was yet a boy, there was a man sailed from my country." Assiolo leant back in his chair. His tone was light and brittle, his eyes fixed on the old woman's face, and she found she could not move, not even put up her hand to shield her eyes from the light that burned so bright about him. "His ship slipped from the harbour, a flag of green and gold fluttering at its mast, four and twenty sailors standing on its deck, its captain at the prow, to sail, in and out of dreams, ever into the west."

She could not speak, she could not swallow, she could scarce even breathe. All she could do was look at him, and listen.

"There is no finer sight in all the world than a ship upon the sea, its white sails bellied full of air and hope," said Assiolo. He sat a while in silence, staring out of the light at Yatta Tala, at her thistledown hair, her bent shoulders, her face grey with fear and lack of breath. Quietly, terribly, he asked her, "Do you know the ending of this tale?"

He lifted one finger of his left hand and she gasped, drawing in a great gulp of air. "No," she whispered.

He shrugged. " 'Tis quickly told. There is a king dwells in the west, and jealously he guards it. He sailed to meet that ship upon a summer's morning. With his bronze sword, he killed the sailors, by one and two and three, and cast their bodies to the sea. He stripped the captain and pegged him out upon the deck to die beneath the sun."

The light around him grew ever stronger, casting all the rest to shadow. Her eyes were sore dazzled but she could not close them. She must look and look and know blindness would follow. No woman's eyes could bear this light.

"There is a name can join that tale to this one, mistress," Assiolo said, tightening the noose about her heart, "a name you know as well as I – I've heard it from your lips already in this room."

Again, his finger moved. She spoke, a breath, a broken whisper, "Te-Meriku."

"Te-Meriku." His brown eyes were hard, his voice was level. He knew pity, he knew mercy but not here, not now, not for her. "Why did Marwy Ninek go with him?"

He raised his hand to let her speak, knowing she must answer and, this time, tell the truth.

"Because I bade her go."

Silence between them, broken only by the thunder of her heart.

"Tell me." Two short sharp words flung across the silence and, at each of them, the weaver flinched as if he struck her.

"I shamed her," she muttered at last. "I told her she'd broken faith once with Felluria – to stay would be to break it again."

He drew a breath but said no word. Under his eyes, her tongue limped on, "I told her 'twas I who loved you best and she a poor, weak thing, with neither will nor courage, fit only to huddle here within the walls."

"I'd trusted you to keep her safe, but you sent her to him." Assiolo rubbed his hand across his face and she knew a moment's release. A moment, no more than that. He put down his hand and, if tears had softened his eyes, they did no more. "That, perhaps, I could forgive

but never this: you *shamed* her as you did it. Her love, well that's not
a thing I'll sully by speaking of to you but her courage? Did you
who were born later think it a little thing to live on after the ruin?
You do not know who did not suffer! But here and now you are
afraid. Perhaps you are in pain." His finger moved; she nodded once,
she could do no other and no more. "And this is nothing," Assiolo
snapped, sharp as cracking twigs, "*nothing* to her fear and pain, no
more than a candleflame set against the summer's sun. Be grateful,
mistress, that I am not a man like Torùkotu."

His fingers moved against the air in a pattern she knew well. So
had her own fingers moved many times, winding in a spool of yarn.
Round and around, he wound the unseen thread and she felt cold,
heavy as hemlock, settle on her hands and feet; saw, from the edges
of her eyes, the shadows thickening around her. He did not speak, he
did not smile, and, in the end, he held out his left hand, a little light
burning on his scarred palm, a candle in the night time. She stared
and stared until, with one quick movement of thumb and forefinger,
Assiolo pinched out the light and all the rest was darkness.

-+— —+-

The ship pulled into the shore, grounding itself upon the shingle. A
cheer went up as the king leapt lightly to the beach. He turned back
in the shallow water, holding out his hands to catch Marwy Ninek
as she jumped after him. His red cloak swung around her as she
stepped onto the grey stones of Lyikené and knew herself the sight
in the eyes of all the Sea People. Thodùhah followed, unable in his
age to leap as lightly as his king.

"Bide with Thodùhah," Te-Meriku told her, "there's women
enough in his house to keep you company. I'll away awhile; the
dead are gone and I must have a care for the living left behind."

He strode away and the crowd gathered round him, the women
of the Sea People come to welcome home their menfolk and their
king. She saw wives embrace their husbands, children their fathers,
mothers their sons, lovers their sweethearts. And she saw the other
women, their faces suddenly grown old with bitter knowledge, their
outstretched arms holding nothing but the wind; she heard their
lamentations, alike in every way to mourning women all across the
world, even in Felluria. She saw Ardùvai, white-faced, mouth set,
offer his mother a lock of sandy hair; saw her sink silent to the
shingle, hands pressed across her mouth, tears spilling from her
eyes. And in the midst of grief and joy, she saw Te-Meriku the king,
straight and tall upon the shore, the still centre of it all.

When the ship was empty and each man gone to his own, she
felt Thodùhah's touch upon her arm and followed him up across the

shore. A slender, grey-eyed woman held out her hands in welcome. Thodùhah embraced her, and swung up onto his shoulder the smaller of the children clinging to her skirts. "My daughter, Liùthánwy, and these lasses," Thodùhah told her, laughing as the child pulled at his braid, "are my granddaughters, Eilis and Thodùwy."

"Marwy Ninek, you are welcome here," said Liùthánwy, taking back her daughter. The elder child put back her hood. Her face was her mother's copied in miniature but the hair whipping round it was red as a firestar leaf in autumn or the flames at the heart of a fire.

And so to Thodùhah's house, to meet Maris nar Ardùwy, his wife the old king's daughter.

And so, to wash in warm water at a fireside, to dress in her own clothes again and spend the afternoon sitting at rest whilst Liùthánwy sewed and her daughters demanded stories of their grandsire of the Later Lands, where men and women thought to charm the sun itself by dancing.

And so, to the evening and a room with a bedplace piled with white sealskins where, at last, she could be alone. There was a spray of briar roses in a vase of green glass on a shelf beside the empty hearth. She bent down her face towards the flowers, the sweet pink petals set above their jagged thorns. Their scent was the faint echo of other roses, far away across the sea.

She opened the window and let the wind blow into the room. There were no stone walls in Lyikené, nothing to turn the wind from its path across the green hills to the sea. Mixed with the wind was a song she had known her whole life long; even here, at the edge of the world, there was a blackbird claiming the evening for its own. She pinched out the lamp and settled herself into the windowseat, giving herself up to the evening and the blackbird's whistle that meant everything and nothing.

Sharp and sweet the memory: red roses on a summer's evening, Assiolo at her side and a blackbird singing in the twilight. Closing her eyes, whispering his name, she reached out her empty hands to a man that was not there.

He was not there. Yet she held him so clear and certain in her mind that, when the door opened and she saw a figure outlined against the light, it was a dozen heartbeats before she could believe it was not him. But it was only Liùthánwy bidding her to dinner in the king's hall.

Time out of mind, the king's hall of wood and whalebone had stood above the shore. Each beam was carved with a pattern of apple leaves and little gilded apples hung by the wall. Fresh rowan leaves were bound above the door and the rushes on the floor were strewn with thyme and rosemary to scent each footfall. Walking into the hall between Thodùhah and Liùthánwy, Marwy Ninek saw Te-Meriku in his own place and stared to see him so altered. Upon the sea, his garb had been no whit finer than any other of the Sea People; only his red cloak and other men's manners marked him the king. Now she saw him combed and clean-shaven, with the gleam of gold at his throat, his cambric shirt broidered over with green leaves and golden apples, and a briar rose pinned in his collar. At her side, Liùthánwy paused, setting her shoulders and standing straight.

Kenu Vanithu said, in a tone somewhere between mockery and meaning, "There are three sights in Lyikené I think no one could forget: a dragonship upon the sea, white flowers upon the apple tree and Te-Meriku the king with all the fires of sunset in his hair. A fair seeming, has he not?"

"No seeming but the man himself," said Liùthánwy. She took her place beside her mother's; Maris being yet the mistress of the women's side, stately as any queen. The piper sat down in his old, accustomed place between the empty hearths and Thodùhah at the king's left hand. Marwy Ninek took the chair Maris offered and glanced again towards Te-Meriku. He smiled his quick, harsh smile, and she saw it was only his clothes that had changed for, on his face, she saw the look he had worn each time he asked, "Do you trust me?" And his smile matched her knowledge of the bronze knife at her belt and she found she could eat and drink amongst the Sea People as within her own stone walls so far away across the water.

Then the hall was full of noise and food and music as the Sea People feasted to welcome home their king, but when all the words were spoken and all the songs sung, the broken meats were cleared away and with them all save those with whom the king wished to keep company. Te-Meriku sat drinking his blood-red wine and, in that same small chamber behind the hall, Kenu Vanithu stretched out his hands to the king's fire of applewood, letting its warmth draw the stiffness from his fingers.

"Will you play?" Marwy Ninek asked.

"Later, perhaps. The wind makes its own music tonight, and who am I to set myself against the wind?"

"Had you the wish to play you'd pay no more heed to the wind than to any man that walked in it."

She saw his twisted smile. "Aye, Marwy Ninek, that's about the truth of it. But you are here, and I am here, and Te-Meriku – there's a tale I wish to tell him tonight, when he has a mind to heed me."

The king was playing fox and geese with Thodùhah. The helmsman's geese had penned the fox in the first game of the pair and now his fox picked off the foolish geese that wandered from their flock.

Te-Meriku laughed as this game too turned against him and counted out the six of ivory that had been their wager. "The advantage lies with you, as ever – you played this game before I was breeched."

"And so I did, Te-Meriku," the old man answered, "but there's younger men than you can beat me, Ardùvai for one. You've never cared to gain the mastery, that's all."

"Nay, Thodùhah," said the king and took up the jug of wine, "there's many in this hall will play you with all their will and all their skill, but few enough like Ardùvai think to set themselves against me. It's in such little things men give themselves away."

The piper smiled. "So, even in Lyikené, there are those who think it flattery to lose against the king. And of the men that sailed with you into the Later Lands? Has each of them taken a game from you to win his place beneath those eagles?"

"Kenu Vanithu, do you think men are as easy to read as ripples on the water, that knowing one thing of them you know all?" answered Te-Meriku, laughing. "If it were so, it would be a very simple thing to be a king."

"Well now, Te-Meriku, I know many things of many men and tonight you shall have the proof of it, if you'll listen to my story."

"I'll listen, if Thodùhah will put away his winnings and his smile, and drink a cup of wine with me."

Thodùhah held out his cup in answer, though his grin deepened.

"It begins," Kenu Vanithu said, "as so many stories do begin, with a man and a woman. The man made himself a king but not king in Lyikené." He laughed, a little laugh that had no humour in it. "Nay, I'll give him his name, since all here have it already: Torùkotu was the beginning of this tale."

The fire was warm; the night, being so close to midsummer, mild but each of the three saw Marwy Ninek shiver and wrap her arms around herself.

"There is no lock upon the door, Marwy Ninek; go out if you wish," the piper said. "It is to Te-Meriku I speak – this tale you know already, all save its end."

Te-Meriku stood up from his carved chair and crossed to her side. She sat stiff and straight and did not look up at him, only into the bright heart of the fire. She closed her eyes against the light and saw the patterns there, the flames flowering across the black walls of Felluria.

The king set his hands lightly on her shoulders and told the dwarf, "You're very brave or very foolish to name that man, here, in this company."

"He is dead and gone into the dark," said Kenu Vanithu. "His name is a word, and no more than a word. A word cannot hurt her."

"You do not know, you were not there."

The dwarf looked up and slowly turned his head to look at each of them in turn and none would meet his golden eyes. "Oh, I know many things, Marwy Ninek. I do not name that man tonight to please me or to frighten you – only because it is necessary to tell this tale, in this company. Will you go out, or shall I begin?"

She drank her wine and did not answer. He shrugged and smiled and took up his tale. "His hair was red, his arm was strong, no man could stand in fight against him, but he was not the king. Another sat in the king's place and Torùkotu was a man among many in the king's hall, who must be silent when another spoke and answer when another asked. These things, he could not bear." His golden eyes stared up into the king's. "Young men think such thoughts, do they not, Te-Meriku, young clansmen in Lyikené?"

"I cannot make windows into men's minds," the king said, "and I ever judged the deed above the thought. But any chooses to set himself against me will find me ready, me and my bronze sword. There are many men in Lyikené but one king only, and – by my life!" his voice fell to a soft growl, "all else will live within the limits that I set on them!"

"Well, the king of those days," Kenu Vanithu went on, "also set limits to the freedom of the Sea People and Torùkotu must set sail to find his kingdom. Across the sea, he killed a king and hung his body from an apple bough and made himself the red king in Eulana, salt in the meadows, blood in the trees."

Marwy Ninek caught her breath into a gasp. The king's fingers tightened a little on her shoulders and she put up her hand to his, a moment's touch, no more than that.

"Men must die," the piper said, "and women mourn them. It was Ketala Iitha loved that dead king and mourned him a threemonth 'neath the tree. Torùkotu saw her, perhaps he loved her at a glance – other men have loved so, in other times and places." Kenu Vanithu paused, to look at Marwy Ninek, at Te-Meriku standing at her side, at the grey helmsman, his cup forgotten by his hand, and then continued with his tale. "But, whether 'twas from lust or love, he laid her down upon the frosty ground and took from her what he wanted."

Marwy Ninek flinched and shivered. "Enough!" she pleaded, her voice throbbing, "Enough!" Her eyes were wide and dark and all her memories of Torùkotu written on her face.

Kenu Vanithu went on, steadily, implacably. He spoke, and so she must listen, though every word tore away the years since the night Felluria fell into ruins. "When he was done, he carried her away, to sit at his side, and pour his wine, and lie with him between the sunset and the morning."

Marwy Ninek bent her head into her hands and her breath came fast and ragged. Te-Meriku took half a step towards the piper. The look upon his face was one Thodùhah had never seen before, though he had thought he knew the king in all his moods.

"Aye, monster, enough!" roared Thodùhah, rising from his seat before the king could speak. His little knife glinted plain as he pulled it from his sleeve. "We all know what he was. If there's some point to this, get to it fast and, if not, beg her pardon and be silent."

"Torùkotu was all you think him, but so much more besides," Kenu Vanithu snapped out, not one whit afraid that the helmsman raised his knife against his life, nor yet touched by the sight of Marwy Ninek crouched in her chair beside the fire. "You'll see the point, soon enough, Thodùhah, if you'll sit down and let me speak."

It was not enough for Thodùhah that the piper bid him sit but the king said, "Let him go on. Of all the tongues in all the world, they say his cannot lie. Let's hear what he's to say and, if we do not like it, we can between us make a reckoning."

Thodùhah sat but kept out his little knife and made a show of paring his nails.

"And in lust or love, Torùkotu kept her close," said the piper, steadily, "pouring his wine and warming his bed. Winter turned to spring, spring lengthened into summer and, as the year waxed great, so too did his child in her belly. But at summer's end, when Torùkotu was at his hunting, Ketala Iitha went to the apple tree where her own king hung, a rotting ruin swinging between the land and sky, and, with her hands upon its bark, she swore the red king's son would never be king in Eulana.

"And, while the king was at his hunting, a-chasing the deer in the wild woods of Eulana, she slipped away, through day and night, to knock at the gates of Felluria, and Marwy Ninek let her in. Why that was, she can say better than I."

"When she asked," Marwy Ninek said, "what could I do but answer?"

She reached out to the king and drew him back beside her. He bent close, his question a breath against her cheek. "Because once you bore another name?"

She nodded, and he set his hands again upon her shoulders.

The piper's voice was hard and harsh as the clash of stone on stone. "But when the king came home and found her gone, he too went a-knocking at those gates and, against him, those gates stayed shut. Well, Torùkotu was not a man to take *Nay* lightly and broke Felluria to ruins. No need to tell that tale—it's been told many times and many. 'Tis what happened within those walls concerns this company tonight." Marwy Ninek's eyes flicked to and fro, looking everywhere save back to him. "Within those walls Ketala Iitha's child was born. Some women love their sons; I think she hated hers, hated it so much she'd kept herself alive only to watch it die. Its throat was cut before the cord. And then," he said, "she drank the cup you offered, easy in the knowledge of its death, and went smiling into the dark."

"She died," whispered Marwy Ninek, her face curd-white, pitiful and desolate, "her story ended, and the child's. I could tell this tale a dozen times out of Felluria, of the year after that night, and each time its ending is the same."

The piper shook his head. "A hundred times this tale's been told, of that night and of that child, but not once has it been true."

Kenu Vanithu took a sip of wine to wet his throat and set the cup down beside him. "See, Thodùhah, I am coming to the matter of my story. Shall I tell it, Marwy Ninek, or you?"

She made no move and said no word but sat silent, stiff and still as a figure of wood, staring into the distance beyond the fire. The king stood behind her chair, agleam with gold, his hair, bright as the fire's red heart, tumbling across his shoulders. The helmsman sat back, waiting, watching, his little knife still in his hand. Silence swelled and grew between them, the fire burned steady in the hearth, until, with one swift gesture, Kenu Vanithu stooped and threw a log onto the flames and patterns changed and shifted across the night.

"Such a little thing, a newborn child," he said, his face hideous in firelight, "such a little weight upon the world. You held it in your arms and could not do its mother's will; you let it live against her wish. You told its father it was dead to keep it from his kingdom. And, in the morning, when the door was opened, you carried it beyond your ruined walls of tumbled stones, across the water to the further bank and borderlands beneath the other sky, where the quiet king waited beneath the tree. But you cast aside his welcome to steal an apple and return, alone and lonely, to the waking world to make a man into a monster."

Her whisper was thick with hatred. "That he was already. I did no more than strip away his laughter and his smile."

"What of the child?" asked Thodùhah, leaning forward, his knife pointing at the piper. "What of the child?"

The piper's eyes met his, easy, unafraid. "It lay in its nest of sheepskin on the streambank. The wind blew upon it, the stars shone upon it, sometimes it woke, sometimes it dreamed the neverending dream of borderlands. It could lie there forever beyond the ending of the world and perhaps it would have done, had I not come upon it.

"Like Marwy Ninek herself," he said, into a silence deep as the sea, "I had come into the borderlands when I could bear the waking world no more. I found it at the streamside and saw starlight reflected in its eyes. It was a child of men in a place where it could never learn to be a man. In the borderlands, there were no loving arms to dandle it, no soft lips to kiss it, no hard hands to strike it down, no cruel words to mock it. There, in the borderlands, it could never be more than it had been at the moment when she laid it down: a newborn baby staring at the stars.

"*This is not your place*, I said to it. *I will give you all the future your own kin never gave you.*

"So I took up the babe and, together, we crossed the water into a wild night in Lyikené. In the time before the dawning, we found shelter in a sheepfold and, in the morning, the shepherd found the child and brought it to his master. And when I saw it had come to safety, I slipped away into the day."

Te-Meriku's grip must have tightened on her shoulders for his knuckles stood out white against the dark stuff of her gown. Marwy Ninek looked up at him, her lips moving in broken words he could not hear. For a long, long moment, they stared into each other's faces and then he lifted his hands and stepped away towards the winejug.

"Scratch the surface of any tale..." muttered Thodùhah.

"Even so, Thodùhah, even so." The piper's smile twisted his face into a grimace. He bowed his head, once to the king, drinking his wine; once to Marwy Ninek, her head pressed into her hands. "That is the ending of my tale and, having told it, I'm away to find my bed; the rest you can have from any in Lyikené."

"That's not quite enough, piper, to join one story to another," Thodùhah said, slowly. "There were three feathers – how did you come by those? Such feathers do not grow like flowers by the wayside, beneath this sky or the other."

Golden eyes reflected firelight, a terrible bright beauty in that dreadful face. "No more they do," Kenu Vanithu answered drily, "but the sea eagle is a bird as any other, for all three eagles are the symbol of Lyikené. Did you think that man in Eulana the first to shoot an arrow and bring one down to earth?" He looked the helmsman in the eye and cut across his answer. "They do not love the Sea People in the lands across the sea. An easy blow to strike against you and, besides, they take the newborn lambs. Often and often, in the Later Lands, have I seen one by the wayside, hanging from a keeper's gibbet."

The king laughed, hard in his throat, as Thodùhah spat into the fire. The piper shrugged and stood up from his place, buttoning his coat and turning his collar up against the night.

"One question more, before you slip away into the dark," said Te-Meriku, holding out his hand to stay him. The king's face was grim and, seeing it, Thodùhah thought it well for the piper that he was not a man.

"Ask, and I will answer."

"Did you tell this tale to Hadùhai?"

The piper smiled, and the king's hand clenched on his knife. "Aye, Te-Meriku, I did."

Kenu Vanithu limped from the room; Thodùhah paused a moment longer, to wait upon the king's wish, but Te-Meriku shook his head and so the helmsman bade him, "Good night."

Marwy Ninek looked up into the king's face. His eyes were hooded, unreadable in firelight. The silence between them was filled by the crack of branches in the fire, by the wind rattling at the shutter, by the blood thundering in her ears. Years slipped away: another room, another fire, the smell of blood and birth.

It was Te-Meriku who broke the silence. "Once," he said, "the piper asked, *What is Marwy Ninek to you?* Now he has answered his own question."

She had not the words to speak to him. Not yet. A child's eyes, clouded blue, stared out of her past; she felt again a child's weight heavy on her arm, a broken promise heavy on her heart. She held out her cup for wine and the king filled it nearly to the brim. She drank it fast and marked, as one outwith herself, how much her hands were shaking.

"Well," he said at last, "now you know me for myself. Twice the piper has turned my future to another shape but 'twas you made any future possible. Tell me," he asked, his eyes fixed on her face, "why did you do it?"

Her whisper was a thread no stronger than gossamer, drifting across the little space between them. "There is no *why*, Te-Meriku. Only a thing I could not do. I knew what it was, what it could be. I knew its mother's hatred; I knew its father's wrath... Such a little thing... So easy to make an end when all around was blood and death. And yet it was a child, naked and helpless." She did not look at him, only into the fire, seeing the shapes shift and change across the evening, patterns forming and falling, remaking themselves in another shape. "And, in the morning, I took it up thinking only of its father – to keep his own from him when in all else he had the mastery."

Silence again. The night was mild, the fire was warm, but she could not stop herself from shivering. At last she set down the cup and stood up to take three steps towards him. "When I first saw you, a red-haired barbarian come out of the west, standing so certain in your pride beneath the stone walls of Felluria, it was as if all the years between had never been." She stared into his face, tracing again the lineaments of another man. "It is written on your face, had I the eyes to see it sooner," she whispered. "Not your father but your father's son, a living memory of all that was done that night. I kept one kingdom from you and Kenu Vanithu gave you another."

"Now I know," he said, softly, "I know why Liùthánwy put Hadùhai's knife into my hand and bade me give it you. *She will be afraid, Te-Meriku, to sail with you upon the open sea.*"

"I was afraid," she answered, "and yet I held you in my arms when you were but a babe newborn."

"A child that should never have been born!" Te-Meriku laughed, and she saw a flash in his face of the boy he had been once, the pride that was the cloak he wore to hide himself away. "When I was a boy, they mocked me in Kistoru's hall because I did not know my father. We made up tales of him, Imacah and I, some strange, some wonderful, but none so wild as this. Now, in one night, I have a father, and a mother, and a—"

Marwy Ninek broke in, "No! What I am, I am. There are words must not be spoken, things that cannot be."

The laughter died from his eyes. She shook her head, trying to sift the past from the present. She drew the bronze knife from its sheath and held it in her hand, letting the firelight run along the shining blade. "Torùkotu locked me in a room between the sunset and the morning..."

He did not move and did not answer. After a long silence she said, "You are his son."

"I told you what I was on that first morning of our sailing, when I gave you that knife." The king reached out and took her hand that still held the knife. The look upon his face was never seen upon his father's. Quite softly, he told her, "This knife is still the same as on the water 'neath Cal Mora, and so am I. Does it change me from one man to another to know my father's name?"

"You are his son!"

"No man can choose who sires him, nor yet the manner of that siring. You know that who took Allocco's son to your heart and to your bed. Torùkotu gave me nothing, not even my name."

"Except your life!"

"And that I think I may fairly call my own, since I have gambled it against the kingship," he countered, his harsh smile on his face. Gently, firmly, he took the knife and laid it down on the table. He pointed to the pattern of the apple tree, at the golden apples picked out by the glow of firelight. "You saw more clearly on the sea, Marwy Ninek, when the wind began to blow your fear away. I know my place within the world and thought you had begun to learn it. Do you think I am my father come again?"

She stared at him, at his red hair, at the hard lines of his face, at the question in his eyes. This king had called her from the nightmare; had given a knife to guard her in the moonlight; had smashed the bones beneath the trees; had shown her how to kill a man. She looked and saw and knew the only ghost was in her mind.

"No, Te-Meriku," she shook her head as the dead king slipped away into the dark, leaving the living behind, " 'tis but your faces that are alike."

His smile started in his eyes, lighting his face brighter than the firelight, kindling his hard features almost to beauty. Te-Meriku held out his hands and she came to him, putting her hands upon his breast, feeling his heart beat out the strong rhythm of his life.

"When I sailed from Lyikené," he said, "I knew only what you'd done; I knew only the stolen apple and the broken troth. Almost then I hated you, for giving Averla what she needed. Since then, I've come to know why you did it."

"What does that change?" she answered, softly, sadly. "Still the thing is done."

Te-Meriku touched her cheek, as if he would wipe away the tears that were not there. Softly he told her, more like a brother than the dread king of the Sea People, "It changes nothing but my heart."

The words she wanted would not come to her tongue and she put up her hand to his.

"The world is as it is," he said, "you are my kin, if not my kind, and so my future is tangled in your past. I owe a debt to you; aye, and to Assiolo too, for my mother's sake. That is not a little thing." She felt his sigh as she rested her head against his shoulder. He closed his arms around her, holding her lightly, loosely. "Sometimes, I think the piper plays us like tunes upon his pipe. To tell that tale, tonight – I wish I knew his purpose."

She drew her breath to answer but then came a light rapping at the door. The moment passed. As the door opened, Te-Meriku turned from her and sat down in his carved chair beside the fire. He had shaken off whatever it was bound him in thought and was his hard, harsh self again.

Liùthánwy stood at the doorway. There was nothing in her face to say what she had seen; there was nothing in her eyes to tell her thoughts. She bowed her head to the king. "Te-Meriku." Her voice was smooth and empty, and likewise the king's, "What is it, Liùthánwy?"

"An it please you, Te-Meriku, my father sent me fetch his guest away. He did not think you would wish to walk alone, Marwy Ninek, in a place you did not know. Come," said Liùthánwy, "I'll take you home."

"Go to bed, Marwy Ninek." The king dismissed her without another glance, pouring the last of the wine into his cup. "It is late, you are tired. I will see you in the morning."

As they walked in the halflight the little way along the shore towards her father's house, Liùthánwy said, "My father is affronted because he has learned two things of the king he did not know, and the more so to find I have known one of them since I was nine years old."

"Kenu Vanithu told a child that tale?" She was sickened at the thought of it. He had told her many stories in Felluria, in that golden summertime amid the roses, but never such as that. The swifts had screamed above her, and the swallows darted to their nests below the eaves while he sat cross-legged beneath the stone walls and spoke of dancing trees and shooting stars; of seals and swans and great grey whales singing in the deeps of the sea. He had never spoken of any of the things a man might do on the night of the moon's darkness. Such tales as that were learnt at childhood's end, and then there was no need to tell them.

"He told it to the king my grandsire," Liùthánwy said, "but I was there, close by his knee, and I heard every word. And later, after he had gone, the king gave me his knife. He stroked my hair and told me, *You heard one tale tonight; in time, you will hear others. Listen to the stories that are told and remember them across the years.*" Liùthánwy's voice was steady, her eyes still as water fifty fathoms deep; she could not read the thoughts that moved across their depths. Lightly, as if the two were in no way linked, Liùthánwy said, "At the next moon, he sent up into Kistoru's hills for Te-Meriku to come to him. On the day he walked into the king's hall, he had nothing but his borrowed sword and his patched cloak and his bastard's pride but he stood before Hadùhai as certain of himself as of the sunrise."

So had he been beneath her high stone walls, a man knowing neither fear nor doubt. So had he been in his ship upon the sunlit sea, king of the bronze blade and the apple tree. Marwy Ninek paused on the path, turning to look back at the lighted windows of the king's hall. The warm red glow of firelight shone out from between the shutters of the little chamber and she pictured Te-Meriku sitting there alone, drinking his wine. All the time since Felluria she had scarce been a dozen paces from his side. She had thought, on that first day of their sailing, she never could grow used to him, so great was the space between them. Yet he had reached out to her across that space and tonight he was closer to her heart than any living man, save only Assiolo.

They had reached the door of Thodùhah's house. Within, children's voices called out in play.

"The sea eagle died," Marwy Ninek said, "his sword was broken. What does this mean?"

Liùthánwy paused, her hand upon the pin, her face stark and white in the gloaming. "The king can do what other men cannot; the sea eagle flies free in the high sunlight, knowing neither love nor hatred. But, when all is said and done, Te-Meriku is only a man. You know that, who listened to the piper's story."

The door was opened from within and the children flung themselves into their mother's arms. No time for further talk. Lifting the little girl and holding the other's hand, Liùthánwy stepped across the threshold of her father's house and, with a thought and a backwards glance, Marwy Ninek followed.

-+— —+-

"Assiolo." Though he had been interrupted in the middle of some reckoning, the mercatman smiled in welcome and set down his beads amidst the scatter of tally-sticks. "I had heard you were come back again – 'tis good to see your face after so long. The southlands... Cincern Dùn my homeland, was it not? I saw a kerchief of that country round your boy's neck."

"Only in passing, along the way," Assiolo answered. "Faranon."

"I know it only as a word, a story told by the piper when I was yet a child."

"The place is of no matter," Assiolo said, shortly, " 'Twas not to exchange travellers' tales I came to you." He sat down across the table without waiting to be asked. "Edo Incithu, I would do business with you again, and I would do it now."

"Of course," the mercatman bowed his head, "how may I be of service?" He indicated the counters for his wares, marked with the signs of wine and weaving, grain and rare spices, half the goods of half the world spread out upon the table. "Not this time a halfweight of saffron out of Marihon? I saw the dress that saffron dyed, and I've marked it to remember;" he touched his forefinger to a counter scratched with the weaver's sign, "there's a lady in the queen's court in Escen might fancy such a gown and I'll show her the cloth to cut for it."

Assiolo smiled, a bitter smile that did not reach his eyes. "Not saffron of Marihon, nor red wine from Escen nor even walnuts out of Cincern Dùn. I want your ship, Edo Incithu, and the crew to sail her, and I want them soon as saying. A five days sailing, and, when I'm where I want to be, they can away with the next tide."

"And if we could agree on terms for my ship and my crewmen, and, mind you, I'm not saying more than *if*," he leaned back in his chair, placing his fingertips together, narrowing his eyes, a fat man with a hennaed beard, gaudily dressed after the manner of his kind, but neither a weakling nor a fool, "if we agree terms, where is it you wish to take her, so soon before midsummer?" He took the jug of wine and poured two cups, offering one to Assiolo, who took it with a second smile, bitter as the first.

"Lyikené." Assiolo dropped the name into the room hard as a stone cast upon the floor and surely a gust of wind must have blown through the open window for, at the word, the door banged shut behind him.

"Lyikené!" Edo Incithu first stared, then shook his head. "No. More than my life's worth to go there unlooked for out of season. If you've a mind to see a king there's one in Tarhn lives in a golden hall."

"I've heard Te-Meriku promised you a game of fox and geese," said Assiolo, drily. "That sounds to me much like a welcome."

"Well, maybe I'm welcome there but you are not, full certain," he said, his tone dry as Assiolo's. "I have eyes, and I have ears, and I listen to the things men tell me, especially in Lyikené. You are a man of Ohmorah, certain as that fool who set himself against the king a score of years ago and longer."

"That's my concern, not yours." Assiolo sipped his wine. "I want passage to Lyikené and I want to be ashore before the dawning on midsummer's day."

The mercatman spread out his hands. "I never make a bargain I'll regret nor meddle in things that don't concern me."

"There are four mercatmen in Felluria this day and 'twas not chance, out of the four, brought me to you." Assiolo set down his cup and there was too much light within the room. Edo Incithu put up his hand to shield his eyes. "I've heard besides that, when Te-Meriku stood beneath yonder wall, you greeted him by name. He took away something of mine. I want it back."

The mercatman's eyes were dazzled but his answer was steady. "Marwy Ninek went of her own will."

"So have others said. I did not believe them, I do not believe you." Assiolo leaned forward across the table, a quiet man unhurried in his movements, a soft-spoken man whose mildness merely veiled a will implacable as the noonday sun. "It was by your speech Te-Meriku first passed the gate. For that reason, if no other, I will have your ship and your crew."

The mercatman matched him tone for tone. "Assiolo, I am not some foolish fisherman. I know men and I know dealing. I've seen queens and princelings in my time; I've met magicians and musicians, sailors, liars, mystics and thieves; aye, and traded with them too. That I've not met this trick before does not mean I cannot know it as a trick." Screwing up his eyes behind his hands, Edo Incithu said, "When I can see clearly, then I'll talk. You cannot threaten me with tricks and seemings. Each man of mine's signed on for honest labour, not to lose his life at the thrust of a bronze spear because you are disappointed in your love."

Assiolo shook his head. "The threat is neither trick nor seeming: from courtesy I ask, not necessity. I'll have that ship, with your agreement or no."

As he spoke, the light grew thicker, pressing down upon the mercatman like a weight of water, slowly, inexorably, crushing the breath from his body. Behind his beard, his face turned red, then slowly blue and, at the last, Edo Incithu held up his hands, gesturing defeat.

The light was only sunlight falling clear as water through the open window, nothing hidden in its depths. The mercatman could breathe again, and did so, deep, gasping breaths that set his flesh a-quivering. "If you set a fair price, I'll pay it," Assiolo said, his bitter smile curving the corners of his mouth, his eyes hard as agate.

There was a space of silence as they sat staring at each over across the wooden table. At last the mercatman's eyes slipped back to his beads and tally-sticks, to the counters marking out his wares. "A fair price?"

Assiolo nodded, once.

Himself again, composed as if Assiolo were not there, as if the moments past were of no matter, Edo Incithu sipped his wine whilst his right hand flicked beads to and fro to complete the calculation begun before this conversation. "I'm not a prince, nor yet a magician," he said, as the beads moved in a pattern only he could read. "I deal merely with the matter of the world, red wine and walnuts, wool and wheatenflour. You've dragged me down beneath my depth, so it's you must tell me, Assiolo, what is a fair price for a man's life?"

He glanced up, perhaps to see if his words had meaning in the other's mind. Assiolo made no move, he said no word but sat still and upright, sunlight on his face, shadows at his back.

"And are all lives rated equal?" Edo Incithu asked after the long moment passed. All the while, his fingers had not ceased to move nor his beads to click-click against each other on the wires. "Or do I say so much for a sailor, add on half as much again for the boatswain, triple it perhaps for the master?" He pursed his lips and paused his fingers, considering his working for a moment. Satisfied, he began again. Click-click went the little beads, counting out in ones and tens and scores the value of his trade. "What of the cabin boy of twelve years old? Is he rated less than a man because he knows so little, or higher because he has much more to lose? Can lives be weighed out like saffron or measured out like barleymeal? I never had to think on such things before this moment." His reckoning complete, he marked the total on a tally-stick and set it aside with a stack of counters.

He cast a measured glance across the table to Assiolo, who sat still as a figure carved in stone and kept his silence. Leaning his elbows on the table, placing his fingertips together, meeting Assiolo's eyes levelly, Edo Incithu asked, "And when we have agreed our price, how do I pay it? To each ahead of time, so he can get dead drunk in the spending or slip away to another ship? Or in arrears, and save us both the cost. Or should I find each man's mother, or his sister, or his sweetheart, and say to her, *Here's the price of your flesh and your blood, and here's some weaving from Felluria might tempt you part with it again?*"

Still Assiolo kept his silence and the mercatman laughed, a tight little laugh with no humour to it. "That you give no answer tells its own tale. Yours is the mastery but I've my own honour: I know some things can be neither bought nor sold. There can be no fair price for this sailing."

"Your honour is of little interest to me nor, in truth, whether you name a price or no. I have the mastery and I will have my sailing. That is enough."

"Assiolo, you push a man past reason! I'll charge you dayrates in silver for a twelve day sailing and a five man crew. In advance. An you take my ship, their lives are on your conscience." Edo Incithu held out his hands and the only look upon his face was sorrow. "When first we met you were an honest man, give me now a promise that they'll come safely out of the west?"

"I can give no more promise against the future than any other man. Whilst I'm aboard the odds are in their favour; once I'm ashore your crew's own skill with sail and weather must suffice to get them away."

The mercatman sighed. "They're good lads, but it's little enough to set against the Sea People."

Assiolo's smile was wider than before, stretching his face in bitter mirth. "Once I'm ashore the Sea People will have other concerns than your ship, Edo Incithu. I think it not impossible they'll come safely back again." He stood, saying, "I'll leave you to make all ready. Your ship's master knows the stars and currents well enough to set a course, I'll warrant, but, if not, send him to me soon as you can. By my reckoning, the ship must sail tomorrow on the afternoon tide to be there an I wish it."

"If the winds be fair set from the east."

"They will be," said Assiolo, leaving the door open behind him.

XIII, Lyikené: An end and a beginning

We know by the moon that we are not too soon,
And we know by the sky that we are not too high,
And we know by the stars that we are not too far,
And we know by the ground that we are within sound.

The Gower Wassail, *Traditional*

"Are you ready, lad?"

He nods, dry-mouthed, unable to look the king in the eye. They walk out together and all in the hall fall silent as they pass by. They pass by clansmen from the mountains and whalemen from the north; pass by fishermen from every coast and shepherds down from their pastures; pass by the ragged piper from away across the sea. Men's eyes watch and women's too, looking their last upon their king, but all around are silent. What use are words at such a time? Even the child stands stiff and straight at her mother's side, her face like thunder and tearstains down her cheeks. She watches with the rest, witness as to who it is walks out today beside the king towards an end and a beginning.

When they are alone upon the shore, the king speaks. "Don't worry, lad. I'll not walk your dreams."

Strange to laugh at such a time but laugh he does. "Was it writ so clear upon my face?"

"You're young yet. In time you'll learn to hide your thoughts."

Shingle crunches beneath their feet, the salt wind lifts their hair. The tide is nearly at its peak, the spring tide after the equinox, running swiftly up the shore to the highwatermark.

The king marks its rising. "You've had many things of me, Te-Meriku, this year, to keep or to discard, here's the last of them: when you are king you'll know no man your master, not even me, but, if you can, let there be one to whom you are only a man."

"Who'll take a bastard for himself, for love of his red hair?"

Now the king's great laugh rings out across the shoreline. "There's many'll see past the bastardy and others past your hair, it's your heart will give them pause."

He does not answer. There is no time for him to answer, even if he had one. The tide has peaked and turns now to the ebb. The pebbles shift and rattle, cold as old bones and wet with the salt of the sea.

" 'Tis time," says the king, "and here's as good a place as any."

Beautiful and terrible, the sea eagle rises on the wind, sweeping above the land and water. The king casts his cloak aside, taking care to let it fall well above the watermark, and looks all around, at the bracken on the hillside and the blue sky, at the sunlight on the sea. A long, long time he stands, an old man looking his last upon the world, but in the end he kneels stiffly down where land meets sea, bowing his head, he who has been near fifty years the king.

"All that is mine, Te-Meriku, I give to you, if you will take it."

He takes a step towards the king, standing between him and the sun, and raises the sword. As he brings it down he catches sunlight with the blade, turns it a moment from bronze into a flame. The sword strikes hard, far harder than is needed to twine an old man from his life, hard enough to kill a king and conjure another out of the moment of his death. The thing that had been a man falls slowly aside whilst the red tide ebbs from the shore. The head is tumbled by the waves until it comes to rest beside his foot. Those grey eyes are open still, steady and unblinking, not blinded by the light.

A little while, a lifetime, later, when he has lugged the body up the shore to lay it on the turf cropped short by rabbits and by sheep, when he has set its head decently beside it, when he has washed blood from his hands in clear, cold saltwater, he picks up the king's red cloak and drapes it round his shoulders, standing for a little time on the tideline to watch the patterns of sunlight on the sea before he walks, alone, back to his hall.

All through the afternoon he sits in the king's hall, in the king's carved seat, the king's red cloak about his shoulders, and all Lyikené gathered there to see him. Sunlight falls through the windows at his back to pool on the stone floor and conjure colours from the silks knotted in the clansmen's hair, azure and ivory, sea-green and heather purple, the gay gold of gorse. Morigu mor Inistai, first and greatest of the clanlords, comes forward. He kneels, smoothly graceful as a cat, to rest his head between his palms and stretch out his hands to take his oath.

"You are my king beneath this sky. My sword is your sword and your word my law. Your will is my will, your enemies are my enemies and your friends my friends. When you ask me, I will answer; where you lead me, I will follow, though it be into death. May the sky fall down and crush me, may the earth gape wide and eat me, may the sea rise up and swallow me if ever I am foresworn."

He leans forward to kiss Morigu upon his brow, acknowledging his fealty. His duty done, Morigu rises and steps back, a touch of sardonic humour in his black eyes. The world is turned all upside-down that a man of his degree, a thousand years of clansblood in his veins, should kneel before a bastard. The next man follows and the next, then it is Kistoru's turn to kneel and promise. He slumps ungainly to his knees, a heavy man in middle age grown quickly old within a year. The words slur and slide out of his mouth, his hands shake in their patterning, but he manages well enough for all that.

A pause after the kiss, a beat too long of silence, time enough for their eyes to meet and "You were not there!" to swirl unspoken on a haze of barleyspirit across the space between them, then Kistoru backs away, mopping his brow on his grass-green cloak.

Clansmen give way to shoremen; shoremen to fishermen. Who would have thought so many men were in the world? His mind is swimming on a sea of faces. The words of the oath beat through his brain, hammerblows of short, sharp words shaping him into a king.

The piper stands in the strangers' place between the hearths, wearing his coat of ragged blue. Those golden eyes stare into his and he wonders what would happen if, today, he bade him too come forward to take his oath by land and sea and sky. Wild laughter rises up at such a thought. He chokes it down, mindful of men's eyes. The piper is not a man; he stands outside the laws of men and cannot be bound by rule or custom. He turns his gaze back to the fisherman before him. "You are my king beneath this sky..."

At last, as the sun stoops down towards the west, the line of men draws to its end. He stands to walk through men's voices to the open door, an apple in one hand and a sword in the other, looking only straight ahead towards the sky and sea. Red light behind him, his shadow stretching black before him.

The shout goes up, a thousand tongues moving as one, "Te-Meriku the king!"

14: Blinded by the light

"O boatman, boatman, put off your boat!
Put off your boat for gowden money!
I cross the drumly stream the night
Or never mair see my honey."

Annan Water, Traditional

Women must age and women must die, but children still play upon
the shore and fill the day with shouts and laughter. Assiolo stood
above the highwatermark, watching his son run and jump with
Enwy Issa, listening to the children shriek with delight as little waves
chased them up the beach. Beyond the gate, men dug a grave; within
stone walls, Baesina Yatta sewed a winding sheet and her daughter
mixed clay to seal a mouth forever. Seeing their grief, he had wished
he could regret the death. Gru he had mourned, blaming first Averla
and then himself, but he knew no cause for Yatta Tala's ending but
her own deed. Yet his ship would not sail until the morrow and so,
coming from his garden and finding the women distracted by sorrow
and their needful tasks, he had taken their child with his, first to
find sweetmeats in the kitchens to coax away her tears and then out
onto the foreshore to forget sorrow awhile.

The children built up their dams of sand and stones and seaweed
to catch the streams left by the ebbing tide and Assiolo walked along
the beachtop, pausing by a scrub of sweetbriar to pluck a single wild
rose to wear the day upon his coat. There were far finer roses in
his garden, roses red as blood, sweet as love, drooping their heavy
heads against the summer's warmth, but she was not there and,
without her, those roses had no meaning in his heart. This rose grew
without the wall, a poor flower with just a touch of sweetness, falling
to pieces with the evening and yet with strength enough in root and
stem and thorn to stand against the salt spray and the wind. He
had expected to find the garden a blazing mess of firestar and found
instead the blacksmith's boy, a boy no longer, clipping off deadheads
with a certain touch, whistling a tune to a girl from the kitchens, a
girl no longer, whilst their babe kicked on a bit of sheepskin in the
shade beneath the rowan tree. Looking, seeing, he had stood a long
moment in the shadow of the wall and turned away without a word.

Now, beyond the walls, above the shore, his own son in sight
and out of mind, he saw their happiness again behind his eyes and

clenched his teeth against it, marvelling he could so hate a man he did not know.

The day was lovely, full of sunlight, with high cloud only in the east. The sun rose slowly up the sky to noontime, shortening the shadow of the mountain, drawing a path of light across the water, flashing and scintillating in freckles of gold. At his back, Cal Mora reared into the sky in a mantle of heather and bracken and the patterns of the mountain stood again reflected in the sea before him. He looked into the distance and the west, wondering if he would see the eagle banking against the east wind or else square sails on the skyline. He saw nothing. There was nothing to be seen. The sea and the sky were blue, and that was all.

Assiolo turned himself around and looked to where the light was brightest. "If you are there, show yourself," he said, and Averla stepped smiling out of the light.

"Thorn told me you were ready, Assiolo, and I am here."

"You are here," he said, and he did not smile, "and nothing has changed between us but the place. You gave me my son, madam, and I shall keep him safe within stone walls. You gave me my life but you do not command my will. You'll have nothing of me – no joy and no desire. In Faranon, I made my choices and went free of you."

"And so you did, choosing Marwy Ninek above the world."

"Tell me, madam, how far did I get along the road before you found me?"

"An hour, maybe a little longer. I had but to follow the light. You shine, Assiolo, when you feel love or anger." There was a note in her voice he had not heard before: wonder perhaps, or admiration. Averla paused at his questioning look but, when she spoke again, he heard her familiar, mocking tones. "And you love that black-haired fool, for all you are your father's son. And now she is not here! Poor Assiolo, to come all this way for her sake and find she did not wait for you. Are you so certain of her love?"

"That I believe in, certain as the sunrise. This whole matter has your reek about it – I think this was your doing."

"My doing?" A flicker in the light like laughter. "Oh, Assiolo, Assiolo, this was the king's thought and the king's word and the king's deed."

"Why did he want her?" he cried out. "Why? There is none here can tell me truth."

"There is no mystery – 'tis as you said yourself: he seeks to make certain he is long remembered." She laid her white hands each side of his face, caressing him with a touch light as a lover's, gazing at him from eyes deep enough to drown in, whispering to him through lips red as summer roses. "And Marwy Ninek? Well, you are a man, Assiolo. A woman never forgets the man who has her maidenhead. I never saw one man so like another as Te-Meriku to Torùkotu. He snapped his fingers and she went with him."

"Madam, you are as much a liar as any in Felluria!" Assiolo caught Averla's wrists and pulled her hands from his face, hating her, fearing her. "She loved me full as well as I loved her."

"Words, Assiolo, words. Many men have told themselves this tale before – all of them were fools. You cannot change the truth with words." Averla laughed, rubbing the red marks of his fingers from her wrist. "Maybe 'twas from fear she went with him, maybe desire, but certaintimes Te-Meriku has her. Certaintimes, he's had her. Think on it, Assiolo, your black-haired trull in the bed of that barbarian."

Her laugh rang out across the day, rippling like birdsong.

He gasped for breath like a man suffocating. "Is that the truth? Tell me, is it true?"

She smiled. Never had there been a sight so lovely and so terrible; the sun in splendour was not so glorious as Averla's smile, not yet the world so cruel. "Do you think she has the strength to say him, *Nay*? He with his bronze sword and his iron will? And if she said him, *Nay*, think you that he would heed her? There is no one in Lyikené says to the king, *Thus far and no further*."

Assiolo held his left hand to the sky, his right to the sea, and the world fell to silence. The wind was paused upon Cal Mora's braes, the waves upon the shore, the children in their game; all and about were still and silent as a dream.

"I will," he said, "by land and sea and sky, I swear it."

—+— —+—

Maris was in the king's hall, setting the factor about his business, and Thodùhah walking with his granddaughters upon the shore. In a daychamber of her father's house, Liùthánwy sat, quiet as a grey shadow, smocking a child's nightgown.

"This was yours, I think, before it was mine." Marwy Ninek laid the bronze dagger down upon the table beside a jug of wildflowers, sweetbriar and scabious, harebells and seathrift, a tall spike of yellow iris.

"I have other knives," said Liùthánwy, "and you do not. I think it better that you keep it. It's served you well, my father says. Maybe you'll have need of it again."

She bowed her head in thanks and courtesy. "A gift well given. I thank you, Liùthánwy."

"What do you want of me, Marwy Ninek?" Liùthánwy set down her sewing and folded her hands in her lap.

"You know the king better than I can. I'd have you speak of him."

Liùthánwy smiled, a sad, soft smile, weak as sunshine through the rain. "What can I say? He lost what most he loved and, often and often, he has taken what was offered in its place, always hoping it would be enough, always knowing it was not."

"There must be more than this."

Liùthánwy's eyes were grey as the light before the dawning; Liùthánwy's face was still and sad; Liùthánwy's words were soft as raindrops falling on the surface of the sea. "If you'd hear tell of his kingship, best speak to my father or to Ardùvai or any in his hall. I can tell only of the little there was between us. Te-Meriku's not a man to sleep alone – one night he asked, and I gave him what he wanted. And, after, when I knew I went with child, I made a bargain with Ithánu the whaleman."

Marwy Ninek remembered words overheard upon the sea and asked, "Because he had red hair?"

"In part, because he had red hair." Liùthánwy laughed, and if there was a joke it was one she told against herself. "But more because he would take me far away into the north to a place where I could begin the world anew." Her laughter died away. She passed her hand across her face and sighed. "Don't believe all my father says. My husband was not a foolish man, only a kind one. Kindness is not a virtue overrated among the Sea People. When Eilis was an hour old, a red-faced, mewling mite, Ithánu showed her to his kinsfolk and his clan and named himself her father. And it was no less than the truth: all a father can give, he gave to her."

Marwy Ninek snapped out, "Except her life!" and saw Liùthánwy's eyes darken, like stormclouds above the sea. "What of Te-Meriku who sired her in a night and thought no more about it?"

"You do not know – you were not there!" Liùthánwy cried. "Do you dare pity or despise me? Are you like my father, naming Ithánu a fool, seeing in me only a woman that bedded one man and wedded with another."

Marwy Ninek shook her head and pointed to the knife. "In truth I did not think of you at all, Liùthánwy. I thought of other women, other times."

Liùthánwy reached out a thin hand towards the briar, the sweet dusky pink petals set above their jagged thorns. "There's not been a bairn laid to the king's account but that he's done his duty." She no longer sounded angry, only very tired. "Te-Meriku told me no lies and made me no promises – 'twas my own choice took me into the north."

Marwy Ninek looked at her and saw at last the lines traced by her life around her great grey eyes. Liùthánwy bowed her head and sat in silence, pulling the petals from a rose, her eyes bright with the tears she was too proud to shed.

Softly, slowly, watching the petals drop by one, by two, by three, Marwy Ninek asked, "Were you happy, Liùthánwy, in that land beneath the northern lights?"

"No," she said, "not very." Her answer was a thread of misery stretching its way across the silence between them. "I should have been a man, to sail my ship towards a distant star. Instead, I had the promises Ithánu had made me, and my children. For a while, it was enough. Ithánu was a good man, a kind man, and there is no place so lovely as the north country in the summertime, sunlight on the water and seabirds calling across the shore. At such a time I could believe I had set my past behind me. But the wind blows cold across the ice in winter and the sun forgets to rise. And children die."

Her hand gripped the briar; when she looked up, the grief that had woken in her heart had made a desolation of her face. "Bonny at night, dead at the dawning," said Liùthánwy.

Marwy Ninek felt a cold hand clutching at her heart. She did not want to look; she did not want to listen; she did not want to learn any more of sorrow or of suffering. There was enough in her own past to fill a life twice over. She could close her eyes but not her ears and so she could not help but hear her, each word an icy drop falling to a bitter pool. "The winter sickness took my baby and left behind a cold, hard thing, a stone with his face." Liùthánwy's words tailed off into a jagged silence, and, when she spoke again, her voice was small and tight. "He was also Imacah – I did not wish it but it is for a father to name a son. It is of no matter, now that he is dead."

Liùthánwy opened her hand and let the crushed flowers fall. Three red beads welled up from her finger where thorns had pierced it. Tiredly, stupidly, she wiped them away, smearing her sleeve with her own blood. "And after that," she said, "what I had with Ithánu was no longer enough, for all there had been love between us of a kind. When he died, I pulled my hair across my face to hide I could not weep. I had spent my store of tears on Imacah and there were none left for him."

Hesitatingly, Marwy Ninek reached out but stopped before she touched her. What comfort could she offer to such grief? She was not a woman – all the rest she could know but never that. She bowed her head, unable to look her in the face. No stone walls had ever crashed across Liùthánwy's life; she had never smelled the smoke of fires reeking in the night time but there was no lesson in despair left for her to learn.

So in the end it was Liùthánwy who drew her close and kissed her as her mother might have done. But her mother was many lifetimes dead and had never kissed her but the once as all around the world fell into ruin. She would rather have looked anywhere but at Liùthánwy at that moment, for fear of seeing Ketala Iitha reflected in those rain-grey eyes.

"It is harder than I thought to begin the world anew," said Liùthánwy. "Now here I am again in my father's house, the widowed mother of two girls, and still my eyes slide sideways to Te-Meriku and I think of all the things that might have been. And part of me hopes midsummer's day will bring an ending."

Their eyes met, and it was Marwy Ninek who first looked away.

—+— —+—

Beyond the walls, Yatta Tala lay, clay cold in a stony bed. Her daughter had said all that was needful, and her granddaughter too, their faces wet with tears; the lantern they had set upon her grave had burned the short summer's night away and faltered only after the morning. Women grow old, and women die; she had lived longer than many another in Felluria – no need for wonder at her passing. Assiolo stood inside the gates of Felluria, his mind on other matters. Beyond the gates, upon the water, the ship waited, for him and for the tide, but he took a moment to look about. The walls stood high and grey above him, the stone walls of Felluria traced across with lithia's false fire, and, over and about them, woven to and fro between the gateposts, another tracery that he could see only from the edges of his eyes. He smiled, pleased with his skill to make a place of safety for his son and weave so fine a web, one so subtle in its patterning, none of this place could even think that it was there and yet so strong and so unyielding none of Faranon could pass it, in flesh or thought or seeming.

He crouched down beside his son, placing his hands upon his shoulders. "I'll be back again before the moon reaches its fullness, or sooner like enough," he said. "You're to mind Issa Baesina and her mother, and play within the walls with Enwy Issa. Stay within the walls, lad, but don't get underfoot in the kitchens or they'll bake you in a pie."

As he had intended, the boy laughed at such a thought but, when Assiolo tried to stand, he put his arms around his neck and clung tight and would not let him go.

"Nay, Imacah," Assiolo said after a little time of the child's sobbing, "this time you cannot come with me, howeverso much you ask it. There's enough here to amuse you whilst I'm gone. The steward's younger sons are near your age if you tire of playing with a girl. No doubt they know every corner of Felluria, from the wall top to the cellars."

The boy whispered, his face pressed against Assiolo's shoulder, "I want Oca. She promised it would not be long."

Assiolo sat back on his heels, looking into his son's tears. "Oca is not here," he said, firmly. "You left that life behind when you came away with me: Oca and Casarca and your mother and all. This is your place now, Imacah, and, when I bring its mistress home again, we'll make a new beginning, you and she and I together, forever and for always."

"Gru was here," the child began, but then fell silent. Assiolo embraced his son, holding him close, but did not ask what he had seen, for fear to hear the answer. He closed his eyes but saw Gru's empty stare gazing back at him. In the silence and the dark, he could hear his son's gasping breaths, feel the flutter of his heart. Such a little thing within his arms, a child, half-formed and delicate.

Longtimes the ship would wait for him, but not the tide. Assiolo peeled away the small hands clutching at his coat. "I've said all that I can say," he told the boy. "No more words, Imacah. I must away and you're safer here within these walls than any place beyond them, even at my side." He held his son's hands within his own. "Dry those tears, lad, and bid me farewell with a smile."

Still the child clung to him. "You will come back?"

"Here's a promise, Imacah, and a token of that promise." Assiolo pulled his ring from his finger and slipped it onto his son's thumb, closing his fingers around it in a fist. "I love two people in the world and you are one of them. The other gave me this. Keep it safe for me and give it back when I return."

The boy stared at the ring, running a finger over the chipped edge to the stone. "Which king is here?"

Assiolo smiled and ruffled the boy's hair. "I'll leave you to guess at that, Imacah, and tell me when you give me back my own." He kissed his son upon the brow and walked out of the gates of Felluria towards the waiting ship.

—+— —+—

Night time, and Marwy Ninek could not rest within Thodùhah's walls. Thoughts ran round and around her mind of the king and Assiolo. Barefoot, quiet as could-be, she slipped through the dark and silent house and slid back the bolts upon the door. She pulled on her shoes upon the threshold, gathering her courage about her like a coat, and stepped out into the halflight. She had not taken a step, a step but barely three, when she heard her name spoken behind her.

She turned to see Thodùhah standing at his open door. "Where," he asked, "might you be off to, so late into the evening?"

"Not so far. I could not sleep and had a mind to see the king. 'Tis so close by I had not thought it needful to wake you."

"Old bones sleep lightly and I know all the sounds of my own house. Remember too, I'm a man with a daughter – there's a loose board or two outside my chamber I've never thought to tighten." She heard his smile in his voice, as often when he spoke of his daughter. "I thought the days long done when I'd hear them creaking in the night time."

She laughed, soft in her throat. "Not so many years left until you hear them creak again. Children grow, Thodùhah."

"Aye, lass, and when they have no doubt I'll listen for them in the night time. But the bairns are asleep in their bed and so too is my daughter and it's you I must have a thought to." He closed the door quietly and came out to stand beside her. "If you've a mind for starlit visiting, I'll walk with you to the hall door and see you safely in."

"I'm not a child," she said, "and I have my knife."

"So you do," he said, drily, "and that thought might have eased my mind and let me keep my bed, had I not seen the way you use it."

She bit her tongue upon her first answer. He was her host and due her courtesy. "Think of it from my side," he told her. "Te-Meriku put you in my care and I'd rather face your wrath than his – I've seen him use a knife too, often and often. Believe me, it's more than my life's worth to let you walk alone by night."

She saw his smile and let her own match it. "I'd not want you to suffer for my sake. Walk with me and welcome." He folded her arm into his and led the way along the path above the shore.

The summer's night was soft, scarce dark at all with shreds of sunset lightening the west and the long-haired star a stain upon the eastern sky. Down by the water oystercatchers whistled, one to another, and now and then she heard the strong, quick beat of wings against the wind. "You've come a way," Thodùhah said. "It was a poor, quivering shadow we picked up in Felluria and now you'll take up your knife to dare the night time in Lyikené."

"I did not then know the king," she answered, flushing and glad there were shadows enough to hide it, "and no more of Lyikené than fire and blood and death."

"I'm sorry for it, lass," the helmsman said, an old man speaking quietly in the halflight, a father who loved his daughter well, "that the old tales are all true. The shame is ours that shaped him."

And yet, she thought, without him there would not be Te-Meriku. That was a hard, harsh truth within her mind. "He is dead," she said, "dead and gone into the dark. No need now to think on him."

Thodùhah's fingers tightened a little on her arm. "Ah, lass, you've come a way indeed, and glad I am to see it."

Their footsteps rang on the courtyard stones and a shadow waited at the door, shifting and shrinking into a man as they came close.

"Here's one to see Te-Meriku," said Thodùhah to Ardùvai. "I'll bid you good night, Marwy Ninek." He did what he had not before, held her close in a strong embrace, kissed her cheek as he might have done his daughter's. "Go to him, lass. He needs you full as much as you need him."

She kissed him in return. "For your kindness and your company," she said. "I would I'd known you sooner, Thodùhah."

"I took him, fox and geese, an hour ago," Ardùvai told her as he led her through the warren of rooms behind the hall, "and left him rueing his losses 'midst the wreckage. If you've a kinder heart than I have, you'll give him one game of the pair."

"I know your heart full well," she said, "you take no great care to hide it."

"Oh, I've no need to hide it. There's some born blind and some that will not see. But, since my brother died," he said, and she heard again that note of throbbing pain, "I've felt the burden of it, somewhat harder than before. Sore hearts look for comfort rather more than whole ones." He stopped at the king's door. "Thus far and no further, for me if not for you."

They were nowise alike, the nightwatch and the helmsman's daughter, but for that touch of roughness in their voices when either spoke of the king. And yet, even as that thought hung in her mind and she fumbled for an answer, Ardùvai's quick smile flashed out, full of sidelong mischief. "Nay, spare your tender thoughts for those that need them. All fishermen tell tales of the one that slipped their hook but there's fishes a-plenty in the sea for all that. I land my catch, often and often."

As always, his smile conjured her own. Impossible for melancholy and Ardùvai to keep long company together. "You're a black rogue," she told him, "but a good friend. I hope one day you'll get what you deserve."

"That's little enough," he objected, his eyes glinting in the halflight. "If you're my friend, you'll wish me far more than I deserve."

"What you deserve," she said again, biting her lip upon her laughter, "and I hope they take you fox and goose."

Ardùvai rapped hard on the oak and, as the king answered, "I'm here!" he slipped laughing away into the shadows.

Marwy Ninek closed the door quietly behind her. "Three nights ago," she said, "I did not have the words I needed but tonight, when I did not want to be alone, I thought to come to you."

Te-Meriku stood up from his seat beneath the window, the last of the sunset at his back. The lamplight shining from the sconce beside it picked out the golden threads woven in his shirt and conjured the fire from his hair. He took her hands in his and lightly kissed her brow. "And who else should you come to? Is it play you're after, or to drink the night away, or both of them together?"

His red cloak was cast carelessly across a chair back, trailing to the floor. The game board still lay on the table next to a silver flask, geese and fox beside it all tumbled together with a handful of coloured shells. "I'll drink a cup with you," she said, "but I'll not play you, fox or goose."

"For fear of losing or that I'll let you win?"

"You?" She arched her brow against his smile. "I've seen your game. What did Ardùvai take you for tonight?"

"We played, like boys, for seashells." He grinned, and poured two drams of barleyspirit. "An I did not cap the stakes, he'd have half Lyikené by now. I've no mind to end my days a beggar." He raised his cup and his tone turned to mockery. "To Kenu Vanithu," he pledged and drank and filled his cup again, "who, for sake of my red hair, set me on another path."

It was to her a bitter jest, conjuring thoughts of the future out of the past. Long threads of memory tugged her back among the ruins and strangled her laughter in her throat. "Better to be a king than a beggar, no matter what old songs say." She shivered, remembering the wind whistling down Cal Mora, those years among the ruins, those many, empty years, before the black tower fell. "To go most days a-hungry and know no shelter from the wind."

"You're cold," he said, catching up his cloak, "but there's shelter here, and company. This'll warm you without." He wrapped it round her shoulders and gave her a cup of barleyspirit. "And this within."

" 'Tis not cold," she said, though the weight of wool and the rasp of liquor were comforting, "only a memory of cold that makes me shiver. The past seems very close tonight, Te-Meriku, and it is your past too."

"Then come here and let me share it."

She let him draw her down beside him into the windowseat, leaning her head against his shoulder, lapped in the folds of his cloak. Strange now to think how she had feared him. She sipped, and felt the spirit warm her, strong as his arm about her waist. Long moments passed, a counting out of time in slow heartbeats as darkness gathered at their backs.

Three windows to the king's chamber and all of them were open to the summer's night. One looked south towards the dark bulk of Kistoru's hills, one looked west across running water to the tree and the last eastwards to the sea. A lovely sight enough, on other nights, the starlight on the sea, the wind upon the water, but not tonight when the common stars were dulled and dimmed beside the balestar and the sea all stained with sulphur. And slowly, surely, that star was rising higher until at last its yellow light spilled 'cross the sill into the room. The hairs pricked on her neck at such a sight; she crooked her fingers and said aloud, "Banish misfortune!"

"What I can, I'll do," Te-Meriku answered, laughing at her fears, and stood up to close the shutters. "The rest must wait until midsummer."

"Nay, I'm a fool," she said, though the star's meaning was yet a weight upon her heart, "leave it alone." She crossed the room to stand beside him. The starlight slid through the window and cast a sickly yellow pallor across his face. "Were it not for that star's shining, I'd not be here. You'd know no more of me than the Tion of Felluria and I'd yet think you a barbarian beyond the western sea. One choice leads on to others and it changes nothing if we close our eyes. Even now," she said, softly, "knowing what I know, the choice I made I'd make again, for Assiolo. He is the beat of my heart, a part of me, forever and for always."

"Did you think I do not know it? As for you, so once for me. There was a night when, had Averla come to me, I'd have taken her bargain. The beat of my heart, aye, that was Imacah."

Te-Meriku turned his head, staring out into the night, as if he looked for someone standing just out of sight, beyond the light of the long-haired star.

The dead were dead and came not back, howeverso much he wished for it. The night beyond his window was empty as a broken heart, the only face to see his own, a pale shadow reflected in the glass. He put up his hand to the windowpane but did not quite touch it. His voice was a whisper, a murmur, lonely as the wind blowing down Cal Mora. "We thought the world would never change, our deeds would never find us out, and we would live forever and for always. Then Hadùhai sent for me. An end and a beginning."

Marwy Ninek said, softly, to call him back from the place within himself, "I am here, Te-Meriku."

He looked around, as in surprise to see her at his side wrapped in his cloak, and forced a quick, tight smile. "It's true," he said, "the past is very close tonight. Half my life ago and longer, and always it could be yesterday." He closed the shutters 'gainst the starlight and slid the bar into its place.

"No need to speak of Imacah, an you do not wish to."

"You've heard this tale before? It's a poor story, scarce fitting for a twicetold tale."

"I had something of it from Ardùvai, upon the sea. But I'll listen if you've a mind to tell it – I know full well," she told him, "two can bear what one cannot."

"What's to do but bear it?" He sat down in the seat beneath the window, leaning back against the wall. "Oh, I'll tell it and be done, if you've a mind to hear me. Pour me another drink, if you will."

She turned away, taking her time that he might find his balance. "As I walked out of his father's hall, Imacah called me back to give me his sword, because it was finer than my own, and so we parted, laughing at his father's anger. I thought, young fool that I was, Hadùhai sought only to clip a bastard's wings and bid me remember as Kistoru had done, often and often, it was not fit for me to match myself against the clansmen. Well, 'twas not that," he said shortly, taking the cup she offered. "Instead he made me a king and gave me a sword as pledge of it.

"So I went back to Imacah, my head full of dreams and glory. First he stared, and then he swore, and in the end he said he'd not have let me have his sword if he'd known I'd find another one so easily.

"Until then," Te-Meriku said, "we had been equals, two halves of one whole. It was no longer so." The lamplight shone reflected from his eyes, burning away the years between his memory and this moment. He raised the cup and drained it.

No need to say, *He stole an apple.* No purpose in reminding him, *The price of a stolen apple is very high, beneath this sky or the other.* No kindness to make him speak more than need be on his lover's death. She said, to spare him the telling, "And so Imacah went out and you did not."

"Aye, so he did!" She heard his anger and his grief, still raw and rough after twenty years and longer. "And yet we loved each other, Imacah and I. It's a hard lesson, and a bitter one, that love is not enough." Te-Meriku broke off, pressing his face into his hands. "I could not ask, he did not tell, if it was by chance that death had found him out."

Marwy Ninek knelt at his knee and reached out to him, this time to offer comfort not to take it. He bent his head onto her shoulder, stiff and silent in his grief, and she held him close, stroking his red hair. He smelled of barleyspirit, of leather and of woodsmoke, the faint, dry scent of mountain thyme.

Always, since he had first called her to come out from her stone walls and face him, she had seen only his strength and his certainty, the fierce light of his will. He was the king of Lyikené whose part it was to guard the tree that stood between the world and the world's ending. Here, in the quiet night, he had laid all that aside. This could be any man, she thought, mourning his lover gone into the dark, crying out it is too soon. She cradled his head against her breast, her king, her brother, the child snatched from the ruin, and wondered on the price of a man's life. An apple? A sword? A kingdom?

The dead were dead and came not back, but they were very close tonight, lingering long in the shadows at their backs. Imacah had let a wolfspear thrust into his belly; Ketala Iitha had taken the cup she offered in her cold hands. Te-Meriku wrapped his arms around her and they were a long time silent, locked in a close embrace.

At last he raised his head. She saw no trace of tears upon his cheeks but his eyes were very bright. "It's been a long time," he said, "since last I spoke of Imacah, and that the reason."

"If it had fallen out the other way," she asked, "if Imacah had held the king's sword in his hand and said he would not go, would you have courted death that night?"

Te-Meriku was so long silent she thought he would not speak. But, "No, I would not," he answered in the end. "I loved him too well to leave him lonely. It is very easy to die, to slip away into the dark, but the living are left behind to pay the price."

That was a truth he had no need to teach her. Before she slipped away and left her to face the red king's wrath, Ketala Iitha had kissed her with cold lips. "I too was left behind," she said. She brushed the touch of that kiss from her cheek and closed her mind against the memory. "A woman would have died, when Felluria fell into ruin, but I am not a woman and I lived on."

He asked, as if he read the thoughts unspoken in her face, "What was she like, my mother?"

A wraith, she thought, *a shell, consumed by hatred and by suffering, living only as long as was necessary for vengeance.* Aloud, she said, "She loved the king. She should have died when he did—far kinder that than to live on, alone and lonely, past the death of love."

He met her eyes, and she knew he understood all she had not said. "There's many and many must do that."

"I had not your strength to bear it. I could not let Assiolo go. More than my life, I love him."

Te-Meriku laughed, hard and harsh, as he stood up. "Oh, don't think me better than I am—I've scarce lived lonely," he said, crossing the room to take the flask of barleyspirit from the table. "There've been many come to my bed since Imacah died. *Every woman in Lyikené,* they say, *and half the men besides.* An easy way to drive away the dark, a glance, a touch, a night time's pleasure."

She thought of Liùthánwy, a grey ghost in her father's house, of Ardùvai, in the dark beyond the door, but she had seen the loss and longing in his eyes each time he spoke of Imacah and could not judge him hardly. "For me," she said, "there was only Assiolo. All else that might have been, Torùkotu took from me. Longtimes I lived, an empty shell, a broken thing, the Tion of Felluria."

"And Assiolo?" he asked, as he sat again beside her. "What were you to him?"

"All a woman can be to a man." She bent her head to hide her blush, remembering the sweetness of his body in the night time, his tender touch, his joy and his desire. "He did not see in me the Tion of Felluria."

"No more do I," said Te-Meriku. "I do not think it was the Tion of Felluria placed her body 'twixt a babe and a monster, nor more than 'tis the Tion of Felluria sits here now with me. You are not much like the piper."

He poured the last of the barleyspirit into their cups and they sat a while a-drinking, quiet in each other's company. "That night," she said when both their cups were empty, "that dreadful night, when all I knew had ended, I thought there could never be a future. And yet, out of that night this one has come. I am glad to know you as yourself."

"You and I are one blood. Nay," he laughed as she shook her head against such words, "the world is as it is. You said as much yourself."

"I know," she whispered, "but we've lost much, you and I."

"We've found something too." His arm tightened a little, holding her close. "Something neither of us looked for but it is here between us. There are many kinds of love."

She took his hand between her own. "I do not know the piper's purpose – I do not even know if he is friend or foe – but I am glad he told that tale."

"So too am I, whatever happens after."

No need to speak at such a time; all that needed saying had been said already. Later, later, drifting away on a rising tide of drowsiness, warm in the folds of his cloak, she felt his arms about her, lifting and carrying her across the room. "It grows late," he said, laying her down upon his bed. "Too late to rattle at Thodùhah's door. I thought you could sleep here."

She murmured, lapped in the softness of sealfur, "An you will lie beside me, as on the sea, and keep bad dreams away."

He lay down and she rested her head upon his shoulder. She slept first and in a while he followed her, deep into a dreamless sleep. But, in the time before the morning, he woke and rose to sit a while before the window looking out across his country to the tree. Alone within his bed, Marwy Ninek tossed and turned through uneasy slumbers, as the sunrise crept towards her 'cross the floor.

‑‑   ‑‑

For the parting with his son Assiolo had shut up his fears within his mind. Now, upon the sea, they came back to him over and again, in the dazzle of sun upon the water, in the quiet darkness of the night. All through the day and long into the night, as Felluria fell away into the blue distance, he stood at the rail looking ever into the west while the balestar rose at his back. He lay long hours awake, rocked by the waves like a child in its cradle, his mind like the sea, always in motion; when at last sleep came to him, little and late, he dreamed of being blinded by the light, of being tumbled by the flood. Averla lied; surely as she lived, she lied...

And yet, Assiolo wondered, lying in the narrow bunk alone, letting the black thoughts chase the red across his mind, if not for that, then why?

By the morning he had had enough of thinking and of dreaming, and bade a sailor draw up a bucket of seawater. He was Allocco's son and his first affinity was with fire and iron but he could turn other elements to his purpose if he so chose. The sailor obeyed without a word but, when Assiolo turned his back, he felt the man's fingers crook against misfortune. He shrugged it off, as he had every time before. The sailors' distrust was of no matter: they did his will and that was all he cared for. He filled his bowl half-full of clear, cold saltwater and carried it below.

By lamplight in the mercatman's cabin, Assiolo set the bowl before him on the floor and reached for his leathern bag. He pulled out Marwy Ninek's red shawl and spread it across his lap, searching this way and that until he found the thing he needed. He wound the long, black hair around his fingers to keep it safe and lifted the shawl to his face to breathe in rosewater and lavender, the sweet, distant scent of her. It was too much to bear. Anger and fear crashed over him in a towering wave of pain and all his promises pressed heavy on his heart. A long, low moan escaped, muffled by the heavy folds across his mouth. He forced himself to calmness, then folded the shawl carefully and put it aside, turning his attention to the bowl.

The ship was running before a crisp east wind and the water rolled with the motion of the sea. Assiolo frowned to see the reflections in the water change as it slopped around. He said a word and the surface calmed, resting still and clear as glass. His lips curved in satisfaction as he leaned a little forward to see his face reflected in the water and dropped the hair into the bowl.

The hair unwound across the surface, looping itself into a circle. Outside the edge, Assiolo saw the cabin; within, another room, a timber-vaulted chamber where early morning sunshine spilled across grey sealskins on the floor. A man lounged in a windowseat, barefoot in trousers and a shirt patterned with leaves and apples, his hair flaming 'cross his shoulders. From the back of his mind, his father's voice spoke across the years: *A red-haired whelp now bears the kingship; I think Hadùhai grew foolish in his age.*

The king looked around, as a man does when he thinks that he is watched, and Assiolo gasped to see his face. His heart beat fast – it could not be: that man was dead beneath the winter trees with cold stones lying heavy on his bones.

The king stretched and stood and crossed the room. Assiolo saw the bedplace piled high with white sealfurs. A tangle of black across the white, and there she was, curled sleeping in the furs of this barbarian's bed. He caught in his breath. He had known she must be within the room – had he not cast this charm to find her? – and yet it was a knifeblade to his heart to see her reflected in the water, so close, so very far away. He saw her eyes moving beneath closed lids, saw her hands thrust out, and knew she was tossed again by nightmare, as so often in their bed. As on those nights, he said aloud, "I am here, love," but she could not hear him, not even in her sleep. Instead the king put out his hand and she woke at his touch.

Assiolo saw her mouth open, saw her struggle against the red king's grasp. He could not hear her scream but he needed no words to know it was his name she cried.

The charm snapped in that moment. The water rocked and rippled in the bowl, reflecting only his own fear. Assiolo closed his eyes, counting out his heartbeats, letting the quiet dark swallow his panic and his rage. He had made a window on the world and seen what he had looked for, and the seeing was no more than he had known these last days, since he had heard Yatta Tala say, *The king took her away.*

"I am coming, love," he said, turning one hand up and the other down, whilst lamplight settled on his hair. "No man shall stand between us."

—⊢— —⊢—

Fathers decree, grandams command, mothers instruct, but children go their own ways across the morning. Felluria was full of places where a boy and girl might play and they could find content in none of them this morning. The steward's sons had commandeered the empty room atop the western tower as their lair and kept the stair with sticks and stones, lording it over youngsters of six years and five with all the arrogance of seven and ten. They played a while within the court but the blacksmith's wife complained of their noise, and then a while within his father's garden until the gardener's wife came by with her baby, who staggered after their ball, and screamed when they took it back, and the woman spoiled their games with her scolding and her cautions. The gate was open, the road beyond the gate shimmered in the morning sun and beyond the road was a scintillation of light on water. No bully boys or babies there, nor yet the nagging tongues of adults. The boy remembered well what his father had told him, the girl knew what her mother expected of her, aye, and her grandam too, but beyond the gate was the seashore and the rocks of Loch Mora-side. Between the rocks were pools of saltwater left by the ebbing tide and, in the pools, sea-jellies flowered, spreading out red petals. Periwinkles crept between crevices, limpets clung tight to the rocks and crabs hid in the weed. No better place to play upon a hot summer's day, paddling knee-deep in cold, clear water and catching glassy shrimp or tiny dabs the colour of the sand. Or so the girl said, when the steward had driven them from the hall and the cook from the kitchens and they stood again before the open gate, sticky with stolen honeycomb. 'Twas too hot to watch the blacksmith in his forge, and the orphan lamb she had reared was grown too dull and big for petting it to be long a pleasure. If they stayed within her mother's chambers, work would be found for them to do, sweeping of floors and carding of wool for him, sewing of seams and stitching at samplers for her, and, besides, her great-grandam's loom stood there yet, her last web stretched upon it, a pattern broken off before its end, an echo and a memory.

They slipped through the gate beneath the porter's gaze as he supped his ale, a man made thirsty by the heat though the morning was not yet halfway done, and ran hand in hand toward the shore. Oystercatchers rose from mussel beds, uncovered by the retreating tide, and flitted low away across the water, whistling one to another. Turnstones, less wary, pecked at the seaweed at the tideline and the great grey heron, to whom two children were of no concern at all, stood hunched in his place at the water's edge, watching, waiting, a shadow in the sunlight.

The sun rose towards noontime and the shadows shortened across Cal Mora. The children played and splashed and called, one to the other, "Look!"

"A fish..."

"A crab..."

"A sea maid's purse..."

"A feather from an eagle's wing..."

"Look!"

Three shepherds, dozing in the shade of rocks upon the brae, heard their piping voices rising from the shore and thought nothing of it. 'Twas summertime – what surprise that children played by the water? So too had they, a dozen years ago, when they were boys.

Nor did the shepherds think it strange to see two women walking at the lochside, always a little above the tideline. Where there were children, there were always women. So it had been when they were boys; so it would be when they were fathers, and who would want it any other way? Women could mend a quarrel and answer a question and nurse a bruise and soothe and slap and manage all the needs of childhood. The shepherds lay on their backs and planned their futures, not here upon Cal Mora's braes but away across the Inner Sea on the banks of the Eus, where the queen of Escen was ever in need of men with quick wits and strong right arms to keep the peace that she had made.

And, on the shore, the children laughed and played until the boy looked up and saw the women standing there, the grey-haired and the brown, each holding out her arms and smiling, and, with a whoop of delight – "I *knew* you'd come!" – he ran to them, hugging first one and then the other. Their first joyful greeting done, he turned to call his friend and make all known, one to the others.

"Enwy Issa, this is Oca, my nurse, and this Casarca. Oca, Enwy Issa has her own lamb, and I fed it this morning!"

Each stooped to kiss her and thanked her for her care with such sweet courtesy as to make her heart swell with pride. Then, for a while, the shepherds could see, if they cared to look, there were four figures playing in the rockpools at the lochside and, later, an hour or two past noontime, the same four figures sitting in a line, sharing the contents of a basket and throwing crusts to the seagulls and the crows. But the shepherds had their own bread and cheese to eat, with honeycake to follow, and a jug of beer keeping cold in the stream running down the brae, and plans to make of mail and swords and foreign lands. Then one spoke instead of the steward's eldest girl and what he would do if he met her on the hillside on midsummer's eve. Straightways, his companions laughed at him – who had not yet a beard worthy of the name – for boasting and strutting like a grousecock; one twisted his arms behind his back while the other pelted him with heather twigs until he admitted his folly and begged for mercy.

And, hours later, as the summer sun hung above the western sea and the shadows of the walls stretched out towards the lochside, the girl walked through the gates alone, tired and happy, a garland of wild roses and honeysuckle wreathing her hair, her hands full of seashells, to find her mother and her supper and her bed. Of the boy she could talk but vaguely; his nurse had met them, she said, and his mother's maidservant – "Oh, and 'twas she had woven this garland – Isn't it lovely?" – and they had taken him away back to his mother, who was waiting for him in a bower beneath the trees.

And at such words, her mother scolded and her grandam ran away, to tell the steward and rage at the porter and find men to make a search across the hillside and the shore. But, though they searched high, and they searched low, and they searched late into the sweet summer twilight, of the boy there was no sign.

—+— —+—

The doors of the king's hall stood open. Midsummer's eve and what need to close the door against the balmy morning and the sweet winds off the sea? The king sat with his company around him, with Thodùhah at his left hand, Marwy Ninek at Liùthánwy's side among the few women who had not been sent away into the hills and mountains, and the piper in his place between the empty hearths. Midsummer would come with the morrow, and who knew what would happen before the sunset, but no need now to speak of it. The sea was calm, the air was still and the king's bronze sword remade and ready, waiting for his hand.

"And there were three kings standing beneath the bone-bare tree," the piper said, telling his tale to Renùku and half a dozen other boys, "one wore red, and one wore green, the third wore black, and all their faces were the same.

"The red king held out his hand and in it was a sword.

"The green king held out his hand and in it was a rose.

"The black king held out his hands and both of them were empty —"

A man stepped out of the sunlight spilling through the open door, a thin, spare, grey man who cast no shadow, though the light was very bright behind him. He stood upon the threshold, the sight in all men's eyes, and looked about and, though he made no move and said no word, the hubbub in the hall died away to nothing.

Thodùhah stood up and walked between the tables towards the grey figure. "Who are you, stranger, that comes uninvited into the king's hall? Only the very brave or the very foolish walk where they are not welcome."

Suddenly the light was very bright about the stranger in the doorway. Thodùhah put up his hand to shield his dazzled eyes and other men started to their feet, squinting into the light. Only the king kept his seat, toying with the bronze knife he had to cut his meat.

The stranger took a step into the hall and the light faded. He seemed no more than a man standing in the morning sunshine, as any man might, save that he had no shadow.

"My mistress sends me here," he said, "in courtesy and in warning to the Sea People: Midsummer's coming. Te-Meriku will die upon the morrow – that is as certain as the sunrise. But," he looked around the hall, holding out his empty hands, "my mistress bids me tell you this: There need be no other deaths. Many times, the king has died upon the shore," he said, and now he looked at Thodùhah, and at Ardùvai, at each man of Lyikené in turn, and each man turned away from his grey gaze, "and always a beginning has followed from that ending, a new king in the king's hall. Let it be so again. Your lives are yet your own, to live in your own country, an you lay down your swords, your spears and shields and knives."

All in the hall were silent, all watched their king, who drank his wine and set his empty cup down on the table, easy as if all this was of no matter. "Nay, it's not for me to answer," he said into the silence. "You have all your own tongues, you men of the Sea People who guard the west and keep the balance: What say you to Averla?"

A stamping and a roaring, a pounding of knives upon the tables, a hundred voices raised as one in a shout to echo forever 'cross the green hills of Lyikené, "Te-Meriku the king!"

Te-Meriku stood up, his face curving into a mirthless smile. "You have your answer to take back to your mistress. There will be fight upon midsummer's day."

The stranger's voice was a whisper and a rustle, scarce louder than the wind in the leaves of the rowan branches bound above the door. "Then the time is very near, men of Lyikené, when you must fight to keep your own. Are you ready for midsummer when you cannot even see what's hiding in the light?"

"Words," said Te-Meriku, "empty words that have no more substance than you yourself."

He strode down the hall towards the stranger, holding his bronze knife up before him. The grey man smiled to see such folly but the king drove the point into the ball of his own thumb and swept his hand in a wide arc, shaking the red drops into his face.

"I have eyes, and I will see," Te-Meriku cried out. "Let the world be as it is!"

A shimmer and shiver, a thinning and a flickering, sunlight swirling around the king like the current in a stream. Between one heartbeat and the next, the man was gone. Nothing remained where he had been but five drops of blood upon the threshold, red as rowan berries, red as spilled wine.

"A trick of the light," said Te-Meriku, against the crowing and the stamping, "a foolish seeming. May all our enemies be of such little matter."

In the commotion afterwards, Marwy Ninek pulled at his sleeve. "Are you sure, Te-Meriku, are you certain you can bring this to a right ending?"

"And why not? I am the king and this my kingdom."

Hard to look into his eyes, into his quick, harsh smile, and speak her meaning, when it was not clear even to her own mind. She said, "Averla said you were to die tomorrow."

"So might a cat speak to the mouse pressed beneath one velvet paw." She let out a soft gasp and caught his hand between her own. A flash of laughter lit his eyes. "I'm not a mouse, Marwy Ninek! No need to fear on my account – I gave Hadùhai a promise before ever I was king that I'd not die one day before my time."

She whispered, "Assiolo?"

"You have my word: I'll not strike the first blow. That much, at least, I owe him and 'tis Averla is my enemy. Assiolo's safe enough if he keeps his wits about him. And besides," Te-Meriku drew her close, brushing a stray strand of her hair back from her cheek near as tenderly as Assiolo himself might have done, "he is your lover, the beat of your heart. When he sees you here in Lyikené, my guestfriend and my kin, do you think he'll cleave to you or to Averla? How's that for an ending – the heir of Imacah mor Tamarhak standing aside Allocco's son against her?"

She tried to smile and could not: five years of hidden fears beat up out of the hidden places in her mind. "Five years she's had of him, and Averla is very lovely."

"And he a man as other men, led easily astray by sweet red lips and soft round breasts and a fall of golden hair?" He laughed, and his laughter drove such fears away into the dark where they belonged. "Nay, never fear it. So too are you lovely, very, very lovely – sweet as a briar rose in the summertime. Averla dazzles, she commands – a man might burn for her, fear her, desire her, die for her, but never love her."

She held his hand, knotting her fingers into his, though she saw eyes watching from all across the hall. She could say no more; the Sea People were waiting. The king bent his head and kissed her cheek, a touch, no more than that, and walked out of the hall, looking neither right nor left but always straight ahead towards the sunlight. She looked down and saw his blood smeared on her hand and, across the hall, the piper, watching the king with golden eyes. At the look upon his face, she shivered in the sunlight.

The boys had run outside to ape the men and practice with their knives and shortswords. The piper sat down in his place again and took up his cup to drink the king's red wine. Marwy Ninek could not settle and moved restlessly about the hall.

"How goes your tale, Kenu Vanithu?" she asked at last.

"That must depend upon my audience. Always I ask – which would you choose? That boy now," he pointed through the open door to Renùku, lording it among his fellows by virtue of his scarred face and his great deeds beneath the trees, "he chose the sword – boys mostly choose the sword – and so to him I tell a tale of high adventure, a monster lurking in the wild wood and a hero come to set his people free; women, on the other hand," he said, raising his cup to her as in a toast, and she flinched before his steady gaze, "women choose the rose, and so they hear a tale that ends with true lovers never to be parted."

"I remember." And so she did, though she fought hard against the memory. "A rose, a queen, one drop of blood to break the spell and call her from her dancing." She laughed to drive their past away, back into the dark where it belonged; he laughed with her, and both heard their laughter had a bitter edge.

His laughter dried up first. "I gave that choice," said he, "twenty years ago and longer to a boy in Ohmorah."

She counted out a dozen heartbeats, and a dozen more. "Did he choose the sword?" she asked, when she had control enough to hold her voice steady.

"Assiolo? Can you think that of him? He chose the rose!"

She clenched her fingers to a fist. Of course Assiolo chose the rose. Impossible to think of him with a sword in his hand walking out into the sunlight to kill a man. "Can such tales be true?" she asked.

The piper's golden eyes stared up into hers and she turned away as from the sun. "All my tales are true, and this is also true: He is Allocco's son and learned much from his father."

"It did not seem so in Felluria."

"But then he was your lover. Other ties bind him now. Who can know what choice he would make if I told my tale again?"

"Three kings beneath the tree," she said, remembering a distant dreaming. "What of the third?"

"The third king's hands are empty and no one has ever chosen nothing over something."

"But still you know that tale?"

"I know it well, Marwy Ninek, but I have never told it." He sipped his wine, slowly, and his gaze fell on the briar roses Liùthánwy had set upon the tables. "Assiolo killed a king for you," he said. "What will you do for him, now you've come out from your stone walls?

"What can I do but love him?"

"Think you it is enough? It never was before."

She reached out and plucked a rose from the spray; she stooped to tuck it into his shirt and, as she did, she told him, "The roses are in flower, even in Lyikené. Perhaps all will end well."

Their eyes met and, for a long, long moment, the ghosts of other roses hung between them; red roses and an evening in a garden long ago before the ruin; a glimpse of might have been. Then the dwarf scowled and looked away. "I never heard a tale of love that ended well—have you, Marwy Ninek? Love fades with time. In the end, everything fades." He put up his hand to the rose and cast it down, wincing as prickles pierced his thumb. "Poor things enough, full of thorns and withering before the morning."

Marwy Ninek took his hand and wiped the blood away. "You've lived too long, Kenu Vanithu, if you see the thorn before the flower. There's nothing in the world so lovely as a rose upon a summer's evening. Its beauty is no less because it cannot last."

"Fine words, lass," he said, "and maybe they're true. But whether they are true or no, they're not the words you spoke upon an evening in the sallows when Averla came to make her bargain; they're not the words you spoke upon a midsummer's night when she came back to keep it. Other ties bind Assiolo now." He held her hands, as he had held them long ago, but now, as he looked up at her, his face was not gentle. He was the monster as well as the musician. "You cannot undo what you've done and why you did it does not matter."

She pulled her hands from his. "It matters much to me. You're not a man, Kenu Vanithu, and you've forgotten all you ever knew of love. But Assiolo is a man, and he'll not forget. To him too, it will matter."

"Oh, I can remember what matters," he answered, "and that's to keep the tree beneath this sky. Set 'gainst that need, love is a very little thing."

Once, she had longed for him; later, she had hated him; now, she feared him, and so she turned away.

Outside the hall, men clad in their mail gathered by ones and twos and threes, clansmen and shoremen, whalemen and fisherfolk, each with his mark of his own kind, and each and every of the Sea People, all armed against the morrow with shining blades of bronze. She paused to watch the clash of sword on sword and hear the thud and thump of boots against stone. The king in his mail swung hard at Ardùvai, and Ardùvai leapt aside, sweeping his own sword up and round as he did in a slash that would have severed a man's head from his shoulders had the man been there yet to meet it. "It's a fine blade again, Te-Meriku," he called, "if only you'd the skill to match it."

"Insolent pup!"

What the king did next she could not quite see but it ended in Ardùvai upon his back, the king's blade at his throat. Te-Meriku's voice was a soft growl, "Another jest, Ardùvai, and a thousand years of clan's blood runs red across the stone."

Laughter from the Sea People, cheers for the king, jibes against the nightwatch. Ardùvai held out his hands. "No finer man in all Lyikené! I yield, Te-Meriku." The king sheathed his sword and offered a hand to pull him to his feet. "I'm glad of it, man. I've no time to haggle with Morigu over your death-fee."

The piper came limping from the hall and many men drew back lest his shadow fall across them. Thodùhah scowled to see him.

"What was that grey creature?" he asked. "You'll have seen that trick before, I'll warrant."

"A spirit of the sunlight shaped into seeing by Averla's will." The helmsman spat onto the stone and the dwarf shrugged. "It's not his kind that'll trouble you tomorrow. You know that who fought beneath the trees. There are others, far more dangerous, hiding in the light."

"Here and now?"

The piper shook his head.

"That is the truth?" the helmsman asked.

"All I say is true, Thodùhah. I am not a man."

"Nor, Kenu Vanithu, did you speak," Thodùhah said, dry as dust. "As on that night beneath the trees, you kept your silence. If I'd known then what I know now, I'd have had it otherwise. So look around, most carefully, and tell me clear: is anything or anyone hiding in the light among us?"

The piper laughed. "Nay, man, you're safe enough until the dawning and so are all your kind."

Thodùhah scowled and spat again, turning to Marwy Ninek. "You saw before what men did not: are others here, hiding in the light?"

Marwy Ninek looked around, at sunlight and at shadow. "I cannot tell." She shook her head, frustrated that she could not see clearly. The light was too bright and dazzled her; the shadows flickered and shifted in the breeze in an ever-changing pattern. "I think not."

"Look to the horizon, lass," said the piper, pointing into the east.

She looked again, narrowing her eyes against the light. She saw the sea, she saw the sky, she saw the line where sea met sky and the little patch of whiteness breaking it, a tiny thing against the vast sea and the vast sky.

"Well, lass, what do you see?"

"I see a sail," she said, "a white sail in the distance."

"Even so," said the piper, "and where there is a sail, there is a ship."

"Of all the ships in all Lyikené only the king's bears a white sail," said Thodùhah slowly, "and that is beached on yonder shore."

The piper smiled as the helmsman hastened away towards the king. "Do you think," he asked, "that ship carries a fair cargo?" She looked and looked, and did not answer. "If the ship be friend, what need to hide it from the eyes of honest men?"

Thodùhah returned and the king with him, two men screwing their eyes against the light to see a thing that was not there. Te-Meriku set his hand upon her shoulder. "What is there?" he asked. "What manner of ship? How far offshore?"

"I cannot see a ship," she said, "only a sail on the far edge of distance."

"The wind's hard from the east," Thodùhah said, "and steady. As for a ship, if ship there is," a hard scowl at the piper, "there were mercatships when we were by Felluria, like enough 'tis one of them."

The king stared a little longer, his hand resting on his swordhilt.

"That ship," Thodùhah nodded towards the horizon, "what should I do?"

"Bid the men arm themselves ready by the hall, an hour before the dawn. All else left in this place, the women and the children, any man not fit to lift his sword, must away into the hills, quick as can be. Thodùhah, I'll leave that to your lady's charge."

"And the fishwives on the shore?"

Te-Meriku laughed, harsh and short. "Half of them are seals, I'll warrant, and will slip away into the sea at the first sniff of danger. Tell them what's coming and let them make their choice. But mind me, Thodùhah, treat any that choose the hills with courtesy – they too are of the Sea People."

"I would I could see," the helmsman muttered. "I cannot strike an I cannot see the thing I strike at."

"All is made plain across the water," said Kenu Vanithu, "and men may fight on either bank."

The nightwatch span round to face him as all around armed men fell silent. " 'Tis not fit—" Ardùvai began but the piper cut him off, "No, lad, it's not. But you can fight that side the stream, and see your enemy, or keep your honour, and be cut down on this one."

"If it were honour only there'd be no choice," said Te-Meriku. "It's a fine word for stories and for songs but this matter's worth more than any honour – show me the man says elsewise and I'll show you a fool. But," he said, looking from one man to another, "no man of Lyikené will cross that stream with blade or flame whilst I am king and guard the tree beneath this sky. We'll fight upon the nearer bank."

A moment's silence. The king's will was the law, none would contest it, but men could look, one at another, and never say a word.

Then Ardùvai laughed aloud, tossing his knife from hand to hand. "All of us here have fought in the dark," he called out, "we'll fight as well in sunlight."

Other men caught up his laughter and the moment passed. The king grinned at Ardùvai, to meet his eyes and nod his thanks, and Marwy Ninek saw that he started, as if he saw his nightwatch suddenly a stranger or else something in his face that had not been there before.

"So that was Hadùhai's meaning," Te-Meriku muttered beneath his breath, his eyes fixed on Ardùvai. "Well, I'd rather 'twere you than many another, and far above Allocco's son." Aloud he said, "I'm away to clear my head across the water. I'll be back afore the evening. An any wants me, you'll find me on the further bank. Ardùvai, you know your duty for all it's a short night tonight – much light and little darkness: keep a clear head and come to me after the sunset."

The piper too looked to the nightwatch. "Well, lad," he said, so quiet that none there heard him, "seems it's time for you to make good on your wager." He turned away, his eyes creased with sorrow.

The day at noontime was clear and blowy, clouds in the high blue, white horses galloping across the sea driven by the wind out of the east. Here, beneath the tree was dappled shade and shelter, scented with thyme, scattered with tormentil and harebells. A fair, fine day, if you knew not what followed after. Even he, who longtimes had feared no man, shivered, thinking of the morrow.

How does it feel, Imacah asked, out of the shadows at his back, *to know the time a man must die?*

Standing alone beneath the tree, Te-Meriku wondered, as he had wondered many times over many years, if it were he broke faith with Imacah or Imacah with him? He shook such thoughts away. Now was not time to think of Imacah. The dead were dead and never came they back. He set his hand upon the tree and thought instead of other things. He lived, and today was a fair, fine day to rest in the shelter of the apple tree, and look out across his country, whatever followed after.

A blackbird's rattle sometime in the afternoon told him he was no more alone. Lying on his back, looking up into the patterns of leaf and sunlight, he said, "If you are there, show yourself."

Liùthánwy stepped into view, slight and brown in her grey kirtle, barefoot in the summertime.

"Te-Meriku."

"Liùthánwy." He sat up, leaning against the tree. "Does your mother know you're here?" She shook her head. "Your father?"

"My father is with the children, bidding them farewell." She sat down in the shade, close enough to talk easily, too far to touch, and rested her chin on her knees, staring out across the day to the king's hall in the distance and the sea beyond. For a while, there was silence between them, filled by the rustle of wind in the apple tree and the humming of bees in wild thyme on the hillside.

"Why are you here, Liùthánwy?"

Without turning her head to look at him, she said, "I thought you would be lonely and came to keep you company."

"It's been a long time since we kept company. Almost, I thought you were avoiding me since you came back from the north."

"When I was a child, I trotted at your heels." She laughed, and he heard a note of warning like a blackbird's rattle in her laughter. "Life is so very simple, when one is a child. A child can wish for the moon and never doubt her wish will be granted. But, when one is grown, life is no longer simple, so yes, Te-Meriku, I've been avoiding you."

He asked, wondering if this time she would answer with the truth, "Why then are you here?"

"Because I have eyes and I can see; I have ears and I can hear. I've wished longtimes to speak with you and I thought, if I did not today, I must remain forever silent. That thought I could not bear." There was a strange timbre to her voice, like the throbbing echo of a harpstring after the song has ended. She looked up into the apple tree, down at the tormentil, straightways into his face, and leaned forward to clasp his offered hand. Her fingers turned and tightened, lacing themselves between his as he pulled her close beside him. "And so, seeing the children happy with their grandsire, I slipped away to find you."

He tightened his arm around her. "I missed you, Liùthánwy, those years you were in the north."

"Did you, Te-Meriku?" Her eyes were steady, a hint of a smile in their grey depths. "Less perhaps than I missed you."

The past was gone, the future might never come, only the present was left and she felt so sweet and warm beside him. "Let me show you." He put his hand under her chin, turned up her face to kiss her and lose himself a while in her embrace. Her hair was scented with rosemary, her skin with rosewater, her lips opened soft as rosepetals beneath his mouth.

For a moment, only for a moment, she matched him, kiss for kiss, touch for touch, her mouth and hands as greedy as his own, but then she pulled away, her fire damped, a cold, stiff thing within his arms.

"No, Te-Meriku, not even here, not even now."

"Your kiss said otherwise." He had not let her go and, remembering a night she had given another answer, he let his hands roam freely, teasing and caressing, and heard her catch in her breath in a soft gasp. His lips against her neck, he whispered, "I know you, Liùthánwy, I would not ask an I thought you were unwilling. You've told me twice you loved me."

She caught his wrists and held his roving hands away from her. "I do love you." That well-remembered sob of laughter in her voice. "Always and always, I have loved you. But I'll not be used again, not even to drive away your ghosts."

The years she had been gone fell down between them. Desire slipped into unease, sunlight into shadow, to hear her speak so. He had lived too long to be ignorant of the things men do to women in the dark. "That man you married, did he treat you well? Despite..."

"Despite your child in my belly? Despite I did not love him?" Her laugh rattled out, bleak as winter rain upon a roof, a woman laughing at a cruel jest told against them both. "Yes, very well. He was a good man, Ithánu, a kind, good man. It was not his fault I was unhappy." She sat back on her heels, her face suddenly bone-white and filled with that bitter laughter.

Relieved, confused, angered by her laughter, he said, "There was no need to go away. No need to marry without love."

Liùthánwy threw her answer at him, hard as a gust of wind throws rain against a windowpane. "There was every need!"

He ground out, between clenched teeth, "For you, I would have tried. Had you given me one word, one look to say you wished it, I'd have asked you of Thodùhah."

Her great grey eyes glanced sidelong at him. He could not read the meaning in those eyes: strange passions swam in their depths like fishes in the sea. "Would you, Te-Meriku?" she asked, lightly. "I am glad you did not. My father," she paused, gathering her thoughts, choosing her words, "my father loves me, and loves you near as much. Had you and he joined forces, I could not have stood against you. But each time he spoke, you kept your silence, I kept mine, and in the end he gave up, baffled, thinking after all he was mistaken."

He remembered an afternoon beneath this tree, her face so white and wan, her answer, half a laugh and half a sob, *When you want me for myself, I'll kiss you.* He said, "I'd not have had you unwilling. You told me, *No!* and what could I do but take it, even with my child inside you, yet you never told me why."

"Why? I'll tell you why!" she cried, and all the passion he remembered flooded her face. "Because I love you. And, loving you, I could know no greater pain than to lie with you, to touch you and taste you, to feel your flesh in mine and see in your eyes I meant nothing to you, to know that *any* body in the dark would do as well to banish memory. I said you, *No!* and meant it, and went away so I could not be tempted. And still," she said, her eyes too bright, her face too pale, "it is the same. You ask me because the one you want is gone."

His heart beat hard and fast, blood pounding as in anger or with fear. So strange, to see himself through another's eyes, as if he were another man. So much of her he had not seen, had chosen not to see, because he could not render love for love, had felt for her never more than fondness which sparked, sometimes, into desire.

"Liùthánwy!"

"Love grows or it does not," she said. "Some things are beyond even the king's command. But there was a night, Te-Meriku, near eight years ago, when I put my hands upon this tree to wish you might never come to peace nor yet find comfort in a lover's arms."

At that, he laughed hard and harsh, seeing the kinking patterns their lives made as they twined against each other across the years. "Did you illwish me, Liùthánwy? That was not kind."

She shook her head and sighed, trying to smile. "Oh, I called back that wish afore I went into the north. 'Twas but a twisted thing conceived in darkness and strangled in the morning when better thoughts returned. If your heart's raw yet for Imacah it's your love and not my hatred makes it so."

His face must have betrayed him, for her eyes softened and her voice grew gentle. "Why him, Te-Meriku? You could have had any woman in Lyikené and half the men besides. Why only him, forever and for always?"

"Why does any love another? For a little thing – the way his hair fell across his cheek. For a great one – he stood beside me when all else mocked me as bastard. For all the things that made him *him* and not another." He held out his hands and after a moment she sat down again at his side. Ruefully, he asked, "Are you quite sure you called back your wish? It surely has been granted."

"Quite sure. Even in those days I loved you too well to make a binding of my ill humour. I made you a promise once, and I've kept it, after a fashion."

"Almost you sound as though you hate me!"

"Hate you! Oh, my dear!" She flung her arms around his neck, holding him close, whispering into his shoulder. "You're only a man, Te-Meriku, alone and lonely in the dark. You took me once for your pleasure and, had I been another woman, I'd have taken you now for mine and that would have been an end of it. But I am myself and, if I cannot have all, I'll take nothing; if I cannot give all, I'll give nothing, not even comfort."

He shrugged himself free of her embrace, his heart somewhere between pity and anger. "Is that what you wanted to say to me?"

"No. I had no thought to say any of this." She rubbed her hand across her eyes, her father's gesture in face of things he did not understand. "I had finer words, better ones, ready in my father's house. They slipped away when I saw you. They always do." Her voice died away to nothing, a whisper of breath upon the wind.

Anger faded. Pity deepened, and shame crept in to join it. He turned her hand until he could see the line across her thin brown wrist. Tracing it gently with his finger, he said, "I'm sorry, Liùthánwy, I should not have asked, that night or now."

"Hush, now," she said, "you asked and I answered. And that night, between the sunset and the morning, you gave me all I could desire, whatever followed after."

"Did I, Liùthánwy?"

She sighed, biting her lip, swallowing her answer. Her eyes grew silvery as rainclouds 'cross the water and she shook her head to banish the tears gleaming on her lashes. He let go of her hand, ashamed of a broken promise. His turn to sigh, at forlorn hopes and empty hearts; at dreams, conjured in darkness, slipping away with the dawning; at himself, unthinking cruel. "I was never worth such folly. You should have found a better man than me to love you."

"I could look a hundred years and never find one. There's none but you for me." She sat beside him, her hands clasped round her knees, so close, so very far away. "We are very much alike, Te-Meriku, casting all the world aside for love we cannot have."

He had no answer that could give comfort. The past was gone; the present could not be altered. "What will you do?" he asked.

"An we live to see tomorrow to its ending? All that I can. Bide in my father's house and be a mother to my children, grow old watching the light upon the sea." She looked into his face and all the ghosts and shadows of their past stared out of her rain-grey eyes. "And you, Te-Meriku, what will you do?"

"Lie a-waking in the night, thinking of might have been," he answered, his voice near as dull as hers.

The summer clouds passed across the sky: sunlight, brightness, shadow, making up a day as any other in the year. The east wind blew across the hillside to the tree; above his head, the leaves whispered in a tongue he did not know. He looked to the emptiness above the heather hills, thinking to see a birdshape, his other self, his namesake, drifting there, as when he roamed them as a boy with Imacah. But for the clouds the sky was empty; Imacah was dead, and the sea eagle. Only he remained. *One is one, and all alone, and ever more shall be so!*

Liùthánwy rose to her feet and stood looking down at him. For a moment, he wondered if she would speak again. But all that could be said had been said already and so she turned and left him. He watched her out of sight, a slight, grey figure slipping across the afternoon into a place he could not follow.

XIV, *Felluria: Do I yet please you?*

Sir, I will accept from you the keys to your heart
To lock it up forever that we never more may part
And I will be your bride, your joy, and your dear
And I will walk with you anywhere.

The Keys of Canterbury, *Traditional*

*She wakes slowly and smiles, remembering the night. He lies beside her,
every limb relaxed in sleep. No second skin of wool or linen between them
now, no shift, no shirt, no coat or kirtle. His warm body, his side pressed
against her breasts and belly, his shoulder where her head is resting, his
arm encircling her waist, his legs entwined with hers, is mother-naked as
her own. She lies still a little time, listening to the gentle rhythm of his
breathing, gazing at the curve of his cheek and the arch of his brow, at the
sweet, supple lines of his lips. Her lover now in every sense. She does not
speak, she does not move, but joy fills her, rising up out of the night as
the spring tide up the shore.*

*Beyond the room, day has begun. Carefully, slowly, she slides from
his side and from the bed. He stirs and murmurs, reaching blindly out in
search of her, and she leans over him to rest her hand against his cheek
and whisper, "Hush now, I am here."*

*He sighs, turning back into his slumbers. She pulls on her shift, slips
her arms into the sleeves of his coat and opens the shutters to a grey,
dull morning. Beyond, below, the business of the day goes on: a flurry of
women before the kitchens, the iron ring of the blacksmith's hammer, a
bleating of sheep and goats from pens beneath the wall. She turns away.
All that matters in the world is here within this room, sleeping between
patched sheets beneath a pile of mismatched blankets.*

*She crouches on the hearth to coax the embers into life, feeding the spark
with twigs and dry moss until it is strong enough to bite into the clods of
peat she stacks around it. The room is cold, the air is chill; waiting for the
fire to catch, she shivers and hugs the heavy folds of his coat close around
her. It smells of him, of the sharp, clean scents of his herbals, of the wool
fat he uses in his liniments.*

*His voice speaks across her thoughts. "Come back to bed, love. I'll
warm you far better than an old coat."*

*Looking around, she sees he has propped himself on pillows against the
bed-end. His brown hair is tousled, his brown eyes alight with laughter;
smiling, he holds out his hand, inviting her to come to him.*

"*I thought to boil a kettle and make tea. There's rosehip here, and camomile.*"

"*Sweetheart, so there is, and you'll find raspberry leaf and tansy there besides; also mint and agrimony, feverfew, nettle and dandelion, fennel and sage, citrus and sorrel, and doubtless others I cannot now bring to mind. I want none of them. Come here and let me kiss you.*"

When she sits down upon the bed, he cups her face between his hands and brushes his lips lightly across her brow.

"*That's not how you kissed me in the night time.*"

"*How did I kiss you in the night time?*"

She puts her arms about his neck, and pulls him close, and shows him.

He says, doubtfully but his eyes agleam, "*I'll rub you red and raw, love, an I kiss you like that afore I've shaved.*"

She presses her answer all across his face and he grins. "*Oh well, sweet, if you're certain sure, I'll do it.*"

His lips are soft as rose petals against her skin, a teasing contrast to the roughness of his cheeks. He kisses her long and lovingly, and slips his hands beneath the coat. She sighs at his touch upon her breasts and then his left hand goes a-wandering, before, behind, between, below.

"*Take off the coat,*" he whispers. His hands help her slough it free. All the while, she kisses him, his cheeks, his chin, his neck, over and again his mouth. "*And the shift.*"

He turns back the bedclothes and settles her upon his lap. As she slides onto him, a long, low groan escapes him and his grip tightens about her waist. She laughs at such proof of his desire; he laughs with her and his grasp relaxes a little, though still his breath comes fast. They face each other, breast to breast, clasped in each other's arms, each smiling at the joy and wonder reflected from the other's eyes.

"*Last night I led you,*" he says, "*now you lead me.*"

"*What should I do?*"

"*Just as you like, love. I'll take my cue from you this morning.*"

She starts to move, slowly at first, testing sensations and possibilities, then finds her rhythm, rocking them to and fro until all around her shatters into light and fire.

When they can speak again, they speak of love, whispering to each other, their fingers interlaced, interspersing promises with kisses.

"*Until the seas run dry...*"

"*Until rocks melt...*"

"*Until the world's ending...*"

Longtimes they whisper together beneath the bedclothes, reluctant to leave their warmth or one another. In the world beyond the window, the morning passes by. In the room beyond the bed, the chill lies heavy on the air. He had called her from the fire before it quickened and it is again only hot ash and embers beneath the peat bricks, giving no useful heat. When at last he gets up, he tucks the blankets round her before he puts on shift and shirt and britches. She watches him walk, barefoot and shivering, across the room to fill the iron kettle from the jug. He hangs it from the hook above the grate and speaks a single word in his own tongue. The fire roars and rushes into life. At once, even across the room, she feels its warmth and sees its heart burning red and steady.

He turns towards her, laughing. "Foolish, perhaps, to use such tricks, but you were cold."

"What are you, Assiolo, that you have fire at your command?"

Then memory shapes itself into meaning: a man to stop the sun at noontime and make a world of light and fire. "Of course," she breathes, "you are Allocco's son. I had quite forgot you told me so yourself."

The words leave her lips before the second thought. Seeing his face, she wishes she could call them back.

"I had not thought you listened, love, that night, but I told you true. I would it were not so."

He comes to kneel beside the bed. Her heart catches at the question in his eyes, a nakedness of spirit far more revealing than ever flesh could be. She has not thought before that he could look so young nor yet so vulnerable, this man who walked into the year's dark eye to kill a monster. "Well," he asks, a little roughly, "do I yet please you?"

She leans forward and cradles his head in her arms, kissing his ruffled hair. "Oh, Assiolo, dear, dear love, there are not words enough to say how much you please me. You are mine, forever and for always."

He puts up his hands to hold her tight. Then both are still, locked in a crouched embrace. The moment stretches out into another and another; is broken only when the kettle starts to sing.

"Time for that tea," he says, himself again. "Camomile, I reckon. Soothing to mind and body."

15: The matter of a wager

'Tis down in yonder garden green,
Love, where we used to walk,
The finest flower that e'er was seen
Is wither'd to a stalk.

The Unquiet Grave, Traditional

Seven years Ardùvai had served as nightwatch to Te-Meriku, seven
years he had watched his oaken door and marked all who went
in after the sunset, all who came out before the morning, but still,
tonight, he paused a moment before knocking. "Te-Meriku?"

"I'm here."

Ardùvai stepped into a room full of shadows. Two of the windows
were shuttered fast but the west window was open, a touch of
brightness lingering in the far beyond long after the sunset. The king
lounged in the seat beneath it, cup and winejug to his hand upon
the ledge and a gaming board beside him.

"Waking alone?" Ardùvai arched a black brow towards the sealfurs
in the bedplace, white and smooth as fresh fallen snow. "That's not
your wont."

"I'd not a mind for company, nor yet for sleep." He gestured to
the board, its geese pale figures half-seen in halflight, the fox a clot
of shadow. A touch of bitter humour in his voice. "I played until the
light was lost to drive back the thoughts I did not wish to think."

"Thoughts of the future?"

"Nay, of the past." Te-Meriku picked up one of the geese that had
been driven from the game and tossed it hand to hand. "I'd told
myself I'd do no harm, taking only the willing – I was a fool and
another pays the price of my folly." The nightwatch kept his silence
and, after a moment, Te-Meriku shrugged and stretched, then set the
goose again beside its fellows. "What's done can't be undone, and
brooding on it in the dark will aid me nothing. Since you're here,
man, make a light so I can see you."

It was too mild a night to need a fire but a firepot stood on the
empty hearth. Ardùvai found the tongs to lift the lid and lit a taper
at the embers. Aware all the while that the king's eyes were following
him around the room, he set the lamps on mantelshelf and walls all
a-burning. As he lit the last lamp in the sconce beside the window,
he glanced down at the goose-game, reading the pattern of the pieces.
The set was a fitting thing for a king's chamber, the geese of ivory,

the fox of amber, the board of walnut-wood inlaid with mother of pearl. "The geese will win in three. Your game's improving."

Te-Meriku snorted with laughter. "So it must be – I played the day away and never once lost."

Another night, Ardùvai would have caught up that laugh and matched it with his own. Another night, he would have reached for the winejug and issued his challenge. Instead, he asked, "What of Marwy Ninek? I doubt she'll sleep tonight with her mind full of the morrow. Unkind to leave her lonely."

"I sent word for her to stay with Thodùhah. She'll be company for him with his womenfolk away and it's you I wanted."

"Then the honour's mine, Te-Meriku." Ardùvai bowed his head and spread out his hands with all the gracious dignity of his grandsire, a clanlord's scion awaiting the confidence of his king. Only the gleam in his black eyes spoiled the effect and caused Te-Meriku to shake his head and rue aloud the day he named him as nightwatch.

"Ah but so you did, and so I am, and we must both live with your folly," he answered, relaxing with the king's good humour. "So is it a game of fox and geese or something else you want of me, Te-Meriku?"

"Only to talk of this and that before the morning. I have forgot to thank you, man, when upon the sea you stepped in between a fool and his folly."

"You saw it, then?" Ardùvai asked. "I'd thought you'd lost your touch."

"Saw enough, and smelt too much. She fair stank of herring that last night." Te-Meriku's grin near matched his nightwatch's. "Often and often, I'd a mind to ask her why she wore your shirt to see what answer she could manage."

"Oh, I gave her one of mine I knew would satisfy."

"Did you now?" Ardùvai's smile was bland and guileless beneath Te-Meriku's hard stare. "Aye well, I've three things I wish to say to you, if you've a mind to listen. To thank you was the first and least of them but it leads on to my second. Sit down beside me, man, and let's have a drink."

He poured wine into his cup and gestured to Ardùvai where he might find another. The nightwatch held it out for filling but did not sit. Instead, he leant his back against the wall, watching the shadows play over the king's face. The gloss of easy laughter had slipped away, leaving his heavy mood behind. "What's to do, Te-Meriku?" he asked in a little while. "It's not like you to sit a-brooding in the dark when there's men a-drinking in the hall."

The king stared into the dark surface of his wine, as if he sought to make a window on the world. But he had neither the knowledge

nor the skill for such a thing and, after a moment, set the wine
a-swirling and his reflection splintering and scattering across the cup.

"Since the piper closed the gates of morning," he said, "there's
been a reckoning due. Averla wants her own again – a day to last
forever, a world without an end. She asked me once to aid her – I
said her no, as has every king before me. But Assiolo is not of the
Sea People – how has he answered?"

Ardùvai did not know and could not answer; he drank his wine
and waited for the rest. The king passed his hand across his face,
pushing back his hair, and the nightwatch saw how sharp and deep
were the lines about his eyes. He was not old but here and now the
kingship pressed heavy on his shoulders.

Te-Meriku went on, "It took the Liùthion's flood to undo his
father's deeds but I've not the sea at my command. I've only my
strength and my will and Marwy Ninek." He forced a laugh but it fell
back to nothing, the shadows of his thoughts chasing the laughter
from his eyes. He set his cup down half-empty by the gameboard.
"We've made monsters of ourselves, across the years," he said, "all
we kings since Imacah, keeping the tree safe with our bronze swords
against fools and fishermen, and now, at our greatest test, what
matters is not a sword, not the king's will, but a lover's heart. I tell
you, Ardùvai, it's a bitter thing to be the king and know it."

"Aye well, I'd not think on it overmuch," the nightwatch answered
lightly. "You do what you can and what you must, and if the heart
breaks there's your sword behind it, and mine and many another.
Assiolo's but a man – he cannot stand against us all forever."

"We've seen before what's hiding in the light."

The nightwatch shrugged and drank again. All in his manner
said such things were of no matter but his black eyes told another
tale. Te-Meriku sighed and said, after a moment, "What will come,
will come. But I must have a mind of Marwy Ninek – I brought her
into this and if Assiolo loves her, I'll warrant Averla does not. She's
sent a man against her already in the moonlight." He looked up,
grinning as if all bitter thoughts and doubts were driven from his
mind. "I don't reckon much to my chances an she comes to harm
whilst in my care. Assiolo's killed one king already for her sake."

Strange to laugh at such a thing but laugh Ardùvai did, seeing
the king's face, though he crooked his fingers too against misfortune.
"Don't jest on it!"

"I'll give you a better reason," said Te-Meriku. "She's my close
kin, my own mother's daughter."

"That tale I had from Thodùhah." A sidelong look, a wicked smile.
"I wondered if you'd tie up your hair now you're a clansman – I can
show you the way of it."

"I'd rather you cut it to the scalp! Don't joke on such a thing–the old tales are all true and she must every day remember it. Better a bastard than son to such a father. Aye, I know," spreading out his empty hands against the nightwatch's answer, "the whole's a damned tangle, and I'm not such a fool as to think any of it's chance. If the world were as it should be, I'd be sitting down aside Assiolo and calling him brother–instead, all I can do is give Marwy Ninek my word I'll not strike the first blow. That leaves me hamstrung 'gainst Averla and 'tis Averla I must give first thought to in the morning. Keep her safe, Ardùvai, if I cannot."

"You're a fool to think you had to ask, even without the kinship." He put his cup beside the king's. "That's two things of three and neither of them worth the saying. Why am I here, Te-Meriku?"

"I could not speak of it afore Marwy Ninek," the king said, steady and unhurried, "but if Assiolo means to do Averla's will, he'll come for me. He has the knowledge from his father but my death gives him the right."

Ardùvai's hand reached for his winecup but, suddenly clumsy, knocked it from its place. It shattered in the space between them. He saw the red drops roll and pool upon the stone and his first thought was not of wine but blood, his brother's blood warm and sticky on his hands. Looking towards Te-Meriku, he found he had no need to ask the question that had stabbed sharp as a shard of ice into his heart: its answer was written on his face.

The king began, "An I—"

The nightwatch leaned forward in an agony of rage and grief to stop his mouth. Gripping the king's shoulders hard, glaring into the king's eyes, he hissed, "Not a word more, Te-Meriku, not one word."

He had spoken to the man but it was the king struck down his hands and stood to face him. "When I speak, clansman, you will listen!"

"Not to folly!"

Their eyes met, a fierce, brief struggle for the mastery. Then, beneath the surface of Te-Meriku's rage, Ardùvai saw again what he had seen before and looked away. There were sights he could not bear, though he had seen his brother broken beneath the trees and never flinched. In the silence afterwards, Te-Meriku turned to the gaming-board and moved a goose sideways out of the shelter of the flock. "The geese in three, you said." His voice was his own again, easy and unhurried, his eyes calm as the surface of the sea beyond the window. "You take the fox–let's see if you're right."

Ardùvai moved the fox on a square and then the bold goose came forward. Upon the board, he saw what he had seen before: all futures narrowed into one. "Fox takes goose," he said, and did so, though his hand trembled.

"But there are other geese," the king moved one, "this one comes on, thus, and fox is trapped: no move to make, no place to turn. You saw the end a-right." He swept the pieces from the board, rattling them carelessly back into their box. "You've more skill than any other in my hall but you joined this game too late to turn it."

The nightwatch whipped around, his eyes a-blazing. "It's not a game, Te-Meriku!"

The king said sharply, "The piper said it true. What matters – *all* that matters, Ardùvai – is to keep the tree beneath this sky and Averla from the mastery. I'll do what's necessary, and so will you. Or else you're not the man I think you."

"You know full well I'll keep my place beside you, no matter what's hiding in the light. You've got my measure well enough in seven years: ask, and I'll answer."

A touch of laughter in the king's face. "But I must not ask tonight?"

Stubbornly, Ardùvai shook his head. "Such thoughts as those will give succour to your enemy and confusion to your friends. You are the king beneath this sky."

"And one like to see the sunset, and many sunsets after?" Te-Meriku asked, and Ardùvai clenched his hands tight at his sides. At his foot, spilled wine from a broken cup trickled slowly 'cross the floor. "Sure, man," said the king, grimly smiling, "and that's the tale I'll tell in the morning, but 'twould be another kind of folly to give no thought to what might be. Marwy Ninek trusts Assiolo but Averla's had five years to shape him to her will."

"I'll not give flesh to fancy. You've sat too long a-brooding under the light of that damned star. Put your mind to other things."

For a long moment he wondered if again he had gone too far, then the king's words cut across the thunder of his heart, saying, "As you will it; I'll not waste my breath with words – you've never been a fool and the morrow will come soon enough." The nightwatch let out the breath he had not known he held in a shuddering sigh, steadying himself against the wall. Te-Meriku reached for the goose-box to shake the pieces out across the board. "Will you play instead? It's a short night and I've no desire for sleep nor yet for further brooding."

The nightwatch paused a little space, one thought chasing another round his mind. Then he made his choice and reached behind his head to pull at the twist of azure silk knotting up his hair and dropped it down amidst the pieces. His hair fell about his shoulders, black as the feathers of a crow's wing. "I've taken you fox and geese over and again these seven years. Let's play another game before the morning."

Te-Meriku looked him slowly up and down, then shook his head. "I think not," he said. "We'll keep to our old custom, you and I: either you play me fox and goose or you go out and leave me here to think alone upon the morrow."

Having gone so far, Ardùvai could not help but take the last step, even if it were into folly. He grinned, wide and reckless, and said, "You've taken to thought too much tonight and it's worse than drink for making a man melancholy. You've played this game with many another. Why not with me?"

A moment's pause, a bitter laugh, and the king reached out to the winejug. "Your stake's too high, man. I have not one to match it and I'll not play beyond my means again."

The nightwatch spread out his hands, protesting that such things were of no matter. Te-Meriku's eyes were steady in the lamplight, his cup was steady in his hand, and the distance between them yawned wider than it had ever been. "Enough, Ardùvai," his voice was quiet and empty, "thus far and no further."

Ardùvai arched his brows in shocked surprise. "And me so braw and bonny, with a thousand years of clansmen at my back. Ah well, you'll not think less of me for asking."

Te-Meriku's lips twitched in an unwilling smile. "No less indeed. You always were a chancer, and I can't say I'm not tempted, but I'll not fall twice into the same folly, not even for sake of your black hair."

"All the rest you've given me – why not that?"

"Because I gave it to another, long ago, and what's left behind is not enough for you."

Ardùvai said, a little roughly, "It was enough for all the others."

"No, it was not," Te-Meriku told him, "and even if it had been, it changes nothing. You should not lie in a dead man's bed, not tonight."

"You're thinking again," the nightwatch warned, "and no good will come of it. Your ghosts, not mine – and what need for a bed?"

"Enough, man." Te-Meriku put up his hand to make an end to jesting. "You've asked and you've had your answer. Don't push your luck or try my temper."

Silence between them. The king drank his wine. Ardùvai stood staring out into the night, the dark glitter of his eyes reflected in the glass. No trace now of laughter in his face. He could not keep his voice quite steady but there was one thing more to say. "Whether you'll have me or no, I'm your man, Te-Meriku, heart and hand."

"Aye, that I know," Te-Meriku said quietly, "but still the world is as it is. All the rest I'll give you, but not that."

"Te-Meriku!" Ardùvai turned, quickly fluid as a cat, to pull him close and kiss him hard upon the mouth, then span on his heel without a word and let the door close quietly behind him.

Slowly, very carefully, Te-Meriku fitted the game pieces back into their box and dropped the scrap of azure silk a-top them before he closed the lid. Then he stood an hour or more before his window, staring out across his country. And all the while, bright and dreadful in the night, the long-haired star rose to hang above his hall, its yellow light reflected in the stream snaking down the hillside from the tree.

Beyond the hall 'twas night time in Lyikené. It lacked perhaps two hours of dawn and those who could were sleeping whilst others kept look-out 'gainst the morning. A balmy summer's night, though in the east the balestar spread its sulphurous glow 'cross land and sea, casting the common stars to dimness. The nightwatch stood on the threshold of the king's hall, a shadow amongst the shadows. A shiver of white swept across the court, freezing the night time with its call: *Who will? Will you?*

The question called to mind another night, another owl, and, even through the confusion of his thoughts, Ardùvai laughed. "Nay," he said, "I'll not again be frighted."

Then all around was silence, broken only by the little sounds of Lyikené, the rise of waves against the shingle, the cry of seabirds 'cross the shore. He stood a while to mark the moment for, on the morrow, all might change and memory alone remain. But tonight was a short night, little darkness and much light, and he had only a little time to listen and to remember.

A door opened and shut behind him, and then came the sound of footsteps 'cross the stone floor. Hearing the drag and shuffle of a twisting foot, the nightwatch turned his head to glance into the hall.

"There's more men than one slipped out tonight, thinking to prove their manhood. If you've a mind to do likewise, try the fishwives' huts along the shore."

"I doubt I'm to their taste, any more than they to mine," the piper said, against Ardùvai's mocking smile. "What I need, I'll not find in the fishwives' huts: 'twas you I looked for, since the king has no more need of you tonight."

"For certain sure, you're not to my taste, Kenu Vanithu, and you'll have nothing from me." He grinned down into the dwarf's face, hiding his thoughts behind his smile. "Or think you you can take me?"

"That, I've done already," the piper said. "I've a claim on you, Ardùvai mor Ardùvai, in the matter of a wager. Tomorrow, you must pay the forfeit."

"Ah, the price of folly." The nightwatch snapped his fingers. "And there was I thinking you'd forgotten or at the least would let me slip away into the dark, leaving the debt to my sisters' sons. What must I give? A pipe of ivory perhaps, to charm a seal out of her skin, or else a coat of cloth of gold to show the world you are the prince of beggars?"

"Nay, I've need of neither ivory nor gold. The wager was you'd answer when I asked and do what I required."

Something in the piper's tone caused hairs to prick on the nightwatch's neck and he shivered, for all the mildness of the night. His laughter slipped away and his fingers crooked against misfortune. "Tell me the matter of this forfeit."

" 'Tis no more than this," said the dwarf, "soon after dawn as can be, I'd have you take Marwy Ninek across the water and let her bide upon the further bank. Oh, she'll go with you," he said, drily, across Ardùvai's protest, "you ever had a tongue to charm and she trusts you next only to the king."

"And am I to say who bids it?"

"If she asks, answer as you choose. All that matters is, when noontime comes, she is one side the water and Te-Meriku the other. Noontime, Ardùvai," he said, though the nightwatch shook his head, "the very moment of midsummer when the light is at its brightest and the world all out of true. After that moment you fetch her back quick as can-do—'tis but a step across the stream."

"You've shown them what they are, the ties that bind them one to the other—oh, aye, I can see the pattern you've woven across the years—and at the very end you'd have them either side the water. Kenu Vanithu, what is your purpose?"

The dwarf stepped from the shadows, a hideous thing, twisted and stunted, no touch of grace about him but his eyes. "I seek to shape the future to one of my own liking."

"They say yours is a tongue that cannot lie," said Ardùvai, "I'm but a man and make no such claims for mine. Yet," a knife glinted in the sickly yellow starlight, "this at least is true: I'm the king's man. So, piper," a fluid movement, quick and supple as a cat's pounce, a hard hand twisted in the piper's hair, a knifepoint pressed beneath his chin, "tell me: what of Te-Meriku upon the morrow, an I do as you bid me?"

The piper did not flinch though the knife pricked at his throat. "Most like Te-Meriku will die upon the morrow at Assiolo's hand."

"And so you show yourself Averla's creature at the last." Ardùvai's tone was low and dangerous; his black eyes, hard and sharp as the knifeblade, glittered in the starlight. "Imacah named you rightly, *Monster*."

"And so he did," the dwarf agreed, hideous beneath the balestar. "So too did Marwy Ninek name me rightly, *Musician*. Had the world been kind, I'd have walked a different path." Ardùvai's hand moved a very little and a thin trickle of blood ran down the blade. "Had the world been kinder still," Kenu Vanithu said, "I'd have died what I once was, the piper at the gates of morning. But, since the world is as it is, I live and, as I live, I'll keep the balance I made long ago."

"No balance, an Averla's puppet has the mastery." The knife pressed harder and the blood flowed faster. "A wager's a little thing against the things that matter. I'll end your traitor's life tonight and keep my place beside the king tomorrow and we shall together turn the future to one of our own liking."

"Then you'll burn together in Averla's fire." The piper's fingers closed round the nightwatch's wrist, pulling down his hand with strength surprising in such a little, twisted creature. The bronze knife clattered to the stone between them. "Ardùvai, longtimes I've moved my pieces 'cross the board and the stakes are always highest in the endgame. You know as well as I, often and often, a goose must be sacrificed to make the win."

The nightwatch reached for his knife but the piper's hand was there afore him. Black eyes stared a long, long moment into gold, and then looked away, unable to bear longer what they saw there. "I like not the game," Ardùvai growled, "that counts kings as geese."

"No more do I!" the piper snapped. "But since I must play, I'll put my own desires aside and play to win: my geese against Averla's fox. You want the truth – I'll tell it: 'tis the king's purpose to keep the balance but only Assiolo has strength and skill enough to stand firm against Averla's wish to break it. An he holds the kingship, he can match her, aye, more than match her – quench her fire forever."

Ardùvai drew a long breath, whistling through his teeth, his face stark, staring white. "High stakes indeed! And if Te-Meriku thinks otherwise? You know as well as any in Lyikené: the kingship's a gift to be given full as much as a prize to be taken."

Kenu Vanithu met his eyes, level and steady, a rock that would not shift though the spring tide crash against it. "I'll shape the taking and the giving, setting one love against another. Marwy Ninek must be across the water when Assiolo meets Te-Meriku. Love's not enough to end this – there must be hatred first." The piper leaned forward and five drops of blood, black in the yellow starlight, fell from his throat down to the stone.

"So I'm to forsake Te-Meriku and make a king out of Allocco's son and all for a wager!"

"Aye, lad, and, if it helps, I'm sorry for it," the piper said, softly, very sadly.

"I do not like the part you give me.

"What matters that?" No hint of softness now in those golden eyes. The piper's words were hard and sharp as broken glass; his face a monster's from a child's nightmare, most dreadful, most terrible. "You lost the wager and your promise binds you: it's for me to ask and you to answer to my will."

In the east, the long-haired star had climbed higher in the sky. Ardùvai looked around, seeing the familiar made strange by the balestar's light, and shivered. He leant his back against the wall of the king's hall and called old tales to mind. "You made a king of Tamarhak's son," he said, after a little time, and the piper nodded, "a king to guard the tree beneath this sky with his life and with his sword. There have been many kings since Imacah and each has kept that promise."

"Bronze swords have served well enough across the years 'gainst fools and fishermen but they'll not serve against Averla. That you saw beneath the trees." Kenu Vanithu pointed to the east. "The proof is written there."

Ardùvai looked at where he pointed, and then a long, long silence stretched out between them, uneasy, unwilling, broken at the last by the owl's asking, *Who will?*

A tear shone on Ardùvai's pale cheek as the last flicker of hope died in his heart. If the piper saw, it was of no matter nor had any power to move him. He set the knife down by the nightwatch and pushed himself onto his feet. "Te-Meriku cannot do it," he said, "nor can you. Only Assiolo."

"Tell me," Ardùvai put out his hand to stay him, his voice but a hoarse whisper, "what you'd have done, had I not taken your wager. Would you have still have asked this of me?"

The piper sighed, no longer terrible, no longer dreadful. "I'd have asked it, lad, and you'd have answered. But, this way, you can call a choice necessity. Maybe it'll help you sleep a-night in the years to come."

He limped away towards the gate leaving the king's hall stirring into life behind him, a clatter of boots and a rumble of men's voices, the hard clash of bronze on bronze.

—+— —+—

As the short night faded, Assiolo came ashore, unseen by all and any of the Sea People, a shadow amidst the deeper shadows. There were

many on the tideline of Lyikené had watched for him and none had
seen as the little boat sculled quietly to the shore. He climbed out
and bid the sailors, "Good speed". They said no word but made it,
oars dipping fast across the water. By the balestar's light, he watched
them go and, because they had served him well these five days past,
kept them sheltered in shadow until they were two arrowflights from
land. No more than that. He cast them from his mind and walked
unseen along the shore, past the ships beached above the watermark
and the watchfires, past the king's hall and the houses, across the
grass cropped short by rabbits and by sheep.

Unseen by all and any of the Sea People. But there was one
that night in Lyikené who was none of the Sea People and his eyes
marked his passing. The little piper stood in the shadows by the gate
and watched him walk by, towards an end and a beginning.

And there was one more besides who watched him, hiding not
in shadow but in the balestar's yellow light; watched him, smiling,
stroking her sleeping son's pale hair with her white hand, knowing
that, when she asked, he would answer to her will.

Assiolo paused a moment where the stream ran out upon the
shore to drink a little of its water. A man could not drink much of
that water; it ran colder and deeper than any other in the world. To
the eye, a little thing that stream, burbling and laughing in its stony
bed down to the sea, as wide as a man could jump without an effort,
as deep as he could reach with his arm wet to the shoulder, as quick
and clear and ordinary as any other on the hillside. Only to the eye.
It was a fool who stepped in it. This stream ran far deeper than an
eye could see, it flowed far faster than a man could swim, and its
further bank was not always the one seen from this side the water.
But these were all things Assiolo had known from his boyhood and
so, when he had drunk, he went on steadily, a quiet, calm man with
murder in his heart.

After the dawning it would be midsummer, that day of light and
fire, much light and little darkness, when all the world was out of
balance. He let his heartbeats measure out the moments between
night's ending and the beginning of the day. At his back, the eastern
sky was painted all across with brightness. The sun rose, a ball of fire
casting a golden path across the water, and, at the very moment of its
rising, Assiolo turned around to face it, holding out his hands. With
eyes blinded by the light, he said the words and made the patterning,
binding it to his own purposes as had his father long ago.

He did not speak loudly but even Averla caught in her breath in
wonder to see Allocco's son upon the shore, holding fire in his bare
hands, mantled by the sunlight. Then she stepped out of the light to
stand beside him.

"Look there, Assiolo." Averla's white hand pointed back along the shore.

He looked, and what he saw near froze his heart within his breast. He cried out, "Let the world be as it is!"

But the world was as it was and his eyes saw truly a dancing boy with sunlight in his hair. Averla smiled. "He is here, as you are here, and I."

"He cannot be here!" Assiolo said, rubbing his eyes as if to change their seeing. "I left him safe within stone walls."

"Oh, Assiolo, Assiolo, you've always been a fool. No wall or gate can keep me out if I wish to be within. Have I not shown you, over and again? I told you on the shoreline in Felluria that you were ready." Averla laid her hand upon his arm. "The time is past for trades and bargains so let us speak plainly: you came here to kill the king."

"Aye, madam, but not for you," he said. "I have my own will and make my own choices. Te-Meriku took what was not his, and will suffer for it. I want his life but not his kingdom."

"If a man should kill the king, what does that make him?" Averla's shrug was the ripple of sunlight on the water. "There are two futures beyond that moment and you must choose between them. For your son's company, Assiolo, you would kill a man, what would you not do for his life?"

Assiolo gasped, winded as by a heavy blow.

"Even so. An you'll not serve my will, I'll twine him of that life."

"You would not!" he choked out, sickened by the thought. "Your own son born of your body."

"Do you think I am jesting? I had no thought of it. 'Tis true, I gave him his life twice over, since you got him with the life I gave you. But what price the candle 'gainst the summer's sun." She leaned close and whispered softly in his ear, "My heart is not tender – what I want I take and I do not mark the price. An you go free of me this day, your son dies before the sunset."

That then was the trap and now it was sprung. "He is a child – your own child! Even you'd not stoop to such an act!"

Again the ripple in the light, a shimmer and a shiver. "My child got for my purpose. This purpose. His life is in your hands. If you would keep him safe, you will do as I desire." Averla stepped from the light; she cupped his face between her white hands and made him look at her. "He is a fine boy, our son. Shall he lie with the flotsam at the watermark?"

He could not look away and knew she saw his answer in his face. She was stronger than he, and he would, in the end, give way before her. He could run, he could close his eyes against the light but never against the knowledge in his heart. For his love, he would kill a king; for his child's life, he would bring the world to ruin.

He closed his eyes and saw Averla clearly. No place of darkness left in his mind where he could hide. Her whisper was the caress of sunlight cross his skin. "I knew you from the beginning, Assiolo: all I need do after was wait for the moment I could make you mine. This is that moment. Yonder on the shore your son is playing. I will not touch him, if you give me back my own. But if you will not, if you will not use your strength and knowledge to suit my purpose, I am myself to the tideline. Such a little thing, a child's life; so fine a thread binds it to the world."

Averla smiled, most beautiful, most terrible. She had hid herself before but now her fire blazed, driving back all the rest. "You know as well as any in Lyikené: *He who kills the king, is the king.* If you wish your son to live, when Te-Meriku is dead and you the king, right and knowledge in one person, you will close the gates of evening and then the firstborn tree will grow no more beneath this sky, but always and forever in my brother's borderlands, withering no more towards its end."

"It is the king's purpose to keep the balance," said Assiolo. "An that gate closes and the tree grows no more beneath this sky and all in this world endure forever and for always, am I not foresworn as my father was before me?"

"What matters that to me?" Averla put back her shining hair, running with light and fire, rippling like the white heat of flames beneath the summer sun. "I sang my song before this world began. I remember the light that never dies, the light unmixed with dark beyond the gate. All that was mine – I was that light! Now I am little more than you: a shell of flesh around a rattle of bone that walks and talks and waits fearful for its ending. It is not enough! You will keep the promises your father made me, and I will have my own again."

Her laughter rang out across the day, rippling like birdsong through the air. Assiolo felt the future press down on him, suffocating, choking.

"Now I see why Te-Meriku took Marwy Ninek from Felluria," he gasped. "He holds a knife against my lover's throat and you another to my son's. I am left to walk the line between the sunlight and the sea, coming to ruin in the end whichever choice I make."

She laughed again and kissed him. "No ruin, Assiolo. A new beginning as the man your father should have been, a king in light and fire."

A balance was such a delicate thing – such a little weight upon the pan could tip it. Oh, such a little thing, not an apple, not a sword, not a kingdom: a bright-haired child who should never have been born. "He will live, Averla? An I do this, my son will live?"

She took his hands in hers, in seeming a woman but for the light shining in her eyes. "Assiolo, my sweet fool, kill the king and close the gate and you shall have your heart's desire. No need to wither from the world. You may have your black-haired love forever and for always, your son at your right hand."

Averla kissed his cheek, she kissed his eyes, and Assiolo saw the future stretched out before him, a child's shadow pointing out the way.

-+- -+-

In the hour before the dawning, Marwy Ninek walked again with Thodùhah to the king's hall. In the court armed men had gathered, in knots of three or four or more, torchlight glinting on their polished helms. As she came close, she saw that the nightwatch had threaded a sprig of gay gold broom into the mail on his right breast. He smiled and plucked another from the bush, tucking it into her hair. "It suits you fine," he said, "being you're dark as I. Better," he told her, standing back to judge the effect, "since it's a flower to match your gown."

She smiled to see him so light-hearted, seeing a good omen for the day. Te-Meriku nodded his welcome to Thodùhah and offered her his hand. The shadows shifted and shuddered in the wind and torchlight and she saw the piper at the open door. He made no move, he said no word, he stood upon the threshold wearing his coat of ragged blue but the look upon his face was the one that he had worn long ago beside a garden gate when he bade her, *Farewell.* And then she saw the nightwatch's eyes flick from him sideways to Te-Meriku and, all at once, knew his laughter was no more than a seeming.

"Te-Meriku," Ardùvai asked, "what of Marwy Ninek today?"

"My place is with the king," she answered quickly.

The piper was very still upon the threshold. His face had changed. His golden eyes reflected only the fires of the torches and showed nothing of his thoughts.

"Aye, so it is," said the nightwatch, "if all were as it should be."

The king shook his head but he persisted. "Nay, think on it a moment: You said yourself last night, Te-Meriku, Averla loves her not, and she knows as well as you she's like to stand between Assiolo and her desire." He grinned, looking into the king's hesitation. "If I were Averla and had men could hide themselves in light, I'd make sure of her out of Assiolo's sight, aye, and shift the blame to you. Tell me you'd not do the same?"

"I would for sure," grunted Thodùhah, "and there was that cur beneath the trees. What's happened once can happen twice."

Ardùvai said quietly, "You bade me keep her safe today. So shall she be, across the water."

Marwy Ninek glanced from one man to another, reading their faces, and took a step towards the king, taking his hands. "I want to be with you," she said.

Ardùvai's black eyes, serious now as she had ever seen them, met hers, level and unblinking. "Marwy Ninek, had you the strength and skill to match your courage, I'd be honoured to stand a-side you but the battlefield's no place for a woman, and less so after. You know that, who saw Felluria fall. Far better wait across the water 'neath the tree, where nothing and no one can hide in the light."

Te-Meriku's hand tightened at the mention of Felluria; his throat convulsed, swallowing back some bitter taste. The piper drew back into the shadows, the sight in no man's eyes. She said again, "I want to be with you."

"And I with you, but Ardùvai has it a-right and 'tis best you're where Averla cannot reach. We'll keep beneath the tideline much as we can but there'll be blood spilled today on every side and I want none of it yours. You'll be safe upon the further bank and yet close by if you are needed."

"That's the place," said Thodùhah, and Ardùvai said quickly, "I'll take you there myself, an you can spare me an hour, Te-Meriku."

There was good sense in all the nightwatch said and yet she did not like it. "Te-Meriku," she said, "I've not the strength or knowledge of the least of your company but I'd rather take my chance with you this side the stream. I trust your strength and your sword as much as I do Assiolo's love." She looked up into his face and said, "You called me out from my stone walls to stand beside you 'gainst Averla on this day, and so I shall, above the tideline or below."

A flicker of a frown drew his brows together. "Then I knew you only as the Tion of Felluria, a tool to suit my purpose and use as I desired." He pulled her close, speaking to her alone, "But now I know you as yourself, my closest kin that kept me safe and suffered for it, I'll not treat your life so lightly. You will cross the stream and bide beneath the tree until I call for you."

Marwy Ninek looked up into his hard, harsh face and saw his love and certainty. After a little time, she nodded, knotting her fingers into his.

"Have you some word or token I can give to Assiolo that when we meet he may know that you are here?"

She had no token, no broken ring, no torn kerchief, as in old songs by which one lover knew again the other. Instead she said,

"Tell him I'll dance with him at midwinter wearing slippers of the finest red leather."

He grinned at that and yet kept his arms close round her, putting off the moment of their parting. A shuffle and a scraping, and the piper came out from the shadows, his golden eyes bright in the torchlight, to stand between the nightwatch and the king. Ardùvai stepped forward, setting his hand on the king's arm. "I'll see her safe across the water," he said. Still the king held her in his warm grip. "Te-Meriku, you know I'll guard her with my life. An we go now she'll be across before the daybreak."

She stood up on her toes to kiss the king farewell. "I'll wait for you to call for me," she promised. "Ask and I will answer."

"We part until the noontime, lass," the piper said, "noontime at midsummer when all things are made clear."

Ardùvai held out his hand and together they walked out, taking the shore path towards the stream. For a while it ran beside them, too wide to jump, and both knew only a fool would try to wade these waters. Behind them, the sky brightened and, despite his mail, his shield and spear, Ardùvai quickened his pace, wanting to reach the crossing point before the day began. Marwy Ninek kept her place beside him, kilting her skirts up above her knee. And yet they were too slow. Their shadows stretched before them between the hillside and the stream, the sun cast its path across the sea and Ardùvai spat and swore, a thin, fluent hiss beneath his breath, cursing the day that had begun awry. His face beneath his helm was grim and set, his mouth a hard, straight line, his eyes 'most like a stranger's. Almost she feared him. She had seen such men long ago, capped with bright bronze, clad in bright mail; she had seen the use they made of shield and spear and sword, giving no quarter, knowing no mercy. Only the broomflower at his breast marked him as the man she knew.

"Tell me of Assiolo," he said, as they went on. "Is he a hasty man? One quick to anger?"

"Assiolo? No! Of all the men —" Movement from the corner of her eye. A shimmer and a shiver, light flickering to form. Marwy Ninek started back, crying out, "Ardùvai!"

"Run!" he told her.

The first man moved towards her, the second towards Ardùvai, swinging a foul mockery of a thistle upon a black chain. As she turned and ran, the nightwatch flung his spear towards the first and bared his sword. She heard a thud and grunt behind her, and heavy footsteps gaining on her. Hard hands caught her around the waist, hot breath panted down her neck. All this she had known before, but then it had been Te-Meriku, preparing her against this moment. She kicked and twisted against the weight of iron and muscle, feet skidding and sliding on the loose stones beneath the hill. They span about upon the path and his hand came up across her mouth, choking, suffocating.

"Our mistress bid us bring you to her." A low, lewd chuckle in her ear. "I think we'll play with you first a while."

She bit, hard as she could, and spat out blood, as his curse rang in her ears and her head rang with his blow.

His right arm was a rod of iron across her throat, his left arm clamped her against his chest. Trapped by his strength, she could not move, she could not think, she could only watch. As in the slow thickness of a nightmare, she saw the armsman on the streambank, a glorious sight in blue and steel, his hair spilling like light from beneath his helm, swinging spiked death lightly as a child his toy. And then the blow, a strike with the iron handle against the nightwatch's shield to make the prickled ball flick around the edge. As his red blood spilled and splashed, Ardùvai's shield sagged, only a little, but a little was enough for the other's shield to buffet into his face and knock him hard down to the ground. Her heart stopped in her breast as his foe stepped back, swinging up his weapon for the deathblow.

And then he was tumbling and crashing, his leg severed at the knee by the sweep of Ardùvai's bronze sword, his mouth open in a scream that brought back all her memories of ruin, a scream that died away into a rattle as Ardùvai's bloody hand thrust a knife into his throat.

In the silence afterwards Marwy Ninek could think again. The man had an arm around her neck, the other round her waist, but her hands were free and he distracted, measuring the little distance to Ardùvai hasting towards his spear, his sword in his left hand. She found her knife within her sleeve and stabbed it deep into the inside of the armsman's thigh, close under the skirt of his mail. IIe gasped and lurched, and she was free, wrenching the blade out as she pulled away. Ardùvai stooped and rose again in one fluid movement and, as he rose, his spear flew from his hand. The armsman made no further cry as he fell, the spear full through his neck, so only the ringing clash of steel on stone marked out his ending.

He was dead and worth no further thought of hers. She left him lying 'neath the hill and ran back towards Ardùvai. He stood upon the path above his broken foe. She paused beside him, looking where he looked, seeing the hoarfrost of its hair, the sun and the moon upon its arm. Averla's mark, Averla's man, dead on the streamside, no more to hide within the light from the eyes of honest men. And then she realised why the nightwatch looked so long. "Ardùvai, this man," she said, "I saw him first beneath the trees."

He kicked the corpse to turn it on its back. "Aye, had it been a hundred years, I'd have known him. Many's the time since Almecu died, I've dealt that blow in thought and longing." In the depths of his black eyes she saw again his grief. "It's little enough to give my mother but she'll sleep better knowing 'twas that I cut him down and spoiled his beauty. Stand back, Marwy Ninek, there's one thing left to do."

Ardùvai caught up the thistle on its chain and swung it down upon the dead man's face. A sickening crack, a flowering of blood and bone, and Ardùvai's lips curved into a smile of satisfaction. "My brother's blood," he said. "My mother's grief."

He dropped the iron beside the corpse and turned towards the stream to wash his hands and clean his sword and knife with a handful of damp grass. Blood dripped slowly from the gash torn in his left arm. Marwy Ninek crouched beside him, cupping water to her mouth. She could not drink much. No water had ever been as cold as the waters of that stream, as if the sun had never touched them.

"Wipe your knife," Ardùvai said, shortly. She did and slid it back into its sheath. Her hands were shaking now though they had not before. "You did well," he told her. "Keeping your head, marking the time to use your blade." He pulled a flask from his pocket, drank and offered it. "We should away," he said, looking around. "Where there were two there may be others."

"You're bleeding." She turned back her stained skirt to rip a strip from her shift. He let her bind his arm, grumbling the while it was a scratch, no more than that, until she let him go free.

"Now let's away," he said again, impatiently. "Sooner you're 'cross the water, sooner the piper's will is done and I can take my place beside Te-Meriku."

" 'Twas the king wished me to cross."

"I misspoke. For sure it was the king." A moment's flush on Ardùvai's pale cheek. "You're certain sure Assiolo is a man to think before he acts?"

"He's a good man, Ardùvai, a kind, good man."

"Aye well, good men can be twisted out of their proper shapes." He picked up his shield before she could answer, striding away to set his foot upon the second corpse and pull the spearhead free. The flies were gathering already, shining blue and green in the sunlight as they buzzed round the carcass.

The path climbed up the hillside. The stream rippled and bubbled beside them, a rush of clear water laughing in the sunlight. A little way further and they reached the point where it narrowed. A tangle of briars grew on the bank, green leaves and pale, sweet roses tumbling down and trailing in the water.

"Here's the place," said Ardùvai. His face was paler than she had seen it yet, bleached bone-white despite the morning sun. "See, it's not so very far away. I'll be back for you come noontime, sooner if I can shape the day to my liking."

Marwy Ninek gathered herself to jump but Ardùvai held out his hand to stop her. "Set down your knife," he said. "It is not fit that even the bronze blades of Lyikené are carried 'cross these waters."

So she drew her knife from its sheath on her left arm and laid it down beneath the briar and leapt the running water. As she passed over she thought she heard music, a song with words she did not know. The light was brighter, her shadow short as noontime. Yet the further bank was no other than it had seemed, the same green grass beneath her feet, and she could see the king's hall small in the distance and sunbeams slanting across the morning to the sea. It had been no more than the sound of the wind across the hillside, no more than the shimmer of sunlight on the running water. Ardùvai was already striding away. He did not look back and soon she turned from the water to walk up the hillside to the tree.

Not knowing the bargains adults made in the sunlight, the boy was playing on the shore. Armsmen stood guard, halfseen where the light was brightest, women watched, sitting on the shingle above the highwatermark, but he paid heed to neither men nor women. He had found a rockpool and was teasing sea-jellies with periwinkles, watching the blindly grasping fingers reach out until, by chance, they seized their desire and held it fast, contracting back into themselves until but a red clot upon the rock remained. There were crabs there too, tiny shore crabs, no bigger than his thumbjoint, and hermits scuttling sideways clad in borrowed whelkshells. He chased a while a blenny, which darted to and fro between the strands of weed, always too fast for him to catch, slipping each time between his curving fingers. Entranced, enthralled, he pounced and poked and splashed and gave no thought but to the moment. He was a child, engrossed in this new world beneath the water, and gave no thought to the sudden silence of the gulls; he was a child and did not think it strange that shadows should shrink almost to nothing, though it was three hours and more 'til noontime; he was a child and knew of his mother only that she was beautiful and smiling, that she gave him toys and told him stories and called him by a name his father did not like.

So much he did not know, until the day exploded into a rush and roar, a wave of men across the shore and another come to meet it from the land. They clashed in a fury of bronze and iron, in

muscle-shredding violence without quarter, casting a red veil between
the seashore and the sun. In all the midst of noise and light and
blood, the boy stood still, screaming for his nurse. Who did not
come. And did not come. He saw Casarca start towards him and fall
outstretched, a spear quivering in her back; saw men leap and fight;
saw swords flicker and twist, plunge into a man's side and come
out bloody; saw a man's cheek sliced away beneath his helm; saw
a fallen man writhing on the shingle, his severed arm lying by his
foot. After that last sight, the boy crouched down in the shadow of
the great humped rock, his hands across his eyes, in terror beyond
screaming.

Te-Meriku had not known the boy was there until a fishwife,
chance met at the tideline, told of what she had seen upon the shore
before she slipped away to join her sisters in the sea. Nor had he
thought far beyond the knowledge that this was a prize worthy of
the taking. He was the king: it was his part to stand as long as could
be 'gainst Averla's fierce desire and keep the tree beneath this sky.
What was a child's life set against such a purpose? And such a child,
the son of his enemy, Averla's ill-gotten whelp, a child that should
never have been born, a tool for others' using.

He stood now in the sea's edge, staring at the boy crouching in
Kalanu's shadow, frozen in terror because all around the day had
fallen into ruin. The men of his company crowded close round, wary
and ready for what might step out of the light when he set foot
across the tideline. Te-Meriku held his bronze sword in his hand
and thought how easy it would be, so very, very easy, to bring such
a little life to its ending.

Then he remembered this child's name. 'Twas likely chance, no
more than that, yet still enough to give him pause. Te-Meriku stared
into the light, remembering bad dreams, balancing the child's fate
against his own. The future was not yet written. He could not know
the deeds to turn it to one of his own choosing, only those fitted
to his kingship. He sheathed his sword and told his company, "He
should have no part in this."

Men stared, amazed, and Ardùvai stepped forward, black-haired,
grim-faced, the sprig of gay gold broom yet tucked in the breast of
his mailed shirt. Te-Meriku saw his eyes flick to the boy, then squint
into the light.

"That's a pretty thing to let slip through your fingers," he said.
"Some might counsel you to keep him close to force his father's
hand."

A beat of time before he answered, light and laughing, "Other
men, perhaps, Ardùvai, but not you, not today. No child chooses his
father."

Ardùvai flushed. "As you will it, Te-Meriku; I'll deal with him as you bid me."

"I want him the other side of the water, where his mother cannot reach and his father cannot hide. There's one there can keep him company."

"Aye, well," said Thodùhah, spitting into the waves, "there's a deal of ground to cross between the tideline and the stream and more hiding in the light, I'll warrant, than we've seen yet."

Te-Meriku grinned. "I'll do it an you're with me."

"Am I not always with you?"

"All the years of my kingship." Then Te-Meriku stepped onto the shore to crouch beside Averla's son. "Open your eyes, lad, look at me."

The child shrank away, pressing his face into his hands. He had seen too much already: the crumpled heap that had been Oca; the monstrous creature with his face half cut away; the blood running down between the stones.

The king touched him gently on the shoulder. "No need to look, but better to look than to imagine. I'm but a man. And no man will strike at you while you are with me." The child looked up, gazing wide-eyed into his face. "I'm Te-Meriku, and you, I know, are Imacah."

He sat back on his heels waiting patiently for the boy to find his voice. Armed men stood by, watching, wary. At last the child whispered, "Yes."

Te-Meriku laughed, short and hard. "It's a good name. I once knew a man called Imacah."

"My father chose it."

"No better choice. Well, lad, this is no place for you. Let's go find you a safer one."

The light grew stronger; shining out across the shore brighter than living eyes could bear. Averla stepped from the sunlight, taller, more lovely and more terrible than any there could have imagined, all the light in all the world shining in her golden hair, casting the rest into shadow and darkness. Te-Meriku lifted the boy, stepping quickly back below the water's edge.

"The boy is mine."

"Well, Imacah, she's asked it. Would you go to her?"

The light was too bright for the child's eyes and dazzled him. He clung tight to Te-Meriku, twining his arms around his neck, pressing his face into his shoulder, and whispered, "No."

Te-Meriku's answer rang out loud and clear, "The boy's below the tideline, Averla. You shall not have him, though he be a hundred times your own."

Averla frowned, a thickening of the light like water. Men pressed closer to Te-Meriku, bloody blades poised and ready. He laughed and said, "Aye, I know full well you could kill me with a word. Alas for you, my death would serve no purpose here and now and so 'tis I have the mastery."

From Averla's back other men came, bright and bold in the sunshine, armed with black iron, the sun and the moon blazoned on their shields. "Give me the boy and I will bid Assiolo kill you quickly."

"Assiolo's choices are his own." Te-Meriku's eyes narrowed against the light, but still his face was full of mocking laughter. "But, Averla, do you think he'll judge me hardly because I got his son to safety? In truth, I think the day is mine for all the brightness of your light."

"Do you think love enough, Te-Meriku?" she asked, with a shrug of her white shoulders. "It might have been, had not the piper called in his wager. Whose will is done today?"

With a hissed oath Ardùvai moved to stand in front of the king, shield raised, sword ready. Others joined him, men of the Sea People clad in bronze and blood, making a half-circle of grim intent. A moment's pause, a wave of Averla's hand and the tide of blue and steel rose up against them.

"No one will touch you, Imacah," Te-Meriku said, quietly in the boy's ear, "I'll get you to the stream bank but now's the time to close your eyes."

He did as he was bid, turning his face again into his shoulder. He heard the clang and clash ring out, heard grunts and groans, a scream, shrill and too close beside him that ended in a dreadful, bubbling gurgle. Te-Meriku was running now, with other men close round him, splashing through the water. The boy felt the rhythm of his stride, the rattle of stones beneath his feet and heard the jeers and whistles of the armsmen on the shore. He clung tight, his arms around Te-Meriku's neck; heard his voice, a whisper and a promise, "You're with me, Imacah, I'll see you safe onto the other side."

He opened his eyes when their pace slowed. A man, grizzled grey with age, walked at Te-Meriku's left side. Like him, he held his sword in his right hand; each was stained with red blood to the shoulder, but, looking from one face to the other, the boy could not think them fearful. Soon Te-Meriku paused, knee-deep in saltwater. His company pressed round him, catching their breath, measuring their chances above the tideline. They had reached the point where the stream that tumbled and bubbled 'cross the grass-green hillside ran out across the beach, its waters mingling into the sea. Te-Meriku leaned forward, pointing through the wall of men and past the armsmen waiting on the shore, to the crossing place, an arrow's flight away up across the hill. "Imacah, an I get you there, can you jump the stream?"

The boy screwed up his eyes against the light and saw the stream was but a little thing, scarce wider than the waters in his mother's garden. He swallowed, and whispered, "Yes," then, "Will you follow?"

"An I could, Imacah, I would." Te-Meriku shook his head. "But I'm the king, see, and must stay this side the water until the sun sets. But, in the evening, Ardùvai here will find you. You'll know his face again, won't you?"

He gestured to Ardùvai beside him. The boy looked up at the nightwatch, at his bronze helm and black eyes all a-glitter in his hard, pale face, and whispered, "Yes."

"Then wait for him beneath the tree."

"Will my father find me there?"

"I'll tell your father where you are. You have my promise, Imacah."

'Twas time to go and yet Te-Meriku lingered a moment, watching the red tide lap against the shore. Later, the crows would come, and the kites, but for now only a seagull drifted across the day, screaming out for its lost soul to any who would hear it. He felt the boy tug at his sleeve. The child held out a ring set with a red stone that hung on a leather thong around his neck. "My father gave me this," he said. "He said to think which king it was. I think it must be you."

He traced a finger over the carving on the stone, feeling its chipped edge, and thought of things that might have been, had he not once said *Yes!* to Hadùhai and taken a sword in his right hand and made himself into a king. He shook his head and told the child, "No, it's not I – see, this king's hands are empty." He turned from the boy to look from one man to another, shaping his face into a grin. "Well, lads, are you ready?"

Their cry went up, "Te-Meriku the king!" and with one mind and one fluid, flowing motion they passed the boundary of sea and land.

And then all around the dreadful clang of bronze on iron, the thud and crunch as blades bit deep in flesh and bone. The boy pressed his face against the king's neck, closing his eyes against the horror of the day. Te-Meriku smelled of sweat and leather, the salty tang of the sea. "Not far now, Imacah." Above the din, he heard the drumbeat of his heart, the thud of his boots upon the shingle, a clattering and a rattling, and then the duller pad of footsteps over turf, his breath rasping in his ears, the bubbling music of the stream.

Te-Meriku set the boy down upon the bank and squatted beside him, looking him level in the face. "We part here, Imacah. There is no blood and death the other side the stream, no light to dazzle, no fire to burn."

Above them and around them, battle raged; not far away, men cursed and struck and screamed and died. Armsmen in their steel and blue, by the dozen and the score, stepped smiling from the light to press hard upon the king's company. They were fewer now, a flicker of swords about their king. The old man was down, blood leaking from the hole in his left side, and Ardùvai stood astride him, dealing out death with every stab and thrust. The boy set his teeth and looked only at the king. He felt his grip firm upon his shoulders, steadying him in the midst of devastation.

"You must away." Te-Meriku pushed him gently to the stream's edge. "Jump, Imacah, and let me see you safe."

He jumped and found himself upon the further bank and that it was not the one he had seen from the other side. A man was waiting there, holding out his hand. For a moment, looking up into his face, he thought the king must after all have crossed the water, but then he looked again and saw the stars tangled in his hair.

XV, Lyikené: Flame across the water

Oh, the day of his funeral there was such a fine sight
There were four-and-twenty young men all dressed up in white.
They carried him along and they laid him on clay
They said adieu to young Willy, then they all marched away.

The Lakes of Cold Flynn, *Traditional*

Hadùhai's corpse lies upon its bier of rowan branches: green leaves and blood-red berries. Someone—Maris, perhaps—has washed the blood from the head's grey hair and rebound it with red silk into the clansman's knot. "No," he thinks, watching Maris's face as she wraps a plait of hair around its wrist, "it was not her." Thodùhah, then. She kneels at its side, its hand in hers, and her whole body shudders. She presses her hands across her mouth, not quite hard enough to stifle her sobs.

As if they were alone, as if a multitude of watching eyes were of no matter, Thodùhah steps forward from his place to wrap her in his arms and hold her close against his breast. Maris clings to him and his hand strokes her rough hair, soothing away the rawness of her grief. What he says only she can hear but it is enough. When he stands back, her face is calm again but for the brightness of her eyes. She leans forward to kiss the cold cheek and then she turns away.

Her daughter takes her place. The child reaches out a hand but does not quite touch her grandsire. She bites her lip to still its trembling and then raises her face to his.

She is only a child, and what she thinks is of no matter, but still he flinches, seeing himself reflected from her rain-grey eyes. Then her face crumples and, weeping, she runs the few steps back to her mother.

It is his turn. He steps forward to kneel by its right side and place a sword in its right hand. The bronze blade gleams in the long evening light. It has lain near a year in the dark, this sword, in a kist within his chamber beneath a tumble of patched clothes, out of sight but not forgotten. His hand is steady as he lays it down, a scrap of grass-green silk still wound around its hilt. There were many swords in the king's armoury, older ones, finer ones, ones better suited to a king, but none like this with meaning in his heart and so, for his first and only gift to Hadùhai, there can be no other.

He walks around the bier to fold the apple into its left hand. An old man's hand, gnarled and knotted with its years. Its fingers are stiff with death and he must press and force and fumble. Imacah's hand had been smooth-skinned and slender, such strength in its white fingers as they

*closed on his wrist to pull him down into the heather. He bites his lip
upon the memory. No burning ship for Imacah. No flame or fire or sunset.
Only cold clay to stop his mouth and a winding sheet to swaddle him in
his stony bed. They are nowise alike, Hadùhai and Imacah, save both are
dead for sake of him.*

What is the price of a man's life? An apple? A sword? A kingdom?

*He kisses the cold brow, the skin like wax beneath his mouth, so little
like a man, and calls to mind the answer.*

*The sea eagle sweeps across the hill, free of the past and of the future,
a dream of liberty beneath its burnished wings. Heavy in his flesh, he
watches it out of sight, knowing himself only a man, sharing nothing but
its name. The past is a hole where his heart should be; the present is
reflected in tears spilling from a child's eyes; the future presses down upon
him with the weight of a thousand oaths.*

*He stands straight and nods to Thodùhah. The helmsman steps forward
with five others to lift the bier into the ship. Men's boots crunch across
the shingle, and then the rattle and roll and splash as the ship takes flight
onto the sea.*

*The night is dark now, save for the flower of flame across the water. A
lovely sight, red and gold shining against black, if he knew not what it
was: the rush and roar, the shrivelling of flesh, the snap and crack of wood
and bone. He cannot turn away but watches from the shore with twelve
clanlords at his back until, like an eye closing, the light blinks out and
there is only darkness.*

Later, later, a long time after the sunset, the rattle at his door might be
the wind but the thud cannot be other than a hand banging against the
wood. Awakened from his first deep sleep, he lies naked between the sealfurs,
considering who might dare disturb the king at such a time, then rises up
to open the door. The child bursts in, screaming, sobbing, flinging herself
at him.

Quicker than thought, he twists sideways and catches her wrist, holding
her an arm's length from him. She sinks her teeth into his arm, beats at
him with her free hand, her face swollen and ugly with her grief. "You
killed him," she cries, over and again, "you killed him."

He lets her rant and rage until she is exhausted. When he releases her,
she crouches upon the floor sobbing, hopelessly, helplessly, pressing her
hands across her face. He looks down for a long, long moment, seeing in
her loss the echo of his own. Without a word, he turns away to light the
lamp and pull on his shirt and trousers.

At last her sobs grow quiet. "I taught you better than that," he tells
her. "I should be dead or dying, you with a knife like that one to your
hand and I but a naked man."

She raises her face, puts back her damp and tangled hair, to look hard at him and see if he speaks in jest. Her wrist has turned from white to red where he held it; tomorrow there will be bruises. He has not been gentle, no more than she came at him in play.

"*I wish I'd killed you.*" *Her voice is flat and empty, and her knife again in her right hand.*

He sees her trembling with fear or rage or cold—perhaps all three—and turns his back. Pouring wine into two cups, he tells her, "*Then do it. You have the knife—you know the places.*" *He hears no step behind him and, when he turns back to face her, she has laid down the knife.*

"*I hate you.*"

"*Do you, Liùthánwy?*"

She looks him in the eye and her face changes. Again, she flings herself at him but this time she clutches and clings so hard he can scarcely breathe.

"*Hush, hush,*" *he soothes, picking her up and carrying her to the fireside. Such a little weight in his arms, bird-light and delicate. He sets her down and wraps her in a sealskin, soft as feathers, white as snow, gives her a cup of wine to warm her and sits beside her with the other.* "*If you're yourself again, we'll talk.*"

"*You...*" *her words tail away to silence.*

"*I did what was necessary,*" *he tells her,* "*as Hadùhai once did what was necessary.*"

"*Oh,*" *she says, reaching out to lay her hand along his cheek,* "*you are changed. I can see it in your eyes. Now you are the king.*"

He takes her hand but does not answer. There can be no answer. The thing is done, the burning ship sent beyond the sunset. The old king is dead and the young king come into his kingdom. She swallows once, she swallows twice and asks him, "*Was it quick?*"

That he can answer. "*Very quick,*" *he says,* "*the sword is very sharp, my eye is keen, my arm is strong. As easy a death as any man could wish for.*" *Except, perhaps, that time of knowing that it must be so. All men must die but only the king knows when and how and who. He has made a beginning today; one day, far, far from this moment, another man will make an ending. So has it always been; so will it ever be.*

Her tears run down her cheeks and she turns away to hide them.

"*A man is dead. There is no shame in mourning him.*"

She cries out, "*I wish it had been otherwise. He could have lived and you still been the king.*"

"*Come here,*" *he says, and holds her close to comfort her. So had he wished before the dawning but now he can see the pattern that had been hidden.* "*There cannot be two kings in one land,*" *he tells her, stroking her rough hair,* "*he knew it, Liùthánwy. It was the last thing he had to do.*"

But, late into the night, she weeps for her grandsire, pressing her face into his shoulder, and he sits, holding her in the crook of his arm, remembering the sword's weight in his hand, its bite into a man's flesh and a man's bone, the grunt and groan of life departing. He does not weep; he spent his store of tears a year ago.

"How does it feel," asks Imacah out of the shadows, "to know the time a man must die?"

He answers, whispering so that the child will not hear him, "Lonely."

16: Forever and for always

If ever thou gavest meat or drink,
Every nighte and alle,
The fire sall never make thee shrink;
And Christe receive thy saule.

A *Lyke-Wake Dirge*, Traditional

The sun rose up the sky to noontime as men fought and died upon the shore. To Assiolo such sights were of no interest. All men must die: what matter that they died on this day rather than another? He walked the path above the shore and none saw clearly he was there at all. His mind was filled with his true love, and all she had suffered at the red king's will between the sunset and the morning. That king had died upon the riverbank – so too would this one, so like to him in face and thought and deed.

And after?

He shied away from thoughts of after. He had made his choice. His son would live, and he would give him everything his father had not given him. He walked the shore and thought the while upon a garden with neither gate nor door, a garden where white roses grew within the wall, where smooth paths of stone passed by the pools wherein golden fishes swam, where arching trees gave shade and shelter from the summer sun. A lovely place, that garden: bees humming in the lavender, butterflies dancing above the mallow, honeysuckle twining 'cross the day, the honey-heavy scent of elderflowers. A child could play beneath the trees and two lovers sit handfast on the grass, contented in each other's company forever and for always. No need at such a time, in such a place, to think of the world beyond the wall.

At last he saw the sight he looked for, the red king on the riverbank, his bloody company around him. And at that sight Assiolo put aside all thoughts of past and future and stepped out of the light beside him.

"I am here, Te-Meriku, to make an end and a beginning."

The king turned at once towards him, holding out his hand; almost, he thought, as in a greeting. His mouth opened but what the barbarian would say was never said. Assiolo held out his empty hands, he said a word, and the king dropped to his knees and all about was light and fire, the king but a crouching man, screaming his agony to the four winds. From the corner of his eye, Assiolo saw a clansman with a ragged broomflower at his breast drop shield and sword to leap away across the water, a coward fleeing the field. The little part of his mind not filled with fear and vengeance pitied him – there was no place of safety on this day, not even on the further bank.

A little way away the piper sat beside the stream, watching all, saying nothing. And, close by, Averla, her red lips open, her eyes and hair bright and beautiful as the midsummer day. "My will is done," she said. "Soon the end will come and a new king, to give me back my own."

"Soon indeed, Averla," said the piper, "Allocco's son shall change one future to another."

Averla smiled, and a world of light and fire was reflected from her face. "Oh, my monster, all those years lost between us, but in the end you turned back to me, delivering the king to Assiolo's wrath. I'll not forget it in the time that is to come."

The piper gazed at her, his golden eyes wide and unblinking despite the brightness of light. "If I had been a man," he whispered, "how I could have loved you. Alas that might have been will never be."

Whatever men did within the world, Marwy Ninek was safe beneath the tree, beyond the boundary. Beyond the water swords could thrust and fire could burn but here the wind rustled the leaves of the apple tree and a blackbird sang in the sunlight of midsummer's day. There was green grass beneath her, blue sky above her, and all the rest was far away. *Bide there until I call for you.* She would wait, and she would keep her promise. Until then it was a fair, fine day to rest beneath the tree, if she looked to the leaves and to the sky, if she listened only to the blackbird, if she did not turn her eyes across the water. She leant her back against the tree and closed her eyes and let her mind drift this way and that between a dream and waking.

Three kings stood beside her 'neath the tree. One wore black and one wore red, the third wore green and all their faces were the same. The red king spoke her name, and she opened her mouth to answer, "I am here!" but the black king put his finger gently 'cross her lips for silence, pointing with his left hand to the blackbird perched on the topmost twig, its yellow beak open in song. Then tears shone like summer raindrops on the green king's cheeks as all that might have been was washed away forever and for always by the bubbling ripple of birdsong, lovely and empty as the midsummer sky.

A rough hand shaking her shoulder dragged her back into the moment. She opened her eyes to Ardùvai, pale-faced and bloody, his black hair straggling from his helm. The look upon his face tore the

day to ruins and yet, in the tree above them, the blackbird was still
singing.

"You must come," he said, "*come now!*" His hand left a stain upon
her golden sleeve. Slowly, stupidly, she wondered if it was his blood
or another's. "The king – Assiolo..."

He faltered into silence. She curled her hand into his and did not
know if she sought or offered comfort. Ardùvai pulled her to her feet
and they were running, running down the hill towards the water,
and all the time the blackbird was still singing as if all the world
were of no matter.

And then, a world away across the water, a man screamed out
her name and, at that cry, the bird took fright and fluttered from
the tree, rattling its warning as it flew. Another moment and they
were at the stream bank and she kilted up her skirts to leap the
running water to where her knife was waiting on the further bank,
with Ardùvai's shield and sword beside it. She slipped it home into
its sheath and looked around for Assiolo.

It had been full daylight 'cross the water but here was light
beyond the sunlight, light the like of which she had not seen though
she had lived a long, long time. Light shone. Men fought. Light
burned. Men died. Ardùvai cried out and put up his hands to shield
his eyes. No man could look into such light and not be blinded,
nor see what stood at its white heart. But Marwy Ninek was not a
woman and she saw the man drawing fire down from the sun to cast
it at his enemy.

She screamed, "Assiolo!" and made to run to him, to pull down
his hands and kiss his face and turn him again into the man that
she remembered. She had not taken a step towards him when light
itself took form and caught at her arm, tangled her all about with
strands of golden hair, whispered in her ear, "My will is done today
and I shall have my own again."

Marwy Ninek turned and twisted in Averla's hands, those white
hands that looked so fair and whose grip was stronger than any
man's. "Do you trust Assiolo's love?" Averla asked. "As well believe
oranges grow on an apple tree as a man who swears he loves you.
He turned from you the day his son was born. I called across the
world, he got up from your bed and came to mine, to lie in my arms
and tangle himself into my hair. He is mine, forever and for always.
Look yonder at the proof of it!"

Marwy Ninek looked. She saw the sun stopped still at noontime
and dead men lying in their blood, Thodùhah among them, his
sword by his right hand; she saw the piper, bent by the weight
of knowledge and of sorrow, witness to this as to so much before;
she saw Te-Meriku upon his knees, his mouth open in a scream so

terrible her mind closed itself against it lest it too be broken. The king's hands, his face, his hair ran red with fire; he burned and burned and was not consumed. Consumption would have granted death, and death, mercy, but Assiolo was his father's son: he had learnt much from Allocco but nothing of mercy.

Grief and anger boiled and bubbled in her breast, raging and ranting into the sunlight. "That is a monster! My curse on you forever that made such a thing of Assiolo!"

Averla held her left arm and she could not reach her knife but Ardùvai was close beside her. She snatched a dagger from his belt and stabbed upwards into Averla's face.

The point was true, the blow was sure, but it never met its mark. Averla, quick as lightning, caught the blade in her right hand. No flinch of fear, no gasp of pain, only molten metal spilling between the fingers of her fist. Yet even Averla must let go her grip to catch a knife and, in that moment, Marwy Ninek broke free and ran to Assiolo.

She screamed his name but he could not hear her, and Averla smiled to see her will made manifest within the waking world. Marwy Ninek stared and stared, and saw a man she did not know. She reached out to touch his face, she looked into his eyes; she saw light and fire and hatred looking back at her, but never Assiolo.

Averla's laughter rang out, echoing across land and sea as a ring of golden bells, most lovely and most cruel. The sun, paused in its path, beat down upon the world as the moment of noontime stretched out towards forever, driving away all shadows and all hope of safety.

Marwy Ninek had not known that she could weep but weep she did, a rush of heavy tears bitter as brine. In despair, she turned away to embrace Te-Meriku, placing herself between him and Assiolo so her shadow might give a little shelter, her arms a little comfort and her tears falling down upon his face a little balm.

All the time there was stretched out into the light and a man's agony, his face transfigured so by suffering he scarce seemed a man at all. She clasped him close and saw in wonder that his eyes were yet his own, no fire there, only the shifting colours of the sea, grey and green and blue. He could not move, he could not speak, he could scarce even breathe, but he was still the king who could not be driven easily into the dark.

Marwy Ninek held onto Te-Meriku for all the sun shone fierce and fire burned hot and death hovered over them, certain in sun as in shadow. She was too close to the light and every drop of blood running through her veins burned with Assiolo's borrowed fire. A woman would have died but she was not a woman and she would not yield nor stand aside though light shone, and fire burned, and love itself fell into ruin.

"Now comes the choice I've gambled all on," the piper muttered, seeing clearly though other eyes be dazzled, hearing her sob of grief ring out across the day. And Assiolo heard it too and paused to listen. And, in that pause, the light flickered and the piper smiled to see Averla's frown. And, in that pause, Marwy Ninek said softly, sadly, stroking back her brother's hair, "Assiolo, please, no further."

A whisper, a murmur, a thread fragile as gossamer twisting on the breeze between them, a thread fine as silk, subtle as cobweb, tied with a laugh, an oath, a promise, on another midsummer in a garden of red roses. Assiolo caught in his breath as the golden thread pulled him from one moment to another. Marwy Ninek, crouching over Te-Meriku's agony, looked up into her lover's face. At the sight of her fear and her pain, the thread drew tight about his heart. Assiolo said no word, he made no move but the light about him died into nothing.

"Thus far, and no further," he cried out to Averla. "I gave a promise to my love and I will keep it."

There was a fearsome darkness to the day, as when the sun slants beneath the thunderhead. Averla held out her hands 'cross land and sea. For a moment she seemed tall as the sky, most lovely and most terrible, and Assiolo but a little thing, a puppet made of flesh and blood to be crushed with one blow of her white hand. He looked up and met her eyes, only a man, but, as he shook his head, it was he who had the mastery: she had no hold upon him but the boy.

Silence across the day, broken only by the babble of the water, until with a rush of wind and a flicker of light, Averla was gone. Assiolo sank upon the grass and pressed his face into his hands, knowing he must pay the price of this refusal.

Men could move again and did so, closing about Assiolo, bronze swordpoints pricking at his neck. Ardùvai pulled off his helm and dropped it down upon the streambank, his hair tumbling lank and tangled all across his shoulders, his eyes black pits of pain to see the king lie broken and dying. The piper pushed through the throng and the nightwatch spat and stepped aside to avoid his short shadow, as a man draws back from foulness.

Shadows gathered at the edges of Te-Meriku's vision, fluttering like a black crow's wing. A curlew cried sweet and sudden in the distance. So close, so very far away, the tide was ebbing from the shore. He was so heavy in his flesh he could not feel his sister's fingers in his hand. Black feathers brushed his cheek, soft and cold as snow upon the meadows. He closed his eyes against the light and knew again the eagle's flight across the hill, a dream of air and freedom, no weight upon the world.

A touch, a breath, a whisper, drew him back across the line between a dream and waking. He tasted the salt of his sister's tears as she bent her head to kiss him. "I am here, Te-Meriku, and I will not let you go."

Te-Meriku opened his eyes and saw no crow's wing at the edge of darkness, only his sister's hair falling down around him. He pulled himself back into the moment, back into light and pain and flesh: he was yet the king and could not slip quietly away into the dark. Marwy Ninek smoothed back his hair and kissed him; he reached up to wipe away her tears, whispering painfully through cracked lips, "Truly there are many kinds of love."

A little way across the grass, Assiolo raised his head and spoke her name. She did not look and did not answer. He said more strongly, "Look at me, love."

"How came you to this?" she asked. "To kill a man that never lifted arms against you."

"Such thoughts," Assiolo said, "such fears since I found you gone with him." He stared at her, holding Te-Meriku so tenderly. "But this looks not like a rape."

"Is that what you thought it?"

"I found you gone!" he cried out. "Gone from your stone walls, and none could tell me why! Only that he'd taken you and sought for me. I'd seen the long-haired star and read its meaning: what could I do but think it?" He rubbed his hand across his eyes as if that would change the seeing or the past. The flat of a swordblade pushed it down towards his side.

"He is my brother, my own mother's son," she said, her eyes raw with tears. In her grief he saw only truth, and yet still he stared, not seeing how it could be so. "But what are you, Assiolo, to do such things and turn your back on all you held dear?"

"A man," he answered, brokenly, "my father's son, my son's father. I wanted to be only your lover but other parts were forced on me." He did not say, *'Twas you who forced them first*, but the words unspoken hung in the air between them. "Now Averla has gone to the tideline to twine my son of his life."

Slowly, painfully, Te-Meriku raised his head. "She'll not find him. The boy is safe across the water." Assiolo caught his breath in hope and shame. "He'll not suffer for his father's deeds. Whatever I am, I am not that."

Assiolo bowed his head and marked, as a man marks little things at times of great moment, the daisies scattered here and there across the grass. There was nothing he could say. Not now. Later, perhaps, his words would return but not just now. His love was safe, his son likewise, and he himself a murderer. The Sea People stood in a circle round their king and the moment lengthened into another, and another. The sun was above them in the bright sky and, beyond them, the tide was ebbing from the red shore.

The moment was broken when Kalanu the shoreman took three steps forward, his knife in his right hand. He caught Assiolo by the hair and pulled back his head. "Shall I kill him, Te-Meriku?"

Ardùvai drew a quick, deep breath and made to move towards them but the piper was already there. "Don't be a fool," he snapped at Kalanu. "This is Allocco's son and he must make the ending, as his father made the beginning." He looked past the shoreman to Te-Meriku. "To do that he must be king this side the sunset."

Marwy Ninek looked up, first at the piper, then at the nightwatch and saw the colour stain his cheek and his hands clench at his side.

"No chance, then," she asked him bitterly, remembering his manner of the morning, "nor even courtesy that I was across the water?"

"No chance at all," Ardùvai began, but the piper broke in, "I'll take that on myself, lass, guiding the day towards this moment and this choice."

She spat at him, crooking her fingers 'gainst ill-fortune.

The king said in a halting whisper, "To me, Ardùvai!"

The nightwatch span round to face him. In a rush to tell his tale, he began, "I'm your man, Te-Meriku, but the piper used me for another purpose."

Te-Meriku's hoarse whisper cut across him, "I'm yet the king. Whatever the piper did, or you, or Assiolo – the rest is mine. To me, Ardùvai."

In one swift movement the nightwatch knelt beside him and caught up his hand to kiss it. "You knew last night," he said. "Even before he called in his wager, you knew."

"No, man, not that. Only the kingship. I tried to speak on it but you'd no mind to listen." Te-Meriku's broken body shuddered, his breath came in harsh gasps. "I saw clearly yesternoon: there's nothing can change that seeing. The time's come for me to ask," he whispered, reaching for his sword. His hand was clumsy, fumbling and slipping, until Marwy Ninek caught it and closed his fingers around the ivory of the hilt, helping him to lift it. "Will you take this of me? It's a fine blade again – I think there's none finer – but I've no more the skill to match it."

Ardùvai looked up, his black eyes shining with grief. "I am not fitted to the kingship."

The king's laugh was a rattle and a cough. "And you with a thousand years of clanlords at your back? You'll take it, Ardùvai, or you're not the man I think you."

"Te-Meriku!"

For a moment their right hands clasped the sword together, fingers entwined upon the haft, then Te-Meriku's grip loosened and his hand fell back. Ardùvai stood up, pale-faced, black eyes a-blaze. He brought up the sword, shifting his grip on its hilt of ivory and gold, hefting it in his hand to find the balance of the bronze blade.

"When I ask it, Ardùvai, you use that blade to twine me from my life."

The nightwatch nodded. "Aye."

"Te-Meriku, this cannot be!" The piper pushed himself forward to stand before the king. He was little, he was twisted but in him was the strength of a great boulder that does not shift though the waves crash down upon it. "Ardùvai can no more bring this to an ending than you or Kalanu or any of the Sea People. It must be Assiolo. He has the skill and strength that you do not."

Assiolo laughed, a bitter, broken laugh that ended in a grimace. "We are all dancing to your tune today."

"Always, lad, since the gates of morning closed."

Then Ardùvai swore and Assiolo said to the piper, as if they were alone, as if no bronze blades were raised against his life, as if all the rest were of no matter, "When I was a boy, I loved you." His voice was taut with anger, throbbing like a lutestring, the thickest string that yields the deepest, darkest note. "But you left me to my father."

"Aye, so I did. I knew what he would teach you."

Assiolo made no move beneath the shoreman's knife, he said no word, but the piper recoiled from the fire that flickered in his eyes. He took a breath and said, "I knew Allocco, lad, I knew Averla. And I knew you. I knew your love would be no little thing and sent—"

Assiolo's glance flicked to Marwy Ninek, cradling the king against her breast. "Do not speak to me of love! Do not dare! Not after—"

"This pattern is not of Assiolo's weaving," Marwy Ninek cried out, looking around in desperation, "he did not come here to make himself a king."

"He who kills the king is the king," the piper answered. "It was ever so in Lyikené."

Ardùvai took a step towards the piper, the sword in his right hand. "You are the king," he said to Te-Meriku. "No need to do his bidding an you do not wish it. Give me your word and I will make an ending."

"The world is as it is," Kenu Vanithu said, terrible, implacable, "and not as you would wish it. You accepted as much this morning, Ardùvai mor Ardùvai, when you took Marwy Ninek across the water. If not Assiolo, no one. If not now, never. Te-Meriku, you are the king beneath this sky and this is the last thing you must do."

And then there was a clamour and stamping as the Sea People raised up their voices 'gainst the piper. Te-Meriku put up his hand for silence, his strength near spent. He said to his company, "He ever spoke the truth. Let Allocco's son approach."

Bronze blades drew back from Assiolo's throat. Slowly, slowly, like a man wading through a dream, he walked forwards towards an end and a beginning.

"Well, Assiolo," the king gasped, "are you the piper's plaything or Averla's?"

Assiolo flushed. "I was both, I think. Now I am neither." He knelt beside the king, holding out his empty hands. "Te-Meriku, believe me when I say I never wanted this. I wanted only a quiet life with my own love beside me."

The silence thickened between them until Te-Meriku rasped, "Does not a man make his own choices?"

"Aye, so he does, and then others twist them awry," Assiolo answered bitterly. "But this last choice is yours: Will you trust me, Te-Meriku, or kill me?"

Strange to laugh at such a time but laugh he did, though each heave of laughter rose on a wave of pain. Assiolo's voice was a whisper across great distance. "An you give me the kingship I'll quench Averla's fire, forever and for always, and keep the tree beneath this sky."

His sister's face swam into view; his sister's touch drew him back into the light. "Do you trust him?" he mouthed.

Marwy Ninek looked to Assiolo whose brown eyes, full of sorrow, full of shame, were fixed upon the king. She swallowed once, she swallowed twice, and nodded. "He gave me a promise once," she said, "today he kept it, though 'twas I broke faith first."

"Then what I can, I'll do." A tremor and a quiver, a sheen of sweat upon his brow. Te-Meriku set his teeth and stretched out a shaking hand to beckon the nightwatch close. "Today all ways run crookedly. You have the sword. The rest another must give you after the end." A breath. A pause. His weak voice strengthened. "And, Ardùvai, take what is yours if he will not give it freely."

Marwy Ninek whispered, "No," and Te-Meriku reached up to trace a tear's track across her cheek. "Te-Meriku, please —"

He pressed his finger 'cross her lips and she tasted the salt of her own tears. "The king knows the king," he told her, his whisper so faint she had to bend her head to hear him. "Some things not even the piper can change."

She looked to Assiolo and to Ardùvai, and saw no comfort in either of their faces. The future stretched before her, an empty place, drear and dreadful where there was no shelter from the wind. The piper stood between them, the price of a man's life reflected from his golden eyes: not an apple, not a sword, not even a kingdom. She wanted to scream, to rage and shout, to rush at him and spill his red blood across the grass. To do that now would change nothing: what had been broken never could be mended. Instead she kissed Te-Meriku, one kiss upon his brow in sorrow and in parting.

"Give him your knife," Te-Meriku whispered. "Let it be by a bronze blade – that is the proper way for the king to die."

She offered it to Assiolo, biting her lip in grief and pain. Te-Meriku asked, "You know how to use it?" Assiolo nodded, his hand steady for all the paleness of his face. "Then all that is mine I give to you, Assiolo, if you will take it."

Marwy Ninek felt a shiver and a shudder, a harsh release of breath, and the thing that had been Te-Meriku resting heavy on her breast. She bent her head, biting her lip to keep back her sobs, and cradled her brother in her arms as on the day when he was born.

Assiolo did not weep but tears could have added nothing to the sorrow in his face. After a moment, he laid his hand, very lightly, on her shoulder. "I've feared and failed, love, most dreadfully, and now the thread is snarled, the pattern broken, but what I can I'll do." His voice throbbed, a lutestring out of true. He paused to steady it. "I'll not betray your trust nor misuse the gift he gave me."

Marwy Ninek looked up into his face and could not see a monster, only the man who loved her. "Oh," she breathed, "you are still Assiolo."

"Such things I've done, such things I've become, but yes, love, for you, forever and for always Assiolo."

She reached out to him across the body of her brother, curling her hand into his. Somewhere, across the water at the edge of hearing, a blackbird was singing its song of love and freedom.

He kissed her softly on the brow. "We will talk after the end," he said.

"After the end," said Ardùvai, hard-faced, hard-eyed, a shadow in the sunlight, "you will answer for that death, be you a hundred times the king."

Assiolo stood to face him and nodded, curtly. "As you will it, clansman."

He turned his back on the king's company and walked a little way alone along the stream bank, the sight in all men's eyes. He wore no mail and bore no sword, no red cloak fell about his shoulders, he was in seeming but a brown-haired man with empty hands held out to sea and sky but, when he spoke, the world fell quiet to listen.

"Are you there?" he asked the light, and Averla answered, "I am here."

She could do no other and no less. He was the king and here and now he held the mastery.

"Te-Meriku is dead," he said. "I am the king this side of the sunset, to hold a little while by day all your brother holds beneath the other sky. A broken world cannot be mended but I shall keep the balance. You'll not have your will of me: I'll not give you back your own."

"Oh Assiolo, Assiolo," she leaned towards him, sweet red lips, and soft round breasts and a fall of golden hair, " 'Twas I gave you your life, gave you your son – would you turn from me into death?"

"Aye, madam, I would. I am many things beneath this sky but I am not my father."

"You have lost much," she warned him, "you will lose all an you do this."

A little light laugh. "Madam, I have all any man could desire. My son is safe, my love is waiting for me yonder – that will not change whatever happens after."

A moment's pause, as blue eyes stared into brown, red lips curved into a lovely smile, and in that pause the world caught in its breath in fear at what would follow. And then a roaring and a rushing, a shifting and a shivering, as the fire that had burned beyond the sunrise before the world began shrugged off its shell of skin. Golden hair swirled into strands of sparks, flesh shimmered into flame. Fire flickered, lapping across the day; fire blazed, driving away all darkness and all shadows – all shadows save the one: a black-clad man outlined against the flames; the fire about him burned and burned but he was not consumed.

Assiolo said no word, he made no move, but all the light that was in the day settled upon him so he alone was illuminated, shining brighter even than the fire. All the time there was stretched out beneath the sun, his to do with as he willed. He held out his empty hands and stepped towards Averla and caught her around her waist. Those who watched beyond the bank saw there was not a woman of flesh between his hands but one of flame. Fingers of fire closed round his wrists but all her strength and all her will were not enough. She writhed and twisted in his grasp but slowly, slowly, he pressed her back towards the stream. For a moment, all saw them balanced on the bank, a man and a woman caught in an embrace tight and close as love, burning more brightly than the sun. Light burned. Light blinded. Even the piper needs must close his eyes against the glare. Then Assiolo pushed her down into the water and all was hidden behind a rainbow haze of light and spray.

After a long, long time, when struggles ceased and flames were quenched, when the stream ran cold and clear again, when the midsummer sun was the only light left within the day, Assiolo pulled the body from the water to lay it gently down upon the streamside, as if Averla did but sleep and he did not wish to wake her. It lay upon the riverbank with all the fire and glory of her life gone from it. He sat beside it, shaking, staring at his empty hands.

Ardùvai came forward with Marwy Ninek beside him. The piper limped behind, a little, broken, twisted thing, his head bowed down.

"The only end is death," said Assiolo, dull-eyed, grey-faced, tired beyond all measure. "The flesh died today – the light will die at the world's ending. All the rest was washed away, name and thought and memory, forever and for always."

He made to rise but had not the strength or will and sank down beside the water.

"You are changed," Ardùvai said. "Much was washed from you too, I think."

"My fire is quenched and my skill spent. I could do nothing if I did not give all – Averla deserved that as much as she did my hatred. I am at last a man as other men." A bitter laugh, a hollow smile. "Less, in this company, seeing that I have no knife."

"That I can grant you," said Ardùvai with a mocking smile, "if you've a mind for a fight."

"And is not the kingship a gift to be given?" answered Assiolo in a tone to match him. "Or will you break the pattern after all? Nay," he said, setting all mockery aside, "I've been too long a tool for others' using – all that I have is yours. Take it and be done. I ask only that you do rightly by my son. He is a child," he said, his hands open in supplication, "no child can help who sires him."

"So said Te-Meriku, and bade me find him after the sunset. What I can, I'll do – give him a sword and a ship, teach him to be a man amongst many in the king's hall."

Assiolo bowed his head and Ardùvai turned to the piper. "I am not yet king," he said, "and you are yet free to go your way across the world, to sing your songs and tell your stories, the piper from the gates of morning. But," he said, soft and dangerous as ever Te-Meriku had spoken, "when I am king, I will remember only that your blood runs red as any man's across the stone. If I see you, I will kill you," he moved his hands through the wide patterns of the oath, "I swear by land and sea and sky."

The piper raised his golden eyes. "I did what was necessary."

A short, hard laugh. "And yours the tongue that cannot lie! You made a choice. So too did I, so did Te-Meriku, so Assiolo. Today all our choices lead to one end. If you wish to live beyond the sunset, Kenu Vanithu, find a ship, find any that will carry you far from this country."

Marwy Ninek had watched as in a dream as he turned one future to another but now she ran to Ardùvai and took his hands. "No, this must not be," she pleaded. "Assiolo's a good man twisted out of his proper shape. Give him to me – I will stand surety for him. He will live out his life and never set foot beyond the stone walls of Felluria."

Ardùvai's eyes were dark and deep, black as a night without stars. No friendship there, no pity, only the ghosts of might have been moving like monsters through the depths. He did not move. He did not answer. She looked up into his pale, cold face and saw a stranger, a man of the Sea People knowing no end but one. She flung her arms about his neck, whispering, "Ardùvai, I loved him too but there's been enough of death today."

"I can offer nothing. You heard Te-Meriku as clear as I did. *Take it*, he bade me, and so I shall."

She turned from him in despair to Assiolo, wrapping her arms around him, pressing herself against him, holding him tight, never to let go.

"No, love, it cannot be," Assiolo told her softly, stroking her hair. "I've done such things, even within your own stone walls, I am not fit for loving. And besides there is the kingship."

"I will away a little while," said Ardùvai, "to see to the dying and the dead." He drove the king's sword into the grass. It cast a short, sharp shadow 'cross the bank and he set a knife down a little way beyond it. "All the time that's left is here. The sword knows its own purpose and I know mine. You have until the shadow reaches the knife, Marwy Ninek, to say what can be said."

At their backs, the dead were gathered up and the king's ship made ready for its last sailing. Armed men stood by, an arrow's flight away, wary, ready, but their watching eyes were of no matter. Only the other mattered. Handfast, they sat together by the stream, talking of little things because the great ones were too terrible to speak on.

"Do you remember, love, the first time I kissed you?"

"I was so afraid," she said. "I could scare see you, I was so afraid."

"And now?" he asked, softly.

"Now?" She looked down at their knotted fingers. "Now I have stabbed a man by moonlight and another by the stream, now I have set myself against Allocco's son who said a word and stopped the sun, I do not think I could be afraid again."

Assiolo brushed his lips against her cheek. "All that made Allocco's son was washed away. Only I am left."

Heartsick, she said, "I gave you to Averla."

His fingers tightened. "I killed your brother."

All they had done fell down between them. They looked into each other's faces and then they looked away, hands sliding from the other's grasp. The light was longer now, slanting from the hillside to the sea. A splash of red lay upon green branches and men stood all around it, their heads bowed, their hands empty. Down on the shore the ship was waiting, for the sunset and the tide.

"Will you go to him? Your place is at his side."

She shook her head. "He is not there. Flesh and blood and bone but nothing of Te-Meriku. Only you are here."

The shadow crept towards the knife. All the time there was was melting down into a moment. If words were not said now they must remain unspoken forever. He said, "I cannot change the past, love, nor give you good memories to set against the bad. I can say only that I love you, forever and for always."

Marwy Ninek plucked a wild rose from the briar beside them, though its thorns pricked at her fingers sharp and hard as love and sorrow at her heart, and tucked it into the laces of his shirt. "Such joy I had of you, Assiolo, such sweet delight."

"And I of you." He kissed her poor torn fingers. "Alas, the sweetest roses have the sharpest thorns."

She pulled him close to kiss her. Then, for a little while, the world was far away. Skin against skin, touch matched with touch, kiss with kiss. This was what mattered – this was all that mattered. But, always, from the corners of their eyes, they saw the shadow stretching out towards the knife. He held her close, he held her tight and told her, "There is a place for you, love, within the world."

"But not for you."

He shook his head. "No, sweetheart, not for me."

Half a laugh and half a sob. "Oh, Assiolo, dear, dear love, what is the world to me without you in it?"

He tried to speak but she closed his mouth with a kiss. Slow tears ran down his face, as warm as blood and salty as the sea.

The light slanted across the hill, the stream was a ribbon of gold as the long day lingered and the evening rose up to meet it. The shadow reached out to touch the knife and armed men stood straight as Ardùvai passed by. Down by the shore oystercatchers whistled, one to another, and then a curlew called, sweet and sudden in the gloaming.

Marwy Ninek stood beside the briar, watching them walk away. She watched as Assiolo knelt down where land met sea; watched as Ardùvai swung up the sword; watched as the sunset kindled the blade to flame; watched as the thing that had been a man fell slowly aside. The curlew cried, once, twice and again. At its third calling she drove her bronze knife home into her heart.

Acknowledgements

There are many people who helped during the writing of *After the Ruin*. Three, first and foremost: Louisa Tsougaraki, who supported and encouraged me all along the way, and choreographed the fights; Jane Dougherty, who read and reread so many different versions she must fairly have the tale by heart; and Douglas Reed, who, besides providing coffee, biscuits and a shoulder to lean on, drew the map. My love and gratitude to all of you.

I'd also like to thank the members of the Phoenix literary group for their comments on an early draft, and Terri-Lynne DeFino, my sagacious editor at Hadley Rille, for helping tweak the book into its final shape. A grateful mention is due too to Antonis Tsolomitis for advice on typesetting and fonts.

And, finally, I should thank a large number of folk, living and dead, I've never met: Francis Child, Cecil Sharp, Ralph Vaughan Williams and all the other song collectors of the nineteenth and twentieth centuries, and the many, many singers and musicians who have kept and keep those songs alive in all their forms. Without them, I doubt anything would have been written at all.

Harriet Goodchild,
Edinburgh, January 2014

About the Author

Harriet Goodchild was born in Glasgow, and lives in Edinburgh. This is her first novel.

CPSIA information can be obtained at www.ICGtesting.com
Printed in the USA
LVOW12s1226050415

433361LV00002B/299/P